TOR BOOKS BY APRIL CHRISTOFFERSON

TRAPPED

APRIL CHRISTOFFERSON

TOR®

A TOM DOHERTY ASSOCIATES BOOK • NEW YORK

This is a work of fiction. All of the characters, organizations, and events portrayed in this novel are either products of the author's imagination or are used fictitiously.

TRAPPED

Copyright © 2012 by April Christofferson

All rights reserved.

A Tor Book
Published by Tom Doherty Associates, LLC
175 Fifth Avenue
New York, NY 10010

www.tor-forge.com

Tor® is a registered trademark of Tom Doherty Associates, LLC.

ISBN 978-0-7653-6475-3

First Edition: November 2012

Printed in the United States of America

0 9 8 7 6 5 4 3 2 1

For Steve,

with love

ACKNOWLEDGMENTS

I have been going to Yellowstone my entire life, and to Glacier National Park my entire adult life, but my familiarity with and love for both have climbed to new heights since my children became rooted in these two incredible landscapes. First and foremost, I want to express my love and gratitude to Ashley and Ryan, who over the past few years have generously shared their endless passion for and knowledge of Glacier and the Blackfeet culture with me, especially during the writing of this book. It's impossible not to fall in love with Glacier and the town of East Glacier when you see them through Ashley and Ryan's eyes.

A heartfelt thank you to Dale McCormick, who once again served as my technical adviser on all matters pertaining to law enforcement, and to Eric Morey of Yellowstone National Park, whose willingness to share his expertise and intimate knowledge of both Glacier and Yellowstone was immensely helpful. I also called upon Yellowstone "Rev" Michael Leach, who is nothing less than a walking encyclopedia on all things Yellowstone, as well as its passionate ambassador.

To Natalia Aponte, Tom Doherty, Linda Quinton, Paul Stevens, Tom Cornack, Miriam Weinberg, and Edwin Chapman, whose support and hard work on my behalf are greatly appreciated. I'm privileged to have worked with this talented, dedicated group for so many books and so many years.

To Alan Centofante and Brad Bunkers, both of whom work miracles, thank you.

To my readers: Connie Poten, Ashley Sherburne, T. J.

Carroll, Lisa Christofferson, Randy Ingersoll, Jane Aldrich, and Michael Leach, thank you for your wise and valuable input.

I have come to know, love, and respect many people working at the grassroots level on the issues I write about in *Trapped*. It's not an easy path to take, and I thank each and every one of them, in particular, Kathleen Stachowski, Chris Barns, Jerry Black, Sue Eakins, and Footloose Montana, for the difference they are making.

I lost two beloved dogs and a cat—the best companions I could ever hope for—while writing this book. To Sparkie, Lila, and Mookie, you are indelibly imprinted on my soul and my heart. You live on in both.

To my mother, Isabel, whose light (and fight) still shines bright and guides us, and to Crystal, for her love, support, and that beautiful spirit and smile.

And to Kamiah, my little angel.

In the considerable amount of time I've been blessed to spend in Glacier and Yellowstone, I've met many people whom I consider heroic. They patrol the roadways and trails, do hands-on work in the field, sit behind desks, and man entry gates. They live in the gateway communities where they observe and explore, with childlike wonder, and help visitors do the same. I intended for the heroes in this book to reflect upon these very real people—the important work they do, their sacrifice and commitment, and the difference they make for visitors to and inhabitants (two- and four-legged, winged and finned) of these sacred wild places that we dare not take for granted if we want them to endure for generations to come; if we want their majesty and their wildlife—from the great spirit bear to the smaller, but no less magnificent, wolverine—to survive.

Here's hoping I succeeded.

TRAPPED

FOREWORD

In 2011, the State of Idaho opened a five-month trapping and snaring season designed to kill wolves.

"I am haunted by memories. I go to Stanley and there are no tracks, no wolves, no howls. The lone survivor of the Basin Butte pack, B450, I can pick up on my telemetry radio and at least know he is still alive. I have not seen him for over a year. He is now three, very elusive, thank goodness. . . . Sometimes I get quite sad, but I will never give up."

—LYNNE STONE,
Idaho wolf activist and grandmother,
November 16, 2011

"I have noticed in my life that all men have a liking for some special animal, tree, plant, or spot of earth. If men would pay more attention to these preferences and seek what is best to do in order to make themselves worthy of that toward which they are so attracted, they might have dreams which would purify their lives. Let a man decide upon his favorite animal and make a study of it, learning its innocent ways. Let him learn to understand its sounds and motions. The animals want to communicate with man, but Wakantanka does not intend they shall do so directly—man must do the greater part in securing an understanding."

—BRAVE BUFFALO (late nineteenth century),
Teton Sioux medicine man

PROLOGUE

Whisper Little Wolf's heart pounded in her brown chest as she peeled her eyes off the photo propped against the wall on the counter and lowered herself into the padded swivel chair. The harsh fluorescent lights overhead cast a glare on the framed image, but she could still make out the body of a mountain lion, massive head propped up by a beaming, near bald, camouflage-clad man. His eyes were hidden by sunglasses.

Whisper had seen plenty of similar photos, enough to wonder why the rifle that took the animal's life wasn't also prominently displayed. But never before in a dentist's office.

The technician—a surly, squat woman whose age Whisper couldn't begin to pinpoint—barely waited for her to get settled before she spread the blue paper apron over Whisper and snapped its fastener at the side of her neck, catching a long black lock of hair.

"Ouch," Whisper cried.

The technician either didn't hear or didn't care. Whisper figured she was a typical Flathead-area white woman and didn't much like having to touch a full-blooded Indian—especially if that Indian was Blackfeet.

Maybe Spencer and Cole were telling the truth. A powerful instinct to bolt came over Whisper—but merely turning her head caused knifelike pain to sear through Whisper's jaw and up into her temple, and she knew she had no choice. Her tooth had to be tended to. And the Indian Health Services' dentist's day in Browning was four days away. And even if she could wait that long, it was first-come first-serve for dental care on the reservation. Whisper remembered all too well the time she had accompanied her grandmother, Sky Walker—who had held a position of great honor as the eldest person in the Blackfeet tribe, until she died the previous year—to the IHS dentist as a little girl. One woman told them she'd slept at the clinic's door for two nights, just to ensure she got her aching tooth pulled. Whisper couldn't afford to spend a night away from the job, so there were no guarantees she'd even be seen on Friday.

Bridger Brogan, the only dentist between Kalispell and East Glacier, had an opening that day.

Besides, she was sure the guys at work were just kidding her. Cole and Spencer, her coworkers at the Snow Slip Inn, loved to tease all the girls, especially Whisper.

Whisper may have been less endowed than the other waitresses at the Snow Slip, but she attracted plenty of attention from men, especially once they got to know her. She had a sweet way about her, a blend of naïveté and openness men found appealing. Of course she also had a fiancé, a local, which in East Glacier was akin to being part of a brotherhood, so the guys at work pretty much stuck to kidding her a lot. Which is what she hoped they were doing when they heard she had an appointment with Dr. Bridger Brogan.

That's what they were doing, she'd decided the night before. Kidding her. Still, something about their comments prompted her to make a few more phone calls that morning, just to see if there were any openings somewhere else. While Brogan's location in Columbia Falls would save at least an hour of driving, at the last minute Whisper tried dentists as far away as Kalispell and Whitefish, but she would have to wait a week to see anyone else.

"Could be a while," the technician said after she'd laid out an alarming number of instruments on the tray beside the chair in which Whisper sat. "He's just fitting you in. Want me to turn the radio on?"

Whisper nodded numbly, then watched as the woman crossed the room and turned a switch on a portable radio that looked like something out of an old Sears catalog. Then, without another word or glance Whisper's way, she waddled out of the room, leaving Whisper with her thoughts and fears. And a local radio talk show, which Whisper had obviously joined in the middle of a heated exchange—at least Whisper at first assumed it to be an exchange. She soon caught on that the host and caller were in agreement, and the heat, it seemed, came from sharing the same right-wing views.

"*This country is going to hell in a handbasket,*" a man's anger-riddled voice proclaimed. "*Next thing you know, they're gonna try to take my guns from me. And I tell ya, you know what will happen when that day comes?*"

A female—obviously a white female—with an annoyingly airy and twangy voice responded, "*I hear you. Our constitutional rights, that's what're at stake. And we have to fight for those, don't you think?*"

"*You bet.*"

"*You know the other thing I'm tired of?*" the female continued. "*I'm tired of the tree huggers and wolf lovers and all those elitist environmental types who spend their time whining about protecting animals—animals!—when our kids can't even count on finding a job when they graduate from college. And the health care we were promised that didn't change a damn thing. How many people out there are still without insurance?*"

The caller jumped on this one.

"*I don't have insurance!*"

Whisper found herself wondering what these people would do if their only health care was what the IHS provided.

"*There you go. What did I tell you?*" The host paused for effect. "*It's depressing, that's what it is. But we have to stand together, and we have to fight. And you know what else you can do?"*

"*What?*" the caller eagerly replied.

"*You can take those guns of yours, the guns you're not gonna let them take from you, and you can put them to good use in our predator derby.*" She laughed then. A contrived laugh. "*I hate to change subjects on you, but I'm damn proud to have come up with the idea of a predator derby sponsored by my KTEA talk show, and I did promise the other proud sponsor of the derby that I'd give them just a teensy weensy bit of mention every now and then.*"

Whisper cringed as the annoying voice practically shouted, "*Thank you, Cabela's!*"

In contrast, the voice Whisper heard next was actually quite nice.

"So what do we have here?"

Despite the pain, Whisper twisted her neck to get a glimpse of Dr. Bridger Brogan as he stepped into the room and walked over to the radio, switching it off.

The pleasant voice seemed totally incongruous with the man.

While his voice was smooth, rich, and pleasant, none of those adjectives could be used to describe Bridger Brogan. He stood about six feet tall. Block-headed with small, dead eyes, a wide, flat nose, and thinning brown hair slicked back and sprayed into a helmet, he looked Neanderthal. But it was his eyes that disturbed Whisper. Something about how he looked at her, as if he were appraising her. She'd had plenty of white men look at her that way.

Self-confidence practically oozed from him.

Turning to shut the door behind him, he approached Whisper, his eyes taking on more life. He pushed the back of her chair and she fell back into a half-reclined position.

He pulled the examination light overhead toward the chair.

"How long's that molar been hurting?"

"I've had some dull pain for a while, but yesterday it got really bad."

"X-rays show an abscess," he said casually, almost as if to himself. "It has to go."

"You mean, be pulled?"

Brogan straightened, looked at her blandly.

"Yes, that's what I mean."

"Now?"

Brogan was already reaching for a mask that dangled from a white tank that had a DANGER: NO SMOKING tag prominently displayed on its surface.

"What's that?" Whisper asked.

"Something to keep you comfortable."

Whisper's hands went up.

"I've never used gas at the dentist before. I don't think I want to."

Brogan straightened, mask still in his hand.

"Novocain isn't going to do what you need."

"Can't we try, and then if it doesn't . . ."

He dropped the mask. It dangled in the air between them. Reaching for the clasp at Whisper's neck, he unsnapped it.

"I've got too full a day to be experimenting. I worked you in because I heard you were in pain. I'll prescribe something to help get you through until you can see someone else."

Just as he turned to walk out of the room, a zap of pain shot through Whisper's jaw.

"Wait," she cried.

Brogan stopped, but at first, he didn't turn. Didn't look at her.

"Please," she said. "I can't deal with this. And I had to

take time off work today to come down here. I'll try the gas. Please."

Slowly, Brogan turned. He still looked annoyed at her. She wished she hadn't been such a baby about the whole thing. Damn that Spencer and Cole.

"Okay," he said dully. "Let's get started."

Trapper Chatter Web site:

COYOTEMAN: *Anybody here? Looks like two of you online right now. It's a fuckin awesome day in the State of Montana and C'man's in a good mood. You guys hear about the predator derby KTEA's sponsoring? Ten grand for first prize.*

MOUNTAIN MAMA: *Mtnmama here. You bet. I've already got three coyotes, but you know what's gonna take the prize, doncha?*

COYOTEMAN: *Mornin pretty Mama. Hell yes, I know. It's gotta be a wolf. Especially with the former governor of Idaho running the show. LOL. She aint got no love for wolves.*

MOUNTAIN MAMA: *You said it. I hear there's a new pack just over the state line, near Thompson Falls. I'm headed over there this week-end.*

DOCTOR D: *I'm setting my sights higher than wolves these days. And not for that contest.*

MOUNTAIN MAMA: *Morning Doctor D!*

COYOTEMAN: *Hey, Doctor D. Wondered if that 3rd person might be you. So you're not going for wolves?*

DOCTOR D: *Hell no. Right now I'm focused on the Holy Grail.*

MOUNTAIN MAMA: *Holy Grail . . . only one critter trappers think of that way!!!*

COYOTEMAN: *You gotta be shittin us. You mean the one Tanner saw, up near Iceberg Lake?*

DOCTOR D: *It could be her, but there's more than one wolverine up that way.*

COYOTEMAN: *Tanner said she was collared. Part of that study they're doing.*

(Pause.)

COYOTEMAN: *Doctor D . . . You still there? She collared???*

DOCTOR D: *Not anymore.*

MOUNTAIN MAMA: *Holy shit*

COYOTEMAN: *Holy shit's right. We better change the subject. Well how's this: all I got myself yesterday was another fuckin dog.*

DOCTOR D: *Same thing happened to me this week.*

COYOTEMAN: *How many that make for you this year?*

DOCTOR D: *I stopped keeping count.*

COYOTEMAN: *LOL. They don't call you dr of death for no reason. Hey, you got a real job, besides trappin I mean?*

DOCTOR D: *We agreed, nothin' personal on here. I come here for information and to support trappers. Not to get to know anybody better.*

MOUNTAIN MAMA: *So you gotta buyer yet?*

DOCTOR D: *Hell, I can pick from a dozen. I've been getting requests for years. I've got a list a mile long.*

MOUNTAIN MAMA: *Better be careful who's on that list. Those anti's are getting pretty tricky.*

COYOTEMAN: *I tell ya, some anti comes to me, into my shop, trying to trick me into selling something illegal, I'll know it. I'll smell it, see it by the way he looks the minute he walks in. Some anti tries to buy anything from me, he'll end up underground. And that's a promise.*

DOCTOR D: *Exactly. SSS*

COYOTEMAN: *LOL. You see that story where that Idaho sheriff's gettin' in trouble for holding a wolf hunting contest? Offerin a rifle and shovel as a prize. LOL.*

*He's saying SSS stands for safety, security and survival,
not shoot, shovel and shut up? Don't you just love it?*

DOCTOR D: *As if anybody in these parts buys that. Even
the stupid fucking reporter. I give the sheriff credit for
originality.*

MOUNTAIN MAMA: *Hey, I see somebody new just joined
us. Who's there?*

(Pause.)

COYOTEMAN: *Hello? Please ID yourself.*

(Pause.)

COYOTEMAN: *Listen you motherfucker, either let us
know who you are or get the fuck outta here.*

(Pause.)

MOUNTAIN MAMA: *Maybe we better take this conversation offline.*

COYOTEMAN: *Doctor D?*

MOUNTAIN MAMA: *He's already gone. I'm signin off
now too . . .*

One

Will McCarroll's foul mood escalated with each of Kola's steps down the rocky trail that led from his backcountry cabin to the Pebble Creek campground.

Goddamn fools.

He'd been waiting for this to happen, for the middle of the night call he'd just received on his two-way radio.

"Hurry down here, Will," Betty Stanmeyer had shouted over the two-way radio she wasn't supposed to have. Betty and her husband, Hal, served as campground hosts at Pebble Creek. "Someone's been shot."

Will had to count on his mare's familiarity with the narrow, rocky trail, as well as her surefootedness, to move at the slow gallop he'd pushed her into. A hint of a full moon filtered through branches of Douglas fir, but not enough to give light to the ground beneath. As they finally broke through the tree line, Will gave Kola a knee in the ribs. She'd developed a habit of pausing at this point, in response to knowing that's what Will wanted— to pause at his first chance of the day to look at the

Lamar Valley unfolding beneath them; to look out at the land he loved, the land he'd devoted his life to.

A life that had become a lot more complicated since the arrival of Magistrate Judge Annie Peacock.

Tonight Will couldn't afford the pause.

"Keep moving, girl," he urged.

Will knew what to expect when he first caught sight of the campground. He'd been doing this—serving as law enforcement inside the park—for twenty-eight years now, so very little surprised him.

At the park's big camping grounds, kerosene lamps and flashlights usually danced like fireflies around smoldering campfires until the early morning hours, but the only thing Will could see moving were the untended flames of at least a dozen campfires. Tent flaps had been zipped tight for a false sense of security. The lights in Betty and Hal's RV signaled they'd obeyed Will's order to return to it and lock up.

No sign of the law enforcement backup that Will had radioed for. Will glanced at his watch. He and Kola had made it down the hill in twenty-three minutes. The drive from Mammoth was forty-five minutes at best, without incident, and that was taking it at a pace that invited accidents.

A shout drew Will's attention to the back of the campground, the row of campsites that bordered the creek. Betty had identified campsite number twenty as where the shooting took place.

Will dismounted and looped Kola's reins around the trailhead sign. Then, drawing his 9-mm, he crouched low, heading toward the campground, which had now fallen silent. At this hour, he would have expected to see adults getting to know each other around campfires, after the kids had gone to bed. Usually he was called because someone had had too much to drink and was getting a little rowdy.

The silence as he approached was absolute.

Something had gone horribly wrong this August evening in this nation's first national park.

As Will passed the outhouse that served the campground, he noticed the door facing the Northeast Entrance Road slightly ajar. A sixth sense, tuned by decades on the job, told him it wasn't empty.

Gun aimed squarely at the door, he approached and kicked the door open.

A slender East Indian woman holding a baby hovered against the back wall, pressed into it, crouching low, between the side wall and the toilet. She was dressed in a traditional sari.

She pulled the baby into the cave she'd created of her chest and torso, whimpering. Will lowered the gun, and in the moonlight filtering through the plastic skylight above, her eyes registered relief, especially when Will stepped into the light and she saw his uniform. Reflexively she straightened a bit.

"He killed a man," she said, as if trying to convince Will that something terrible had happened.

"Stay in here," Will said softly. Nodding toward the door, he added, "And lock that."

"My husband tried to help but he called him a rag head. He shot him, too. Hashmuk, he told me to run, to come here and hide. I'm afraid he's dying, too. . . ."

"I'll find him," Will replied. "Now lock the door behind me."

Will waited outside the door, eyes trained on the campground now, to hear the click of its lock.

Skirting the north side of the campground, the side rimmed by Pebble Creek running down from Sunset Peak, Will heard another shout as he moved between RVs and tents of every color, size, and shape. With the moonlight blocked by lodgepole pines that sheltered the campsites, Will sometimes felt rather than saw the tent flaps open as he passed. Each time, he put finger to his lips to shush the relieved camper about to blurt out. When he got to the RV of the campground hosts, Hal Stanmeyer had been waiting, eyes glued to the path he knew Will would take. He stuck his head out of an open window.

"Two of them with guns," he whispered, "at twenty. Two guys down. I think one's dead."

Will nodded, kept moving.

"Wait for me," Hal whispered.

"No. You stay in there. Call for backups."

"Betty already did. They're on the way. Closest LE was at Roosevelt Lodge. Should be here within ten minutes."

A lot could happen in ten minutes.

Still, aside from the shouts, it was the silence that bothered Will most. He moved forward.

Campsite twenty was one of the most coveted sites at Pebble Creek. Adjacent to the creek, campers loved to fall asleep to the sound of rushing water and wake up to the sight of sunshine reflecting off the current, and the expansive view, to the south, of Round Prairie. Getting a site anywhere near twenty was considered lucky.

But not tonight.

Will saw the twisted legs first. Hiking boots still crusted with mud from the rain earlier in the evening jutted out from between two tents packed closely together at campsite twenty. Both tents stood dark and silent, but as Will crept forward, he could hear a voice. He thought it was the same one he'd heard earlier, only now, instead of shouting, it was more of a rant. Will couldn't make out the words.

He paused at the boots, felt for a pulse. None. A handgun lay still partially clasped in the man's right hand, and blood trailed off into the dark.

Will inched forward alongside the tent, toward the campfire, toward the voice.

A solo man sat hunched over on a ring of short logs that surrounded the fire pit, head in his hands, alternately sobbing and talking to himself.

"What did I do? What did I do?"

A Colt .45 lay at his feet.

Will's eyes surveyed the rest of the campsite before he straightened, walked toward the man, his own gun drawn and aimed at him, finger off the trigger.

"Police officer, don't move."

Kicking the gun out of the young man's reach, he added, "You're under arrest."

The young man—he couldn't have been over twenty-five—looked up, anguish in his face.

"What have I done?"

"Stand up. Hands in the air."

Complying, the young man looked over, and, as if seeing the body for the first time, began to crumple. Halfway to the ground, Will shoved him face down on the dirt.

"Hands behind your back," Will ordered, kneeling over him as he lay prostrate on his stomach. Double locking the handcuffs, Will began reciting his Miranda rights as he patted the skinny torso and legs down.

"He's my best friend," the young man sobbed.

Rage engulfing him, Will rolled the young man over, forcing him to look into Will's eyes.

"He *was* your best friend."

The young man, clearly still drunk, lunged for Will, as if Will had been the one to pull the trigger.

Will took him down with a knee between his legs.

Gasping for air, he moaned, writhing on the ground.

Hal had materialized, and behind him, other campers.

"How many shooters were there?" Will said to no one in particular in the group.

Several shook their heads. While at first they seemed relieved to approach Will, when he kneed the kid, several fell back. But a heavyset man in long underwear stepped forward, saying, "Just two. Him"—pointing toward the kid, still writhing on the ground—"and him"—he pointed at the body.

Handing his gun to Hal, Will said, "Watch him."

Walking back to the body, he trained his flashlight on the trail of blood and followed. It led to a tidy campsite, number eighteen, that hosted a new, family-sized tent.

Will stepped inside and found what he was looking for.

An Indian man lay on his side, holding his stomach. He appeared unconscious, but when Will touched him, his eyes opened.

"My wife," he gasped. Blood trickled out of the corner of his mouth, where it held on briefly before falling to the nylon floor. "My baby."

"They're fine. They're safe," Will said quietly. "I give you my word. Now don't talk. We'll get you out of here, to a hospital."

"My wife . . ."

A face appeared at the mesh window above where he lay. Will heard a gasp and looked up. Betty Stanmeyer.

"Get his wife," he ordered. "She's locked in the bathroom. And see if we have a doctor in the campground."

Wide-eyed, Betty nodded then disappeared.

Will could hear her shouting, as she ran toward the outhouse, "Is there a doctor in the campground? We need a doctor!"

The sirens drowned her out.

Chaos ensued. Sleepy-eyed children emerging from tents were pushed back inside by terrified parents. Campers of all ages stood or squat, ready to flee if necessary, their faces lit only by the screens of their cell phones as they texted frantically to friends and family back home. Those lucky enough to have RVs locked windows and doors, cowering inside once they'd slid the last dead bolt in place.

As Will applied pressure to the bullet's entry point—the man's lower abdomen—two figures appeared simultaneously at the tent's door. One wore a ranger's law enforcement uniform. Josh Kennedy. And the other carried a duffle bag, which he began opening as he hurried into the tent, falling to his knees next to Will.

"I'm a surgeon," he said. "Move aside."

Within seconds, the woman from the bathroom rushed in, sobbing.

"Hashmuk, Hashmuk . . ."

Her husband opened his eyes, reached for her hand, and muttered something in Hindi.

"Ma'am, you'll have to back away," the surgeon said. He looked from Will to Josh. "Who's going to assist?"

Will looked to Josh. "You alone?"

"Yes, but there's an ambulance on the way."

"We can't wait for the ambulance," the doctor declared. "This man needs surgery. Now."

"You stay here, help him," Will said. "I'll make sure there are no more perps."

As he stepped out of the tent, Will's head swirled. He could not blot out another doctor's voice, earlier, many years earlier. Just miles down the road. . . .

"*I'm sorry, she was already gone when I got to her. I tried to save the baby. . . .*"

Demons taking him over now, even the heavyset man in long underwear stepped back when Will reappeared at the campfire at site twenty.

The kid still lay on the ground.

"Get up," Will yelled, pulling him to his feet by his shirt collar. "What was worth killing your best friend for? *What?*"

The kid looked dazed, totally out of it.

"I dunno. I didn't mean to. We got in a fight. He kept saying I cheated."

For the first time, Will saw the cards scattered on the other side of the campfire.

"He drew his gun first." The young man looked around at the crowd of six or eight campers, mostly men. Zeroing in on one, he added, "Didn't he?"

"What about the guy who tried to stop you?" one of the campers yelled angrily. "The guy from India. He wasn't even playing cards with you punks."

The look of terror and shock on the kid's face made it clear. He'd been so drunk that he'd forgotten about shooting the second man, who tried to intervene. He was sobering up quickly.

The camper in long underwear looked at Will. "They'd been drinking and playing cards and arguing all night. I'd asked them to quiet down a couple times. The last time, all I saw was that both of them were waving guns around. That's when the Indian fella came over, to try to calm them down." He looked pained. "I didn't see who got shot first. When I saw the Indian guy dealing with it, I figured it wasn't my problem. I shoulda backed him up. I'm ashamed of myself."

There was some mumbling and more than a few sheepish looks.

Will turned back to the kid and grabbed him by the elbow, shoving him.

"Let's go."

He shepherded him in the direction of the highway, toward the Law Enforcement car that Josh had arrived in. But they had an entire campground, filled with campers, to pass through first.

Now that Law Enforcement had arrived, Pebble Creek campground came back alive. Almost in unison, people began venturing out of their tents.

Some swore at the kid, some prayed out loud. Most stood in dead silence, watching.

More lights and sirens announced the arrival of the ambulance.

Will and his prisoner marched on, ignoring the shouts and stares. Relieved of his duty in the tent, Josh appeared, silently walking on the other side of the kid. But then something caught Will's eye.

A middle-aged, balding man, wearing plaid shorts and a T-shirt, had just turned to reach for a camera that his wife held, arm extended out the window of their RV. A handgun stuck out of the back pocket of his shorts.

Will's arm shot out in front of the kid, stopping him. Turning to Josh, he barked an order.

"Take him on to the car."

Then, without waiting to see if Josh obeyed, Will stormed over to the visitor, who had now aimed the camera his way. Grabbing it out of the man's hand, Will tossed it on the ground, then reached behind his bloated belly and one second later, held the revolver he'd seen in the man's back pocket in front of his face.

"What's this?"

Will's eyes burned with barely controlled rage.

The tourist ignored the camera but reached for the gun.

"Give that back," he said. "You can't take it from me. I have a permit."

He called over his shoulder, toward the RV. "Grace, get the permit."

Gun in hand, Will turned back toward Josh, who hadn't moved an inch.

"What did I tell you?" he said. "Take him to the car."

"Will . . ." Josh muttered.

By now Grace had appeared with a piece of paper in hand. She stepped in front of Will and waved it angrily in his face, her husband behind her, looking just as angry, but happy to let her take charge.

"You can't take that from him. Look. Here's his permit. The new rule's in effect now. We can bring guns into the park, as long as we have a permit."

Will stepped toward her. She was a big woman. He wanted to deck her.

"Not in *this* park," he said, shoving the gun into the waistband of his uniform. "Now get out of my way."

A crowd had gathered around them.

"Who else has a gun?" Will shouted, his eyes scanning the group, which kept growing as more campers felt safe emerging from their tents and RVs.

"You heard me," Will yelled. "Who in this campground has a gun?"

"On us?" one man's voice replied.

"Here. In the campground. In your tent, or your car, or a backpack."

Timidly, a woman stepped forward.

"We have one in our car. . . ."

"Go get it," Will ordered. "Who else?"

A burly man wearing a SARAH PALIN 2012 T-shirt stepped forward. "I have a gun, but I'm not giving it to you. It's legal. *I'm* legal."

Will crossed the ten feet separating them. Came eye to eye with the man.

"Get the gun or spend the night in jail."

"You can't do this," the man said flatly, angrily, sizing Will up.

"Yes, he can," a woman's voice cried out. "Thank you!"

More voices joined hers.

"Take it. Take it from him."

Will ignored them.

Reaching for a second set of handcuffs, he pulled them off his belt. When the man caught sight of them, he stepped back.

Will's hand shot out and grabbed him by the neck of his T-shirt.

"Get the fucking gun," Will said in a low voice, but one so filled with rage that even a sixty-pound advantage, and arms muscled by hours in front of a mirror at the gym, seemed no match for it.

The man stood there for at least thirty seconds, his chest heaving with his own anger.

"I'll file a complaint against you, you son of a bitch."

It looked like he might come unglued when his threat brought a snort of laughter from Will.

"Be my guest. Now get the gun."

With one last withering look, the man turned and headed toward his campsite.

"Anyone with a gun had better produce it," Will said to the crowd. "Now."

With some campers cheering him, while two or three who'd turned toward their campsites to retrieve their weapons shot profanities his way, Will followed the belligerent camper to his tent.

"Tenny, *come*!"

Claudette Nillson waited thirty seconds for a response. When one did not come, she stuck two fingers between her lips and let out an ear piercing whistle. That usually brought her German shepherd running.

"Tennyson!" If anyone were around, Claudette Nillson's whistle, as well as her shout, would have been heard up and down the Paola Creek drainage, which channels its waters to a section of the Middle Fork of the Flathead River especially favored by adventure-seeking kayakers and rafters.

Now her voice shrunk to a worried whisper. "Where the heck are you?"

At first she'd just been frustrated, even uncharacteristically irritated at her errant German shepherd. After all, she only had a month to finish her thesis. She'd already taken Tennyson out for a hike, earlier that morning, and his running off on her now meant she'd have to take another break from writing, just as she was on a roll. That was the problem—she was so intent on her work that she hadn't kept track of the time. It had been over an hour since Tennyson had whined to be let out, and now Claudette Nillson's instincts had her hurriedly slipping on her Chaco sandals and stepping off the porch of the tiny cabin she'd talked her University of Montana professor into letting her use; she was to spend the months of August and September finishing the paper he, as chair of the wildlife biology department, had rather reluctantly approved: *The Case for Ecoterrorism.*

She jumped off the porch and cut across the dry, prickly growth, this time paying no heed to the noxious knapweed—a tall multibranched plant with purplish pink flowers—that she usually stopped to pull out by its roots. That had been one of the deals she'd struck with her professor. Left unchecked, knapweed could—and would—take over native species. Claudette had bargained with Professor Vrable: if he let her stay in his remote cabin on the border of Glacier National Park for the two months she predicted it would take to finish her thesis, she would remove not only the knapweed, but the equally noxious leafy spurge as well. But now she was oblivious to her bare legs brushing against the invasive plants as she hurried toward Paola Creek, Tennyson's favorite haunt. She was pretty sure that's where she'd find him as, that morning, he'd been almost impossible to draw away from the small creek, which had dwindled in size by half in the five weeks Claudette had been there. She'd had to call and call to get Tennyson to return to her side, and even then, he'd turned back twice before Claudette finally clipped the leash she always carried on their outings—but almost never used—onto his collar.

"You're trouble today, aren't you big boy?" she'd said.

He'd looked up at her with big, loving eyes, tail wagging. Stopping to hug him, she added, "Don't try to charm me."

Now as she headed back to the same spot, she pictured those sweet eyes again.

"Tennyson!" she called.

Minutes later, her heart leaped when she saw his white shoulders, hit by a streak of sunlight filtering through the dense Western hemlocks lining the creek bed.

It took just seconds for it to hit her: he had not moved, not even shifted, at the sound of her voice.

"Tenny!"

She was running now, crying.

"Tennyson . . ."

Two

Will stepped out of the late afternoon sun and into the vestibule of the Albright Visitor Center, where he had to work his way through a group of tourists who had just stepped off a bus. Once inside the next set of doors, he nodded at two young rangers working the desk, both of whom looked up at him, through a virtual ocean of park visitors, with nothing less than a sense of awe. Then he headed through the door behind the counter and up the rickety stairs.

He'd known he'd be making this trip to Mammoth, climbing these stairs. It had been two weeks since the shooting at Pebble Creek, but that's about how long he'd expected them to take to figure out how to handle the situation.

Sometimes—laying in his bed, unable to sleep, or camped under the stars in the Thorofare the previous three nights—he'd actually found himself entertained just picturing the chaos that was no doubt taking place, the frantic paranoia he'd brought to the normally placid, uncomplicated lives of the power structure at Yellowstone.

He hadn't told Annie much. She, of course, had heard about it right away, and he had to give her credit. Other than at the preliminary hearing for the kid, she hadn't asked him anything—not what happened, not to explain what was going through his mind, not why he had jeopardized his career. No, she'd just looked at him with those worried, sad eyes, and that had been enough. That had been plenty.

Now he pushed the door open to Peter Shewmaker's office and drew back when he saw that Peter wasn't alone.

Albert Gonzalez, newly appointed Superintendent of Yellowstone National Park, sat in the chair next to Will's boss.

As many times as he'd envisioned this meeting, Will hadn't pictured Superintendent Gonzalez as part of it.

While Pete remained seating, Gonzalez, whom Will hadn't yet made his mind up about, stood and extended a hand.

"Ranger McCarroll," he said sternly.

"Superintendent."

Will grasped it, nodded at Peter, and sat down in the only unoccupied chair.

An uneasy silence filled the room. Will wasn't going to make this any easier for them by breaking it.

Finally, Peter cleared his throat. His eyes dropped to the table between them, and for the first time, Will noticed not only the stapled document, placed facedown, that he knew to be for him, but also a sealed envelope. Peter picked it up and handed it to Will.

"This is for you."

The return address was the Office of Senator Irene Halliday, United States Senator from the State of Connecticut.

It was clear that Peter and the Superintendent expected Will to open the envelope in front of them. Will debated briefly, then decided there was little to be gained by not cooperating. Prying his finger under one corner of the flap, he unsealed it and slid out its contents—a single sheet of paper. It was an invitation.

To testify before a Congressional committee. On the law that went into effect in February 2010, for the first time allowing loaded guns into national parks.

Will stared at it, then looked up.

"This isn't what I was expecting."

Peter Shewmaker and Gonzalez exchanged glances.

"What were you expecting?" Shewmaker asked.

"You know what I was expecting," Will answered, clearly unwilling to play any games.

"It appears your opinion about the recent legislation that allows guns in the park has garnered the attention of Congress," Superintendent Gonzalez said. "You became a much respected and loved figure when you saved the alpha female of the Druid pack. A hero, some might say. Now Congress wants to hear what you have to say about allowing guns in the park."

"I'm happy to tell Congress, or anyone else who wants to listen."

Shewmaker butt in. "It looks like you'll get that chance. But first, Will, there's something else that we need to address." A heavy pause followed. "I think you know what it is."

Will would not oblige him by responding.

"Your actions two weeks ago, in taking guns away from citizens allowed by law to have them."

Will couldn't resist. "It doesn't look like Congress is too troubled by my actions."

"Well, we are. What you did was a blatant violation of park policy and the new Code of Federal Regulations."

"Park policy? Since when does park policy put visitors at risk by allowing loaded guns in crowded campgrounds? People—law abiding citizens—come here to enjoy nature, solitude, the beauty and magnificence of this place, and now it's *park policy* to make it unsafe for them to do that?"

Gonzalez wore the exasperated look of a lawyer who'd had to listen to too many outbursts from indignant, but guilty, clients.

"This park did not institute the gun policy. You know that. But it's law now, and park policy is to observe and implement the laws of this nation and this state."

Shewmaker took a more direct approach.

"You know damn well what the situation is, Will. And you know I'm as angry and disillusioned as you are about Congress and the Interior Department letting this happen. But you can't do something as blatant as take away every fucking gun—legal guns—in a campground and then expect us to turn our heads. It simply can't go unpunished."

"Here we go," said Will.

"You've put us in an uncomfortable position," Gonzalez said. "Ordinarily, for an act this blatantly out of line, a ranger would be fired. But . . ."

"But what? You know I did the right thing. You know by taking what—twelve, wasn't it twelve?—loaded guns away from people in this park I might have saved another visitor from being shot, or a wolf, a ground squirrel . . . or even one of your shiny new signs? Hell, a bear won't even have to charge now to get shot at. Some asshole carrying a gun will just shoot on sight, then say he was being charged."

Peter Shewmaker knew Will well enough to know there was no point in arguing the matter. Nor did he appear inclined to. He, too, seemed furious about the guns-in-park ruling. But like most Park Service employees and supervisors, he felt powerless to express himself about it.

"You've become a hero. You saved 22. And the truth is, most of the country is celebrating your actions two weeks ago. We're not stupid. We know what would happen if we fired you. Once news got out, we'd have a public relations mess on our hands."

Will picked up the envelope, shook it in the air.

"And then there's this," he said. "Isn't there? How's it going to look to Congress and the world when I go in there to testify on the guns-in-parks policy when they hear I've been fired for what I did?"

Silence met his questions.

"So, tell me, guys, does this mean I get to keep my job?" Will asked, already leaning back in his chair, ready to push out of it. This was going way better than he'd anticipated.

Shewmaker and Gonzalez looked at each other. Gonzalez had an expectant look, almost as if he was ordering Peter to reply. But Peter dropped his gaze to his hands, crossed in front of him on the table. If it was an order, he'd just refused it.

Superintendent Gonzalez inhaled deeply.

"Not exactly," he replied.

When her cell phone rang, Sally Gordon was standing at a cash register in the leather goods department of Nordstrom. She was second in line.

She lifted the face of her phone toward her, from where it hung from her belt, to see the caller.

Damn. Wouldn't you know it?

She quickly turned, dropping the Louis Vuitton handbag she'd spent half an hour choosing onto a display of gloves. She snapped the phone free and said a crisp "hello" as she headed for the door.

"It's me," he began, as he always did.

Annoyed at having her shopping trip interrupted—they didn't have a Nordstrom in Palos Park, where she lived, and Sally loved Water Tower Place, so she often saved her shopping for the times she had to drive into Chicago for a meeting—Sally felt like saying, "No shit, Sherlock," but instead replied quietly, "What have you found out?"

"It's official."

Sally slowed momentarily, stunned, even though she shouldn't have been.

True to form, she regained her composure almost instantly, before her caller could have detected even an ounce of unease.

"No uncertainty about it?"

"None. How fast can you act?"

Sally had entered the revolving door that led to Michigan Avenue, the Loop's busiest street.

"A week, ten days at the most," she replied, "but I'll need help." She looked around. The sidewalks were jammed with lunch-hour workers and shoppers. "I can't talk now."

"Tell me when and where," the caller replied. "And I'll be there."

The line went dead.

Sally continued out to the sidewalk and began walking slowly toward her parked car. As she crossed the street, the sun glistened off Lake Michigan. She usually loved being here, in the city, but she was no longer in the mood for shopping.

They had been hounding her more and more recently, especially since her kids were out of high school now, to move into Chicago, where she could keep a closer eye on things, become more hands-on and chummy with the local leaders. But Sally didn't like the idea. She'd grown up in the suburbs, still lived near several of her friends from high school, none of whom pried into her life, they were so caught up in their own mundane existences. Her kids were both going to a community college nearby. Sally had no desire to move.

And hell, if what she suspected turned out to be true, she'd have to leave soon enough anyway.

Unfortunately, it wouldn't be to move to Chicago.

No, if her worst fears were about to come true, she wouldn't be leaving the suburbs. She'd be leaving the country.

"Come in," Annie Peacock said, turning away from the window that had held her attention for the past ten minutes when her loyal court clerk's reflection suddenly appeared in its glass.

Justine stood at the door to Annie's office. In stark contrast to Annie's short black hair and the silk blouse that she'd tucked into a slim black skirt, Justine's graying locks appeared to be in riot mode, springing wildly from her head. Her V-neck sweater had also picked up its fair share of the mane Justine had recently let go natural. She had hurriedly slipped it on minutes earlier, after finding it tossed over the back of her office chair, where she'd left it the night before.

"Hearing starts in ten minutes," she said briskly. "Roger just poked his head in the door to ask if you were available, but I told him you were on the phone."

Annie smiled. Justine could read her from just a glance. The two women hadn't spoken yet this morning, as—aside from the security guards—Annie was always the first to arrive at the Justice Center and it was Justine's practice to come in and get right to business. No chitchat. Still, Justine had apparently picked up on the fact that Annie was preoccupied this morning.

"Thanks," Annie replied. "I'll be right down."

Closing the door behind her, Justine hurried off to tend to the other duties she efficiently performed as Magistrate Judge Annie Peacock's court clerk.

Annie couldn't help herself. She turned back to the window.

At the old courthouse, she would not have known Will was in Mammoth because she wouldn't have been able to see his car. Her chambers in the old courthouse, the Pagoda Building—fashioned by Captain Hiram Chittenden after the architecture he'd observed while serving in the Boxer War—had faced south, toward Minerva Hot Springs and the Stone House, where, as Yellowstone's Magistrate Judge, Annie resided, along with her mother, former Magistrate Judge Sherburne, and Archie, her Lab. The new courthouse was only 150 yards north of the Pagoda Building, but the summer before, the doors to the new and vastly improved Yellowstone Justice Center had finally opened, and the building that now housed the courthouse, security—state-of-the-art as opposed to virtually nonexistent in the Pagoda Building—and two divisions of Park Service law enforcement, served as a showcase for Yellowstone and its commitment to the dictate—given back in 1872, when President Grant established this nation's first national park—to protect Yellowstone and its resources "for the enjoyment of the people." While it meant that Annie's commute—on foot—had now been lengthened by at least thirty seconds or more, Annie welcomed the change as the new building not only increased the size of the courtroom from 262 square feet to almost five times that size, it also provided rooms in which family and friends could meet with defendants, and lawyers and clients could consult before, during, and after a trial—all of which Annie, once a federal prosecutor in Seattle and now the head of Yellowstone's unique judicial system, considered essential to affording every person accused of a crime the best shot at good representation.

The only downside, in Annie's mind, had been that she could no longer sit at her desk and look out the window, toward the Stone House, and see Archie romping alongside her mother and Judge Sherburne as they took their daily walk along the trail at the base of the Mammoth Hot Springs. But that was about all she missed about her old office. This new one, in the northeast corner of the second floor, not only had temperature controls to ward off Yellowstone's extreme desert heat in the summer and harsh cold of winter, it also had large, paned windows, windows that gave her sweeping views that no other judge in the world could boast of: Mount Everts to the east. Directly across the street, Mammoth's century-old buildings, which once housed the military troops called in to protect the park from 1886 to 1918. Beyond the historic district, an indescribably vast expanse that included Tower, the Grand Canyon of the Yellowstone, with its river meandering in and out of sight, and beyond that, Yellowstone's Serengeti—Will's beloved Lamar. Lawns that filled with bison and spindly calves in late spring, and rutting elk in the fall, and, next to the post office, Annie had an almost unobstructed view of the back side of the Albright Visitor Center.

Which was where Will McCarroll's beat-up Jeep now sat. Empty.

Annie was certain why he was there. The fact that Will hadn't informed Annie that he would be coming out of the backcountry and in to Mammoth—Yellowstone's headquarters—pretty much confirmed her suspicions that he'd been called in to discuss his most recent transgression two weeks earlier: confiscating the guns of every camper at Pebble Creek campground after the death of a young man during a drunken fight over a card game. Both Annie and Will had known this would come, but, knowing the consequences likely to follow, they'd both done their worrying, and suffering, in silence.

They had both perfected the art of suffering in silence.

Annie hadn't been surprised by what happened—the shooting had surprised her, as there had only been one killing in Yellowstone in the past three decades, a killing that had come, all these years later, to impact Annie's life. What hadn't surprised her was Will's reaction. Ever since she'd seen—and shared—Will's outrage over the Bush ruling that allowed loaded guns in national parks, she'd known Will couldn't help but do something crazy. Eventually. She just hadn't expected it to be disarming an entire campground.

Annie knew the Park Service would not—could not—tolerate this latest disregard for its rules.

She glanced at the clock—just seven minutes now until her 9:00 A.M. hearing—grabbed her judicial robe, and hurriedly exited her office. Justine was standing with a hand on her hip at the top of the stairs just beyond her office, which was adjacent to Annie's chambers. Quickly, Annie turned in the other direction, toward the back stairway.

Two steps at a time, she descended to the first floor, and when she burst through the side door of the building, she saw him, just getting in his car. At a run now, she dodged in front of the line of cars, trucks, and RVs slowed to gawk at elk, and crossed to the center median. But it was too late, Will hadn't seen her. His rusted Jeep turned right, cutting through the historical district on a road closed to the public.

Annie stood, staring after him for several seconds, before she became aware of the fact that a cow elk and her baby had also stepped onto the grass median. Traffic had now come to a standstill. It was hard for Annie to tell which spectacle was catching more attention: Yellowstone's robed judge or the wapiti.

By the time she'd reached the courthouse's steps, two guards stood holding the door open for her. She averted their questioning gazes, pulled at her robe to straighten its lines, and headed into the courtroom.

Claudette stood over the lifeless body and stared at the half-empty kerosene container beside it.

She willed herself to go through with it.

She had wanted to take Tennyson back to Missoula to bury him, but she was just renting an apartment, and she didn't know anyone well enough, or to whom she was close enough, to consider burying him on their property. No, she wanted to keep Tenny with her. Forever. She'd called a vet in Kalispell and was told it would cost $300 to have him cremated. Claudette didn't have $300. And the woman on the phone showed no emotion when Claudette told her what had happened. She wasn't going to leave Tennyson—even if only for a matter of a couple hours—with someone that cold and unfeeling.

She'd finally decided what to do. Carefully, and with great reverence, reciting prayers to the Creator, with tears dripping from her face, Claudette lovingly dug a pit beside the trail she and Tennyson had created over the past two months, the one that led to the creek. She lined it with a sheet of metal siding she'd removed from the back of the shed on her professor's property. She didn't feel good about that, but she made sure it was in a spot that wasn't visible. She had to make sure, make absolutely sure, that she would be able to collect every ash.

She had spent the past twenty-four hours grieving.

Now, as she touched a match to the kindling she'd

arranged so carefully, before gently lying Tenny on top of it, she cried out in anguish. As the flames took her best friend, she collapsed to the ground, exhausted but knowing she would not sleep that night. Nor the next.

She'd already realized that she would not be able to function, not be able to move on, until she avenged Tennyson's death.

Three

Will clenched his jaw, eyes still glued to the rearview mirror—still visualizing the sight of Annie standing there, watching him drive away. He'd pulled over as soon as he got out of sight, too shaken to drive. How could he do that to her, let her stand there watching him drive away? Pretend he hadn't seen her?

He knew the answer all too well. The explanation was, in fact, simple. He'd followed his instincts. Will had not only lived for almost thirty years with wild animals who survived based on instinct, in many ways, he'd become just like them, operating on instinct, the foremost of which was the survival instinct.

And Will's survival, ever since the incident that had threatened to be his undoing, ever since Rachel and Carter's deaths, had depended on the wall he'd built around himself. Annie Peacock had penetrated that wall, cracked it open, and nothing had ever terrified Will more. Will knew, when he saw Annie crossing the grass median toward him, that he wasn't prepared to see her, to tell her the news. He had to process it himself first. So he'd taken off for the place where he stood the best chance of doing that. The Lamar Valley. The place that over the past twenty-eight years had given him his sanity, had offered him comfort. But today, sitting, hiking, staring out at the herds of bison had only made things worse.

Most of the courthouse stood dark when he pulled back up to it, but he could see lights in the upstairs corner of the building—Annie's office.

As he nodded at the security guard, who had allowed him passage into the courthouse without being screened, he started up the steps and almost collided with Justine, Annie's clerk.

Justine looked at him with that knowing look, and nodded toward the second floor.

"She's up there."

Will rapped lightly on the frame of the door, which stood open several inches, then stuck his head inside.

Annie was seated at her desk. He sensed that her eyes had already been on the door before he knocked. She smiled at him, but he could tell that she knew he'd seen her in the rearview mirror.

"Come in," she said. "I won't bite."

Will crossed the room, sat down facing her, met her eyes. Those big, luminous eyes that he'd once considered cold and hard, but that now enabled him to see the hurt he'd caused her.

"I'm sorry," he said simply.

Annie nodded, swallowed.

"How did it go?"

"I would have called you to tell you they called me in, but I didn't want to worry you. I wanted to wait to hear what was going to happen. . . ."

"I understand, Will. Really I do." She paused. "I just thought we were in this together."

"We are, Annie. At least we're in it together as much as someone like me can be in it with another person." He reached for her hand across the desk. "You know how fucked up I am. How bad at this I am."

Annie looked at Will's hand—strong, deeply tanned, palms calloused from days on end on horseback, looking for poachers, for anyone who dared threaten this park he loved . . . more than anything in the world. She knew that; Will had told her he loved her, and she believed it, but she knew that his great love, the one he could not survive without, was Yellowstone. And because of this, and because she loved him more than she'd ever loved another man, she reached for his hand and clasped it.

"That's enough," she said. "Now tell me how it went."

Will's laugh startled Annie. He shook his head.

"I didn't get fired."

Annie's face lit instantly.

"Suspended?"

"No." He took a deep breath. He'd spent the entire day trying to wrap his head around it, but he hadn't succeeded. He couldn't.

"They've transferred me. To Glacier." The words almost stuck in his goddamn throat.

Annie gasped.

"No."

Will's eyes met hers again.

"Yes, Annie. It's true. I can either leave the Park Service altogether, or take my punishment. Go to Glacier."

"Permanently?"

"They wouldn't say for sure. Peter mentioned it would just be one year, but then Gonzalez said they'd have to wait and see. I think they wanted to fire me—I know Gonzalez did. But they gave me this."

Will reached behind him and withdrew an envelope from his back pants pocket. Annie took the envelope, opened it. Will watched as her eyes took the letter in, word for word.

She was wearing her courtroom face, the one that he'd

tried to read in countless hearings as he waited for her to pronounce punishment on an offender he'd arrested. The one she'd worn during the bison hearings.

When she finished, she looked up at him.

"They couldn't fire you. Not when you've been asked to testify about the guns-in-park law. Why can't they just let you stay?"

"They told me people are coming to Yellowstone now and asking to see me—like I'm one of the sights—and that after what I did, they felt compelled to show they'd taken steps to get me back in line. They said I'd forced them to do this. And let's face it: I did."

Will's eyes moved automatically to the window behind Annie's desk, where a cow elk and her calf grazed on the lawn in front of the medical clinic, seemingly oblivious to a tourist who, despite the fading light, snapped photos less than ten feet away. But Will knew better. That cow knew exactly what was going on, and how close the man was to her calf. A twitch of her ear confirmed it. Will's melancholy was placated by a sudden desire for the 400-pound animal to charge the picture-happy bastard.

"But I thought they'd fire me. I thought I'd stay, get a little place in Cooke City but pitch a tent somewhere in the Thorofare, somewhere they'd never find me. That I'd stay in Yellowstone and keep on doing what I do . . . just not in this uniform." He paused again. "They acted like this was a good thing for me. Like I should be grateful."

Annie hadn't taken her eyes off him.

"They'll bring you back, Will. I know they will. They'll have to. You're the best ranger they've got, and visitors to this park love you. You're their hero. This country loves you. This letter"—she nodded toward the envelope still clasped in her hand—"their requesting you to testify before the commission on allowing guns into the parks, says it all."

For the first time, Will smiled at Annie—at her efforts to console him.

"You are such a good woman, Annie. Don't feel sorry for me. I'll be okay. *We'll* be okay."

Annie didn't respond. She'd dropped her eyes to the desk separating them—space that seemed far greater than a couple feet.

"Hey," he said, walking around the desk to her, lifting her chin with his forefinger.

When Annie's eyes met his, he saw it coming.

"I don't know, Will."

"What don't you know?"

"About us."

Damn. He'd royally screwed up. Even more than he'd realized.

"Annie, listen to me. I apologize for how much trouble I'm always getting into. But that's just me. If you can't deal with it, I understand. But I can't promise that will ever change. I can't promise *I'm* going to change."

Annie looked as anguished as Will felt.

"It's not that, Will. I've always admired you for standing up for what you believe in, at any cost. Even when we were on opposite sides of an issue, even when I knew you despised me and blamed me for the bison slaughter."

Will still had trouble believing that he could have blamed Annie for not stopping the slaughter. That he couldn't see the grief in her eyes when she ruled that there was no legal basis for an injunction. It wasn't until later, until they'd teamed up to help find Annie's mother, that he'd seen just how much damage and hurt that ruling had caused her.

Now, he shook his head in anguish.

"I wish I could take back what I said back then. The pain it caused you, when you were already suffering."

"That's not why I mentioned that, Will. What I'm trying to say is that I'm willing to stand by you. But . . ."

"But what?"

Annie turned her gaze on him then.

"Did you see me? When you were leaving the Albright building this morning? Did you see me walking toward you?"

Will dropped his hand. It would be so easy to say no. It was, after all, what she wanted to hear.

"I was pissed off, Annie. I was shaken. Hearing I had to leave, or quit my job, give up any chance of having it back in the future, in order to stay. I had to think. I had to work through it myself before I could face you. Don't you understand?"

Visibly wounded, Annie replied, "I understand, Will. I understand that's what works for you, but I'm not sure I can accept a relationship where you go off alone to deal with bad news."

"And I'm not sure I can change. Even if I want to."

Annie fell silent and Will knew he'd wounded her again. How was it he managed to fuck up every good thing in his life? Had he spent so much time alone, so much time in the company of four-legged and winged creatures that he simply no longer knew how to negotiate the hazards of a life that included relationships?

But wounded or not, one thing Will had learned about Annie was she would not back away from difficult situations. She'd endured not only harsh criticism while presiding over Yellowstone's legal system, but, also, in an attempt to force Annie off the bench, the kidnapping of her mother.

It hadn't worked.

"I'm scared, Will. I can't imagine you not being here. But as hard as you've been working on this—on us—I know you still have your doubts about whether you want a serious relationship. It hasn't been easy for me either. I didn't expect this. I didn't expect us to happen."

"It's not whether I want it, Annie, it's whether I can

be any good at it. I want it. I want you. I just don't want you to have to settle for less than you deserve."

"Maybe some time apart will be good for both of us."

"That's not what I want. But it looks like that's what we're going to get. Unless I decide not to accept the transfer."

"You can't do that, Will," Annie said. "Please. Don't do it to yourself. Don't do it to us."

Will wandered back to the window.

"I'll go along with it," he said, his back to her as he watched the cow elk and her calf cross in front of a row of RVs and cars. They had had enough and the mother was taking her young one up toward the Old Gardiner Road, away from the craziness that was Mammoth. He continued, "I'll go to Glacier because I have no choice, but if it turns out that they don't bring me back, I'll come back on my own, and I'll be their worst nightmare—a one-man watchdog over this park and this new administration. One year. That's what I told them."

Will turned, returned to Annie, and pulled her to her feet. Face to face now, he took both her hands in his. A strand of coal black hair fell across her eyes and he pushed it away so that he could read her. He didn't know what scared him more—the thought of leaving this place, the only home he'd known for almost three decades, the only place that made him feel sane. Or the thought of leaving Annie.

"You can wait a year, can't you, Annie?"

Annie didn't look away this time.

"I can't make any promises either, Will. But I'm not about to give up."

Will kissed her then, but it was tentative. It already felt as though something had changed between them. He pulled back.

"Will you come visit me in Glacier?" he asked.

He saw a stab of pain in Annie's eyes.

Whether it was those words, or the kiss, he couldn't tell. Maybe it was the same pain he felt merely vocalizing the fact that he was actually leaving. But Annie's next words confirmed that, for that moment at least, they both felt the same raw need for the other.

"Make love to me," she whispered.

It was lunchtime, and Bridger Brogan sat at his desk reading a *Penthouse* magazine. When his receptionist buzzed him, he was just about to unzip his Carhartts and jerk off.

"What?" he practically yelled through the intercom.

"You have a call on one," she replied.

"I'm busy. Have whoever it is call back."

The intercom went dead.

Bridger took another look at the picture lying open in front of him. Two fantastic-looking women. Naked. Together.

He reached for the zipper.

The intercom buzzed again.

"This better be important," he practically growled.

"She says it is. She says to tell you it's urgent."

"Who the hell is 'she'?" Brogan replied.

"Her name is Sally Gordon. She said she met you last year at an American Rifle Foundation conference in Texas."

"What the hell?"

Tugging the zipper back up, Bridger Brogan reached for the phone.

It snowed in the Lamar as Will set out for Glacier.

Will kept his eyes fixed straight ahead as he drove through the valley that had served as his haven from the rest of the world. It was as if he knew the possibility of a wolf sighting—the chance that he might catch a glimpse of Number 22, or other members of the wolf pack that he'd lived peacefully with: the Druids—would change his life forever. Would cause him to pull his Jeep over, park it, grab his pack out of the back, and start on foot into the backcountry, never to emerge again. And that possibility might well have become a reality were it not for two realizations Will had had since all this came down. The first was that he'd never wanted anything more than he wanted to come back to Yellowstone one year from now, to return to the life he'd known for over two decades. A life that now included Annie.

The second was the Congressional hearing.

If he bucked the system now, he would probably doom his opportunity to testify about guns in the park, and that alone—the chance to impart some reason, to influence Congress to reverse course and keep loaded weapons out of the parks—was worth the sacrifice Will was going to have to make in order to be heard.

And so he drove right through the Lamar, past Tower and the Roosevelt Lodge, right through Mammoth Hot Springs, past Annie's house, and the new Justice Center where they had made crazy love that night—a mere week earlier, though it now felt like an eternity—in Annie's office.

Right past park headquarters.

By the time he'd descended the five miles of road winding alongside the Gardner River from Mammoth to Gardiner, the flurries had turned to a light rain. His Jeep slowed through the town, then picked up speed heading north on Highway 89, to Livingston, in wind that howled through the crack in his windshield and that, once he turned west and began climbing the pass between Livingston and Bozeman, rocked it wildly side to side.

Will had spent far more time over the past two and a

half decades on horseback than behind a steering wheel. Perhaps that's why it felt so damn unnatural.

He drove like someone numbed by grief, someone struggling to survive, a little like the whitefish left to die on the shores of a Montana river by a fisherman too blind to recognize its beauty. Too stupid to know it—like the cutthroat—was native to the waters.

"You should have gone with him."

Annie looked up from the brief she'd been reading, which lay on the kitchen table in front of her, one corner tinged brown by the coffee she'd just spilled. She had a hearing today and despite spending hours analyzing both parties' briefs, felt uncharacteristically unprepared.

Annoyed, she looked up, over her shoulder, to where her mother stood in the doorway to the living room.

"What are you doing up at this hour?" she said to Eleanor Malone.

Eleanor stepped into the kitchen. She walked much more slowly these days, and always with her cane, but still, for a woman her age, especially one who had been through such a terrible ordeal, she looked good.

Sixteen months earlier, Eleanor Malone had been kidnapped—surprised and taken violently one late August evening in that very room, as she stood at the stove boiling water for bedtime tea, as she had done every morning and evening for Annie and herself. Annie had switched to coffee after that, and thrown away the teapot that she had found still scalding to the touch, though empty, when she had returned home that night to find that her world had just imploded.

"I heard you get up," Eleanor replied, hanging her cane over the chair facing the window, then lowering herself carefully into the chair opposite Annie. "I wanted to talk to you."

"Mother," Annie said impatiently. "This is none of your . . ."

And then, as Eleanor turned and bent to pet Archie, Annie's Lab, who had followed Eleanor in from her upstairs bedroom and now settled on her feet, Annie saw her mother's ear. Actually, what she saw was what was left of her ear, after the kidnappers had cut it off to send to Annie as a warning that they would do more if she did not vacate the bench.

And all annoyance, all impatience, drained from Annie. She reached for her mother's hand, across the table.

Eleanor looked up and something in her expression— a sheepishness—suddenly made Annie suspect that she'd deliberately bobby-pinned her hair back that morning. Usually she wore it meticulously combed over the disfigurement.

Still, when her mother's frail hand met hers, Annie grasped it tightly.

"I'm okay, Mom," she said. "I'll be fine, no matter what happens."

Eleanor's eyes met Annie's.

"He loves you, Annie. I could see that. You should have gone with him."

"He didn't invite me," Annie replied firmly. "And I am not leaving this place. Ever. Even after I'm through on the bench, I'll stay. It's home now. For all of us—you, me, the Judge—" The reference was to Annie's predecessor, Judge Sherburne, who through the course of events after Eleanor was kidnapped, had come to live with Annie and Eleanor in the Stone House. Annie bent to stroke the warm mound of fur beneath the table, and added, "And Archie."

The thick tail thumped twice against the linoleum floor.

Annie pushed the plate of fruit she'd been nibbling across to Eleanor. "Here, you eat this. I have to run now. I'm late."

Eleanor sighed. While Annie was frequently unable—often painfully so—to give visual show to her emotions, her mother tended to be a drama queen.

"I knew you wouldn't want to talk about it."

Annie finally smiled.

She stood, walked to her mother's side, bent and kissed her cheek.

"Would you like coffee? I made a pot."

"Coffee would be fine," Eleanor replied. "Thanks, dear."

Annie gathered up the brief, slid it into her briefcase, gave Archie one last pat, and exited the Stone House through its back door.

The front door, which looked directly out on the park headquarters, was a more direct route to the courthouse, but the back door gave Annie a moment's privacy from tourists already flocking toward the popular hot springs and one of the area's most recognizable geothermal features, Liberty Cap, situated right next door—less than twenty yards from Annie's residence.

It gave Annie a chance to simply stand in the late summer sunshine and absorb this world, take it in—a world which, in many ways, still felt new to her. The childlike wonder had been stolen from her sixteen months earlier, but even that—what had happened over the course of those grim days after Eleanor was kidnapped—hadn't dimmed Annie's passion for this life, or her job, nor—especially not—for Yellowstone itself.

Minerva, one of Yellowstone's most famous and photographed springs, which had lain dormant for over a decade, had recently come back to life. The fact that it had done so virtually the same day that Will rescued her mother hadn't escaped Annie's attention. Now, she looked beyond Minerva, to Bunsen Peak, then her eyes turned east, toward Tower. That—the sight of the road leading to the Lamar, the road Will had no doubt taken earlier that morning—almost dropped Annie to her knees.

They had agreed that he would not stop to say good-bye.

Before walking by the kitchen window, where she knew Eleanor would still be stationed, waiting for another glimpse of her daughter, Annie slipped her sunglasses on. She briefly debated about not looking Eleanor Malone's way, but at the last second she caved in. Concern for Annie etched deep lines on Eleanor's time- and trauma-ravaged face. Annie tried to muster up a reassuring smile, but settled for a nod instead.

Annie could feel her mother's eyes—they never left her—as she forced herself, measured step by measured step, toward the courthouse. A walk of about 300 yards, this morning it felt much longer.

Had it been possible at that moment, at the reality of facing her first day in Yellowstone without Will, she may well have reached for her cell phone and called him back.

One week earlier, after they'd made love in her office—while they were holding each other, silent—she sensed Will was waiting for her to ask him not to go. Maybe she'd made a mistake in not doing so. But the die was cast. Will abhorred cell phones and had no contact information to give her, so the possibility of pleading with him to turn down the relocation no longer existed once he drove past Annie's house, past where she worked, and out of Yellowstone National Park.

Annie had just passed the General Store and cafeteria and was crossing the busy walk in front of the Mammoth Hotel, when she saw a law enforcement car racing toward the intersection from the North Loop road that led to Tower and the Lamar.

Could Will have changed his mind?

The car slowed as it approached the Albright Visitor Center, just as two uniformed men ran down the steps to greet it. Annie recognized Peter Shewmaker, Will's boss. The other man was a biologist but she couldn't remember his name, nor the field he specialized in. Park biologists always came with two-word titles: bison biologist, bear biologist, wolf biologist, but right now the first word escaped Annie.

The LE car—a Jeep—had stopped, lights flashing. Shewmaker and the biologist crossed in front of where it had stopped. When Shewmaker bent low, the driver opened the front window. The biologist had hurried to the back of the vehicle and Annie watched as he lifted the top half of the cargo door open.

Shewmaker blocked her view of the driver, but when he hurried to join the biologist at the back of the car, the front driver's door opened.

Wylie Darlington emerged. A young ranger who had just recently gone through law enforcement training at the Federal Law Enforcement Training Center in Georgia, Will had told Annie that Wylie had been assigned back-country duty. Annie knew him from his days as an interpretive ranger, when she would see him working the desk of the Albright Visitor Center.

Traffic from the east had begun to back up. Annie saw Peter Shewmaker point toward the Pagoda Building—the building that used to house the courthouse and Annie's offices. As Annie picked up her pace to try to see what was going on, the LE Jeep crossed the street and disappeared behind the Pagoda Building. Shewmaker and the biologist began jogging to keep up with it.

Annie's timing was nearly perfect.

"Peter," she called out.

It took Shewmaker several seconds to pick her out of the tourists streaming along the sidewalk between the Visitor Center and the hotel. When he did, he seemed taken off guard to see her, but immediately turned to his companion and said, "You go ahead, Sam. I'll join you and Wylie in a minute."

Despite the hurry he'd obviously been in, it was clear that Shewmaker realized that this was an opportunity to minimize any damage he'd done to his relationship with the park's judge.

"Judge Peacock," he replied with a tentative smile.

Annie reached out and grasped his hand. Peter Shewmaker had been tireless in searching for Eleanor Malone. Even her displeasure over Will's reassignment could not outweigh her immense gratitude.

She smiled, her first genuine smile of the day.

"It's still Annie, Peter."

Visibly relieved, Shewmaker leaned his six-foot-two-inch frame toward her. "I hope you know I fought to keep him here."

"I'm sure you did."

She hesitated. As desperately as she wanted Peter to expound, to confirm what Will had said—that Peter had promised Will could come back after one year—she knew that she could not do so. As Yellowstone's magistrate judge, Annie could not appear to be exerting any influence over Peter.

Peter nodded toward the LE Jeep, lights still flashing, that was sitting, still running, behind the Pagoda Building.

"Wylie's taken over for Will. He'll cover both the Lamar and the Thorofare, at least for now," he said, "until we decide how to deal with the next year."

Annie wanted to throw her arms around Peter and thank him for that no-doubt planned reassurance.

"That's a lot of territory for one person," Annie said instead. She refrained from adding: *especially someone so green*.

Peter's scowl indicated the addition wasn't necessary.

"We just got proof of that."

"What?" Annie replied.

"Wylie's got a dead wolverine in the back of his vehicle. He found it in a trap, just up beyond Thunderer."

"A study trap?"

A multiagency study was being conducted in the park on wolverines. Annie had just read an article about the compact, misunderstood animal. It had touched her to read of its courage and stamina, its absolute need and instinct to steer clear of humans. Until recently that instinct had meant that little was known about the wolverine, but now, through GPS collaring and microchip implants, a team of scientists that had set live traps throughout the park was gathering valuable information—information they hoped would convince the Department of the Interior to grant requests to list the wolverine as an Endangered Species and save it from extinction.

"No, it wasn't a study trap, but unfortunately, it was a study animal—the wolverine was collared. He'd already been caught in a box trap—up above Trout Lake. We just lost an animal that we've invested a fortune of research dollars in. Sam's absolutely beside himself he's so angry." Now Annie remembered who the biologist with Shewmaker was: Sam Blount, wolverine biologist. The article she'd read had quoted Sam numerous times as the lead biologist for the study. "If only it *had* been a box trap. . . . Wylie found him, barely still alive, in a leghold trap. He died before he could free him."

"That's horrible," Annie cried. "In all my time here, I've never presided on an illegal trapping case."

All Annie could think about was Will.

"I know just what you're thinking," Peter replied, his eyes fixed on Annie. "The timing was terrible. Will pulled out of that area just yesterday morning. He would normally have been out there." His expression made Annie feel half sorry for him—the second guessing he had to be feeling about forcing Will to leave. "Listen, Annie, I have to run."

"Of course. I'm sorry about the wolverine, Peter."

Peter had turned and started toward the Pagoda Building. Now he paused and turned to look at Annie one last time.

"I dread Will hearing about this."

His expression told Annie that these weren't idle words.

"If he hears about it today, I wouldn't be surprised if he turns that old jalopy of his around and heads right back." Another pause before he hurried to catch up with Sam and Wylie. "Who knows what'll happen then?"

Four

The small Montana towns and expanses of golden prairie that stretched forever, always rimmed in the distance by mountain ranges—with names like the Crazies, or the Tobacco Roots, or the Sapphires—barely drew Will's attention. Even the Missions on the Flathead Reservation—magnificent goliaths that seemed to spring from out of nowhere, humbling and silencing the most jaded of travelers—did not cheer him. However, when he dropped into Polson and first viewed the waters of Flathead Lake, Will's gloom lifted just a little.

Mountains, water, wilderness—he told himself—they would still be a part of his life.

But then he made the mistake of stopping at the Safeway for a sandwich. A Starbucks was the first thing he saw when he walked in the door.

The nearest Starbucks to Yellowstone was eighty miles away, in Bozeman.

In Gardiner, when he shopped at a grocery store, it was the Food Farm, where half the shoppers wore the green and gray, and the rest were tourists, buoyed by their visit to this country's first national park, bent, puzzling, over a selection of local beef, bison, or pork roasts.

The shoppers in this Safeway looked like they'd either just stepped off a commuter jet in Los Angeles or the pages of an REI catalog. Will realized that he had spent so much time around it that he hadn't recognized the sense of wonder that ran beneath the surface of just about every person he encountered in Yellowstone. He felt like that whitefish along the shore again—about to take its last gasp of air.

It only got worse as he drove north, along the east side of Flathead Lake—the largest freshwater lake in the western United States. Ringed on one side by the Mission Mountains, and on the west by the Salish Mountains, Flathead had once been the domain of mainstay Montana locals, but its stunning vistas and the growing awareness of Montana in general had drawn wealthy out-of-staters who built million-dollar lakeside estates, with gates and names pasted across signs or hand-hewn log arches over their driveways.

Will's Jeep crawled along the lake in a stream of cars, passing one cherry orchard after another. By the time he reached Big Fork, an upscale, artsy community where the Swan River joined the lake, he began contemplating a U-turn.

Maybe he couldn't do it after all. Maybe he didn't have the courage or the heart, for even one year. Desperate for a distraction, he turned the radio on and began scanning for a station that his broken antennae could pick up. When the static finally cleared, he stopped twisting the dial, just as an annoyingly folksy voice, that of a woman, said, "Of course I stand by my decision to shoot wolves from helicopters!"

Will continued down the main drag north of Big Fork. If he'd wanted distraction, he'd found it. He may have lived in the backcountry of Yellowstone for almost thirty years, but even he knew whom the voice belonged to: the recent governor of the state of Idaho, Faithe Unsword. Unsword, a right wing born-again, had been tapped by fundamentalists to run for the U.S. Senate, but then a series of bad PR moves—including a state-sponsored predator killing derby that some Idahoans may have loved but that enraged others (although more for tourist dollars lost than for the twisted cruelty that had outraged the rest of the country)—had forced her to withdraw from the race. Will hadn't heard what she'd been up to since then, but he was always at least a few months behind on any national news, so that came as no surprise.

Will despised Unsword for her views on just about everything, but especially for her aerial gunning of wolves, her administration's indiscriminate killing of entire families and packs—pups and all. He squinted to get a glimpse of where on the dial his scanning had stopped. Twelve eighty. That seemed too high up to be a national station, but then again, what did he know about such things?

"I was governor of a state that depends on hunting—not just for income, but for its residents who live below the poverty level, and who, you know, depend on hunting to put food on their tables, to feed their kids. And big game hunting—hunters who come in there and take home a beauty of a bull elk, or a moose. I have no affection for wolves. They kill for sport. Just for the fun of it. And when they do, they hurt the people I was charged with taking care of. You betcha, I have no regrets about aerial gunning. And if I ever served in a political office again, and I tell ya', I have no political ambitions, none at all, I'm telling you the truth, I'd push for hunting wolves year round. And grizzlies. Don't even get me started on grizzlies. 'Cause my loyalty is to my country and my family, not to man-killing beasts."

Big Fork had now begun to fade behind Will, and up

ahead he spotted the first sign signaling his destination, a sign for the turnoff to Highway 2.

GLACIER NATIONAL PARK. 26 MILES.

"No sir, my loyalty's not to some animal that a group of extremists think is more important than feeding some little kid—and her sisters and brothers, her grandma and grandpa. That's disgraceful, and if those big groups, groups like Protectors of America's Wildlife, want to go after me, well, go right ahead. I consider it an honor that they do, 'cause I'll be a scapegoat all day long if it helps my kids. Or my country."

"Now," she said, "let's go to line two. Trent Wiles from Troy, Montana. Go ahead, Trent from Troy."

Unsword was apparently hosting some kind of talk show.

"Yes, Senator," the caller said

Unsword responded, "Now didn't I just tell you I no longer have political ambitions?"

Trent Wiles guffawed appropriately before continuing. "I'm a huge fan of yours, and I for one am proud to know you've chosen the Flathead for your next home."

"And I'm honored to call myself a Montanan now," Unsword replied.

Will almost drove the car off the road. Faithe Unsword, living in Montana?

The caller continued, "I agree that it's time to take back our country and that's what my question for you is all about. How do you feel about the guns-in-parks legislation?"

"Oh my. You really wanna' get me going, doncha? Here's how I feel, Trent. It's our right as citizens of this great country to bear arms. The Constitution, article three—I mean two, article two, er amendment two—gives us that right, God gives us that right and I tell you here and now that I will fight to defend it. That's how I feel."

"I couldn't agree with you more. Tell me, Senator, is

there any truth to the rumor you moved to Montana to run for office here, because we could sure use you. We got ourselves a Democrat for governor and two Democrats for Senators. . . ."

"I never say never, my friend, because in the end, I know I'll do what God calls on me to do, what the right thing for my family and my country is. But for now, God wants me here, talking to you on the radio and helping spread the word that all is not lost in this great country of ours. We just need to stand up and fight for what's right. That's all I'm about right now, but thank you, Trent, and all of you who've been calling in during these first weeks of my new show. You've given me great hope and I promise, I won't let you down."

Even more sick at heart than when he started his trip, Will listened to another half-dozen callers before switching the radio off, just as he slowed for the traffic backed up to enter West Glacier. Souvenir shops, guide businesses offering anything from fishing to helicopter tours of the park, and motels grew thick along both sides of the highway.

As Will passed the West Glacier turnoff, he found himself relieved he hadn't been instructed to report to the park headquarters. Peter had told him to go straight to East Glacier, where he was to meet with Shewmaker's equivalent, Rob Deardorf—Glacier National Park's director of law enforcement. From what Will could see, West Glacier seemed the equivalent of Yellowstone's Old Faithful in that it appeared every tourist deemed driving Going to the Sun Road a necessity. In the mood Will was in, he didn't need crowds and a meeting with all the Park Service higher-ups. He'd become a backcountry ranger twenty-eight years earlier in part to avoid just that scene—that of the ass-kissing, rule-abiding career bureaucrat. Still, it seemed odd to him not to be reporting to headquarters.

Just past West Glacier, as Will picked up speed again, and another sign came into view—East Glacier 56 miles, Browning 69—even the hardened, disillusioned old ranger he'd become began having trouble feeling indifferent to the scenery playing out before his eyes.

As he drove on, the mountains became wildly jagged—more like the Grand Tetons, south of Yellowstone, than any of Yellowstone's peaks. The Middle Fork of the Flathead River, with the sun glinting off its roiling waters, hugged the left side of the highway, creating the divide between the vast and inaccessible Bob Marshall Wilderness on the right and Glacier on the left. The sheer vastness of the landscape and the incredible beauty comforted Will. He imagined the countless grizzlies roaming out there, just starting hyperphagia—the period during which they gorged themselves on berries and cutworm moths in preparation for winter and hibernation; the wolves he would soon be living amongst. His heart lifted. It did not soar as it did on almost a daily basis in Yellowstone, but it recognized that he would have the same mainstays—wildlife and wilderness—that had sustained him ever since Rachel and Carter's deaths.

Some things, however, would be no different. Just after he'd passed a highway sign saying Entering Glacier National Park, Will saw the trademark cars parked alongside the road. People stood, pointing cameras up the rocky hillside that climbed steeply no more than twenty feet from the road. Instinctively, from the topography, Will knew they had to be looking at either mountain goats or bighorn sheep. The next sign, Goatlick, answered the question. Within minutes, another sign told Will he was leaving Glacier. He would travel another thirty-five miles just outside its eastern border before he reached the town of East Glacier.

It was a spectacular thirty-five miles.

How many grizzlies were out there, roaming the Nyack

Valley he was passing on his left? How many wolves would be his neighbors this time around?

The knowledge that he would soon be back in the wilderness gave Will a new confidence about what lay ahead—even a spark of excitement.

He couldn't wait to get in the backcountry.

That would be his salvation.

Sam Blount reached for the radio collar lying on his desk. He'd been staring at it, numbly, for several minutes now when suddenly it registered. The scent.

Sam Blount knew his scents.

The fury inside him, which he'd somehow managed to contain throughout the morning—as he allowed Number 2 M to be taken away for the last data he would ever provide, the report on his death—erupted when he brought the collar to his nose.

"Goddammit!" he yelled to the empty room. "Son of a bitch."

In less than a heartbeat, the door to his office opened.

His student intern, Danette Kirst, stuck her head inside warily. She'd been standing in the hallway, wondering whether to come in or leave her boss alone.

"I was waiting for you to let it out," she said.

Blount turned to her, his face a portrait of frustration and grief.

"*Son of a bitch used a scent lure.*"

Eyes wide, Kirst stepped into the room.

"You're sure?"

Blount jumped up, hand extended, and pushed the collar under her nose.

"Smell it! That poor animal must've rubbed himself raw with it. Must've been downright giddy by the time he stepped into that trap."

When Kirst inhaled deeply through her nostrils, the

smell caused her to fall back. Scent lures often consisted of wolverine urine and anal gland secretion mixed with other chemicals known to attract wolverines. Blount's research team used scent lures to attract wolverines to the live box traps used in their study.

"Whoa. You're not kidding. Do you recognize it?"

"I sure do," he answered. Blotchy-faced with anger, he pried his eyes away from the collar and met Kirst's loyal gaze. "Get Yellow Kidney on the phone."

If you blinked driving east along Highway 2, you might miss the town of East Glacier. And if you did that, you'd soon find yourself in Browning—the heartbeat of the Blackfeet Reservation.

East Glacier was an odd blend, nothing like the gateway communities to Yellowstone that Will was familiar with. Not that he was enamored of Cooke City, or West Yellowstone, or even Gardiner, but they were all similar in many ways, and Will was used to them. To start with, East Glacier sat on the reservation. Its residents were a quirky blend—Blackfeet, old time residents, many of whom were descended from settlers who'd never left, hippies, recluses, "lodgies"—those who came solely to work at the lodge—and part-time second-homers, usually loners, who were drawn by the raw quality of both the land and the people. Like the rest of the Blackfeet Reservation, with its long, brutal winters and dangerous roads, East Glacier was not for the timid, nor the faint of heart.

A place where homeless dogs roamed the town, moving from one storefront to a motel, to a favorite house or garage, where they were inevitably fed and looked after; where conversations with a stranger on the next barstool turned out to be as straightforward and lacking in pretense—and sometimes as wildly out there—as the locals themselves. A place that survived economically because it served as the portal to the east side of one of the world's most famous and spectacular national parks, but that sometimes resented the tourists who flocked there and considered the park their own playground, or resource. Or, for many, church.

Most people didn't linger long in East Glacier, but those who did often stayed a lifetime and eventually—not easily, but almost always, eventually—became part of a tightly knit, dysfunctional community that took fierce pride in what it meant to live there.

When you entered East Glacier on Highway 2, you could either drive straight through and on to Browning, which was thirteen miles down the windswept road, or you could take an immediate left, under the Burlington Northern tracks that serviced the remote outpost, and follow the road leading to the magnificent Glacier Park Lodge, past the nine-hole golf course that in the spring was frequented by grizzlies, and several modest, family owned motels, and on up to Two Medicine, the entry gate to the park.

Will had attended several law enforcement conferences at the lodge over the years. Not one to mingle with other attendees at the end of a long day of sitting in conference rooms, at night he'd taken off hiking on his own, usually until well after dark, and then, when he couldn't bear the thought of returning to a hotel room, he'd often headed to the bar, where he'd broken up more than one or two fights over the years.

As he turned left, under the tracks, and passed the first hole of the golf course, he remembered the night he'd slept on a fairway, staring at the sky—homesick for Yellowstone after only two days and taking solace in falling asleep to the same constellations he'd closed his eyes to countless times in its backcountry. That thought led to thoughts of Annie, the night in her office—the look in her eyes when he kissed her good-bye—and a pain so visceral hit him at that moment that it almost caused him to double over the steering wheel.

"What the fuck have I done?" he asked himself aloud.

When he finally reached the entry gate, he was in no mood to deal with a jackass of a young ranger.

Will had pulled his Jeep over, out of the line of vehicles waiting to enter the park. As he got out and began walking to the booth that served as a poor version of Yellowstone's log cabin entry stations, a uniformed ranger leaned out its window. "Hey, buddy, back in your car."

Will didn't miss a step. He flashed his LE badge as he approached and the door of the booth opened, but the ranger—a fresh-faced redhead—had already turned his back on Will.

"Whatever it is," he said over his shoulder in a nasal Chicago accent, "it'll have to wait until I get these people into the park."

Will took a deep breath as he listened to the kid deliver a litany of admonitions and instructions to the driver of each car. Finally, when the last one had cleared, he turned to Will.

"Your first season?" Will asked.

Red-faced, but unable to come up with a suitable reply, the kid said, "How can I help you?"

"I'm supposed to be meeting Rob Deardorf here."

The kid finally smiled.

"Are you Will McCarroll?"

"Yes."

"Supervisor Deardorf asked me to give you this." He reached into the drawer where he had been depositing entry fees and withdrew a white envelope with a Glacier National Park logo on it.

Will took the envelope, ripped it open, and found a key inside. What a joke, they actually locked their back-country cabins.

"Supervisor Deardorf told me to give you directions

to your cabin," the kid said. "You can turn around after this RV has cleared."

"Turn around?" Will echoed, eyeing the oversized RV with Washington plates heading their way.

"Yes. Did you notice a little café called Brownies when you drove through town? It's between here and the lodge, on the left. Your cabin is just past that. It's kind of hidden behind Brownies but you won't have any trouble find-ing it."

Will simply stared at the kid.

"There must be some mistake. I'll be working the backcountry, the Nyack."

The kid lifted his shoulders.

"That's all I know," he said. "Excuse me for a minute."

He turned to greet the RV. As he did so, another car pulled up behind Will's, parked, and a woman wearing a Park Service uniform got out. She looked to be in her mid-fifties, with graying brown hair tied in a ponytail. She headed for the booth.

When she stepped in, she smiled at Will, donned a quizzical expression, then moved on to the window and began thumbing through a pile of credit card receipts the kid had been sticking in a file organizer. Neither she nor the kid greeted each other as he gave the welcome spiel that Will had already almost memorized.

Suddenly she stopped, mid-pile, and turned to look at Will.

Her name tag said Rhondie Wilkins.

"You're Will McCarroll."

Still grasping the key and reeling from learning he was supposed to live in town, Will frowned at her, almost ir-ritated that she was interrupting his thoughts about what to do next.

"Yes."

Rhondie looked at the envelope on the floor, the key in his hand.

"Oh my god," she said. "He really did it. I can't believe it."

She'd piqued Will's interest.

"Who?" he asked.

"Deardorf. He actually gave you the house in town."

She simply stared at the key, shaking her head.

"I told him you wouldn't put up with it. . . ."

The RV cleared and the kid had turned their way. For the first time, Will noticed his name tag. Brent Marshall.

"What are you doing?" he said to Rhondie. "You shouldn't be telling him"—he nodded toward Will as if he weren't there—"what Supervisor Deardorf said. That conversation was privileged—it was just between the three of us."

Rhondie looked at the kid and said, "The three of us? You had nothing to do with it—all you did was eavesdrop. I knew I should've kicked your ass out of here yesterday when we were discussing this. Do you know who this is? This is Will McCarroll."

The expression on Brent's face made it clear he wasn't the least bit impressed.

"I don't care who he is. You shouldn't be sharing a conversation you had with Supervisor Deardorf with him."

She swatted the air his way.

"Rob Deardorf couldn't hold this man's jockstrap. And you should be down on your knees. Do you know all he's done for the parks? Do you even know why he's here? He's here for trying to protect people like you and me. Don't even get me started. Your shift's over. Now skedaddle, before I really lose my temper."

Ordinarily Will might have found Rhondie's tirade amusing, but right now nothing could make him smile, even the feisty ranger in front of him.

When a sullen Brent departed without saying another word, Will watched Rhondie wave two cars through the gate. Then, when she turned to him, he said, "So what's the story?"

"The story is that Rob Deardorf got instructions to house you right there, in town. He can be an asshole, but this time it wasn't even his idea. It came to him from some higher-ups."

"How do I work the Nyack from East Glacier?"

"That's what I asked Rob. He didn't give me an answer."

Will took two steps over to the counter, slammed the key down on it, and said, "Thanks for your honesty Ranger Wilkins. Tell Supervisor Deardorf thanks but no thanks."

She reached out and grabbed his hand, stopping him.

"Wait. Think about it."

Will tried not to lash out at the woman. She was innocent, after all, and clearly more friend than foe. But he had trouble containing his anger.

"What's there to think about? I could no more live in that town—any town—than that ground squirrel out there could fly."

"That's what I mean," Ranger Wilkins replied. "Think about it. They know that about you, yet that's what they told Deardorf to do."

Will froze. He'd been so upset that he hadn't been thinking straight.

"They want me to quit."

Rhondie pursed her lips and nodded her head.

"That's how I figure it. But why? Who?"

Will shook his head.

"It has to be Gonzalez, the new superintendent. Peter gets sick of the trouble I cause, but he wouldn't want to get rid of me. Gonzalez probably wants a fresh slate. He knows the new administration's going to be looking at him."

Rhondie had been waving cars through right and left, talking all the while.

"Son of a bitch doesn't have a clue if he thinks getting rid of you is a good thing. Just another asshole politician, climbing the ladder," she said indignantly. "But the question is, what are you going to do about it?"

Will's eyes dropped to the key. He stared at it, silent.

Five

"H'lo?"

Johnny Yellow Kidney sat in his usual spot—at the back table of Brownies. A dark, two-story log building on the west side of the town of East Glacier, Brownies served as both a convenience store and café on the ground floor and, up a flight of creaky stairs, a hostel that, during its Old West days, housed a brothel. These days it was not only a favorite of old-time locals, like Johnny, but also, because of its location—any vehicle entering the park through the Two Medicine gate passed by it—it had caught on as a place to stock up on sandwiches and incidentals for a backcountry hike. At eighty-three, its owner, Vilma, still worked the counter mornings, though she'd turned over the espresso machine to the young girls from places like the Czech Republic and Sweden who flocked to Glacier National Park each year looking for summer excitement and romance. The lucky ones ended up at Brownies, where Vilma took them under her wing, teaching them not only how to make a damn good sandwich, but also how, and when, to put obnoxious customers in their place.

As Johnny pressed his cell phone to his ear to be able to hear over the chatter from nearby tables, Vilma topped off his coffee. He rewarded her with one of his boyish, shit-eating, glorious smiles. Aside from his head of shiny black hair, Johnny Yellow Kidney wasn't a handsome man. Until he smiled.

"Johnny, it's Sam Blount."

"Sam," Johnny replied, pressing the phone closer. "I'd say it's good to hear your voice, but you don't sound so happy."

"I'm not happy. In fact, I've never been so pissed off."

Laughter from the next table, where two couples sat decked out in new hiking clothes, almost drowned Sam out. Their accents indicated they were French.

"Hold on a minute, Sam," Johnny said.

He rose to his full six-three self and leaned toward the table.

"You folks mind quieting down a little?" he said politely, but with a steel determination. His eyes moved from one of the men to the other. The message was unmistakable. He nodded toward the phone in his hand, and added, as if anyone in his right mind would understand: "Important call."

Neither of the men looked happy about it, and the women seemed equal parts insulted and taken with this striking stranger. His actions had the desired effect. The table went silent.

Johnny looked up, toward the cash register, to see if he'd annoyed Vilma, but she merely shook her head, with a *tsk-tsk* kind of look on her face, then handed another young couple their change.

Johnny sat back down.

"Okay, Sam. Tell me, what's going on down there?"

"A backcountry ranger found Number 2 M in a trap this afternoon."

Johnny laughed.

"Greedy little bugger."

"I don't mean one of our traps. It was a leghold. He's dead, Johnny."

Heads turned when Johnny's fist came down on the table.

"Son of a bitch."

There was a moment's silence, then Sam said, "How's the hand?"

Ignoring him, Johnny was intent upon finding out more details. "Where? North of the park? East? Cooke City? Last reading you sent me, he was on the Thunderer."

"That's where it happened. Near Thunderer."

"Goddamn! Inside the park?"

"Inside the park."

Johnny shook his head. "Shit, Sam. I'd expect that here—traps are nothing new. But not there. Not in Yellowstone."

"Why the hell doesn't Glacier crack down on trapping?"

"Two things. For starters, we don't have the backcountry LE you have. And this is between us, but those we have aren't as well trained as your people."

Johnny heard Sam's groan.

"Yeah, well, we just lost our number one deterrent. Will McCarroll."

"McCarroll left?" Johnny straightened in his chair at the news. "I never met the man but I've heard enough to be surprised he'd ever leave Yellowstone."

"This is just between the two of us, 'cause it's apparently something they don't want to advertise. I just learned it today, because of what happened. Will's leaving wasn't by choice. Got himself in trouble again and they decided the best way to deal with it was sending him away for a year. Actually, he just left today and he's headed your way."

"To Glacier? Goddamn. We could sure use him. I've been coming across legholds in the Nyack."

"You think they're trying for wolverine?"

"Not where I've been finding them. We've got a couple study animals in the park, but they're up high, near Iceberg Lake. I suspect this guy's not in good enough shape—or else not motivated—to get up there."

"You said there were two reasons you've got more trapping going on there. What's the second?"

Johnny watched as the two couples at the next table got up, still practically silent. Both men shot him angry glances. One of the women tilted her head playfully and waved good-bye.

"Indians," he answered. "Trapping's part of our heritage, and my people have treaty rights—they can hunt or trap in the park as long as they eat what they kill."

"You gotta be shittin' me," Sam replied.

"Nope. The park used to be Blackfeet land. They took it from us. About the only thing we got out of the deal was that—the right to hunt for food. And to be honest, it's pretty rare when it actually happens. But I tell you, it makes finding traps a complicated issue.

"But my people would never do what just happened in Yellowstone. They don't kill for sport, and they sure as hell wouldn't go after a wolverine. Animals aren't trophies to us. They're sacred. When someone kills an animal for food, it's done with reverence." Suddenly Johnny caught himself. "Hey, I'm sorry. Didn't mean to get all holier-than-thou. But I'm so pissed to hear what happened there. I'm sorry, man. Don't know what I'd do if it happened here. Especially to one of my study animals."

"That's okay, Johnny. I knew you'd be almost as angry as I am."

"So what can I do for you? I'm sorry as hell about Number 2, but I suspect you didn't just call to notify me of his death."

Now that the loud tourists had departed, Johnny could actually hear Sam close the door to his office.

"I want to send you something," Sam said. "Number 2's radio collar."

"Why would you do that?"

"Because it reeks. The trapper used a scent lure. I think it's one of yours."

"You're shitting me."

"Wish I were, but I've worked with your scents enough to recognize it."

For years, Johnny had been creating compounds to use as attractants to lure wolverine to the live box traps used in his studies. Similar to semiochemicals—natural substances like urine and anal gland secretions, which one organism uses to communicate with another—researchers coated trees and branches with these substances. That usually got a wolverine close enough to the trap to smell the meat left inside to coax it into taking the final step.

"Or at least I think I do," Sam continued. "If you tell me I'm right, maybe it can help lead to the trapper. Let me ask you something: who else have you given your scents to?"

"No one. I haven't wanted them to get in the wrong hands. I designed them for research only, and as you well know, you and I are about it when it comes to wolverine research these days."

"Damn," Sam replied. "How the hell could a trapper have gotten hold of it then?" There was a silence, then Johnny heard him call out. "Danette, get in here."

Johnny listened as Sam ordered, "Get over to the lab

and inventory the vials of Yellow Kidney's scent we have there."

A female voice replied, "Got it."

"How about you," he said to Johnny, when he came back on line. "Are you at your lab?"

Johnny snorted a half laugh.

"Lab? I don't have an office, much less a lab."

"Why the hell not?"

"I'm based in East Glacier. I'd have an office if I were over in West, at the headquarters. Maybe even a lab—at least a shared lab. But I've been over here for about six years now. And believe me, I don't have an office or a lab."

"Why would they put you in East Glacier then?"

Johnny was used to the disbelief he heard in Blount's voice.

"They didn't. I put myself here. I worked out of West for a couple years, but once I had a little clout—meaning, as you well know, got published and got some funding for my research—I used it to move here."

"What the hell's in East Glacier?" Sam pressed.

"The rez, that's what. I grew up here. Actually about twenty miles from here, in Heart Butte. Funny, I grew up wanting to be anywhere but here, but once I left, I realized there's nowhere else I want to be. Gets in your blood."

Sam Blount clearly didn't get it.

"You can't even get them to find you an office?"

"I've got all the office I need," Johnny replied, looking around. Most the customers had departed, bellies and backpacks full for a day of hiking. "I keep my scents in a freezer in my shed. I'll head over there and make sure none's missing. Meanwhile, overnight me that collar. I'll know right away if they used something I came up with."

"Done. And get back to me, will you, as soon as you check it out?"

"Will do."

Johnny snapped his phone shut and gulped the last two ounces of coffee. As he headed out the door, he reached for a piece of bacon that one of the tourists he'd chased off had left untouched on his plate, stuck it in his pocket, then stopped at the cash register.

"Sorry about scaring your customers away," he said to Vilma.

"They were a pain in the ass," she replied without looking up from the notepad she was scribbling a grocery list on. She would take it with her later, to Browning, where she would stock up for the next week's business.

Johnny waved a five-dollar bill under her nose, but Vilma pushed it away.

"You can't keep not charging me, Vilma," he said. "Hell, I not only scare customers off on a regular basis, I've pretty much turned that table into my office. Take it, please."

Vilma nodded toward a jar sitting on the counter. It was half full with a combination of money—change and dollar bills—and lilac-colored rubber wristbands, like the Lance Armstrong bands, or the pink cancer bands. The rag-eared, handmade label taped to the jar's front said, HELP US FEED THE LOCAL DOGS.

There were dozens of dogs roaming the streets of East Glacier. Many were rez dogs who had the good fortune to be dropped off or to work their way to East Glacier, instead of Browning, or Heart Butte, or Babb. The people of East Glacier had always taken care of these dogs. Despite brutal winters and equally harsh summers, year after year the same dogs moved from one business to another, one home to another, where they were fed and, on the rare occasion they chose to be, sheltered. Part of the funds to do so came from the jar that had sat on Brownies' counter for a decade or more. The locals never chose to grab a lilac band to show they'd donated, but tourists loved the idea.

"Put it in there," she said. "Come winter we always run short."

Johnny didn't mention that he'd already put a five in there, on his way in. Instead, dutifully, like a little boy obeying a half-beloved, half-frightening grandmother, he shoved the bill into the jar and strode out the door, passing a mostly blind, arthritic old hound-heeler mutt lying in the sun on the porch of the building.

Johnny reached down, patted the dog's head, and slipped the piece of bacon under the canine's nose.

"Here you go, Stinky," he said.

It took a moment for the odor to penetrate Stinky's consciousness, but when it did he glommed onto the offering, tail thumping the wooden planks.

"Hey bro," a voice said from over Johnny's shoulder.

Johnny looked up. A big grin immediately spread across his features.

Cole Ingram smiled back.

The two exchanged a hug—not the quick, gratuitous kind, but a bear hug worthy of old friends.

Cole and Johnny had attended high school together. Kids from East Glacier had to be bused the thirteen miles across wind-driven, snow-packed plains to the high school in Browning, where, like Cole, they were often the only white kid in their class. Johnny had gone out of his way to befriend Cole. As it turned out, Cole was not only one tough son of a bitch, he was about as Indian as a white kid could get. That, plus Johnny's friendship, ensured that nobody messed with him.

Since those days, they rarely ran into each other. The last time Johnny had seen Cole was two years earlier, at Indian Days in Browning.

Johnny pulled back, looked at the white shirt with a

Nehru collar that Cole was wearing, and said, "What the hell's that?"

"Chef uniform," Cole answered, clearly proud. "I'm the cook out at Snow Slip now."

"I thought I heard you and Spencer were doing some guiding in the park—backcountry trips."

Cole's other best friend at Browning High had been Spencer Four Bear, who was distantly related to Johnny.

"That's my day job. And my days off. Four nights a week, Snow Slip's my gig."

Johnny knew that Cole had had some bad times over the years—struggles with alcohol and drugs. The man standing before him now looked healthy and happy, like he was in a good place.

"Good for you. You look good, man. What's the secret?"

Cole glanced sideways.

"I'm in love."

Johnny chortled.

"That'll do it. Anybody I know?"

"She's a little younger than us, but maybe you remember her. Whisper Little Wolf."

Johnny let out a long whistle.

"Damn. I see her ride through here some mornings. She's still a sight for sore eyes."

Suddenly Johnny remembered rumors he'd heard, only a few months earlier.

"I thought she was engaged to Lester Winged Foot?"

"She was," Cole answered. "But she went through some kind of tough shit recently, and Lester wasn't there for her."

Cole's face had darkened.

"I work with her at Snow Slip. She's a waitress there. She needed some help after what happened to her, and we hooked up."

Johnny put a hand on Cole's shoulder. He'd seen the expression on his friend's face before. The bitterly cold January day they'd pulled Cole out of class to tell him that his uncle had died of exposure when his car broke down during the night on his way home from visiting a friend in the hospital in Browning.

He'd tried to hitch a ride, but according to the tribal police, who found him around 3:00 A.M., several cars had passed him but no one had stopped.

Over the next six months, before school let out, Cole had gotten in so many fights that he'd finally been suspended.

"Listen," Johnny said now, "if you need someone to talk to, come to me. But don't go getting yourself in trouble, you hear?"

They parted with another heartfelt hug.

When his old friend disappeared inside Brownies, Johnny stepped down off the wood planked porch and jogged across the street. Cutting behind the gas station that also served as a car rental for tourists who arrived via train, he worked his way through a network of rental cabins nestled in the trees, emerged midway down one of a dozen short streets that bisected the town's residential area, and finally—tucked away at the end of a gravel road, with nothing to disturb his views into the park—he reached the little A-frame he called home.

Usually, especially on a day like this—with mountains looming clear and crisp against a sky so blue it could make an artist traveling without his watercolors cry—Johnny headed right for the refrigerator for a beer, which he'd take to the deck that looked out over Midvale Creek and into Glacier National Park. But now he hurried past the cabin and headed for a decrepit wood shack that sat twenty feet beyond the A-frame's back door, literally bumping up against a stand of cottonwoods that lined the banks of the stream.

As he approached, Johnny's eyes fixed upon the padlock he'd put on the door when he'd decided to move the
small meat storage freezer in which he housed his inventory of lure scents into the shed. The early afternoon sun
glinted off the padlock, confirming it was still in place,
but it wasn't until he'd stepped close to the shed, into the
shade of the trees, that he could see it hadn't been opened.
Hell, it had been several weeks since he'd gone in that
shed. He hadn't yet finished the smaller supply that he
kept inside the house, in his refrigerator.

For peace of mind, he wanted to check out the freezer
and its contents. He pulled his key ring out, inserted the
key, and the lock slid open effortlessly. Inside the shed,
he moved to the freezer, lifted its lid, and eyeballed the
contents. He didn't have a sign-out sheet, the kind they'd
used for supplies in West Glacier. Didn't need it since it
was only Johnny who used or distributed the scent lures.
Still, he could tell nothing was missing. The jars were in
order, nothing askew. Relieved, he went back outside,
waved to a neighbor running in the midday heat, and decided he'd better get to work. He'd left his car at Brownies, where he'd stopped, as he did each morning, for a
cup of coffee on his way to Two Medicine.

He'd originally planned on checking the remote camera he'd installed midsummer at a bait station near Rising Wolf, hoping this time it would have caught visits by
the two wolverines he suspected were feeding on the por-
tions of elk carcass he'd suspended from tree branches;
but now he'd decided to change his plans and head up to
Two Medicine Pass instead, to check on the hair snares
he'd set there the day before. The hair obtained would
be used to collect DNA. Ordinarily he didn't necessarily
check hair snares the day after he'd placed them. Despite the deer carcass he'd anchored to the ground with
a metal stake, it usually took wolverines a day or two of
visiting and seeing it was safe before they actually dared

to approach the box trap itself, drawn not only by the scent lures Johnny rubbed generously on downed trees and low branches, but also the ultimate prize—in this case, a dead muskrat inside. Johnny had come across it along a creek on his arduous trek to the elevations where wolverines, who held such a sacred spot in his heart, felt safest.

But what had happened in Yellowstone had Johnny shaken. The possibility that someone might deliberately set out, scent lure in hand, to trap the rare and elusive wolverines that inhabited both parks—two of their last safe havens in a world that was indifferent about wiping them out—had planted a seed of anxiety in his gut.

As he started back to Brownies, accelerating to a jog, Johnny reflected on the other news Sam Blount had delivered. Will McCarroll was coming to Glacier.

Of course, he'd be stationed on the west side of the park—that's where they'd assign someone of Will's standing—but still, the knowledge that Will would be out in the backcountry gave Johnny some peace of mind.

And then, when he got to his car, slightly winded, even though he'd run less than a mile, it occurred to him: he'd checked the freezer in his shed, but he hadn't checked his refrigerator. He'd moved scent lures in there three weeks earlier, for convenience. He kept them in the two drawers at the bottom of the freezer. He'd just opened the top drawer yesterday, to take out the vial he'd used up at Iceberg Lake. But he hadn't checked the bottom drawer since he'd placed the scents in there.

This time Johnny used his car to get back to his house, gravel flying as he spun out of Brownies' parking lot and crossed in front of the line of cars that had turned off Highway 2, headed to the Two Medicine entrance.

When he got to the A-frame, he jumped out and sprinted to the front door, which, like most East Glacier residents, Johnny never locked.

Racing through the sparsely furnished living room toward the kitchen, he already knew—his instinct told him—what he'd find.

Throwing open the freezer, Johnny slid the bottom tray out, then slammed his fist into the refrigerator's door.

"*Shit.*"

Claudette Nillson had already been on the phone for fifteen minutes and still hadn't talked to a live person at Montana Fish, Wildlife & Parks. She'd exhausted all the voice mail menu options, when finally it occurred to her to simply press "0."

A recorded voice told her to hold for a FWP employee.

When a woman's pleasant voice said, "FWP, how can I help you?" Claudette's grip on the phone tightened.

"I want to report that my dog was killed in a trap."

This was met with silence. When the woman finally replied, her voice had changed.

"Where did this happen?"

"Along Paola Creek, just outside of Glacier."

"That's Forest Service land, I believe."

"Yes, it is."

"Trapping is legal on Forest Service land. Was your dog on a leash?"

Claudette began to sweat.

"No."

"Were you with your dog?"

"What does that have to do with it?" Claudette snapped. "A trapper killed my dog. I want to report it."

"Fine. You've reported it."

"You didn't even ask me my name. Or exactly where it took place."

"You said it was near Paola Creek."

"Don't you even want to know my name? Or my dog's name? Don't you care?"

"What is your name?" the voice replied flatly.

"Claudette Nillson." She hadn't even realized that she'd begun yelling. "My dog's name is Tenny. Tennyson." Tears rolled down Claudette's cheeks.

"Claudette," the FWP woman said. "I will not continue this conversation if you don't get ahold of yourself." She paused, waiting for Claudette's response. When none came, she continued. "I will make a note of the fact that your dog died. But since there was no illegal activity involved, other than, perhaps, you having no control over your dog at the time it became trapped, there will be no investigation. But I've taken down your name. And your dog's name. Now, is there anything else I can help you with?"

"Yes. I want the trapper's name."

"Pardon me?"

"The trapper's name. I want to find out who did this to Tenny."

"That's not information I can give you. And even if I could, I wouldn't. Your voice has a very threatening tone. I will make note of that in my report as well. If you want my advice, you'll . . ."

Claudette pressed "end" on her cell phone.

Forty-five minutes later, she strode into the Sportsman's Paradise store in Columbia Falls. In her hand was the steel jagged-toothed trap that she'd pried off Tenny's leg long after it would do her beloved dog any good. She'd kept it, had, in fact, polished it, ridding it not only of bits of Tenny's fur and segments of his teeth, but of dirt and weeds and untold other remnants of creatures once alive and enjoying a day in the wilds.

Two clerks, both men, worked counters that had fishermen and hunters buying licenses, guns, flies for their trip on the Middle Fork. She stood in the haphazard line. While the clerks pretended not to see her, the other customers did not hesitate to stare. Some smirked.

When she finally worked her way to the front, she plunked the trap down on the counter.

"Can I help you?" the heavyset, balding man asked, his voice registering his irritation at the sight of this obviously upset woman. He wore a name tag that read JAMIE. Under the name, it said OWNER.

"I need to know who set this," Claudette replied, eyes grabbing hold of his.

Without even glancing at the trap, Jamie replied, "You'd have to call FWP."

"I tried that. No one will help me."

"I don't know why you think I can, if they can't."

Claudette lifted the trap, tilted it toward the light.

"Look," she said, "there are numbers here. Does that tell you if the trap was purchased here? Don't you keep records?"

This time Jamie did not even attempt to hold back his irritation. Pushing the trap toward her, he said, "No, we don't. But if we did, I wouldn't tell you who bought it."

Claudette refused to accept his message, which was clearly a warning.

"My dog died in this trap. At Paola Creek. You must know who traps up there." She turned to face the men looking at gear—who had frozen, eyes fixed on the scene unfolding—and those waiting in line behind her.

"Does anyone here know who traps near Paola Creek?"

Most of the men, even those who had snickered at the sight of the trap dangling from her hand, now looked away.

Jamie had come around the counter. Now he grabbed her by the elbow and began escorting her out the door.

"You don't come into my shop and cause trouble. You hear?"

Claudette wrenched her arm free.

She could feel herself about to cry. She would not allow that to happen. Not now, not there.

When Jamie reached for her again, she slapped at his hand, turned, and headed for the door. One man beat her there, and opened it for her. She looked up to nod a thank you, but when she did, she realized it wasn't intended as a chivalrous move. He wanted her out of the store, too, and this was his way to hasten it—and to let her know that Jamie's customers stood behind him.

The tears began to fall as Claudette marched, numbly, to her car, which she'd had to park at the gas station next door.

"Miss," a voice called from behind.

The look on the face of the man who'd opened the door for her still in mind, she did not turn.

"Ma'am." It was getting closer.

Still, Claudette reached for the door handle.

"I'm sorry about what happened in there."

Claudette froze. Slowly, tentatively, she pivoted.

A clean-cut man in his early thirties, dressed in a fishing vest whose pockets bulged with fly fishing paraphernalia, stood eyeing her.

"I'm sorry about that," he repeated. "You just have to understand. People in these parts trap. And even if they don't, they stick together. Jamie's not a bad guy, but he shouldn't have treated you that way." He paused. "Are you okay?"

Claudette backhanded a tear from her cheek.

"Yes. Thank you," she said. "It was nice of you to check on me. I'm fine. I'll be fine."

She started for the door again.

"Wait," the young man said.

Puzzled, she turned back to him. He reached for the trap.

"Can I take a look?"

Brow furrowed, Claudette handed it to him.

He took the trap, tilted it one way and then the other in the sun's light. Scowling, he lifted its open jaws closer to his face. Then he turned it toward Claudette.

"These numbers you showed Jamie?"

After repeatedly scrubbing the trap, Claudette had finally been able to make them out: six shaky numerals scratched by hand on the inside.

38 9999

She nodded and cried out, "Yes?"

"Nowadays traps have to have a metal tag with the trapper's name and address or their ID number on them. But used to be they could put any form of legal identification, like a vehicle license, on them. This looks like a license number to me."

Claudette's hands shook as she took the trap back from the man.

"How can I find out whose license it is?"

"Do you know any cops? If you had a friend in the police department, or sheriff's office, he could tell you who it was registered to."

Claudette's enthusiasm transformed instantly into a cold, bitter laugh.

"I called the police about my dog and all they cared about was finding out what *I'm* doing up here. When I told them I'd like to get my hands on the trapper who killed Tennyson, they acted like I was the criminal."

This didn't seem to sit well with the stranger, who began fidgeting.

"Well, all I know is that the *38* means it was issued to a car registered in Glacier County."

Claudette fell silent for several seconds—a frown clouding the natural beauty that had probably drawn the stranger's sympathetic gesture.

"How many people live in Glacier County?"

He drew back, studied her briefly.

"Are you serious?"

He glanced toward the store, where several of its customers stood watching through the window.

"There may not be that many people in Glacier County, but it's big, and wide open." Then, eyes straying back to the window, he added, "And not always friendly." He paused again. "Finding this guy without someone on the inside to track this number would be like winning the lottery."

Claudette's intensity—her determination—clearly made him nervous. He stepped backward, and began making his way back to the store that way.

"Anyway, good luck."

When he turned his back to her and reached for the store's door, Claudette called after him.

"How can I thank you?"

Without speaking, he turned, gave her a thumbs-up sign that he kept discreetly hidden from those watching at the window, and disappeared inside.

Six

"All rise."

Justine marched sternly into the courtroom, turning harsh eyes on the defendant when she saw that he hadn't hopped up immediately upon seeing Annie enter from the back door.

"The Honorable Annie Peacock presiding."

Annie replied with a quick, "Please be seated."

The courtroom was empty save for Ranger Wylie Darlington, the defendant, and a uniformed guard who stood at the back door, which he'd closed as Annie settled into her chair behind the bench.

For Annie, today's arraignment was bittersweet. Knowing what Will would feel when he heard about it made the case of the wolverine killed in an illegal trap, out past the Thunderer, hit close to home. How ironic that it would happen the very day Will left Yellowstone.

Annie saw it as proof of the terrible mistake it had been to send Will away. At least she hoped that was how Peter Shewmaker and the new superintendent saw it. In Annie's eyes, sending Will away was akin to an open invitation to poachers. It had even occurred to Annie that the silence surrounding Will's leaving, and relocation, was designed to avoid just that—poachers knowing that their worst nightmare was over. At least, as Annie continued to hope, temporarily.

Now the very man accused of setting the trap stood before her. His appearance surprised Annie. She'd seen her share of poachers in the park. Usually they were a hardy type, dressed in flannel shirts, T-shirts, jeans, Carhartts. The khaki pants, neatly trimmed goatee, and a build that, while wiry, almost appeared frail was more in keeping with the traffic violations she heard, usually involving a city dweller eager to get through the park, just checking off items on an obligatory list for a family vacation. This man, however, did not look like a young child's father. No patience or humor born of raising kids showed in his dull brown eyes.

"Good morning, gentlemen," Annie began. "Mr. Gladner, you have been issued a violation notice that charges you with the unlawful taking of wildlife inside Yellowstone National Park. As I've seen you've been informed, you have the right to have an attorney present at today's arraignment. If you cannot afford to retain an attorney, you have the right to have a public defender appointed to represent you."

Gladner was quick to respond.

"I am aware of my rights, Your Honor. I don't need, or want, an attorney."

"Very well. Are you prepared to enter your plea this morning?"

"I am. I plead not guilty, and I request an immediate trial before Your Honor."

Annie looked at the papers in her hand, studied them.

"It's this court's responsibility to ensure justice is handed out, Mr. Gladner. I must say that I am always slightly uncomfortable when a defendant chooses not to have legal representation. Your request for an immediate trial, though you do have that right, makes me all the more uncomfortable. While the illegal taking of wildlife inside the park, in this case through the use of an illegal trap, is a Class B misdemeanor, and not a felony, it will still, if you are found guilty, become a permanent part of your record. I would suggest that you reconsider both your decision not to have an attorney represent you, and your request for an immediate trial."

Tony Gladner's tight little chest heaved with exasperation.

"Your Honor, I am fully aware of the potential consequences of both decisions. I am not a lawyer but I did have two years of law school, and I feel perfectly comfortable and confident in my ability to represent myself. And as for my request to have an immediate trial, I am scheduled to fly out of Bozeman tomorrow. I am a busy man, and I cannot afford to stay here for a trial at a later date, or to return for a trial. I am confident that you will find that evidence is insufficient for me to be found guilty as charged. It's my right to request that this matter be adjudicated right now, is it not?"

Annie studied the defendant. Then she turned to Justine, whose expression told Annie her clerk was clearly not liking the tone used by the defendant.

"Can you please approach the bench?"

Justine padded on Chaco sandals over to Annie, shooting eye-daggers at Gladner as she passed in front of him.

"That cocky little . . ." she whispered to Annie when she got within earshot.

Annie cut her off. "Enough. What's on my schedule today?"

"You have a preliminary hearing at one-thirty. Your morning's clear."

Annie turned her eyes back to Tony Gladner.

"It is your right, Mr. Gladner, to request an immediate

trial; however, in many instances, having that right doesn't ensure that it will be granted. But since we have Ranger Darlington present, neither party is represented by an attorney, and if convicted, your sentence would not call for jail time, I'm inclined to grant your request." She looked to Wylie Darlington. "Ranger Darlington, are you prepared to testify?"

Wylie jumped to his feet.

"Yes, Your Honor."

"The government does not need more time to prepare for trial? To subpoena witnesses or secure evidence?"

"No, Your Honor, we can proceed now."

"Very well. Please take the stand."

Wylie stood at the bottom of the witness box and dutifully repeated the oath administered by Justine, then stepped into the witness box and took his seat.

It was his first time in her courtroom and he looked so young, and disproportionately nervous, that Annie gave him a reassuring smile.

"Could you please relay to the court the circumstances that led to the issuance of a violation notice for the unlawful taking of wildlife by Mr. Gladner here?"

"Yes, Your Honor," Darlington replied. "On the afternoon of the second of September, while patrolling the area behind the Thunderer on horseback, I came across a wolverine caught in a leghold trap. It was barely alive."

He shifted his weight nervously on the wooden witness bench.

"The wolverine died while I was freeing it. I removed it and brought it to Mammoth." He paused. "*That* was my big mistake."

"Mistake?" Annie echoed.

"Yes. I should have left it there and set up surveillance to see who returned to check the trap." Two splotchy red circles suddenly took over Ranger Darlington's cheeks as blood rushed to them. "I . . . I'm new to law enforcement. It was my first day taking over Ranger McCarroll's district."

Annie was so startled at hearing Will's name that immediately after, she, too, felt her face turn hot. While Justine definitely noticed, Annie was relieved to see that Wylie Darlington had not.

"When I brought the wolverine in, Pete, er, Peter Shewmaker, my supervisor, explained my mistake. Anyway, first thing the next day I went back and waited to see if anyone showed up to check on the trap."

"And did anyone?"

Wylie nodded toward Gladner.

"Yes, the defendant did."

At this, Gladner jumped up.

"I was not checking on a trap. I didn't even know one was there!"

Annie pointed at him.

"Mr. Gladner, sit down. You'll have your chance to cross examine, as well as to give your version when you take the stand." She turned to Wylie. "Please, Ranger Darlington, go on."

Wylie sucked in a breath of courtroom air.

"The defendant first came into my sight when he emerged from the tree line, about two hundred yards from where I was hiding, in a thicket of lodgepoles about a hundred and fifty feet east of the trap. He headed directly to the trap. I watched as he approached it. He looked around to make sure no one saw him, then he kneeled down next to it and started examining the soil surrounding the trap, looking for animal tracks. It was clear he knew what he was doing."

Gladner shot to his feet again.

"Objection!"

Annie pounded her gavel. "Mr. Gladner, sit down. I'm not going to tell you again—you'll have an opportunity to cross-examine this witness. Until then, let him proceed."

Gladner had already dropped back into his chair, where he was scribbling notes frantically.

Annie nodded at Darlington to go on.

"I approached the defendant, asked him what he was doing. He was very nervous-acting. Said something like, 'What's a trap doing here?' When I told him I'd been watching, and that it appeared that he knew where the trap was, he said that he'd never even been in the park before that morning, so how the hell would he know where the trap was? He got very hostile, said he was going to report me. I told him he should feel free to do so but that I found a wolverine in that trap the day before and I intended to ask him some questions. He told me that he'd flown into Jackson Hole the previous night and that he'd just arrived in Yellowstone three or four hours earlier. That he didn't know anything about the trap, or the wolverine."

"What did you do at that point?"

"I didn't believe him, but I also didn't have any evidence to dispute what he said, about just arriving in the park, so I let him go."

"And then?" Annie asked.

"I figured he'd parked at the Soda Butte trailhead, so I left him and went to the trailhead. There was a rental car there. I looked inside the car, to see if I could see any evidence, anything that could connect him with the trap. As I was looking, Ranger Bolinger drove by. He saw me and stopped; I told him what I was doing. He suggested that I get in his car and that we wait until the suspect returned to his car. About an hour later, when he did, Bolinger recognized him. He said he'd seen him in the General Store up at Mammoth two days earlier, with a woman."

Annie had trouble hiding her annoyance at the ranger's inexperience.

"Perhaps you should have considered the fact that

Ranger Bolinger isn't here today to establish that the defendant lied before agreeing to proceed with the trial."

Darlington rose and pulled a DVD out of his pocket. He lifted his hand in the air, waved it at her.

"I didn't need him here, Your Honor. Bolinger and I headed right to the General Store in Mammoth and went through their security camera videos from two days earlier. As you can see, this establishes that the defendant lied to me about having just arrived in Yellowstone. He was in the park two days earlier, which meant that he could well have placed the trap. I felt the fact that he was in the park, and that he lied about it, was enough to issue a violation notice."

Tony Gladner jumped up. "Your Honor, even if that tape proves I was in the park, there is no way it can tie me to that trap. I object to your admitting it as evidence."

"Sit down, Mr. Gladner."

Annie reached for the DVD.

"I will admit the tape."

By the time she looked over at Justine, the clerk was already headed out the door, saying, "I'll get a laptop to view it, Your Honor."

Minutes later, Annie sat watching a security video of a couple walking through the glass front door of the General Store in Mammoth. Despite the fact that the man wore a ball cap, Annie recognized the defendant immediately. His size and build gave him away. And when he removed his cap, the bristle of hair he ran his hand through erased any doubt that it was Tony Gladner. His companion was about the same height, probably in her mid- to late-fifties, with short sandy hair, which was mostly hidden by a visor. They disappeared from the camera's field of vision for almost two minutes, then reappeared at the cash register, where the wide-angle camera picked them up from behind as they paid for a disposable camera and some snack foods. Annie was used to seeing people in the store stocking up on food and drinks for their backpacks into the park, but Gladner and his partner had purchased little of either. What most struck Annie was the lack of any apparent connection between the two—had they not entered the store together, she would think they didn't even know each other, yet they were traveling together. When they turned to leave, the woman, who had struck up a conversation with the store employee, was smiling. While Annie could only see her in profile, the camera picked up the fact that she wore braces on her teeth.

When the tape finished playing, Annie looked at the defendant.

"Are you prepared to cross-examine the witness, Mr. Gladner?"

"I don't wish to cross-examine Ranger Darlington."

"You do not plan to challenge this video?"

"No, Your Honor. I'd be a fool to try to tell you that's not me."

"Very well, then you're ready to take the stand in your defense?"

"No, Your Honor; actually, I don't feel it's necessary for me to testify."

Annie's eyebrows shot up.

"This is your opportunity to defend yourself. You understand that, do you not?"

"I do, Your Honor, but whether I lied or not about when I arrived in the park, nothing Mr. Darlington said connects me with the trap, or the wolverine who died in it. I trust that this court sees that and I decline the opportunity to testify. I would ask the court to find me not guilty of the charges."

Annie took a deep breath. She hadn't expected this. She shared Ranger Darlington's instincts—that Tony Gladner's actions, including the fact that he lied, indicated he might be involved in the illegal trapping. But she had long ago learned that on the bench, instincts were to be discounted.

"The tape does show that the defendant, Mr. Gladner, lied when he told Ranger Darlington he had just arrived in the park. However, Ranger Darlington, your testimony did not connect the defendant to the act of trapping. Therefore, because you have not proved to me beyond a reasonable doubt that the defendant was guilty of trapping or taking wildlife in violation of the Lacey Act, I have no choice but to find the defendant not guilty."

She turned to Gladner and, making a concentrated effort to conceal her disdain, announced, "Mr. Gladner, you are free to go."

Gladner's lips turned up in what looked like more than a smirk than a smile of gratitude, or any sense of satisfaction that justice had been served.

He reached for his coat, began to turn away from the bench.

But Annie wasn't quite through with him.

"Before you leave," she said, "let me warn you. While I have no choice but to find you not guilty, I am not entirely convinced of your innocence."

Gladner's eyes dulled, masking any emotion, as he turned them back on Annie.

"And if you think you can get away with breaking laws inside this park," Annie continued, her eyes unbending against his now overtly threatening gaze, her voice tight with restraint, "think again. Because Ranger Darlington"—the name almost caught in her throat—"will certainly remember you. He'll be watching."

Annie didn't notice Wylie Darlington straightening in his chair at Annie's pronouncement of faith in him. Her eyes were still fixed on the defendant.

"And so, Mr. Gladner, will I."

* * *

Claudette had grown disconsolate. She'd spent the past week alternately trying to finish her thesis and driving from Columbia Falls to East Glacier, looking for a license plate that read 38 9999.

Writing her thesis was impossible. She'd sit down and stare at the notes she'd made, at research she'd pulled off the Web and from journals, and within seconds, eyes still fixed to the source in her hands, she'd be thinking about Tenny. Actually, what she spent the better part of each day thinking about was Tenny's murderer. After about half an hour of pretending to work on her thesis, she'd get up, climb in her dingy gray 1999 Honda Accord, and cruise down Highway 2. Sometimes she went west, toward Whitefish and Kalispell, pulling into every business's parking lot and scanning the plates of the vehicles parked. Sometimes she'd go east, toward East Glacier, where there were no parking lots, but she'd become adept at reading license plates of oncoming cars. If there were even a number or two in common with the numbers on the trap, she would do a U-turn, catch up, and make sure she got a good, close look. At night, after dark, she'd park near lighted intersections, either in Columbia Falls, or in West Glacier, alongside the road, near the Belton Chalet, and with binoculars trained on vehicles she saw heading her way, have no more than two or three seconds to read the license plates. It helped immensely that Montana was the capital of personalized plates. Ordinarily Claudette might be amused by some of them, or intrigued by trying to make out the meaning, but now when she saw some pathetic proclamation of the driver's identity on the front plate, her eyes just moved on down the road, to the next set of headlights.

She'd become obsessed with finding Tenny's killer. Yet, at the same time, she had reached a point where she could no longer bear to stay alone in her professor's cabin. It was pointless anyway—finishing her thesis in her current state of mind was as unrealistic as her search for the owner of the leghold trap.

The previous night, sleepless again, she'd finally decided to return to Missoula in the hopes that once there she would be able to let go, perhaps even get back to work. Get her master's degree and leave the godforsaken state of Montana once and for all—where killing animals was as acceptable as carrying an umbrella in Seattle.

But she had one last task to undertake before leaving.

Ironically, on this morning, the morning she chose to spread some of Tenny's ashes along the Middle Fork, a river he'd swum and retrieved balls in countless times over the summer, Claudette had deliberately left her binoculars home. She wanted to be at peace, to be focused solely on good medicine, positive energy—on forever relinquishing a small part of him to the river that had given Tenny so much joy. If ever a dog deserved that, it was Tennyson. She'd vowed that for one day, this day, she would banish thoughts of revenge from her mind and focus solely on the gift that he had been to her.

And then, on her way back to the cabin from their favorite put-in on the river—the spot along the highway where the Middle Fork emerges in all its glory from the Bob Marshall Wilderness—she'd spotted the white pickup truck. It was pulled over alongside the road, about two miles east of the Paola Creek turnoff.

It was the GOD, GUNS AND GUTS bumper sticker that first caught her eye. And then the license plate she barely glimpsed as she whizzed by:

38 9999.

Heart racing, Claudette executed a U-turn, sending an eastbound Harley Davidson into a skid to avoid her. Long, ratty hair trailing behind him like some kind of creature in pursuit of his head, the bearded, leather-clad driver stabbed a middle finger into the sky as he passed her car and continued racing down the highway after regaining control of his machine.

Claudette did not notice the gesture.

Hands shaking, she pulled even with the truck, onto the south shoulder of the highway, and sat there staring at it for a good two minutes before getting out of her Honda, crossing the road and circling it on foot.

She hadn't been able to read the rest of the GOD, GUNS AND GUTS bumper sticker when she was driving, but now she stood staring at the second line: THAT'S WHAT MADE AMERICA WHAT IT IS.

Two more stickers adorned the back window: SAVE AN ELK, KILL A WOLF, and in big bold letters: PETA, with PEOPLE FOR EATING TASTY ANIMALS running in small letters directly below the acronym.

Claudette spit on it.

The bed of the truck was strewn with tools, mud-crusted boots. A large metal box with a padlock on it was fixed to the wall between the cab and the bed.

Claudette stepped onto the running board to peer inside the cab. A rifle occupied a gun rack on the back window. A pair of dirty leather gloves lay on the seat next to the driver's side. On the floor, Claudette could see what looked like a black medical bag. In sharp contrast to the rest of the truck, a white piece of clothing that looked more like a smock than a shirt lay neatly folded on the passenger seat. Claudette pulled on the passenger door's handle, but it had been locked.

Rage building inside her by the second, Claudette marched back to her car, grabbed her cell phone, returned, and began photographing the truck. She wasn't even sure why, but she snapped half a dozen pictures before she finally began thinking more clearly. Before she finally developed a plan.

Quickly, she retreated to her car, which she'd left running, and pulled back out onto Highway 2. She traveled east another quarter of a mile, then swung the car around to head in the opposite direction, being more watchful for oncoming vehicles this time, as she could not afford to screw things up. Twenty-five yards behind the truck, she pulled off onto the road's shoulder. Inching her car forward and far enough over to be partially hidden by branches of the dense forest lining the highway and the shade afforded her by the trees on the south side, she finally put the Accord in park. She left the engine running.

Then she waited.

Seven

From his vantage point high above, on the south slope of Mt. Henkel, Will McCarroll glanced down at Wilbur Creek, which wound its way through the marshy wetlands below.

He couldn't help but stop, as he had already half a dozen times, to take in the landscapes playing out in every direction. But he was headed to Iceberg Lake and wanted to get there by sundown. In Yellowstone, that wouldn't have been a consideration, but Will hadn't made this hike before, and he was advised that the four and a half miles could be steep, the trail narrow.

The advice, delivered by Rob Deardorf, his new supervisor, caused Will to bristle.

It had been more than two decades since anyone had had to give Will McCarroll advice on how to get somewhere in the wild, distant reaches—and what to look out for.

Still, just being out in the backcountry again felt damn good. And Will was impressed with what he was seeing.

Not just the bear scat, which he'd seen plenty of, but the scenery—he had to admit it equaled Yellowstone's. It was different: more jagged peaks; more alpine, with the stunted flora distinct to the high country. It shared Yellowstone's gift of waterfalls cascading down sheer walls of rock.

Wildlife was abundant.

The only thing he didn't like was the number of other hikers he came across. In Yellowstone, he could go an entire day without crossing paths with a backcountry hiker. Glacier's reputation as a mecca for hikers and alpine-country enthusiasts drew a hundredfold more backcountry hikers. Which not only detracted from someone like Will's enjoyment of the experience, it also created situations like the one he was called upon to deal with today: Human-bear interactions. Several grizzly sightings had been reported between Ptarmigan Falls and Iceberg Lake. Will was sent to check out the situation and make a recommendation.

Will already knew what that recommendation would be.

He would advise the park to close the trails.

A year earlier, a mother griz long known to park personnel and hikers who favored hiking Logan Pass had been euthanized. She had entered a camp twice, two cubs in tow. Instead of closing trails or moving her, she had been killed. And one of the cubs, while in transport to a zoo, had died. Will had been furious. It would never have happened in Yellowstone.

So he'd already made up his mind that his first official action as backcountry ranger for the Many Glacier district would be to insist upon trail closures.

The scat already had convinced him of the necessity, but truth was, he'd made up his mind before even setting out an hour earlier, after getting the call on his two-way from Deardorf.

"Campers reported a bear frequenting Elizabeth Lake campground."

The hike was, for all practical purposes, a formality—but it was a formality Will welcomed eagerly, the first assignment he hadn't resented since his arrival in Glacier a week earlier.

As Will climbed to higher terrain, beargrass carpeted the hillsides like white velvet.

Will recognized it as prime grizzly habitat, especially this time of year, when bears were entering hyperphagia, and especially in prime berry country, like this high alpine terrain.

As the trail turned to follow Ptarmigan Wall, Will spied a couple in their late forties heading his way. Both carried bear spray in their hands—not in their holster. When they recognized his ranger uniform, they picked up their pace and by the time they reached Will, they were out of breath from running.

"We saw a grizzly and her cub, just off the trail."

"How far back?"

"Just before we started along the wall."

"Did they see you?"

The man took over.

"She definitely knew we were there. They were eating berries on the south side of the trail, uphill about ten yards or so, when we came around a bend. The sow moved between us and her cub right away. We just talked to her, 'hey, bear, hey, bear, don't worry about us, bear,' and she let us pass."

The woman nodded her head frantically in agreement with practically every word. Will had seen the looks on their faces literally hundreds of times in Yellowstone's backcountry.

"Okay, thanks for the information. You should be fine the rest of the way. I've seen some scat between here and Swiftcurrent but nothing too fresh. Just make some noise and keep that bear spray handy."

"Thanks," they cried in unison.

Will moved on, and soon started his descent. He knew that the lake was held by a glacial cirque, but when he crossed a footbridge and rounded a corner, what he saw literally caused him to catch his breath. Towering mountains surrounded three sides of a crystal blue, clear body of water that even now, after the two hottest months of summer, had chunks of ice floating in it. Will was working his way along the shore of the lake in the shadows of the giant cliffs surrounding it when he ran into another couple. They were headed in the same direction as Will, but their heavy backpacks slowed them. They, too, carried spray but it was holstered, and they walked with an air that said they'd spent many a night and day in the company of grizzlies and black bears.

"Hey folks," Will said as he approached them from behind, "seen any bears?"

This time it was the woman who seemed in charge. She turned sideways, gave Will the once over as he strode even with them.

"Three. A sow and a cub, and a lone female. Saw her on our way down, too. We spent the night at Iceberg last night, just decided to head back for the night."

"Any other hikers still at the campsite on the other side?"

"Nope. Just us. That's why we've decided to head back. Not often you get that campsite to yourselves."

Will eyed the heavy backpacks. They'd obviously had a change of mind because the size and way the packs sat on their backs indicated they hadn't just set out for a day hike from the campground above Iceberg Lake. That made the news Will was about to deliver a little easier, logistically.

"I'm afraid we're closing down the trails."

"What? You can't do that."

"I can and I just did. Sorry folks. You still have enough daylight to make it back to Swiftcurrent."

"Listen, we're not afraid of bears. We hike in griz country all the time."

These were the kind of people Will worried about far more than the earlier hikers who'd been visibly frightened by their run-in with a griz. As far as Will was concerned, anyone who said he wasn't afraid to hike in grizzly country was either a liar, or they were actually like Will, someone who dreamed of going out that way—with the great spirit bear taking him. But Will had yet to meet someone else whose motivation was being recycled back into the food chain, and since his plan to do so wasn't something he routinely shared with hikers, he instead said, "You may hike in griz country all the time, but that's a privilege, not a right. If you want to put yourself in danger, that's fine, take up hang gliding or jaywalking. But if your actions are going to put a bear in trouble, that's *my* business. Now move on."

As he spoke, he noticed another hiker appear in the distance, coming from the direction Will was headed— the direction the unhappy hikers wanted to return. They—the hikers—obviously knew the man as they hurriedly departed Will's presence to meet him—out of Will's earshot.

Will hung back, watching, almost humored by the thought that they were seeking allies amongst other hikers, as they proceeded to gesture Will's way angrily.

The man listened quietly. Will quickly realized he wasn't just another backcountry hiker. When he turned to look in the direction they pointed, toward Will's destination—the cliffs north of and high above Iceberg Lake, Will saw that he wore a standard Park Service– issued backpack, and, on his belt, a two-way radio.

The hikers clearly didn't get anywhere with him, as after he nodded toward Will, they turned and passed Will one last time without looking at him. He heard one of them whisper "asshole," but couldn't tell if it was the man or the woman.

Ahead, the man stayed put in the middle of the trail, as if he were waiting for Will. Will obliged and started back up in his direction.

When Will got close enough, the man said, "You can't close this trail."

"Pardon me?" Will replied.

"You heard me," the guy answered. Will had suspected from a distance that he was American Indian, but now, at close range, there was no question. And though he wore blue jeans and hiking boots, the color of the shirt peeking out from under his fleece jacket also confirmed that he was with the National Park Service in some capacity. "You can't close this trail."

"I can and I just did," Will answered. "Who the hell are you? And why did those folks just leave after talking to you if you don't think I can close this trail?"

"I told them to leave because you're apparently new here, and I didn't want to embarrass you in front of them. But now I'm telling you: you can't close this trail. And who the hell are you that you thought you could?"

The two glared at each other in instantaneous hatred. Then, suddenly the Indian man's expression changed from registering anger and bewilderment to something akin to an epiphany. Just as suddenly, a big smile spread across his features, transforming his face.

He reached out a big hand.

"What the fuck. You're Will McCarroll, aren't you?"

Will's extension of his hand was more tentative.

"Do I know you?"

"No reason you would. I'm Johnny Yellow Kidney. I'm Glacier's wolverine biologist."

While it explained the air of authority, and the shirt, backpack and two-way, this did little to clear up Will's confusion.

"Hell, I was just talking about you."

Johnny's grin never left his face.

"About me? Who would you be talking to about me? I didn't think anyone in this goddamn park even knew I existed."

"It wasn't anyone from Glacier. It was Sam Blount."

At the mention of Sam's name, Will got the connection.

"Yellowstone's wolverine biologist," he said. And just saying that, thinking that—the mere reference to Yellowstone, and a biologist Will had crossed paths with and worked with for over a decade—delivered a crushing psychological blow to Will's gut.

The worst part was that Johnny Yellow Kidney actually saw it.

There was an awkward silence before Will said, "So how's Sam?"

Was it his imagination or did he sense that Johnny seemed reluctant to answer?

Yellow Kidney looked Will in the eye and said, "Someone killed one of his study wolverines inside the park in a leghold trap. I guess it happened the very day you left to come here."

Will had learned long ago to mask feelings of grief and anguish; how to hide them from people, especially strangers. But, at the ripe old age of fifty-two, he'd recently been forced to leave not only the park, the home that provided his sanity and sanctity, he'd also left the first person he'd allowed himself to feel any real feelings for since Rachel and Carter died—Annie. It had been twenty-eight years since he'd felt such vulnerability, and Yellow Kidney's news just about destroyed that stoicism.

"Shit."

That was all he said. All he could say.

Yellow Kidney actually looked away.

"Don't tell me," Will finally said. "They don't have a suspect."

Will didn't see how it could get worse, but it did.

"They had one, but they had to let him go."

"Annie let him go?"

He'd blurted it out without thinking, and there was no taking it back.

Yellow Kidney looked at him quizzically.

"Pardon me?"

"Never mind. Sorry."

"Hey, don't be. I was shaken by the news, too. Especially when we realized that the scent lure they used was one I'd developed. It was stolen from my house."

Will sensed the burden this had placed on Yellow Kidney's conscience as the biologist continued.

"I'm used to finding traps in the Nyack—there are a lot of lazy trappers who just hike in from the highway—but this is new. I've found two legholds up here, where my study is focused, in the past few weeks. And if I've found two, you can bet there are four or five times that many out here. I've been out hiking daily ever since. I tell you, if it happens to one of my study animals . . . well, let's just say I'll be one pissed off Indian."

Will shook his head in anger.

"Well, I'll do my damnedest to make sure it *doesn't* happen. You can count on that." The conversation had become a little too emotional, too personal, for Will. "But I'm closing this trail. I don't know why you think I can't, or shouldn't, but I can and I'm going to."

At these words, Yellow Kidney, too, took on an all-business air.

"To start with, I know Rob Deardorf and he won't back you up. This is a hiker's park and this is one of the prime hiking trails, and seasons. If you want to start off on a good note, this isn't the way to do it."

"With all due respect, Johnny, what happened to that grizzly sow and her cubs last year just isn't going to happen on my watch. She'd been around for years and had never had a single incident, then suddenly, she's euthanized. That would never have happened in Yellowstone. We would have closed those trails so fast it would've made your head spin."

Yellow Kidney studied him, weighing how to respond. He took a deep breath.

"You're right. I was infuriated—ashamed—by how we handled that situation."

"Then why would you object to my closing these trails now? I'm not here to be popular. Plus, I doubt you care much one way or the other about how I get along with my new supervisor."

"Actually, that's not true. I'm so fucking happy to have you here it's not even funny. I heard about you long before Sam Blount told me that that wolverine would never have died in a trap if you'd been on the job. We need someone like you here in the Many Glacier area."

"Then I still don't get it."

"Okay, here's how it is. If you close this trail, what's gonna happen is that people like that couple you just pissed off are gonna still go up to the top of Iceberg, but they're gonna use the northside trail. It's longer and tougher, but that won't stop them. And that takes them right through my study area."

Will finally got it.

"Damn," he said.

"You know how you feel about that grizzly? And about the wolves you lived with in Yellowstone, the one you saved? That's how I feel about wolverines. They're not glamorous and sexy like wolves and grizzlies, generally speaking people don't give a shit about them; but to me, they're the real symbol of wilderness. Of what's wild. I mean, did you ever watch one of those little buggers move?" His eyes lit with an excitement that Will had felt a thousand times. A hundred thousand times. "And who do they threaten? What do they really want? Just some peace in some of the most rugged, insane landscape you're ever gonna find. They used to at least have that kind of habitat, but now fucking skiers are being dropped into it by helicopters, and assholes on ATVs are roaring through it when they're trying to den. Trying to survive. So yeah, I don't want you to close this trail."

"Damn," Will said again. "I'm sorry to hear that, but if it's a study versus a griz and her cubs being in danger, it's the griz I'm gonna look out for. That's my job, and that's pretty much what I'm about."

"I heard you weren't one to compromise," Yellow Kidney said glumly. He stuck out his hand again.

"Do what you have to do. And good luck."

As he turned away from him, Will grabbed him by the elbow.

"Wait a minute."

Yellow Kidney's dark eyes turned back to Will.

"What if I closed the other trail, too?"

Claudette reached for the stick shift of the Accord. The sun had risen high enough that its first direct rays were moving across the highway, clearing their way over the tops of the trees whose shadows had sheltered her, headed to where she sat. She'd already moved her car backward once, away from the truck sitting just ahead of her on the side of the road, to stay in the shadows, but soon the sun's glare would make it impossible for her to see. It would also make it easier for her to be seen. She would have to move again.

As she pushed the clutch in to shift to reverse, she saw him emerge from the trees.

Claudette let out a gasp of horror.

One thick hand held a piece of metal, from which a chain about three feet long dangled, its end just above the ground. She recognized it as a leghold trap—the same kind she'd pried off Tenny's forepaw.

The other hand held what looked like a pelt of some kind.

Even at that distance, she could see the trapper's face, his eyes. He looked just as she'd pictured him—not necessarily his coloring or his size, or even his features—but the expression, or perhaps more accurate, the lack of expression, was just as Claudette imagined it would be. He moved like a predator. But not like a predator of nature—his were not the graceful, poetic movements of a wolf.

He moved like a human predator.

She had planned to leave her car—walk toward the truck, as if she'd stopped to pick some of the wildflowers along the highway—to get a closer look once its driver returned, but he placed his loads in the bed of the truck so quickly and moved with such a sense of purpose that Claudette stayed put, hand still grasping the stick shift. Ready.

Suddenly, as if sensing her presence, he turned and looked Claudette's way.

She dropped to the seat. Sweat poured down her face sideways. Claudette held her breath, as if that would help make her and her car invisible. Then a welcome sound—that of several cars, eastbound, toward East Glacier—and she heard the truck roar to life.

Once the rumble of its diesel-fed engine faded, Claudette rose. Seeing the road in front of her empty, a new panic seized her.

She had to catch up to him.

She swung the car onto the highway and pressed its pedal to the floor. She never saw a sign of the truck the entire twenty miles to West Glacier. Furious with herself for the choices she'd made—why hadn't she gotten out of her car and confronted the asshole?—she pushed her Accord harder and harder, causing its old frame to shake, endangering herself on the sharp curves that followed the rushing, winding waters of the Middle Fork, which she might well have joined, dropping seventy-five feet to do so, had she not been an excellent driver.

She passed dozens of small gravel roads, any one of which he might have turned onto.

She'd become convinced that that's what had happened—he'd turned off the highway—when the sight of a police car, lights flashing, ahead of her forced her to slow as she entered the town of West Glacier.

The cop had left his car and now stood at the window of a vehicle he'd pulled over, which sat directly in front of him. It wasn't until she passed both, that Claudette recognized the truck. And the driver.

It was him.

This time she would not lose sight of him.

She pulled into the parking lot of the Belton Chalet inn, fifty yards down from where the two vehicles were parked, and backed the Honda into a spot where she could watch what was happening in her rearview mirror.

She'd assumed the cop was giving the truck's driver a ticket, but in the rearview mirror, she could see the two engaged in friendly conversation. She watched until the cop left, and as the truck passed by the turnoff to the inn, she pulled onto the highway behind him. While she stayed at least 100 yards behind, this time she did not let the truck out of her sight. It passed through West Glacier, then Hungry Horse. When it entered the town of Columbia Falls, it slowed, and at the first light, turned left. Claudette followed, concerned now that if the truck went any distance at all, it would be obvious she was following him. But instead, it turned right almost immediately into the parking lot for a medical and dental building. Claudette moved on, and pulled instead into a parking lot on the left. Again she watched through the rearview mirror.

The driver had emerged from his side of the truck and circled around to the passenger side. She watched as he opened the door, reached inside. When he straightened, she saw that he had the white shirt in his hand. He slid it on over his flannel shirt and she realized it was a medical smock.

The building was clearly labeled: Columbia Falls Medical on the left side, Columbia Falls Dental on the right. Amazed, Claudette watched as he walked at a fast clip and entered the right side of the building.

She got out of her car, crossed the street.

Unable to help herself, she veered toward the truck. As she passed it, she stretched to look inside, and then let out a cry.

A dead coyote lay in its bed. It hadn't been a pelt he was carrying after all. Next to it, a bloodied trap.

Claudette followed the steps taken by the truck's driver.

A sign at the entry door listed that side of the building's occupants. One dentist and an insurance agency.

Knees weak, Claudette pulled the door open, grasped the wood railing as she climbed a flight of stairs to a glass door. She could see the truck's driver, his back to the door, talking to a receptionist. The reception area was empty otherwise.

Just as she reached for the handle, the man she'd been looking for ever since finding Tenny dead in his trap disappeared down the hallway beyond the receptionist's counter.

Claudette took a deep breath and opened the door.

"Can I help you?" said the receptionist, a coarse-looking woman who appeared remarkably like a young female version of the man who'd just exited her office.

"Yes," Claudette answered, forcing her hands to stop shaking as she reached for one of the business cards stacked neatly on the counter.

"I'd like to make an appointment with Dr. Brogan," she replied. She looked more closely at the card in her hand, then raised her eyes to meet the receptionist's less-than-welcoming gaze.

"Dr. Bridger Brogan."

Eight

The white pickup with the government plates spit gravel at Annie and Archie as the two marched doggedly north toward the Church Universal and Triumphant's property.

They were walking along the Old Yellowstone Trail road, which started at the Roosevelt Arch, in the town of Gardiner, and headed west first, then north, toward Royal Teton Ranch, the property owned by the highly controversial group. The wind threw sagebrush across the gravel road that led to what was once the town of Cinnabar, where the Northern Pacific railroad's tracks stopped, just five miles short of the north entrance to Yellowstone. They'd already passed the old Gardiner cemetery on the hill—the one where Annie had stood watching sixteen months earlier as a cadre of law enforcement—from Yellowstone as well as the Park County sheriff's office—dug at the makeshift grave that had appeared overnight. Fearing the worst after they'd received a call from a local who'd reported the new grave in the century-old and long-closed cemetery, Peter Shewmaker and Rod Holmberg, the Park County sheriff, had suggested that Annie not go to the graveyard. They felt certain, as did Annie, when they arrived to ask her to issue a search warrant to allow them to dig up the recently disturbed ground, that it had something to do with the kidnapping of Annie's mother, Eleanor Malone. Still, Annie had insisted upon going along. She'd stood that day, surrounded by good-hearted people who were silently praying, as was Annie, that its sudden appearance was strictly a coincidence, that it didn't relate in any way to the night Annie had returned home to find her mother missing, and Archie shot twice and on the verge of death. But the gasp that she heard from her friend, park photographer Les Bateman, when they reached the bottom of the newly dug grave, had confirmed Annie's worst fears. Actually, that wasn't the truth—her worst fear was that her mother lay at the bottom. What they actually found—a coffee can with a piece of Eleanor Malone's recently amputated ear—came damn close. But it at least signaled that Eleanor must still be alive.

Now, as Annie and Archie marched by it, heads bent to the wind, Annie did not so much as glance the cemetery's way. Archie, who had made a miraculous recovery after Will had rushed him to the vet—saving his life in the process—seemed to pick up his pace as they passed it, too.

Annie would have preferred to walk the Old Gardiner Road, which started in Mammoth, just behind the Chittenden House, and worked its way through the high desert terrain down to the entry gate, but dogs weren't allowed in the park, and when she'd hurried out of the house, Archie had looked at her with such a sense of excitement that she'd instead grabbed his leash, loaded him in the car, and hurried away in her desire to avoid her mother and Judge Sherburne. Right now she needed time alone to think.

The letter had come to her office, but she'd stuck it in her briefcase and hadn't remembered it was there until the end of a long day of work, when she was sitting at the kitchen table, sipping a glass of wine as she watched a group of Tibetan tourists—at least half a dozen of them monks—disembark from a tour bus and stand staring, transfixed, at Liberty Cap. Annie had giggled out loud at the sight. Liberty Cap—to Annie at least—looked like a giant dildo. The expressions on some of the faces circling it now made her think she wasn't the only one who thought that. Momentarily cheered, lifted from the gloom she'd been fighting ever since Will had left Yellowstone, she suddenly remembered the letter, whose return address indicated it was from the American Judiciary Conference. She padded barefoot into the living room, dropped down in the recliner that Judge Sherburne had pretty much taken over since moving in with Annie, and reached for the briefcase she'd plopped on the table beside it.

Curiosity piqued, she ripped it open. She only had to read one line before the sense of confusion, anxiety— and excitement—overtook her.

> *Dear Judge Peacock,*
>
> *We are writing to invite you to be a guest speaker at our annual conference, which is being held this year at Glacier National Park.*

Heart racing, Annie went on to read the committee's apology for such late notice. The planned speaker had suddenly pulled out and they were—sheepishly—asking Annie if she would consider presenting the section on "the Judiciary and National Parks." In two weeks.

When Annie heard the creak in the upstairs flooring that signaled her mother was about to head downstairs, she hurriedly took off with Archie.

While Yellowstone National Park was a haven for its wildlife, it was anything but for dogs, and so Annie had to resort to the walk she and Archie used to take, before Eleanor's kidnapping.

Now, head bowed, Annie's mind revisited the letter. It did not surprise her to be asked to speak at the annual conference—after all, as chief prosecutor in Seattle, she'd been a keynote speaker, but what were the chances this year's conference would not only be held in Glacier, but at the Glacier Park Lodge—in East Glacier?

Will had been gone two weeks now, and aside from when Eleanor had been missing, Annie had never been so miserable. She had come to realize she'd made a mistake in accepting his relocation, in giving in to her fears about her feelings for Will. She had grown so used to her independence, and to holding her heart close to the vest, that she'd been scared to death when she and Will had fallen so hard for each other.

She'd only heard from him once since he'd left: a voice mail left on her office phone while she was in court. Only nine words: "Hey, it's me. Just wanted to . . . hear your voice."

Annie had played it again and again. She knew it hadn't been an easy call for Will to make. They had, in fact, never used the phone with each other. It had always been Will dropping by to see her at the office, or finding her car in Gardiner, or coming by the house when he was called to Mammoth for meetings. Their best times, however, had been when Annie went looking for Will in the Lamar. She'd inevitably end up at his cabin, up near Trout Lake.

The longing she felt for him had been unlike anything she'd ever experienced before. So why was the letter inviting her to speak at the conference in East Glacier so distressing to her?

She walked for two and a half miles, until she reached the archaeological site Will had taken her to—teepee rings that Van Reese, the park archaeologist, had dated as being at least 1,000 years old. She and Archie had stood in the center of the ring for a good ten minutes. And then she'd headed back to her car, which she'd parked at Arch Park.

She passed the line of vehicles waiting to enter the park at the gate, waving at the seasonal ranger, Jim, as she used the lane for park employees. A trio of bighorn sheep, in their customary place, high on the cliffs above the Gardner River, had drawn the attention of several visitors, who'd pulled over and stood watching and pointing at the three, magnificent in the early evening's setting sun.

She smelled the coffee and the spaghetti sauce as she stepped into the back porch adjacent to the kitchen door, which meant she would find her mother and Judge Sherburne sitting in their usual places at the table beneath the window looking out at the lower hot springs. Preparing her poker face, Annie stepped into the kitchen; but before she had a chance to explain her rushed departure, her mother opened her mouth.

"Please tell us you're not going to turn down the invitation to speak at the conference."

The opened envelope, which, in her state of agitation, Annie had left on the table beside the judge's recliner, lay on the table between them, the folded edge of the paper sticking out at an angle, having been hurriedly replaced.

Annie looked at it and gasped.

"Mother!"

Eleanor Malone waved a dismissive hand. But Judge Sherburne acknowledged his culpability—and shame— by not being able to meet Annie's indignant glance.

Annie snatched the letter from the table, pirouetting on her toe as she did so to head back out. She was not in the mood for a mother-daughter chat. The Raven Grill was still open, she'd seen customers lined up outside its Old West barroom swinging doors as she'd passed through Gardiner ten minutes earlier.

But her mother, still adept at some things, even after her ordeal and at the age of eighty-four, reached out and grabbed her wrist.

"Annie, don't go running off again. Please. Sit with us, we've been holding dinner for you."

Annie's mistake was looking at the duo. Despite her blatantly wrong invasion of Annie's privacy, her mother's eyes already looked wounded, and Judge Sherburne, who could still not say more than a half dozen garbled words as a result of the stroke that had cost him his job—his world—in Yellowstone, had learned to play on Annie's emotions almost as well.

"The two of you are pathetic," Annie said. But then she pulled her chair back and slid down into her place between them.

Judge Sherburne issued a happy grunt.

Her mother said, "Thank you dear. And I do apologize. But I was worried about you. It was obvious you were upset by the letter and when you didn't return, after an hour, I"—she looked over at the judge—"*we*, decided we had better find out what upset you. So we could know what, if anything, we could do to help. Please forgive us."

Annie's shoulders heaved with a sigh.

"You're forgiven. You two are always forgiven."

She didn't have to look the judge's way to know he was smiling. He might even have a tear or two in his eyes. He may have had a stroke, but he could still manage to smile and cry at the same time. She'd seen it dozens of times since stealing him away from that rest home in

Livingston and bringing him back to the house that had been his and his family's home—the Stone House—for the three decades he'd ruled over his beloved Yellowstone.

Will had told Annie—one night after they'd visited the judge at Rainbow Living, because Will believed that if anyone would be able to understand why Eleanor had been kidnapped, it was his friend the judge—about the times he'd snuck Judge Sherburne out of Rainbow Living and taken him to the park. He'd told her about the look on his face, the sheer joy, at being back—at being able to see the bison in the Lamar, hear the howl of the wolves. He'd told Annie that the first thing the judge wanted to do every time they came to Yellowstone was go see the Stone House. That they would sit there, in the parking lot across the street, with the judge staring at it. And that tears would fall from his half-frozen face.

That night that Annie took Judge Sherburne away from Rainbow Living for the last time, she'd helped him into the recliner that sat under the window that looked out on the park, out on Mammoth's hot springs. She'd turned the recliner around, so that he could sit there—which he did all that night, and night after night after that—and look outside.

Annie had seen firsthand the tears that could flow at the same time the right side of his mouth smiled, while the left struggled to keep up.

How the hell could she possibly stay angry with either of these two old peaceful warriors, who, in their twilight years, having lost the great loves of their lives, had found such kinship and comfort?

Annie turned loving, confused eyes on them, their transgression forgotten.

"I honestly don't know what to do. Will's only been gone two weeks. I'm not sure how he would feel about me showing up at East Glacier. We'd decided the time apart would be good for us."

It was a sore subject for Eleanor.

"I've always said that's a bunch of baloney. Two people in love need to be together."

"Well, Mom, that's obviously not possible. At least right now."

"Well, it's possible two weeks from now! And you're a fool if you turn that invitation down," Eleanor Malone declared.

Annie sat staring at the envelope. She picked it up. Slid the invitation out.

Such an innocuous thing—an invitation to speak before her colleagues, to share what this new job, this new life, had taught her about working within the legal system; an honor, really—yet it had her gut in a knot.

"Okay," she finally said. "I'll go."

Both Eleanor and the judge seemed to physically lift in their chairs at the news.

"But only on one condition," Annie added. She could feel the four kind, worried eyes on her. She lifted hers. "I'll only go if you both go with me."

Eleanor Malone let out a little giggle, but promptly followed it with, "What you and Will need is time alone, not to spend it with two old timers like us."

"Will and I will get time alone. You two can keep each other company. I've heard Glacier is phenomenal. I want to share that with you. We might as well make it a vacation."

"Then I'll go. Gladly," Eleanor said. She turned to the judge. "Your Honor?"

There it was. The smile and the tears.

Judge Sherburne nodded. Yes. He would go.

"Good," Annie said. "I don't have any idea how to reach Will to tell him." She paused. Why put him through the anguish she felt now, the anguish she knew she would feel for the next two weeks?

"You know, maybe that's a good thing. Maybe it's best that I not tell him."

"I know you, Annie. You're just thinking that if you don't tell him, you can back out."

Annie looked annoyed.

"Mother, I'm a magistrate judge. If I tell these people I'm going to speak at their conference, I wouldn't back out."

Eleanor mouthed an "of course," but her expression still held a bit of doubt.

So did Annie's.

Will stepped onto the porch of Brownies and looked around.

Opening the door, he saw Vilma, the owner, who had finally smiled at him once or twice over the past week.

But not this morning.

He walked past her to the hot coffee, filled his thermos, then walked back to the cash register, grabbing a slice of homemade banana bread wrapped in cellophane from the "day old" basket on the counter.

"Where's the dog?" he said, handing two dollar bills to Vilma as he nodded toward the porch.

"Stinky?" she replied. "He hasn't shown up yet today." She picked a roll of quarters up from one of the metal compartments in the cash register's drawer and banged it forcefully against the counter to break it open before dropping the coins in place in the drawer. "Come to think of it, I don't think I saw him yesterday afternoon either."

"Is that unusual?"

"Not really. Stinky makes the rounds. Half the people in this town feed him." As they were talking, the bell that hung over the door clattered. "That dog can smell a meal a mile away."

A grizzled old timer—beard down to his chest, suspenders holding up worn Carhartts—reached past Will for one of the toothpicks sitting in a shot glass on the counter.

"Talkin' about Stinky, eh?" he said.

"You seen him anywhere, Cleatis?" Vilma asked.

"Saw him headin' down the reservoir road last night," Cleatis answered as he picked at the chewing tobacco between his teeth, " 'bout seven."

"That doesn't sound like Stinky," Vilma replied.

They both seemed to have forgotten Will was there.

"Damn dog's losin' his marbles, I think," Cleatis said.

"Hell, Cleatis," Vilma said as she handed Will thirty-five cents in change, "Stinky's been here longer than you. If that's even possible."

Will dropped the dime and quarter in the tip jar and headed out the door to the sound of Cleatis' hearty laugh.

Outside, he stood on the wood-planked porch, looking into the park at Mount Henry, the 8847-foot peak just beyond the invisible line that separated the town of East Glacier, which sat on the Blackfeet reservation, and Glacier.

It was the same direction as the road that led to the reservoir.

Seeing that Brownies was now open for business, two other familiar canines had arrived to stake out their claims on the porch. Will bent to pet a thick-boned, ratty coated shar-pei–Labrador mix that approached him, a hopeful look on her grizzled face.

He unwrapped the banana bread, broke it in half.

"Here."

She nosed it, then turned away.

Will laughed. She knew there would be better pickin's

soon, as the tourists arrived and ordered egg sandwiches, toasted bagels with cream cheese, and any number of other items Vilma so proudly made from scratch each morning.

Stinky would have been happy with the bread.

For some reason, Will had taken quite a liking to Stinky. Though their appearance had little in common— Stinky's thick coat was mostly black, with some white on his chest and face—in some ways, he reminded him of Annie's Lab, Archie.

Will looked at his watch. He wasn't due to report to work for another two hours. He'd planned to hike around the lake before his shift started, but hell, why not check out that area just west of town instead?

As he stepped off the porch, he heard a sound he'd long ago learned to recognize and love: the thundering of hooves pounding the earth. In Yellowstone, that sound might well be followed by the sight of a herd of elk, or bison, startled by a grizzly, or pursued by a pack of wolves.

Here, in East Glacier, Will knew that within seconds he would see between twenty and thirty horses racing at breakneck speed through the residential streets of tiny East Glacier.

Each morning the herd was moved from its pasture behind Frog Flats down, through town, to corrals across the street from the lodge, where guests would pay to be taken out on trails by guides. Will had seen two cowboys herding the animals several mornings earlier. Today, a young, lithe American Indian woman did so solo.

Though these were not the wild animals Will normally thrilled at, the sight and sound still quickened his pulse. And as much time as he had spent on a horse, riding the backcountry, Will was especially impressed with the young woman's handling of these spirited mares and geldings—moving them just fast enough to create a sight that caused carloads of tourists to come to a dead halt and gawk, but not so fast that an animal ever got hurt. Will knew how much skill that took.

He stood watching as every color imaginable—chestnut, paint, tobiano, palomino, bay—ran, kicked, and whinnied by, to the delight of a group of Canadians who had just stepped out of the car they'd parked in Brownies' lot.

After the herd disappeared down the highway, toward the lodge, Will stepped off the porch and retraced the horses' steps, heading toward the reservoir road, where Cleatis had last seen Stinky. The old dog would have passed by several of his favorite haunts on the way—the Mountain Pine Motel, where Will had noticed him taking shelter in the garage on several rainy mornings, and a dozen or so houses and cabins. Will kept his eye peeled for the shaggy black form. Perhaps he'd found a car or a tree to sleep under after what would have been a rather long trek for Stinky.

The reservoir road started at the end of the short residential street, just before it crossed Midvale Creek—part of the Two Medicine River drainage that ends in the shadow of Mount Henry. In the spring and most of the summer, the creek would be loud enough not to hear it, but now the waters were low, and as he crossed the crude bridge over the creek, he heard the whimper.

Jumping down off the bridge, he followed the sound, and soon he came upon Stinky. He'd gone down to the creek to drink, and gotten himself lodged between two large rocks. Exhausted, he whimpered at the sight of Will, who bent to pick him up. Almost instantly, Will noticed two things.

A foul smell—the smell of rotting flesh.

And that Stinky wasn't just having trouble climbing

out of the crevice between rocks, as Will first assumed—he was actually pinned down by a boulder the size of a garbage can. Stinky had apparently dislodged it in his attempt to get down to the dead muskrat that Will now eyed on the creek's edge.

"Okay, buddy," Will said, "I'll get you out of there."

Thirty minutes later, Will stepped back on to the porch of Brownies, with Stinky in his arms.

The place was now full and a young boy eagerly opened the door for Will.

Vilma rushed toward him.

"Are there any vets in town?" Will asked.

Several people Will recognized as locals, including Cleatis, who hadn't yet departed, had jumped up from their seats and gathered around, gasping and reaching out to pet Stinky, whose left hind leg hung limp and useless.

"Doc Brighton just got here," one of them said. "I saw his car at the cabin last night."

"What happened?" several voices said, almost in unison.

"He was going after a dead muskrat down at the creek," Will replied. "A rock dislodged and crushed his leg. He was trapped there for a while, I think, judging by the looks of him." Will looked at Vilma. "If you show me the way, I'll carry him right to the animal hospital."

"We don't have an animal hospital," Vilma replied. "And Doc Brighton's not a vet, but he's a good doctor. Come on. I'll show you where he lives."

Hands reached out to pet Stinky as Will turned and followed Vilma out the door. Cleatis was close behind.

"Old man," Vilma said over her shoulder, "we don't need you."

"I know," Cleatis said, "but I'm goin' down to that

creek and I'm gonna get that goddamn muskrat out of there before another dog gets stuck down there."

Will heard several other voices offer to go along with Cleatis.

He could feel Stinky staring up at him, but Will couldn't bring himself to look back.

Nine

"So what have we got here?"

Bridger Brogan benignly smiled down at his newest patient as she reclined in the dental chair.

Claudette Nillson smiled demurely back—and that was all it took. She held the smile as Brogan's gaze moved downward. The slobber-cloth the bitchy technician had snapped on her neck hid the low-cut tee that Claudette had chosen for her dental appointment, but it couldn't hide her size C breasts.

Bridger reminded her of a horny teenager drooling over pictures in a girlie magazine. She wanted to reach out and slap the twisted, gleeful expression from his face. Instead, she kept smiling.

"I'm ashamed to say I haven't been to the dentist in a couple of years," she said as he switched on the exam light. "I just moved here and I wanted to get started with someone new. A dentist that is."

"And how did I end up the lucky one?" His smile was so big and transparent, that when Claudette squinted at him against the light, gold fillings glimmered back at her.

This guy was too creepy for words. But that was okay. It was what she'd counted on.

"I saw the billboard with your picture," she answered. Bingo.

Bridger placed a hand on her shoulder as he pulled the light directly over her face.

"Let's see what we have." He poked and prodded tooth after tooth, made some grunting sounds and eventually came to focus on the back left side of her mouth.

Straightening, he said, "That back left molar. The X-rays Pamela took showed the roots are all but gone. Just some remnants left that will cause you big trouble down the line. You're going to need a root canal and a crown." He looked at his watch. "I think I can get the root canal in this morning."

Claudette didn't believe him, but she couldn't tell him that. He might send her packing, and she had to let this thing play out.

"Root canals and crowns are expensive, aren't they?" she said, her voice pitiful and innocent. "I don't have insurance. I guess I'll just have to wait."

This seemed to trouble Brogan.

"You don't want to put it off until the remaining root becomes infected and gives you big trouble." He paused. "There's another option."

"What's that?"

"I could pull it. You'd be fine without it and it'd save you a couple thousand dollars."

Shit, thought Claudette. *What now?*

"Really?"

"Really. It's a very simple procedure, almost no recovery time." He looked at his watch. "And I could still fit it in this morning."

Claudette's heart beat like a drum. Still, she hadn't accomplished what she'd wanted. Her thoughts involuntarily turned to Tenny. His lifeless body, lying half in, half out of the creek.

"Okay," she said. "Let's do it."

Brogan's smile split his bulldog face.

"Thatta girl."

He stood, walked to the door, and stuck his head into the hallway.

"Pamela, bring the gas tank in," he yelled. "Stat."

He turned and smiled reassuringly at Claudette.

"You won't feel a thing."

This had gone too far.

"I don't want to be put out. I don't need it."

"Listen, little lady. I don't have time to fool around. I promise you, you will not want to be conscious when you have that tooth extracted." He glanced at his watch, clearly to make a point. "And I don't have the time to start the procedure and then have you change your mind. It's now or never."

"Couldn't I just have a little time to think about it? The truth is, I'm afraid of anesthesia."

Bridger Brogan had transformed—his entire persona had changed during the debate about her tooth.

And then Claudette realized what was going on. Why he'd been so smiley. Did it have anything to do with putting her out?

The thought sent chills down her already tight neck and shoulders. She wanted to be wrong, but anyone who could kill Tennyson was capable of such things.

Okay, she thought, *if that's what you have in mind.*

"Listen," she said, a hint of an embarrassed smile lifting the corners of her mouth, "I just need to think about it. Learn more." She looked up at him coyly. "Maybe we could meet for a drink one of these nights to discuss it."

Pamela had shown up with a wheeled cart. On its top, linked to the machine by a plastic tube, lay a mask.

Bridger practically pushed her and the cart back out the door.

"We don't need that after all."

When she was out of earshot, he turned back to Claudette.

"I'm free tonight. How does that sound?"

The lone hiker, a woman, seemed to come from out of nowhere. Of course, the campsite was about a quarter mile off-trail, as were most of the trail campsites in this remote part of the park, so even if there were hikers along the trail that connected Pitamakan Pass to Triple Divide Pass, they were hidden from view. The campers—a young couple, in their early thirties—had just finished a breakfast cooked on their camp stove when she appeared.

"Good morning!" She waved a hiking pole cheerfully as she moved their way. She wore a backpack, hiking shorts, boots, and a Chicago Bears ball cap.

She quickly eyed their coffee.

"Boy does that look good," she said, slipping out of her backpack. "I couldn't get my cook stove started this morning, so I had to go without my morning caffeine."

The younger woman looked at the man, who was staring at the woman's backpack on the ground and didn't seem at all eager to extend an invitation. But as much as they were enjoying the solitude of the morning, their time in the park had made them part of a fleeting, but tight-knit, community that greeted one another, eagerly shared information, and helped each other out—the community of backcountry hikers and campers traversing Glacier National Park—and the young woman from Portland took pride in that fact.

"Would you like a cup?" she said, smiling sweetly in

spite of the look of shock on her partner's face. "We made plenty."

"How nice of you to offer! You're sure you have enough?"

"Yes," the young woman replied, angry now that her partner still had not extended any welcoming words. She nodded to one of several thick stumps around the fire pit. "Please, sit down. We'd love the company. My name's Shelby, and this is my fiancé, Blake."

"I'm Haldis," the woman replied with a smile. She extended a hand. "Haldis Beck. From Chicago," she added, pointing toward the cap's logo.

She lowered herself onto the log and loosened the laces on her Keen hiking boots, which drew Blake's eyes from the pack to the boots.

"Your first day in the park?" he asked.

"Oh, no." Haldis followed her reply with a short laugh. "I've been here several days now. I'm headed into the wilderness from here."

This answer finally intrigued Blake.

"Where exactly is that?"

Haldis nodded north.

"Bad Marriage Mountain."

"Alone?" Shelby asked.

"I've been alone the whole time. Never had more fun in my life." She lifted her metal mug of coffee in the air for a toast and laughed again. "To being single." Then she added, "I just got divorced and I'm going to climb my first mountain. And how could I pick anything but Bad Marriage?"

Shelby looked distressed.

"You shouldn't be climbing alone. You shouldn't be hiking alone. Climbing has its own dangers, and this is bear country."

"It's dear of you to worry, but I've lived through worse than grizzly bears and mountains. I'll be fine."

"Really," Shelby persisted. "This just isn't right. Why don't you join us, we're headed to . . ."

"Flinsch Peak," Blake cut her off. In reality, over breakfast they had made plans to head toward the Mad Wolf loop—a loop that started at Mad Wolf Mountain, crossed a ridgeline to Eagle Plume Mountain, and ended on Bad Marriage. But Blake had just changed those plans. Unilaterally.

"No, I'm determined to do this. It's actually something I have to do. To prove to myself I'll be fine on my own. How about this? If you're worried about me, let's meet here again, tomorrow night? We can camp together."

"We won't be back for two nights," Blake said.

"Well that works, too. I'll leave a note for you." She looked around, her eyes finally resting on a large, flat-topped rock at the perimeter of the campsite. "Right under here. Just so you know I made it back okay."

"Promise you'll remember to leave that note," Shelby said.

"It'll be there. I promise. And then maybe we can meet up for coffee or lunch. I'll leave you my itinerary. And cell phone number."

She looked at Shelby, a gleam in her eye. Reaching into her backpack, she said, "Would you mind taking a picture? So I can show my friends back home I really did this?"

Her hand emerged with a digital camera that looked like new.

Shelby smiled, "Of course."

She handed it to Shelby. Donning her backpack again, and picking up the hiking poles lying on the ground beside the trunk, Haldis Beck removed the ball cap and flashed a bright smile as Shelby dutifully took the shot.

"How about one of the three of us?" Haldis said,

looking directly at Blake, who had been making a show of packing up their tent.

Blake reluctantly trudged over to where Haldis and Shelby stood, arms around one another's waists as if they were lifelong friends. He was relieved that Haldis' other arm held the digital camera at arms-length, as he'd half-expected her to want him on the side of her opposite Shelby.

Haldis snapped the picture quickly, efficiently, then another.

"You guys are the best," she said. "I'm so happy we connected."

When she'd finally disappeared back down the trail, Shelby turned on him.

"You were downright rude to that woman."

"Rude? We spent almost an hour listening to her and her divorce story. I can get that kind of shit at work, I didn't drive 600 miles and hike three days to listen to it here."

"I guess you're right," Shelby said, looking less than convinced that they'd done the right thing. "But what if something happens to her?"

"It's not our job to keep her safe. She's a big girl. Plus, she seemed strange to me."

"In what way?"

"For one thing, she said she couldn't get her camp stove to work, but she didn't even have one. And did you see those boots? Brand new. She hadn't been hiking in them more than a few miles."

"Like you're some kind of expert," Shelby replied. "Maybe she had another pair in her pack."

"Nope. I looked it over. There weren't any shoes in there."

"You couldn't tell that."

"I could."

"You just didn't like her. Admit it."

"You're right. I didn't."

Half an hour later, after cleaning up their camp, retrieving their packs from the bear pole and making sure they'd left no trace behind that could attract one of the area's bears to the site, endangering the next campers to come along, as well as the bear—should there be an encounter—Shelby was just making a last trip into the trees to relieve herself when a glint on the ground caught her eye.

"Oh no," she cried when she realized what was reflecting the rising sun's rays.

Haldis Beck's digital camera. She had dropped it.

It landed right beside the rock she'd designated as the place she'd leave a note, upon her return from her solo trip to the backcountry.

Ten

Claudette downed the last drop of her valerian root tea and held both hands out, palms down. They'd finally stopped shaking.

She grabbed her canvas satchel, went to the small mirror in the hallway of her professor's cabin, leaned close to see her reflection in the dark hallway. She rarely wore makeup, but tonight she'd put a coat of mascara on, then added some blush.

Normally at this point, as she was leaving, she would coax Tenny into the living room, pet him as he settled into his dog bed. Tell him that she'd be home soon.

She exited the cabin, climbed in her car, and went back over her plan. She was actually very excited about it. She'd had it in mind all along, even before finding Bridger Brogan, but she hadn't figured out how she could actually execute it. But this afternoon, after leaving his office, it had come to her.

Now everything depended on how tonight went.

When she walked in the Grizzly's Den, she saw him

right away, his back to her, sitting at the bar. She approached him with a big smile, touching his shoulder.

"Hello."

He turned, grinned back at her. He already looked shitfaced.

"Let's move to a table," he said, standing. He steered her by the elbow to a booth at the back of the bar. Claudette slid into one side and, for a moment, thought he might slide in next to her. She felt physically ill at the idea, but instead, Bridger Brogan positioned himself on the bench opposite her.

Their knees touched. He smiled at her through bleary eyes. She willed herself not to jerk away from his touch. Smiled back at him.

The next two hours were the worst she had ever spent. She asked him what he did when he wasn't being a dentist.

"I'm a trapper."

"What do you trap?" she replied, bright-eyed.

He laughed, a big, ugly laugh that caused the flaccid flesh pressing against his shirt to bounce.

"You name it. Coyotes, beaver, wolves. Cats. Right now I'm going for a wolverine."

"Wolverine? Aren't they really rare? Even protected?"

This time he spit beer on her with his laughter.

"You bet that tight little ass of yours they're rare. We trappers call them the Holy Grail of trapping, they're so rare. KTEA's sponsoring a predator derby, and guess who's going to win it?"

"Trapping seems so cruel to me."

"You sound like one of those fucking animal nuts," he replied, studying her without the smile for the first time. "You're not, are you?"

"Not me. I'm just curious. Seems to me animals caught in a trap must suffer a lot before they die. Or get killed.

That seems cruel to me." She forced her voice to become lighter. "But I'm always open to learning that I'm wrong."

The way he was looking at her had her almost regretting directing him to this subject, but it was as if she couldn't help herself.

"Nothing cruel about it. Animals who're trapped just end up going to sleep. Hell, I've caught just about every body part in a trap and it hardly hurts. Besides, animals need to be managed, and that's what trapping does."

Claudette knew she could be risking everything but she had to ask just one more question.

"Don't you sometimes catch animals you don't want? What about them?"

"Nothing we can do about that. I just release them when I find something I don't want. They're rarely even injured. Unless it's a varmint. Then I'm doing the ecosystem a favor by getting rid of it."

Claudette looked down, into the Cosmopolitan she'd been nursing for almost an hour. She didn't trust herself to speak, or to look at him. This wasn't going well—it could all be for naught.

When she felt her hands and knees start to shake, she reached under the table and touched his thigh. All suspicion vanished from Brogan's face, replaced by hooded eyes and his own coarse hand traveling the inside of her thigh.

When she told him she had to leave—that she didn't want to drive the winding gravel road to the cabin in the dark, he leaned toward her and said—she couldn't believe she heard it right, but when she asked him to repeat himself, it came back the same—"Your place or mine?"

He'd been groping her every chance he got—reaching across the table to stroke her arm, brushing the hair away from her face, then letting his hand drift down across the open neck of her hiking shirt, eyes on her, testing her to see just how far he could go.

Had she passed?

She looked at him sheepishly.

"Hey, what's the rush? Unless you're one of these guys who're only interested in one night stands. And if you are, I'm afraid you've got the wrong girl."

This clearly wasn't the response Brogan was going for.

"What? You looking to get married or something?"

"No. Don't get me wrong. I'm looking for a guy to have a good time with. A guy who turns me on." Bingo. "But I like to spend a little time getting to know him first. And to be honest, I'm kind of a nature girl."

She was worried he might not get it, but even though he was two sheets to the wind, the way she said it, the look she gave him, definitely registered.

He leaned forward.

"You mean, you like to do it outside?"

She smiled.

"Yeh. I do. And in daylight." Her eyes met his. "I like to be able to see," she said, and then added, "And be seen."

The groan that emitted from somewhere deep in his twisted soul sickened her. He looked around at the other occupied tables, leaned almost all the way across the surface separating them, and lowered his voice.

"Well, just when can we arrange to accommodate your preferences?"

Claudette couldn't help but draw back. Still, she managed a smile.

"How about next week? Why don't we go on a little picnic, in the park. I know just the spot."

"Why wait a whole week?"

"I have to finish my thesis, that's why. That would give me something to look forward to. My reward for getting it done."

"I have to get into the park, but it can't wait a whole week. It's Tuesday now. How about Thursday?" He looked like a little boy planning a campout with his pals, knowing that they would be bringing along magazines they shouldn't be looking at. "Do you ride?"

She grinned.

"You mean horses?"

Shit, she could see that she totally had him now.

"Those, too."

"Yes. I do. But I can't make Thursday." She had much too much thinking and preparing to do. "Friday's the earliest I could do it."

"I really should go in before then, but if those are the rules, I guess those are the rules."

"You're going in to check traps, aren't you? You trap inside the park?"

He smiled at her, but this time he did not resemble a little boy. He looked like the man who killed Tennyson.

"If I answered that, I might have to kill you."

A chill ran through Claudette.

"Does that mean it's a date?" she said, trying to keep her voice light, and her loathing in check.

Brogan reached for her thigh, squeezed it just above the knee. Another second and she wouldn't have been able to help but slug him.

"You bet your sweet booty it's a date."

Will urged Buddy up the steep, rocky trail. He'd finally finagled a horse out of Rob Deardorf. They'd gotten over the argument about Will closing the trail to Iceberg Lake. Someone had called Deardorf and weighed in on Will's side. Deardorf hadn't told him that, but Will was certain that had happened. He knew the park management style. A supervisor would make a weak decision, then wait to see if, and by whom, it was challenged.

When Deardorf called Will and told him he'd decided to leave the trails closed for another week, and that Will was finally going to get the horse he'd argued was essential to covering the Many Glacier and Nyack, Will knew that someone had gone to bat for him.

Maybe Johnny Yellow Kidney.

For the first time since he'd started patrolling the backcountry of Glacier, he was in a good mood. The horse—a solid chestnut quarter horse, and a veteran of the park's trails—meant he could pack enough supplies for an entire week. He could avoid going back to town, to the depressing little house they'd put him in adjacent to a cheap motel that consisted of cabins so small their occupants spent most of the time they weren't sleeping sitting outside, drinking, smoking, putting together backpacks, and exchanging notes with other hikers, bikers, or tourists. He'd thought he might go mad if he stayed there another night. If he had to get in his car one more time to drive up to Babb, then through the Sherburne Lake entry to the lodge at Swiftcurrent Lake, to get away.

The horse gave him freedom to go where he wanted to go, disappear into the backcountry, explore heights and places, like the one unfolding before his eyes right now, that it would take more time than the Park Service was willing to allow him to spend on foot.

"Whoa."

The gelding eased to a stop, grateful for the respite after the steep climb.

They'd just crested the trail on Two Medicine Pass. Playing out before them was a panorama unlike anything Will had ever seen—directly north, Rising Wolf Mountain. Next to it, standing like a sentinel over Two Medicine Lake, Sinopah Mountain, with Painted Teepee just behind and equally impressive in its bold reach for the sky and near perfect symmetry. Legend had it that Hugh Monroe, the first white man to enter the Blackfeet territory, fell in love with and married Sinopah, the daughter of a Blackfeet chief, who gave Munroe the name Rising Wolf. The two had a long and loving marriage. Now their namesake peaks would preside over the area forever, reminding those who learned of their story that this land was truly Blackfeet land, a land of immense spirituality for their people. When the railroad decided to make this a destination for its ambitions to expand, like other American Indians, the Blackfeet were forced to give up that which was absolutely vital and sacred to them.

Will had admired Sinopah from the shores of Two Medicine Lake on almost a daily basis. He couldn't bear being in town at night, so each evening he would catch a ride through the entry gate and hike around Middle Two Medicine Lake, whose waters were dominated by the silhouette of Sinopah. Two Medicine's waters were not visible from the pass bearing the same name, but seeing Sinopah now—along with Rising Wolf—from this distance, made Will all the more appreciative of their grandeur, and what the Blackfeet had lost.

Directly west of the two lovers, about eight kilometers away from where Will now sat staring out from atop his mount, the arrowhead-shaped Flinsch Peak seemed to list slightly eastward, but as Will examined it, he realized that was an illusion attributable to the fact that the westernmost slope of the mountain was long and gradual, dipping low before his eyes traveled further west to Dawson Pass, whereas the eastern slope plateaued higher. The topography of the mountains Will stared out at seemed foreign to him—unlike anything in Yellowstone. Behind the "dip," layer after layer of rugged mountains, carved out by glaciers tens of thousands of years earlier, led to the immense, snowcapped peaks of the continental divide. So many lakes rested visibly below these mammoth peaks and rims, with tenfold more invisible from his vantage point. Will could not begin to count them, or imagine visiting each one. Some slopes still housed glaciers, with names like Pumpelly and Red Eagle.

Will looked due west, into the apex of the horseshoe-shaped Nyack Valley, which boasted its own majestic peaks, lakes, and pristine, turquoise rivers.

Looking out on all that majesty, all the terrain he had yet to explore, all the wildlife it housed and wildness it represented—for the first time since leaving Yellowstone, Will felt he could breathe again. Really breathe. He took the alpine air into his lungs, the fragrance of its wildflowers—from forget-me-nots, to Northern eyebright, to century-old moss campion—and savored it there. Maybe he could survive this year after all. If he looked at it as an adventure, if he could find some purpose.

If he could put Annie out of his mind.

Why hadn't he encouraged her to come with him? On a practical basis, it was pretty much impossible, but he hadn't even attempted to argue the notion. And then, instead of trying to make up for it by staying in touch, he'd only called her once. Left a voice mail, with no real substance, no suggestion even that she get back to him.

He'd probably done her a favor. Maybe she'd realized that by now.

His moment of elation destroyed by these thoughts, Will nudged Buddy to move again. Ten minutes later, as they began their descent, he heard, then saw, movement about ten yards off-trail.

After almost three decades of his life spent looking and listening for trouble in the backcountry, Will knew immediately what was normal movement and sound, and what was not.

This was not normal.

He pulled back on the reins.

"Whoa."

Will jumped off Buddy, moved toward the sound and the rustling branches of the lodgepole saplings, pushing them aside.

As often as Will had seen dead animals, he had never grown hardened. The sight of a deer or elk or bison lying dead from winter kill never failed to sadden him. He always took the time to say a brief prayer, asking the Creator to guide them into the spirit world, thanking Him for the blessing of having such a beautiful creature in his world.

But the sight of an animal dying—and in particular, an animal injured by a human—engendered a different response from Will—an anger so intense that it overshadowed, at least briefly, his grief.

A coyote lay on its side, still thrashing, still trying to escape what held its half-chewed-off leg in a deadly hold.

A trap.

Will looked at the leg, saw the flesh the coyote had had to bite through in its attempt to free itself. It lay in a pool of blood.

There was no recovery for this poor wild creature.

Will pulled his gun from its holster.

"Aho, Creator, I ask that you watch over this four-legged, guide him into the spirit world . . ."

A single shot brought the animal peace.

Hands shaking, Will lowered the gun. He dropped to his knees beside the animal and continued his prayer, laying his hands on the still warm coyote's once beautiful coat, which was now stained with blood.

"I ask you, Creator, to welcome this animal into the spirit world, where he will feel no pain and no fear. I ask that you let him dance with all the four-leggeds who are no longer with us. And I thank you, Creator, for blessing us with his presence. Aho, Creator."

Will reached for the steel jaws that held the coyote's slim paw. Prying them open, he gently lifted the paw, freed it. Then he stood, eyes still on the lifeless form.

And now, let me find the son of a bitch who did this.

The only thing that helped Will at moments like these, moments that reminded him of the cruelty of man and the innocence and beauty of man's victims, was the intense sense of purpose that took over almost immediately. It literally saved Will's sanity, and he knew it.

Now he reached for the trap. Blew aside the dirt that the coyote's movements had stirred up. He knew that he would not be lucky enough to find a metal identification tag on the leghold, but there was always the chance he'd see something that would give him a clue. It almost never happened.

This time, however, it did.

Just as Will reached for the two-way radio on his belt, it came alive with the sound of static.

"Will," a voice said over the crackling, "Where are you?"

Rob Deardorf.

Will lifted the radio to his mouth.

"Two Medicine Pass."

It took several seconds for Deardorf to respond.

"That's good," he said. "That's actually great."

"Why? What's going on?"

"We received a report of a missing hiker. She was due back from climbing Bad Marriage night before last but never returned. I need you to head that way stat. It's about ten air miles to Bad Marriage, but I need you to stop at the trail campsite just north of Pitamakan Pass to interview a couple who had breakfast with her the morning she took off. She was supposed to leave them a note at the same spot, when she got down from the mountain, but she never did. They have digital pictures of her. They'll be waiting for you." As was always the case in a situation like this, the urgency in Deardorf's voice filled Will with adrenaline. "How set are you to stay out there for a while? Maybe you should come by the station at Two Medicine."

Will resisted saying what was on the tip of his tongue: if Deardorf had stationed him at any of the backcountry ranger stations, especially the Cut Bank ranger station, as he'd been told would be the case by Peter Shewmaker, he would be there within hours. Instead, for reasons still unknown to him, they'd stuck him smack dab in the middle of the town of East Glacier.

"I'm fine for as long as it takes. Instead of coming to the station, I'll just use the trail between Upper and Middle Two Medicine. That'll save a couple hours. I should be there before nightfall." He paused, thinking of the dangers a person could be exposed to climbing alone—even if, as in the case of Bad Marriage, it wasn't a technical climb. Sudden storms, trails and cliffs with steep drop-offs, unstable talus slopes, and bear encounters were not uncommon on any climb in Glacier. "Is she an experienced climber?"

"No. A novice." Silence, then he added, "Just getting over a divorce."

Will grimaced. Why the hell did they have to name that mountain Bad Marriage?

He pressed the button to speak again.

"I'll leave now. Listen, Rob, can you patch me through to Johnny Yellow Kidney?"

Annie stared at the phone, reached for it for the second time, then stopped.

"Call him."

Annie's eyes moved to the doorway of her office. She hadn't realized Justine was standing there.

"You're getting as bad as my mother," she said. Unwilling to allow her clerk to engage her in a conversation about Will, she said instead, "How full is my schedule today? Will I have an hour or so to work on my presentation?"

Justine glanced at her watch.

"You've got a hearing in twenty minutes," she replied, appearing hurt by the rebuff, "and the arraignment for the DUI who hit the griz after that. Then I just need to meet with you before you leave to go over what you want me to get done while you're gone."

"Thanks, Justine," Annie replied with an affectionate smile. "I don't know what I'd do without you. I can leave knowing that everything will be in good hands while I'm in Glacier."

Justine worked up a half-hearted smile in return.

"The reason I came in wasn't actually to snoop. Your mom and the judge are downstairs."

Annie jumped up from the desk that Judge Sherburne had once sat behind. "Why didn't you tell me?"

"I just did. After answering your questions."

Annie went to her clerk and put an arm around her shoulders.

"I'm sorry, Justine. I'm just a little on edge. The truth is, I'm worried that Will won't be pleased to see me. That's why I hesitate to call. If he sounded unhappy about my coming to Glacier, it would ruin the trip, not just for me, but for Mom and the judge. They're like a couple of little kids."

"Are you crazy?" Justine replied, pulling Annie close for a hug. "Will is going to be ecstatic to see you."

They'd reached the top of the stairs. Annie could see her mother standing looking expectantly at the staircase, while the guards hovered around Judge Sherburne, talking and laughing. His wheeled walker, no longer necessary as one giant-sized security officer held him firmly by the arm, stood several feet away. Annie suspected Eleanor was a bit put off at being ignored. Annie waved at Eleanor and her mother's face brightened.

She turned then to Justine, whose feelings had clearly been repaired by Annie's opening up to her and sharing her fears about Will.

"I hope you're right. Still, I'm thinking I won't call him to tell him I'm coming." A trace of a blush colored her fair-skinned cheeks. "I'm the one who feels like a little kid. This is ridiculous."

As she started down the stairs, the scene below caused Annie to slow.

On the marble floor of the entry to the Yellowstone Justice Center, one of the guards—the lone female—had apparently noticed Eleanor standing off to the side alone. To Annie's relief, the two women were now engaged in conversation.

Annie's guilt when it came to bringing her mother to Yellowstone skyrocketed sixteen months earlier, when she was kidnapped by members of the Church of White Hope in an attempt to scare Annie off the bench. Annie had established herself as having environmental leanings in her first year on the bench in the park, and the church—which owned an energy company, and one of whose silent members was Senator Stanley Conroy, a powerful politician in charge of the Senate Commission on Energy Exploration, which had proposed legislation authorizing drilling in and around national parks—had decided it was imperative to get rid of her before the legislation took effect. They planned to install a judge more favorable to their plans to lease the secluded and heavily guarded property above Yellowstone for hugely profitable drilling under the park—drilling that had the potential to irreversibly impact, even destroy, Yellowstone's geothermal features. Eleanor Malone had withstood not only the terror of being kidnapped and held in a once-abandoned mine on the church's property—a mine that had been reactivated secretly, in order to get a jump on the lease they knew, from the senator's involvement, they would be awarded once the bill went into effect—her captors had also cut off her ear to up the ante and increase the pressure on Annie.

Describing Annie's feelings as "guilt," hardly touched the reality of what she'd experienced during that time, and was still recovering from. Still, she had not allowed the kidnappers to get what they wanted by resigning her position.

But on a much lower level, the guilt had started when Annie first moved to Yellowstone, bringing her recently widowed mother along.

Eleanor had struggled upon moving to Yellowstone. She had always lived in a bustling urban setting—first Chicago, where, as the wife of a successful surgeon, she attended benefits and balls on a regular basis; then, when Annie's father died, Seattle, where Annie and her then-husband lived. While Annie's work as the head of the judicial system in Yellowstone ensured that Annie had plenty of interaction and excitement in her life, Eleanor had clearly missed the social life she'd known in Chicago, or the ability to walk to a coffeehouse in Seattle if she wanted to be surrounded by people. Eleanor's social life in Seattle had also been boosted when Annie introduced Eleanor to one of the other prosecutor's mothers, who welcomed Eleanor into her long established bridge group.

Mammoth had been a shock to Eleanor's system, which is why, from the very first day she took office, Annie dutifully went home for lunch, and made a point of encouraging Eleanor to attend ranger talks and community activities in Mammoth and Gardiner. And while Eleanor still clearly longed for attention and companionship, as evidenced by the animation on her face now, as she chatted with the security guard, two things had drastically changed Eleanor's longing for the old days. The first was her kidnapping, which had given both Eleanor and Annie an extraordinary appreciation for every moment they had together, and the second—which was also a result of the kidnapping: the arrival of Judge Sherburne in their lives.

Judge Sherburne.

Annie had heard that name time and time again when she first came to Yellowstone. It had been thrown in her face, most painfully by Will, held up as an example of what Annie was not. Felled by a stroke that left him paralyzed on one side and unable to speak, Annie had been called in to replace him, but she realized almost immediately that her courthouse, Yellowstone, would never belong to Annie. It belonged to Judge Sherburne. And if she were truthful, she would admit now that she had resented it.

And then she'd met him.

And then, by finally succeeding in communicating his suspicions about Jeremiah Dayton, the Church of White Hope's leader, he'd saved her mother's life.

Looking at him now, at the joy in his still mischievous eyes at the reception he was being given upon visiting the courthouse, looking at the response his surprise visit elicited from the security guards and an attorney and a law enforcement officer who had just walked in, Annie could feel nothing but joy and gratitude that this tough old man, a man who made his own rules—as evidenced by the fact that beside him sat Annie's twelve-year-old Lab, Archie, in plain sight of the NO DOGS sign on the door—had entered her life. As did everyone else when it came to Judge Sherburne, the guards were happy to ignore the breach of rules, and so it was Archie who first noticed Annie midway on the stairs.

Tail throwing his body back and forth, he bounded through the metal detector gate and up the stairs.

Annie bent to hug his big block head.

"Hey handsome."

As it usually did, Archie's wet tongue got her lips before she could turn her face to the side.

Annie hurried down the remaining stairs, nodded at the guards, and gave her mother a hug.

"The judge has something he wants you to see," Eleanor said merrily.

With all the bodies surrounding him, Annie hadn't noticed the book the judge had clasped against his chest with his right arm—his good arm. Now he let it slide down to his hand and held it out in offering.

"It's the journal he kept on a camping trip in Glacier twenty years ago," Eleanor explained. "He's been looking for it all morning."

The judge looked pleased with himself, and the offering.

"How great is that?" Annie said, reaching for it. She noticed immediately that several of its pages had neon orange Post-it Notes sticking out in haphazard fashion from the top.

"We've marked the spots we want to visit," Eleanor finished.

Annie's grin grew forced.

She'd invited her mother and the judge to go along to Glacier in a moment of excitement, and later, she realized, a moment of nervousness as well. But the nervousness had soon changed from being centered around seeing Will again, to being nervous that having the octogenarian and her septuagenarian friend along might actually make the reunion with Will more stressful, for both Will and Annie.

Still, when she'd seen how excited the two were about a road trip, Annie had swallowed any sense of regret. But those Post-it Notes brought it all home again.

How was she going to speak at the conference, spend time with Will, and chauffeur Eleanor and the judge from one tourist site to another?

"Let me see," she said, opening the decades-old, leather-bound journal at the first orange flag.

What struck her first was the neat penmanship in which the entries were made. She'd learned to decipher about fifty percent of the scrawling the judge used at times to communicate with her. This penmanship was bold and elegant—the penmanship of a man in his prime.

She began to read:

> *August 12. Woke up in our tent in the Two Medicine campground to glorious sunshine, headed right out to St. Mary, where we sat on the lodge's deck, overlooking Swiftcurrent Lake, drinking margaritas until the sun sank beneath the jagged peaks in the distance.*
>
> *Heaven.*

Annie felt her eyes misting.

"We can do that," she said. "We can definitely do that."

"We also want to drive that Over the Top road, too," Eleanor added.

Judge Sherburne spit a half laugh, half spittle in response.

"Guh . . . in . . ." The hard "g" sent more spittle Annie's way. It was followed by a pause, then "to," another pause, and then "ssssn."

"Going to the Sun," Annie said, after watching his mouth closely. The judge usually managed to mouth a close semblance of the words, at least the words as Annie had come to know them.

The judge nodded.

"Yes, Going to the Sun," Eleanor echoed.

"Well, we'll do that, too," Annie said. "I'm afraid I have a hearing in just a couple minutes, so I have to run, but I'll see you both at lunch. I'm going to start packing so that we can get an early start tomorrow morning."

She knew that with the judge and her mom, early would be some time closer to noon. She tried again to suppress the stress that her invitation had caused.

As she started to hand the journal back to the judge, another page flipped open. This one wasn't marked with a Post-it Note but its contents alone indicated why it had fallen open to that particular page, in that a great deal of time had obviously been devoted to that day's entry.

A map of intricately drawn trails, with at least a dozen notations and arrows added, filled both pages. A tiny, crude drawing of a log structure, labeled *abandoned ranger station, Nyack* with *fire cache cabin* written directly below, caught Annie's eye.

If only she had more time, it might have been fun to read Judge Sherburne's entries before their trip. But she'd had her hands full just getting things at the courthouse in order.

"Okay you two troublemakers," she said, pressing the book between the judge's right arm and his chest, "you'd better get home and start packing, yourselves."

The silence, and a look exchanged between the two, told Annie this had all been part of a plot.

"What about Archie?" Eleanor said innocently. "Have you changed your mind? Don't you think we can bring him along?"

Archie's tail thumped against one of the guard's legs, leaving a patch of gold hair on the spotless black pants.

Annie took a deep breath.

"What the hell," she said.

After all, she was absolutely sure that if he weren't happy to see Annie, Will *would* be thrilled to see his old pal, the judge. And Archie.

"Why not?"

Eleven

Ranger Rhondie Wilkins' "trouble" antennae shot up the moment she spied the truck at the back of the line at the Two Medicine entry gate. After two decades on the job, greeting visitors to Glacier, Rhondie had a sixth sense about these things, and the camouflage-clothed arm sticking out the driver's window—she couldn't see the passenger due to the early afternoon glare on the windshield—immediately sent her red flags flying.

When the truck's turn came and it pulled even with her window, Rhondie made a point of scanning the vehicle's interior at the same time that she sized up the man behind the wheel. A large, hawk-nosed man with pocked skin stared back at her.

"Welcome to Glacier," Rhondie said. "Can I interest you in a national parks pass?"

"Nope. Just Glacier."

"Staying a while? Because if you are, and you plan to do any backcountry camping," she added, bending at her

ample waist to peer at the passenger, who also wore camouflage pants, "you'll need a permit."

"We won't be camping. Just a pass to get in. That's all
we need. And a map."

"Here you go," Rhondie said cheerfully, hanging out
the window with the map and pass in hand. "Pay attention to the rules posted on the back of the map."

As the driver reached for them, Rhondie let both
pieces slide out of her hand, onto the pavement smoldering from the midday sun.

"Oh, I'm so, so sorry," she gushed. "Hold on, if
you'll wait a minute I'll run out and pick them up for
you."

"No," the man practically shouted, holding a hand up
in protest. "I'll get 'em."

Just what Rhondie had been hoping for.

When the man opened his door, she got a better view
inside.

By the time he climbed back behind the wheel,
Rhondie's smile had vanished.

"You need to pull over, into that pullout," she said,
her chomped-short fingernails pointing to a widening of
the road, just beyond the entry gate.

The man leaned toward her angrily. The sun high-
lighted his pock marks.

"Why the hell would I need to do that?"

Rhondie already had the radio pressed to her lips.

"Please, sir, do as I say. Or a blockade will be set up
before you reach Two Medicine and you'll have no
choice but to stop."

"We'll get you fired for this," he vowed, revving his
powerful V-8 before screeching away, gravel flying.

Still, the threat of a roadblock seemed to have worked.
He pulled dutifully into the pullout.

As the truck idled ahead, Rhondie's sense of satisfac-

tion at having detained its occupants soared upon seeing its bumper sticker. So did her sense of alarm.

WOLVES: SMOKE A PACK A DAY

The young couple had been fighting.

They didn't hear Will approaching as they sat on a
stump at the solo campsite, but Will had heard raised
voices as he tied Buddy to the trunk of a Douglas fir.

"Hi folks," he called from about fifteen feet away.

When they turned his way, the woman's eyes were
reddened.

She jumped up.

"Hello. You must be the ranger they sent to talk to us."

Will removed his hat, extended a hand. "Will McCarroll."

"I'm Shelby Ball, and this is my fiancé, Blake Nye."

Blake grasped Will's extended hand.

"So you two spent a little time with a woman who set
off alone to hike Bad Marriage, and now you think she
never returned?"

Shelby responded eagerly.

"Her name was Haldis Beck. She stopped by three
mornings ago, as we were breaking camp. She had a cup
of coffee with us. She was on her way to climb Bad
Marriage, which is what we had actually planned to do,
too . . ." She shot Blake an accusing look.

He was quick to own up.

"I didn't want to hike with her. I hate to say it, but I
found her irritating, and it was obvious she was a
novice—her boots were brand new—so I decided we'd
hike Flinsch Peak that day instead." He looked at Shelby,
halfway pleadingly, halfway just testing the waters. "So
I guess it's my fault she's missing."

"I never said that."

Will raised a hand.

"Listen folks, let's not start blaming anyone. This kind of thing happens all the time. Let's just stick to the facts that might be helpful in finding this woman. This Haldis Beck. How is it that you're so sure she never got back from her climb? Maybe she's left the park already."

"No," Shelby said adamantly. She'd moved over to a large rock, at the edge of the space that had been cleared years earlier for a campsite, and now stood pointing down at it.

"I was upset about her going alone, so she promised she'd leave a note beneath that rock when she got back. We got back here last night and there was no note, so I insisted that we stay until she showed up. This morning we found a spot to use our cell phone and called park headquarters to tell them she's missing."

Will followed her over to the rock, dropped to his haunches, looking for tracks—any sign that someone had been there recently. Perhaps Haldis Beck had returned, placed the note she'd promised to leave next to the rock, and wind or an animal had taken it away.

If anything of significance had, indeed, been there to indicate Haldis Beck's return, the thunderstorm the night before had erased it. All Will could see were several sets of the same tracks in the still somewhat damp soil around the rock.

He glanced at the hiking shoes Shelby wore.

"Can you show me the bottom of those?"

Shelby turned her back to him and lifted her shoe.

It matched the tracks.

Next he scoured the ground within several yards of the rock, working his way outward until brush stopped him in every direction. After he was satisfied that no one other than Shelby had been anywhere near the rock, he turned back to the couple, who still stood several feet apart from one another, watching him.

"I was told she left her camera behind."

Shelby ran back to the log she'd been sitting on when Will approached, reached into a backpack, and returned with a digital camera.

"There's a picture of her alone on it, and a couple of the three of us," she said as she turned the camera on, then with a hand practiced at working digital cameras, brought the shot of Haldis Beck standing alone to the screen and handed it to Will.

The pictures—three in all—showed a woman in her mid- to late-fifties. She appeared to be in good spirits, as she wore a smile big enough to reveal braces on her teeth, and she also looked like she was in relatively good shape, but Blake had been correct—her shoes looked like they'd been taken right out of the box. And her back-pack was a one-nighter—she definitely wasn't carrying enough supplies for a multi-night trip.

Will debated briefly about keeping the camera, for the possibility that something in the picture might later give him a clue that could help him find her; but he decided that the value of posters with her picture on it offset the potential value to him in his search for her.

"I need you to head directly to the Ranger Station at Two Medicine and give them this camera. They already know to get posters up of her picture all over the park."

The young man, who seemed to grow surlier by the moment, did not like this plan.

"But our car is at the Cut Bank Campground."

"Someone will drive you to get it," Will said, giving him a look that clearly brooked no dissent. "Now get going. And hurry."

Will had just climbed on Buddy again when he heard a friendly voice over the two-way radio. Johnny Yellow Kidney.

"Will? You there?"

Will lifted the radio off his belt.

"It's me, Johnny."

"Sorry it took so long to call you," Yellow Kidney said. "I'd been out near Iceberg Lake again. I guess Rob had been trying to reach me for a couple hours to pass on your message. Bad transmission up there.

"I hear some crazy white woman's gone off to find herself on Bad Marriage."

"That's what it looks like. I just got done interviewing some campers who talked to her the morning she left."

"You're already up at Cut Bank?"

"No, they ran into her at the one-man campsite just north of Pitamakan Pass."

"Odd. Everyone who climbs Bad Marriage, Eagle Plume, or Mad Wolf starts from Cut Bank. Had she already been climbing down south of there, maybe Flinsch Peak?"

"She mentioned camping the night before to them, but they both thought it looked like she was just getting started."

"Must've come in at Two Medicine," Yellow Kidney said. "Strange."

Will had worked solo for so many years, and was so accustomed to being the ultimate authority on anything to do with backcountry in Yellowstone that he found himself bristling at Yellow Kidney's inserting himself into the matter of the missing hiker. Yet the uncomfortable truth was that he didn't know Glacier well enough to have realized that her choice to come in from Two Medicine didn't make sense. It must have been another sign of the woman's inexperience, which did not bode well for her. The fact that Will hadn't picked up on it also emphasized his lack of knowledge of Glacier country. He'd been poring over maps and guidebooks since arriving, and had a strong sense of the terrain, but he knew there was no substitute for firsthand familiarity. No one knew Yellowstone's backcountry better than Will. He was always the first one called if a hiker went lost. But Glacier was another story.

Could his lack of knowledge about the details of hiking and camping in Glacier end up costing this woman her life?

How the hell had he wound up in a situation like this, where the skills he prided himself in most, the mission he'd devoted his life to, all seemed to have dwindled in value?

As wounded as it felt at that moment, Will couldn't let his pride jeopardize Haldis Beck's safety.

"Any other information you can give me that might help?" he asked Yellow Kidney.

"I can't figure out what she thinks she's doing, starting from there. Usually people hike Bad Marriage as part of a circuit. They start from Cut Bank Campground, bushwack to the summit of Mad Wolf, then cross a two-mile ridgeline that hooks it up to Eagle Plume. From Eagle Plume, it's possible to continue on to Bad Marriage, but most people don't. Usually they either double back or just come down. The views from Eagle Plume are about the same—they're spectacular, by the way. I hardly recall anyone ever climbing Bad Marriage alone."

"Anything else?"

"The route down from Bad Marriage can be hard to find. I've known hikers—people who've spent a lot of time in Glacier—who ended up just making their way through the woods on the way down because they couldn't find the trail. So the way up has to be even harder. Once she does get down, she'd go to the Cut Bank Campground. You radio anyone up there?"

"Already talked to the campground host, and an interp ranger up there. They went around to every campsite, asked if anyone had seen her. Problem is, she told the couple who last saw her she'd be returning to the campground near Pitamakan Pass. She left her camera behind, so we've got pictures of her now. I just sent them back with the camera and told the interp at Two Medicine to make sure pictures of her are posted all over the park."

"They really ought to send someone else out from up that way," Yellow Kidney said.

Despite his best efforts, this was too much for Will.

"Don't think I can handle it?"

There was a short pause before Yellow Kidney replied, "Sorry, Will. It's not that. I know your reputation. But search and rescue in an area you've never been in is a tricky thing. You know that."

"Yeah, well, they're shorthanded up there due to the fires from last night's lightning strikes, so for now, I'm it." Angry with himself for letting his feelings be known, Will changed the subject. "Listen, I have some other bad news for you. This morning I came across a coyote in a leghold, on the back side of Two Medicine Pass."

This announcement was met with silence for several seconds.

"Damn," Yellow Kidney finally replied. "But I can't say that surprises me. That whole area, especially the Nyack, is a favorite for trappers. It's easy to access, and loaded with furbearers."

"I intend to do something about that," Will replied, his confidence reviving somewhat at the mere thought. Going after poachers and trappers was something he could do just as easily in Glacier as in Yellowstone. "But there was something about this trap I thought you should know."

"What?" Yellow Kidney's voice sounded as if he already knew what Will was about to tell him. Will suspected he did. Hard to surprise a biologist like Yellow Kidney. "They bait it?"

"There was a dead ground squirrel nailed to the ground right behind it. It pretty much had to step into the trap to get to it."

"What else?" Yellow Kidney wanted to know.

Damn, thought Will. He's good.

"They used a scent lure. I could still smell it."

Will heard Yellow Kidney swear. It was in Blackfeet, so he couldn't make out the word, but he had no doubt that it was an obscenity.

"Where's the trap?"

Will had been moving slowly forward on Buddy, but now he pulled back on the reins and reached inside his pocket for the numbers he'd scrawled on a notepad, taken from his GPS.

"Here are the coordinates: 48.478N, 113.3317W. What do you think?"

Kidney snorted a laugh that was anything but jovial.

"What do I think? I think there's a trapper out there using my scent lures to land the holy grail of trappers. A wolverine. Or more specifically, a wolverine from my study."

"That's my bet, too. I want to meet with you when I get back. Maybe you could put together some names of people I could talk to. Someone'll know who's out to get a wolverine. And I'm going to talk to Deardorf about taking me off any duty but backcountry patrols for poaching. It's time to crack down on this bullshit."

"One problem," Yellow Kidney said. "That'll be a little harder in Glacier than in Yellowstone. As you probably know, my people have the right to hunt and trap in the park. It's all they got out of the treaty that took it all away from them. So long as they're doing it for food."

"My guess is a wolverine that's trapped doesn't end up on someone's plate. If I find someone using your scent lures, I'll go after them. Period."

"Can't say I'd argue with that. Of course, nobody's feeling very tolerant of trapping right now, not after what happened to Stinky."

"What do you mean?"

"You didn't hear? That dead muskrat you saw, the one that drew Stinky down to the creek? It was killed by a leghold. We found it half submerged in the water. It had almost chewed its leg off to get free but it drowned before it could."

"How's the dog?"

"He's three-legged now," Yellow Kidney went on. "The doc couldn't save that mangled limb, but now just about everyone in town's wanting to give him a home. Stinky's been a fixture in East Glacier for years. You saved that dog's life, brother."

The genuine appreciation in Yellow Kidney's voice, along with the use of a term reserved for friends, made Will feel petty for having resented the biologist's intrusion.

"Damn," Will said, swallowing hard at the news about Stinky. "I've dealt with my share of illegal trapping in Yellowstone, and you said trapping's always been a problem in Glacier, but what the hell?"

"My guess is this recent stuff is tied to a contest sponsored by a local radio station. Some lazy son of a bitch trapper set that line that ended up costing that muskrat its life and Stinky his leg."

"You mean the Faithe Unsword station? I heard her show the day I was driving up here."

"She's a coldhearted wacko," said Yellow Kidney, "and with her views, and her big mouth, she may be the biggest threat going to everything you and I care about in this part of the world.

"Her station's offering up to $5,000 in prize money for the best 'trophy' catch. Trapping—especially the illegal stuff—has always gone on in Glacier, but nothing like what we've been seeing the past month or so. My guess is it's the prize money."

The trail had just dropped down, and as Buddy began

moving through a portion of it that was hemmed in on one side by sheer cliffs, and steep, rocky terrain on the other, static began to take over.

"You're starting to break up," Will said. "I think my battery's about to run out on this radio."

"Okay," Yellow Kidney replied. "Hey, be careful out there. There's some narrow, steep stuff near the summit of all of those climbs, and lots of scree that makes footing difficult on horseback. Especially if it gets cold and wet."

"Okay," Will said back to him. "Thanks."

Just before he lost reception altogether, Will heard Johnny Yellow Kidney add one more thing.

"And don't forget. There's powerful medicine up there."

Will wasn't sure just what the biologist meant by that—whether it was intended as a warning, or for reassurance.

"Powerful med . . . ," Johnny repeated, before the radio's static swallowed the rest of his words.

"You've got to be kidding? You let those jerks into the park?"

Rhondie Wilkins stood in the doorway, hands on hip, watching the law enforcement ranger she'd called for help trudge back to the entry booth. She'd just seen him wave the truck with the rednecks back onto the road leading to Two Medicine.

Chip Judd put up a hand in anticipation of Rhondie's displeasure.

"Now don't get yourself in a snit, Rhondie," he said. They had worked together for a dozen years, and he knew you didn't want to cross Rhondie Wilkins—not if you didn't absolutely have to. "I called Rob and he said I had no choice but to let them in."

Returning to the booth's window, where one of those boxy-shaped vehicles with obnoxiously loud colors—this one banana yellow—had just pulled up to buy a pass, Rhondie stuck her head out the window and smiled.

"Be right with you folks," she said as she slid the window closed.

Then she turned on Judd, who had followed her inside.

"They had guns in open sight on the backseat," she declared. "And they were dressed in camouflage!"

Judd's expression indicated he was clearly not happy with the situation either.

"I know, I know. But the guns-in-park rule says as long as they're authorized to carry them in the state where the park's located, and they showed me their permits, they can bring loaded, unconcealed weapons in now. And we've never had any rules about dress. You know that."

Rhondie eyed the cars lining up at a fast pace in her lane.

"Did you see their bumper sticker? They're here to poach wolves."

"That's what I'm afraid of, too. I gave them a stern talking to, told them there was no hunting inside the park, but that's all I could do. Rob laid down the law. I had no choice but to let them go."

A honk from several cars back did nothing for Rhondie's mood, but it did, to Judd's obvious relief, force her to get back to work. As she slid the window open again, she admonished him over her shoulder, "You better call Will McCarroll and let him know those creeps are here."

"Already tried. Couldn't roust him. Rob said McCarroll was having radio problems last time he talked to him."

With that, Judd stepped out of the booth.

Rhondie couldn't help herself.

Leaving her post, she ran back to the door Judd had just closed, opened it, and called to him.

"Promise you'll keep trying?"

He didn't look back as he strode to his car, which still sat, lights flashing, at the pullout.

"Promise."

At least the driver of the banana tin turned out to be a good-natured sort. When Rhondie reappeared wearing a less-than-welcoming expression, he looked genuinely sympathetic, which was a refreshing change from some park visitors who, despite being on the doorstep of one of the world's most natural and soothing landscapes, behaved more like they were barking orders for a latte as they rushed, late, to work.

"Everything okay?" he asked. Then, with a sheepish grin, "It's safe to go into the park, isn't it?"

Beside him, a pale, pretty teen lashed out at him with her left arm, slugging him for embarrassing her.

"Dad!"

The driver nodded toward Rhondie, with a wink.

"She knows I'm kidding."

For a moment, Rhondie actually debated about informing the duo about the pickup and what she'd seen. Telling them to steer clear of it. Something like, "memorize that truck, and if you see it parked anywhere—at a visitor center, trailhead, campsite—just keep moving."

But then she looked at the expression of anticipation on the daughter's face. She may have been embarrassed by her father's question, but it was obvious the two were on an adventure together, and excited about it. Another divorced dad trying to make up for lost time.

Pulling her well-practiced smile back out from her let's-make-the-visitor-happy bag of tricks, Rhondie leaned out the window with their pass and map.

"You two are gonna have the time of your lives," she

said. "Someone just reported a griz with three cubs along the north shore of Middle Two Medicine Lake. If you don't have binoculars, you can borrow some from the old guy in the rocker at the store up there. His name's Denny. Tell him I said so."

When the last of the line of cars had pulled through, Rhondie picked up the telephone and dialed Rob Deardorf's number, expecting to leave a voice mail. It surprised her to hear Deardorf actually pick up.

"Rob, it's Rhondie Wilkins. You know I'm not a troublemaker, but someone needs to keep an eye on those two guys you just told Chip Judd to let in."

"I've already put an alert out to all law enforcement in the park," Deardorf replied, his voice controlled. Both he and Rhondie knew she'd stepped over the line already. "You know that's all we can do at this point."

"Did you get through to Will McCarroll?"

Rhondie sensed the pause that followed held significance.

"I haven't been able to reach Will. We have reason to believe he was issued a bad radio. Either that or the battery's gone dead. Or maybe he's just out of range."

Why is it, wondered Rhondie—but this time to herself—that anyone who ever worked law enforcement, no matter how long ago, still used terms like "we have reason to believe"?

"So what're you planning to do?" she pressed. "How are you going to let Will know about those two?"

"Dammit, Rhondie. You know I don't need to explain myself to you."

Rhondie's silence allowed her to hear the sigh of exasperation—tinged with what she suspected amounted to concern—on the other end.

"But you also know that I will anyway," Deardorf yielded.

"Will's on a SAR right now. If his radio's working, he'll get in touch with me as soon as he's back in range. If it's out of commission, he knows to have the first person he comes in contact with radio us. The minute he does either, he'll be notified."

Rhondie expected that to be the end of Deardorf's explanation, but for some reason—a guilty conscience?—he went on.

"I've got extra forces up at the fire by Lake, and two rangers who've called in sick. It's just one of those days. We're all doing the best we can. Now," he added, "is there anything else you'd like to bring to my attention?"

Rhondie knew she should thank Deardorf. That's what lowly entry gate rangers did when interacting with supervisors, especially those based at park headquarters at West.

Despite her tendency to say what was on her mind, she had managed to keep her job this long. Rhondie Wilkins was an institution at the Two Medicine gate, and everyone knew it. It was, after all, the reason Deardorf had given her the time he did, bothered to give her an explanation.

Still, Rhondie wondered if maybe, just this once, she should acquiesce. Cut Deardorf some slack. She knew his job was one of the toughest in the park. The stakes for practically every decision he made were high—lives hung at balance on a day-in and day-out basis. The guy could use a little sympathy.

But then Rhondie looked up and saw a giant RV rolling slowly her way, and thoughts of the endless delays it would cause on the Going to the Sun Road chased any such warm and fuzzy thoughts right out the half-opened, metal-framed window of her ten-by-twelve booth—where they were carried away on a blend of diesel fume and glacial breeze.

"Not at the moment. But if anything else comes to mind, I'll be sure to let you know."

"I'm sure you will," replied Deardorf.

Bridger Brogan didn't realize Claudette was standing in the doorway to his office.

They'd agreed to meet in the parking lot and take off for their "date" from there, but she had been waiting now for over fifteen minutes, and she'd seen his receptionist—the unfriendly one—leave for lunch several minutes earlier, so she'd gone inside, found the waiting room empty, and wandered down the hallway looking for Bridger.

He was sitting in a leather office chair, the kind that rocked back and forth and swiveled, his back to her. His head was bent over the phone—his landline.

"I thought she said it would be this weekend."

He sounded agitated. He listened, one hand pressed against his forehead.

"I had other plans today," he said, "but I've already got the horses loaded up, so I . . ."

Suddenly sensing he wasn't alone, he snapped his head around, turning toward the door.

The look he gave Claudette frightened her.

"Hold on," he said into phone, before pressing a button on its base.

Claudette had leaned against the doorway, pulling at the hem of her shirt to make sure some cleavage showed under the aquamarine LIVE GREEN T-shirt. But now, under his scrutiny, and the anger in his normally dead eyes, she fell back.

"What are you doing here?"

"I was waiting for you outside, but then your receptionist left so I thought . . ."

"Wait in the reception area."

He got up and, with Claudette still standing facing him, shut the door.

"You son of a bitch," Claudette said through the door, reaching for its knob. But even before she twisted it, she realized that she couldn't afford to confront him. Not now, not after all her planning of the past few days. No, she had to respond in an entirely different manner if she wanted to save things.

She walked stiffly to the reception area and sat in a chair facing the door through which Brogan would enter.

In less than a minute, he showed up.

"We're going to have to reschedule our picnic."

Claudette jumped to her feet.

"Why?"

"Something just came up. Other business I have to attend to. And it can't wait."

"I heard you mention the horses. Is it in the park?"

Brogan studied her briefly, as if trying to decide whether to answer.

"Yes."

"It's your traps, isn't it?" she said, smiling. "You don't have to hide it from me. You trap in the park, don't you?"

This time, Bridger remained silent.

Claudette began to panic. She'd had it all so well planned.

"I don't care what your other business is. You must know that. You have to eat lunch, don't you?" she said, moving toward him. "I've got everything out there in the car. Couldn't I just go with you a short distance?"

"'No.'"

She did something then that made her skin crawl. She crossed the distance separating them. She reached down, took one of his crude hands in hers, and placed it on her breast.

"Oh, honestly," she practically purred, "I've been looking forward to this so much. I don't know if I can wait any longer."

Bridger Brogan's façade began to crumble.

He reached down inside her shirt, under her bra, and squeezed her nipple.

"Horny little thing, aren't you?" he said without a smile.

"That doesn't begin to describe it," Claudette replied, pressing herself up against him. "Ever since you told me about that little abandoned ranger cabin in the Nyack, I've pictured us there. Couldn't I just go that far with you? Look at it this way: if you're worried about me knowing about your trapping in the park, let me be an accomplice. That way there's nothing to worry about anymore." This suggestion clearly intrigued Brogan. "Let's have our picnic together. Then you can go on without me."

Brogan took in a deep breath.

He looked at his watch.

"I guess I do have to eat. But I'd have to move on, after we . . . after our . . . little picnic. You'd have to hike back out alone. I'll need both horses."

Claudette pointed down, at the hiking boots she'd known she would need.

"See," she said. "I came prepared. I wanted to get a last hike in the park before I head back to Missoula anyway."

"You're leaving?"

"Yes. I finished my thesis. I'll be leaving tomorrow or the next day."

This seemed to further motivate Bridger.

"Okay, let's get going. It's going to be a long day for me."

Claudette reached up, cupped his stubbly chin in her hand.

"I promise it won't be all drudgery," she said. "In fact, I plan to make it a day you'll remember."

Those words finally brought a smile to Brogan's mutt-like face.

"I'll meet you in the parking lot in five minutes," he said. "I have a quick phone call to make."

Exactly five minutes later, Brogan and Claudette pulled out of the parking lot, with Claudette following behind his half-ton pickup, which pulled a two-horse trailer with a bumper sticker that read SAVE A RANCHER, KILL A WOLF. Almost immediately upon leaving Columbia Falls, headed east, she began having trouble keeping up with Brogan, but traffic lights in Hungry Horse and a backup of traffic heading into the park in West Glacier allowed her to catch up. Once they left West Glacier, however, the next traffic light was sixty-eight miles away, in Browning, and as Claudette pressed down on the gas pedal, her anger grew by the mile.

Son of a bitch, she muttered again, this time to herself, as Brogan disappeared around a bend of the dangerous road running alongside the Middle Fork of the Flathead River.

After meeting Brogan at the bar—having to endure his lewd looks as she sat across from him—she would have thought her hatred of the man who killed Tenny could not get any stronger; but the past hour, his treatment of her in his office, and now, his total disregard for whether or not she was even keeping up with him as he sped down Highway 2 fueled everything she'd ever felt about him. The only thing keeping her sane was her plan.

They were only a few miles from Nyack Flats, and she'd begun to worry that he planned to stop in the short—and only—segment of highway that actually had houses and cabins along it. Aside from the fact that houses meant people, the real problem with that section was that they would have to cross at least a mile and a half of open country before they reached the densely forested Nyack Valley. That would complicate the plan considerably. Claudette had begun trying to rethink her options, when, just after crossing Moccasin Creek, Brogan turned on his left turn signal. Only someone experienced with the area would have known a turnoff even existed—Claudette had, in fact, driven this stretch of highway several times in the past few days and missed it. But now, as she followed the truck and trailer up a short hill, then dramatically down the incline on the other side of its crest, relief flooded her.

Perfect.

What made Brogan's choice of this spot to enter the Nyack so desirable, for Claudette's purposes, was the fact that the Nyack in all its grandeur—wild, forested, and unpopulated, began almost immediately across the river from where they parked.

Claudette pulled her car in next to the truck and trailer. When Bridger Brogan got out of the truck, he walked briskly to the back of the trailer. All business, he began unloading the horses.

Claudette had already put her backpack on. She stood watching as Brogan, who'd entered the trailer, walked one horse—a large Palomino gelding—back and out, on to the dirt ground, and then the other.

He'd already saddled both horses.

Claudette was grateful for the lack of small talk.

Brogan was clearly preoccupied and Claudette suspected it had to do with the call she'd interrupted.

Fearing he was silently pondering backing out of their date again, she forced herself to approach him.

He was yanking the leather strap of the stirrup on the saddle of the smaller of the two horses, a jumpy Appaloosa mare—shortening it—when she reached out and placed her hand on his arm.

"Can I help?"

His expression made it almost look like he was surprised—or irritated—to see her there.

"Let's just get going," he said, dropping the stirrup,
then leveraging his considerable weight—and strength—
down on it to make sure it had cinched in place.

His next move threw Claudette off. He reached for
her backpack.

"I'll tie that on."

Claudette shrunk back.

"I can just wear it."

During the brief second or two that Brogan looked at
her without saying a word, Claudette felt her face flush.
Her mind raced with explanations but he simply shrugged
his shoulders, "Suit yourself. Looks like you packed half
a kitchen in there." A human element finally entered his
eyes. "You sure you want to do this? I'm feeling rushed,
and you're going to have to pack that back out with you.
On foot. Unless I take it, on the horses."

Relief flooded her and Claudette responded cheerfully
with, "It'll be a lot lighter when I hike out." Now that
she had his attention, she knew to make good use of it.
"I have a virtual feast planned for you."

He looked at her, trying to read between the lines. The
way she looked back at him clearly pleased him.

"Okay, let's go. Climb on."

Back in the parking lot of his office, Claudette had
noticed a pile of brown fur on the passenger seat of his
truck.

She nodded now in that direction.

"Is that a bearskin I saw in your truck?"

Questions were definitely not high on Brogan's list of
favorite things. Still, Claudette could tell he'd started to
trust her.

"A griz cub."

"Is it big enough for two adults to . . ."—the pause
was deliberate, and clear in its meaning—"*rest* on?"

Brogan's laugh came straight from the belly that protruded over his blue jeans like an oversized nose over a weak chin.

"Honey, I won't have time to rest afterward, but you bet your sweet ass we can bring it." For a moment, he forgot the phone call that had come perilously close to dooming all of Claudette's plans. "You are my kind of girl, aren't you?"

"I hope so," Claudette replied. "I really hope so."

Twelve

"Oh my," Eleanor Malone's eyes were glued to the backseat window as Annie moved the car up the long circular driveway to the Glacier Park Lodge.

Annie's excitement was tied more to the thought of seeing Will than to the sight of the lodge—which was built by the Great Northern Railway in 1913 as part of its attempt to compete with its rivals, the Northern Pacific and Union Pacific, who'd been wildly successful in drawing masses of tourists to Yellowstone—but she had to admit that the massive lodge and its elegant, sweeping lawns and gardens came as a pleasant surprise. The line of cars ahead of her, however, did not. Ordinarily Annie would have chosen to grab the first open parking space and walk the couple hundred yards to the hotel, but with her mother and the judge as passengers, she was grateful to see a valet standing outside the front entrance.

"Those gardens!" Eleanor exclaimed again from behind Annie, as they passed by rows of colorful, knee-high blossoms. "They're gorgeous."

Next to her, Annie could feel Judge Sherburne taking

the scene in eagerly, too, which surprised her. She didn't expect the judge to be someone easily excited by gardens, or lodges. Not when he'd spent almost three decades in a park that boasted some of the world's most renowned lodges, and wildflower extravaganzas that easily competed with the award-winning gardens lining the walkway that headed toward the small railroad depot across the street, splitting this lodge's golf course–sized lawn right down its middle.

A flood of guilt hit her. She'd rarely taken the judge out to visit the places he loved in Yellowstone. Will had told her about the times he'd smuggled the judge out of the assisted living center in Livingston in which he was miserable—outings where Will had taken his friend for middle-of-the-night drives down the Paradise Valley to visit his favorite haunts in Yellowstone. The Lamar Valley, where they would listen to wolves; Mammoth Hot Springs, where they sometimes simply sat and looked at the Stone House the judge had called home.

Annie knew that inviting the judge to live with Eleanor and her in that same house had changed the judge's life immensely for the better, given him the will to live again, but she suddenly realized how seldom she'd taken him out into the park since he'd moved in.

That no doubt explained the excitement she felt literally radiating from him in the seat beside her.

"We'll come outside to see the gardens tonight," she said, "after my presentation. I promise."

"It's okay, dear," Eleanor said from the backseat. "We can wander around the grounds this afternoon, while you're gone."

When the Subaru finally got its turn and a smiley twenty-something-year-old doorman, dressed in red, opened the passenger-side door, Annie jumped out and lifted the hatchback to start loading the suitcases onto the cart he'd deposited on the curb before he reached inside the front seat to help the judge out.

Archie had been sitting patiently in the backseat, beside Eleanor, but now he bolted over the seat and out Annie's door.

The doorman's smile evaporated.

"The lodge doesn't allow dogs."

Annie, Eleanor, and the judge all froze simultaneously.

"You're not serious," Annie said as she reached for Archie's collar.

"Yes, ma'am, I am. No dogs allowed."

Annie glanced at her watch: 2:25.

"You're going to have to make an exception this time. I'm scheduled to present at a conference here in thirty-five minutes. I don't have time to start looking for another motel. Please."

At Annie's statement about finding another motel, the kid actually blurted out a laugh. The look on his face said something to the tune of, "Are you crazy?" But what came out of his mouth was, "There's no way you'll find another motel in town right now."

When the expression on the three faces in front of him registered, he added, sheepishly, "I'm afraid there's nothing I can do."

Annie handed him a five-dollar bill.

"Please help my mother and Judge Sherburne inside." She turned to Eleanor. "I'll go talk to the manager and get this worked out."

She turned then to Archie. Annie's heart sank at the sight of his tail, which was wagging to beat the band at having arrived at their destination and been given reprieve from the car.

"Back inside," Annie said, gently directing him. "Just for a few minutes."

Leaving Archie and her other companions behind,

Annie strode through the enormous double doors being held open by a second bellman.

Passing by one of the sixty Douglas fir columns that had been shipped in almost 100 years earlier to frame the lobby's atrium—each of which measured at least forty feet in height and three feet in diameter—Annie failed to notice that it bore a poster for the conference, nor did she see the picture of herself as one of the presenters. Panicked upon seeing a line of four or five suitcase-laden guests in front of the registration desk, she looked around for someone who might be able to help her. Dozens of tourists milled around in the lobby, which featured a ceiling that rose three stories, surrounded by log rail balconies on the upper two floors, and shops, a restaurant, and bar on the ground floor. There was a profound sense of history in the heavy logs used to construct the building, and the grandeur of the lobby, that would have made it easy to picture tourists one hundred years earlier, fresh from the train, which stopped directly across the street from the lodge's vast lawns, milling about in a scene much like the one today. But Annie did not have history on her mind.

She'd planned not only to be situated in her room by now, but to also have a quiet hour or so alone to go over her presentation. All that became an impossibility when Eleanor decided to repack her bag that morning, causing them to leave Mammoth over an hour and a half after Annie's target departure, and now the thought that they might not be able to stay in East Glacier caused sweat to bead on Annie's face, and her normally placid heart to race.

As a judge, she was used to pressure, big pressure, but this was something else entirely. Annie felt wet circles under the arms of her blue cotton shirt. Damn, if she didn't have time to change, she'd have to put a jacket over it, and right now, she already felt like she was in a sauna.

Why had she thought it would be a good idea to mix family and dog and business?

The next second, one look at Eleanor's angst-ridden face when she walked through the door, with the bell-man close behind, holding the judge by the elbow, and Annie knew it had been a mistake.

"Please," Annie said, leaning over the shoulder of the woman waiting in line in front of her, "would you consider letting me go next? I have elderly companions who need . . ."

The woman glanced at Annie, gave her a look that told Annie she was out of luck, and then turned back to face the registration desk.

The doorman had deposited Eleanor and the judge on a long log bench facing the piano. He approached Annie with a sense of determination.

"I'm sorry, ma'am, but you can't just leave your car out in front. It's blocking arriving guests."

Annie felt ready to cry.

"But I'm scheduled to speak at a conference here in half an hour. I have to get this settled. I can't leave my mother and the judge sitting here in the lobby. Or my dog in the car. It's too hot out there. Please, can't you help me?"

The kid either had no authority or no heart. Perhaps it was both, for he replied, "I'm sorry but you'll have to move your car."

Annie felt her face flush with anger and anxiety.

"I want to speak to the manager." She had always prided herself in her reputation as being unflappable on the bench, but this was new terrain for Annie, and the tone of her voice shocked her as much as it obviously did the bellman. "Now."

The kid glanced over at the desk, clearly trying to decide what to do. Annie's gaze followed. Half a dozen employees manned different sections—reservations, check in, activity center. None of them looked like they had any more age, experience, or authority than the bellman. Annie's heart dropped.

The kid seemed paralyzed by the situation.

"Annie?"

Annie's head snapped around at the voice behind her.

"Annie Malone?"

A tall, lean man, with thick black hair tied loosely behind his tanned face, stared at her.

Oddly, his warm brown eyes seemed at first to hold some kind of fear, but then a smile spread across his face.

"Johnny?"

Johnny Yellow Kidney laughed and extended his right hand, grasping Annie's hand firmly and enthusiastically.

"It *is* you. I saw your picture on the poster for the Judiciary Conference and wondered if it could be, but I didn't recognize the last name."

Annie felt like she'd stepped into a dream that was half nightmare–half not; or perhaps a different cosmos. In the midst of all this chaos, having just lost her temper with the bellman, with a red face and sweat pocking her blouse, she now stood facing this man from her past.

"I wasn't eavesdropping," Yellow Kidney said, clearly having heard the exchange, "but I did hear you say you want to see the manager."

Embarrassed, Annie stuttered, "We just arrived, and they're telling me I can't have my dog here. I brought my mother and a friend," she nodded in the direction of the bench, hoping the sight of Eleanor and the judge might help excuse her actions, "and my presentation starts in . . ." she looked at the huge clock mounted on the railing that circled the second floor of the atrium, and let out a groan. "Twenty minutes."

Yellow Kidney had judiciously removed the smile from his mouth, but she could still see it in his eyes.

"Stay right here," he said. He strode quickly toward the end of the counter, stepped behind it, opened a door along the wall on the other side and disappeared.

Within two minutes, he reemerged, a pretty brunette at his side. Unlike all the other lodge employees, she was dressed in the attire of a businesswoman in any sophisticated city—sleek suit and heels. She was shapely from top to bottom, especially the long legs. She wore a name tag: STACY.

She smiled as she approached Annie.

"Judge Peacock," she said, extending her hand, "I'm so sorry about the confusion. Johnny explained what's going on. The lodge doesn't allow dogs, but in this situation, we'll make an exception." She looked at the young bellman, whose own face had turned a bright pink. "Casey, please get the judge's family, and her dog, situated in the Roosevelt suite."

She turned back to Annie.

"It's on the first floor, so you can walk your dog right out the back." She flashed another dazzling, warm smile. "If you don't mind keeping him out of the lobby, it would make my life a little easier."

Flustered, sweating, heart racing as she glanced once more at the clock's giant hand, moving ever closer to the top of the hour, Annie felt like hugging her.

"Thank you so much. You can't imagine how much this means to me."

Stacy nodded, then looked Johnny's way.

"Thank your friend here. Now you go ahead and do whatever you need to do"—Annie felt sure she was referring to the sweat-stained blouse—"and we'll make sure your loved ones, dog included, are taken care of."

Annie gave Johnny a quick hug.

"How can I thank you?"

He grinned.

"Hey, just seeing you again is thanks enough. Now go knock 'em dead, Your Honor."

Feeling totally nonplussed, Annie hurried over to Eleanor and the judge to tell them the plan. Then she went in search of a restroom, to try to put herself together again.

Ten minutes into her presentation on Yellowstone's unique judicial system, she saw Johnny Yellow Kidney slip into the room from a door in the back. She'd regained her composure, and with the crisis about Archie behind her, she found herself wondering about Johnny. She hadn't seen him in twenty years but she had never forgotten that he came from the Blackfeet Reservation. She just hadn't connected that fact with East Glacier.

She was disappointed when he disappeared out the same door immediately after her presentation ended. She hadn't thanked him properly, and she had so many questions now to ask him. Unable to follow him—half a dozen audience members had approached her—Annie hoped she'd be able to find Johnny Yellow Kidney again later.

But her recriminations about not thanking Johnny properly were pushed out of mind when Annie recognized another face. Standing back, away from the group crowding around her, Peter Shewmaker smiled at her.

It was clear that he was waiting for the group to disperse in order to speak to her.

When the last person who'd stayed behind headed for the exit, Annie hurried over to Peter.

"What a nice surprise!" she said, giving Peter a hug. "If I'd known you were going to be here, we could have driven together."

"I was on a law enforcement panel this morning. I saw your name on the last agenda they sent me. I would have contacted you about driving together, but Gloria and I had decided to make a vacation out of it. Brought the boys along. We're headed home now. I just hung around to see your presentation and say hi. You were great."

"Thanks, Peter. I was asked to substitute for another speaker at the eleventh hour. I guess I wasn't paying much attention to the information they sent me. I would have been at your panel if I'd known you were here."

Suddenly a thought, one that elicited excitement and dread simultaneously, occurred to Annie. It was only natural to think that Will might have attended a panel consisting of law enforcement officials.

"Was Will there?" she asked, her voice rising an octave.

She regretted asking it the moment the words left her lips, for voicing the question somehow crystallized the fears she'd harbored subconsciously—fears that Will might not be happy about her unannounced visit.

She must have been wearing her heart on her sleeve, because Peter looked painfully contrite, and for a moment she was sure he would say that Will had, indeed, attended. And that he'd left the conference before Annie's presentation.

Anyone who'd attended would have been given a program. And the poster with Annie's picture was posted in the lobby.

"Didn't you hear?" Shewmaker replied instead. "Will's been called into the backcountry. He's out on a search-and-rescue. A hiker went missing."

Annie tried to put the judicial mask that served her so well on the bench back on, but her voice again gave her away.

"How long has he been gone?"

Shewmaker knew he was delivering bad news.

"He was out on his normal patrol when they sent him on the SAR this morning. I'd hoped to see him, too, but I have to get back now, and with this type of thing, you just never know."

He patted her arm awkwardly.

"An inexperienced female, out to climb her first mountain. Alone." He shook his head. "What are people thinking?" He paused. As someone who had overseen hundreds of such searches in his years of law enforcement, Peter was clearly troubled by the all-too-familiar situation. "Will could be out there for days. Especially since they're shorthanded now with that fire that started last night—a lightning strike—near Lake McDonald. All resources are being directed over there. Will's on his own, at least for now."

Annie's could barely bring herself to speak.

"If anyone can find her," she said softly, "Will can."

Peter suddenly reached out and cupped her chin in his hand, forcing Annie to meet his gaze.

"Please forgive me this lapse," he said, his eyes kind and knowing. "But I'm certain of one thing. If Will knew you were here, he'd find her that much faster."

Will dropped his head against the gust of frosty wind that accosted them each time his horse stepped out of the protection of trees on their climb up Triple Divide Pass. He was used to how mountain passes funneled the wind, magnifying what was being felt at lower elevations to a point that one could sometimes actually lean into it and be held upright.

Unfazed, Buddy dropped his head a notch, too, but kept a steady pace.

Will felt frustrated. He'd hoped to run into hikers who had encountered Haldis Beck while crossing the popular scenic pass, which sat at the apex of three major watersheds that flowed toward the Pacific, the Atlantic, and Hudson Bay. But so far the only folks he'd met along the way were a trio of German tourists who spoke little English. Still, their communication through gestures and the few words Will could remember from interactions with the good-natured visitors in Yellowstone had been enough to convince Will they hadn't seen the missing woman.

Was he even on the right trail? Had someone else met Haldis Beck along the way and informed her that her approach to Bad Marriage was, at the very least, not exactly feasible, and at its worse, downright undoable? Had she abandoned those plans, perhaps even left the park?

He felt as though he were looking for the proverbial needle in a haystack, only this haystack encompassed hundreds of miles of dangerous terrain and often treacherous conditions. And what was at stake—a woman's life—upped the ante and had Will questioning every move he made, every move Haldis Beck might have made.

Then, briefly, he thought he'd hit pay dirt.

A lone hiker appeared. At first he was just a dot along the trail ahead. He moved slowly, steadily, a walking stick marking each step. Unlike most hikers, who sometimes spent so much time gawking at scenery that they endangered themselves on the rocky trail, this one moved with head down.

Below stretched a landscape that included views of Medicine Grizzly Lake and a peak of the same name—in honor of a legend in which Flathead warriors killed a Blackfeet who then transformed into the Medicine Grizzly to help his fellow Blackfeet fend off their enemies—but right now, Will zoned in on the hiker. He disappeared from sight, but when Will rounded the next bend in the trail, the old guy stood face-to-face with the wall of red rock that abutted the west side of the trail. He was taking a pee.

The hiker—grizzled, looking like someone who had been in the backcountry most of his life—glanced up, saw the uniform, and said, "You gonna cite me for public indecency?" then looked back down at the erratic stream he'd made on the dry, claylike surface.

His hair fell to the middle of his back, wild and untamed at the neck but ending in a pencil thin braid for the last ten inches that the old man had tied in its own knot.

"Nope," Will replied, bringing Buddy to a halt and turning to eye the valley below while he waited for the stream to stop.

"Ahhh," the old guy finally said, not bothering to zip his pants shut. He looked up at Will. "You got a smoke?"

Despite his mood, Will laughed.

"Nope." He trained his gaze on the old man's face. "What direction you coming from?"

The man nodded behind him.

"You got eyes, don't ya?"

"You been anywhere around Bad Marriage?"

The old man stared out at the lushness below them.

"You know how Bad Marriage got its name?" he replied.

"Nope."

"Used to be called Elk Tongue, but one of the first superintendents, a fellow named E.T. Scoyen, renamed it after an Indian named Bad Married. Poor guy couldn't keep a wife."

"I'm looking for a hiker who's missing. A woman. Maybe fifty years old, short hair. She set out for Bad Marriage, but never returned. She's inexperienced, not enough supplies. New hiking boots. You see anyone that fits that description?"

"I seen someone that fits part of that description. About that age. Don't know about the hair 'cause she had a ball cap on. No ponytail or anything like that, so probably was short. But she looked plenty experienced to me, and she could've lived out of the pack she was wearing for a month."

Will scowled.

"The woman we're looking for only had a day pack. New boots. And braces on her teeth. Did you notice if the woman you saw had braces?"

The old timer's grin revealed teeth that had never seen a dentist, much less an orthodontist. He shook his head slowly.

"She wasn't exactly the smiley type. We passed right by each other. Never said a word."

"That doesn't sound like her," Will said thoughtfully. "This gal's supposedly pretty friendly."

The old guy's grin turned to a cackle.

"Don't s'pose I scared her, do you?" His eyes gleamed with merriment at his own joke. "This one didn't want to talk, and I wasn't too eager either."

Bowing to a particularly nasty gust of wind, he said, "Better keep moving."

Will maneuvered Buddy to the side to let him pass on the narrow trail.

"If you see someone like I described, do me a favor and get word to a ranger."

"I'll do that," the old man lied as he squeezed by.

He was almost around the bend behind him, when Will turned in his saddle.

"Why were you not eager to talk to this woman? Seems to me you might like seeing people once in a while."

The old timer didn't stop or look back.

"Something about her scared *me*," he replied, head down, walking stick clicking on rock.

In the wind, Will could barely make out his next words.

"Don't like that new rule that lets any nut with a screw loose bring a gun in here. Don't like it at all."

"Hey, wait a minute," Will called after him, but by now the disheveled figure had disappeared around the curve of the trail.

The alpine stretch was too narrow to turn Buddy around, and without a branch in sight to tie him, Will urged the gelding forward almost 300 yards, until the trail finally widened to a ledge.

Looping the reins over the saddle horn, he admonished the horse, "Don't make me come after you," then jumped down and, at a run, retraced the portion they had just traveled.

But when Will got to the point where the trail opened back up, just beyond where he'd first sighted the old timer in the distance, with lush woods on one side and a sheer drop-off into the valley on the other—the site where the Blackfeet had ultimately fended off the Flathead—the man was nowhere to be seen.

Thirteen

Claudette Nillson had an irrational fear of drowning.

She'd never actually known anyone who drowned, but she'd grown up spending summers in a family cabin at Squaw Bay, on North Idaho's Lake Coeur d'Alene. Back then, there were no railings along the narrow, winding road along the east side of the lake to stop a car from sliding off and cascading down the steep embankment into the black waters—which had happened with some regularity, causing at least three deaths that Claudette was aware of and one that her parents had refused to let her read about in the local paper.

As a child, Claudette used to secretly undo her seat belt as her father carefully negotiated that road at night. And crack the window open. Just in case.

And then there was the time, her freshman year at Montana State, that she went rafting on the infamous Buffalo Rapids of the Flathead River. Her friends and she had been drinking, but as it turned out, the alcohol had nothing to do with what happened. Claudette and four others floated behind two of the group who were in kayaks and eager to negotiate the Buffalos, in preparation for an "extreme" contest later that month, along what was appropriately known as the Mad Mile—the logic being you had to be mad to attempt to boat the class IV rapids—just outside Big Fork.

Claudette assumed that the kayakers would be the only ones facing danger. She and the others in the inflatable raft had cheerfully watched as their brightly colored kayaks, and then their helmets, were swallowed by the wild waters up ahead.

That's when everyone in the raft began holding tight to the rope running along the top of its perimeter.

They were almost through the worst of the series of four rapids when the raft hit a VW-sized boulder. The front end lifted high in the air. It felt like it was suspended there for eternity, before crashing back down—fortunately for Claudette, right side up. Claudette, who was seated at the rear, was the only one not thrown into the water. She had no choice but to hold tight until the boat cleared the rapids, then she jumped up, looking for her friends. Two heads were already visible in the roiling water. Another popped up almost immediately.

But one did not. Her roommate, Janet.

While the three swam for shore, Claudette balanced herself precariously as she stood, alone in the boat, her eyes searching the water below.

And then she saw Janet—four or five feet below the water's surface, her hand frantically reaching skyward, her face portraying her terror.

Claudette watched, expecting Janet to emerge momentarily, but she seemed to hold stationery—never coming any closer to the surface.

And then Claudette saw it—the reason why.

The boat's bail bucket—a standard on all rafts—was attached to a belt on her friend's life vest.

"The bucket," Claudette shouted, pointing frantically. "Look!"

She could see Janet's powerful legs—Janet was, after all, an AAU championship diver—flailing, fighting to bring her to the surface.

Claudette screamed—mouthing the words precisely—one more time while she pointed to Janet's side.

"The bucket."

Janet was either too frightened, or too oxygen-deprived, to understand.

With thoughts of Lake Coeur d'Alene's frigid waters taking her to a terrifying place in her head, Claudette took one deep breath and plunged into the water.

Janet had stopped kicking. Her eyes, however, were still open. Claudette was afraid to look into them.

She went right for the bucket. Its hook—intended to keep it in place in the boat during rough stretches on the river—had latched on to one of the straps on Janet's life jacket. Filled with water, no amount of strength or valiant attempt to rise to the surface could have succeeded in counteracting its gravitational pull.

When she could not get it loose, Claudette—feeling the last of her oxygen dissolve in her bloodstream—reached instead for the double snaps holding the life jacket in place.

Freed of her load, Janet practically jetted to the surface.

Claudette followed.

Their friends, who had by then reached the shore, swam to meet them; and in the end, it became one of those stories that was told laughingly at parties, again and again—but pushed out of mind in those lonely moments when one contemplates the fragility, and duration, of life.

Maybe Claudette's fear of drowning wasn't all that irrational after all.

Drowning was how Tennyson had died—being held underwater by a leghold trap, until the need for oxygen, the need to breathe, caused him to open his mouth and fill his sweet lungs with water.

Nothing—not even her fear of crossing the river—would deter Claudette from today's mission. Nothing.

Brogan had taken the reins of both horses. He led them down the incline to the water and let each draw a long sip. Then, without another second wasted, he looked at Claudette, nodded toward the mare, and said, "Let's go."

Claudette tried to remain calm. She looked at the water rushing by the horses' feet, saw how even the smallest of rocks—or a recently shod hoof—caused a new pattern to emerge on the surface. Along the river's edge, the early afternoon sun penetrated to the rocky riverbed below. The other shore was a good twenty yards away. The Middle Fork might be at low-water, but those twenty yards still roiled and splashed, and the rocks beneath it quickly disappeared from sight as Claudette's eyes moved in the direction of the Nyack, and the waters deepened.

"Don't we want to look for a better place to cross?"

Already swinging a beefy leg over the saddle, and clearly not willing to humor her, Brogan gave the gelding an almost imperceptible cue and the horse stepped gamely into the river.

Claudette took a deep breath, climbed on the Appaloosa, and followed.

"Shit," she cried, as the mare immediately lost footing on the slippery rocks beneath her.

"Just hold on," Brogan yelled from ahead. He hadn't even turned to look back. "Especially if she starts swimming. Hold on."

Claudette grabbed two fistfuls of mane, clutching that, along with the reins, to the horn of the saddle.

Son of a bitch.

When they got to the other side, Brogan remained silent. Claudette followed as he bushwacked his way toward the dense forest, the Nyack's rolling, forested hills and steep peaks invisible now. Claudette suspected he knew exactly where he was going. In less than a quarter mile, that was confirmed when they reached a trail—used mostly by game—and stepped onto it.

"The cabin's just a couple miles now," Brogan said.

They rode that distance in silence. Claudette wondered if she would be able to find her way back to the highway, and her car, alone. Brogan stopped twice to drop to one knee and examine tracks along the trail.

Claudette suspected he'd be back, armed with traps, but she did not ask. She did not want to.

When they reached the clearing that housed the remnants of the former Nyack ranger station, Claudette quickly appraised it.

The abandoned horse barn was a crude log structure that showed its age—according to the National Park Service Web site Claudette had studied, over eighty-five years. She had read that the other, smaller log structure at the same site was still used as a fire cache. Earlier that day, she'd heard there was a fire in the park—supposedly a lightning strike—but it was up north, near the Canadian border. Either building, she quickly decided as she eyed them, would suit her purpose. However, when Brogan slid down off his horse and began walking around, his gaze glued to the ground, Claudette realized that the description of the ranger station as "long-abandoned" did not necessarily ensure one key component to her plan: isolation.

Brogan looked as unhappy about the footprints—both man- and horse-made—as Claudette felt.

"Motherfucker," she heard him mutter. She slid down off the Appaloosa and hurried over to his side, her gaze following his.

"What is it?"

"Someone sticking his nose where he shouldn't," Brogan responded.

He lifted his eyes from the dirt to Claudette. Along the way, they paused at her breasts. He was tired of questions. And in a hurry. He reached for her, pulled her roughly to him.

"Nothing you need to worry about," he said. "Let's go inside the barn."

Claudette instinctively pushed away, and then, at the look on Brogan's face, stammered, "We can't. Not here. Not with someone around."

Brogan's heavy brows knit together, accentuating the Neanderthal-like quality of his features.

"What do you mean, we can't? That's what you dragged me out here for."

"But I thought this place was abandoned. That we'd have privacy."

Brogan studied her.

"Now you want privacy? I thought you said you *like* to do it outside? That's not exactly private."

"I—I—I did. I mean, I do," she couldn't stop stuttering. "But I never meant I wanted an audience."

He pulled her to him again, and this time she knew not to fight it. This time she let his hot breath linger on her ear.

"An audience might be fun," he said.

Sickened by his nearness, and the smell of him, Claudette pressed back against his hardness.

"I'm afraid it would inhibit me to think someone might come along," she said. "Let's just go off a ways. We'll put the bearskin down and have something to eat first."

He studied her, then, finally, pushed away.

"Okay, you lead. But you better hurry. I'm a hungry man."

They mounted their horses again and Brogan followed as Claudette steered her mare off the trail and into the woods. After no more than two minutes, Brogan said, "This is far enough."

"Just a little farther," Claudette replied. She looked back over her shoulder, smiled and said, "I can be noisy."

"So can I," Brogan replied, his good nature quickly restored.

When she knew they were a safe distance away from the old ranger station, and well off the trail, Claudette pulled her horse to a stop.

She slid off the saddle, dropping to the ground at the same time Brogan did. Seeing how he was looking at her, she quickly slid the backpack off and eased it to the ground before he got to her.

Brogan was all over her in a heartbeat, his tongue practically choking her as he pushed it down her throat, at the same time he slid his calloused hands inside her jeans.

"Take these off."

"I want to feed you first," Claudette replied.

"No. I can't wait."

Claudette's mind raced with the possibilities. She needed a few moments to herself to think. To prepare.

Leaving her hands resting intimately on his chest, she pushed back just enough to let him look in her eyes.

"Okay, but I need to find the little girl's room first. Why don't you gather some firewood—for later—and put the bear rug down." She picked the backpack off the ground. "I'll be right back."

She disappeared into the trees; then, out of sight, she turned to watch as Brogan placed the bearskin on the ground. Hurriedly, she began rummaging through her backpack—its contents had shifted during the ride—strategically placing several items.

When she reemerged from the woods, Brogan was

seated on the bearskin. He was fat and out of shape, and clearly ill at ease. His back was to her. Claudette placed the backpack leaning against the base of a lodgepole pine almost within reach of the bearskin, then she cleared her throat.

Brogan turned and started to rise eagerly. She pushed him back to the ground.

"Stay right there."

Slowly, deliberately, Claudette reached for the hem of her shirt and lifted it off her head. Then, her eyes glued to the rapt look on Brogan's face, she reached behind her back and unsnapped her bra.

Brogan's breath caught at the sight of her. He reached for her again, but she held him at bay.

"Do you like it?"

Her full, perfectly rounded breasts swung free. She took in a deep breath, causing them to rise, clearly offering them to him; then she brushed her fingertips over them and felt each nipple respond.

Brogan groaned.

"Take the rest off."

"Not yet," she replied. "I want to dance for you."

She stepped toward the backpack, bent low, and extracted a portable CD player. She'd already loaded it with a Tina Turner CD. Now she pressed the play button.

"Private Dancer."

I'm your private dancer, a dancer for money . . .

Claudette swung her hips slowly, side to side, to its rhythm, breasts swaying, then finally stepped toward him and reached for the button of his Carhartts.

"It's your turn now."

Brogan stood. He suddenly looked shaky.

He fumbled with the button, slid the zipper down. Claudette could see that he wasn't wearing underwear.

But within seconds, she saw something else. Something was wrong.

"I might need you to touch me first," he said, unapologetic, almost angry. "You shouldn't have made me wait so long."

He grabbed her hand, placed it on him as he stood face-to-face with her, the music the only thing in keeping with the bizarre scene.

Claudette did what he asked.

When that didn't work, Brogan began getting agitated.

"I don't have time for this," he said, reaching for his Carhartts, which were still around his ankles. "I should never have agreed. I have too much on my mind for this."

He pulled his pants up.

"No," Claudette cried. "I know how to fix it."

She stepped back and quickly shed her jeans. Then she let her hands run over her breasts, down her taut stomach. Standing in front of him, she hitched a thumb in each side of her panties.

"You won't regret it," she said.

Brogan couldn't take his eyes off her. He let his pants drop again. Stepped out of them.

This was her last chance. Her only chance.

She slid the panties off. Then she simply stood in front of him, letting him take in the sight.

He became aroused.

"Are you into bondage?" she whispered.

He began stroking himself, his eyes focused at the junction between her legs now.

"I can't say I've ever tried it."

"You won't be disappointed."

Making a show of it, Claudette leaned over. Reaching carefully for the front zipper on her backpack, she extracted a short length of rope.

"You little slut, you," Brogan said, chortling with delight.

His hands groped her.

She nibbled on his thick neck as she pulled his hands behind his back and giggling like a schoolgirl, tied them.

"You have no idea what's in store for you," she whispered, biting the lobe of his ear.

Moving back in front of him, Claudette picked up the T-shirt she'd discarded and began rolling it.

Brogan was rapt.

"What's that for?"

"It's a blindfold. Believe me, you'll love it. It'll intensify everything, what you're about to feel. What I'm about to do to you." She smiled. "All you have to do is trust me."

Brogan leaned his head forward eagerly.

"Are you ready?" she asked softly.

Brogan's meaty legs spread as he grew with excitement.

"I've been ready since the day I saw you."

"Me, too," Claudette said, stroking him.

"Look at you," she exclaimed.

The acknowledgment cemented Brogan's compliance. They were standing near the edge of the bearskin.

"Wait one more second," Claudette said. "I brought lotion."

"Fuck lotion. I don't need it. Not anymore."

"I promise," she replied as she stepped away, "you'll love it."

She turned the volume on the CD player up and, heart in throat, slowly, carefully, slid the heavy contraption out of her backpack. Uncoiling the chain that she'd woven cloth through and over to ensure it would not alert Brogan, Claudette slid it around the base of the tree, and, then, fingers poised, waited for Tina's vocals—"Rolling on the River" had finally come on—to reach a crescendo. When they did, when the song's frenzy filled the air, she pushed the U-shaped piece of metal in place until she heard a muffled click.

Brogan's head instantly snapped in its direction.

"What was that?" He began struggling to wriggle out of the rope tying his hands behind his back.

Heart racing, Claudette moved back to him, pressed her warm body against his.

"It's another surprise for you," she whispered, her lips tickling his ear, "for later." Brogan seemed to deliberate, but with the touch of her tongue, Claudette felt him surrender.

"Hurry," he said.

She pressed her warm body against his, began running her lips down his hairy, bloated stomach.

When he groaned, Claudette began to feel confident.

She looked up at him and said sweetly, thoughtfully, her voice almost little-girlish: "You're almost off the rug. I want you comfortable. Step back, just a little this way . . ."

Dropping to her knees in front of him, her hands on the rolls of flesh at his hips—making certain he could feel her breath, hot, against his stomach—she guided him gently backward.

He resisted, moving only a couple inches, his balance seemingly thrown off by the blindfold, and the heady sensations.

Claudette eyed his position, then gave him one short, quick shove.

The entire Nyack Valley erupted.

An animal-like sound filled the forest, echoing between canyon walls as Claudette bolted away, hands over her ears. Once she was a safe distance, she stopped and, in fascination, turned to look.

A naked Bridger Brogan writhed in pain on the ground, doubled into a fetal position.

"You bitch!" he screamed over and over. His movements, the wild rubbing of his head against the ground, had caused the blindfold to loosen. It hung, draped over his nose, only one eye visible. With the look of a mad man, he turned it on her.

"You crazy bitch. What have you done to me?"

Circling around him, Claudette calmly walked to the tree behind where he lay, checked to make sure the padlock that had almost given her away held the thick chain around the trunk in place, as her victim looked on, writhing in disbelief and pain.

Blood had started to ooze from the line of broken skin, where steel jaws had clamped down on his thick ankle. With a forceful, single snap, they had ripped the flesh away—skinned his ankle, exposing tendons and muscle.

Claudette stared in fascination as Bridger Brogan tried to reach for it. But the knot she had used to tie his wrists—the one taught to her by her father to tie the boat on Lake Coeur d'Alene, a knot that (her father explained) only grew tighter if tested—held firm.

Another scream—so anguished and otherworldly that it sent a cow moose and her calf crashing through the dense brush nearby—filled the air.

Bridger Brogan had just stepped into his own leghold trap.

Fourteen

Annie leaned against the door that separated the lodge's lobby from the dining room, holding it open. Despite Annie's protests, Eleanor refused to bring her cane to dinner. Annie waited as she hobbled proudly through, head held high, trying to hide the grimace of pain that walking without the cane always caused her. The judge followed behind, steadily pushing his wheeled walker. It was the first time Annie noticed the sticker he'd added to its seat, which was folded up when not in use, forcing Annie to read the words upside down.

Dog is my co-pilot.

Despite her mood, Annie had to smile at the tribute to the judge's recently born love affair with Archie.

Only a few of the tables in the dining room were unoccupied, but Eleanor had called ahead and requested a window table. A slender beauty named Isabelle, one of the many "lodgies"—as the locals called them—who came from Europe to do seasonal work in Glacier, now guided them to it, thoughtfully tending to the judge, whose eyes gleamed at the attention.

Annie had barely spoken a word since returning from the conference. She could feel Eleanor glancing at her incessantly. When they'd finally settled into the wood-backed chairs and Isabelle had departed—after proudly announcing that the night's specials included trout caught by "real Native Americans" on the reservation's Duck Lake—Eleanor couldn't contain herself any longer.

"What is it, dear?" she said, leaning across the table toward Annie. "What's wrong?"

Annie had been dreading telling them. But the sooner she did, the sooner they could go home.

"Will's not here."

Ever since Annie was a child, when her mother was delivered news she did not want to hear, Eleanor pretended she hadn't heard correctly. Leaning ever closer to Annie, she said, "Say it again?"

Annie met her mother's gaze.

"Will is not here. He's gone."

The glimmer in the judge's eyes evaporated.

Annie turned away from their gazes, to the window. Mount Henry and Never Laughs Mountain were framed by an evening sky still intensely blue at its zenith, but a layer of cotton candy pink had now been brushed across their jagged peaks.

The raw beauty only intensified Annie's angst.

"What do you mean?" Eleanor pressed.

"He's in the backcountry, searching for a missing hiker," Annie replied drily.

She saw immediately that the nonchalant tone didn't work with Eleanor.

"When will he be back?"

Annie shook her head in frustration.

"How would I know that, Mother? How can I possibly know that?"

Tears springing to her eyes, Eleanor quickly looked

down at the wine menu Isabelle had placed precisely between her utensils.

Eleanor did not drink wine.

Annie reached for her hand.

"I'm sorry, Mother," she said. "I'm sorry."

She had not yet noticed the quizzical look on the judge's face.

Eleanor turned her own hand over and grasped Annie's.

"It's okay, dear. I understand." She attempted a smile. "How do we know Will hasn't already found her? He might be on his way back right this very minute." She turned to the judge. "Right?"

The judge clearly wasn't going to participate in Eleanor's attempt to make the situation all better. A frown creasing the good half of his brow, then disappearing like a worn-out creek on the left side, he lifted his right arm, pointed toward the lobby, which was visible through the glass wall separating the two rooms, and made a characteristic grunt—the one that indicated he had something to say.

After Eleanor Malone's kidnapping, Annie learned—in what almost became a very costly lesson—never to dismiss anything her friend had to share.

"There's something in the lobby you want me to see?"

Looking like a judge who had just heard a defendant confess to tossing his lover over the Lower Falls, he nodded.

Annie pushed back from her chair so quickly and with such force that she had to catch it on its way to the floor. She headed back toward the doors she'd just held open. Heads turned as she passed, some in recognition of her as a speaker that day, others at the urgency in her graceful stride.

The Glacier Park Lodge lobby functioned as the heart of the only official park property in the town of East

Glacier. Other motels, restaurants, and bars had plenty of activity during the peak of tourist season, but the lodge had another air entirely. It was akin to a mini–United Nations populated by people obsessed either with nature or the physical challenges presented by insanely craggy trails and peaks that soared skyward until one lost sight of them. Or both. Tourists checked in and out, registering for activities, shopping in the gift shop. Kids and adults sat side by side, texting from a stool at the coffee bar, or leisurely studying the exhibits in the far corner of the room, reading about the role the Northern Pacific Railway played in the establishment of the nation's fourth national park. If it were a cold day, the chairs in front of the massive fireplace would always be occupied. When it was built in 1905, the goal of the architect, Samuel Bartlett, was to provide the feeling of a sanctuary to exhausted visitors. And while the St. Andrew crosses carved into the balcony railings always lent the room something of a spiritual mood, the atmosphere—especially at night—would usually best be described as bedlam. Energized by a day in the park or relieved at having survived a grueling hike, or a night in grizzly country, or an actual sighting of the great Spirit Bear along one of the trails, North Carolinians and Norwegians, Italians and Taiwanese eagerly shared stories, passing cameras and gesturing to make up for languages they did not understand. Liquored-up guests from across the globe flowed between the bar that opened to the lobby and the piano, where a dreadlocked Jamaican now played reggae.

As she worked her way through a sea of moving bodies, Annie barely noticed any of it; not even the Blackfeet elder, dressed in full tribal regalia, who stood in front of the fireplace, transfixing his audience with an explanation of his people's perspective on the establishment of Glacier National Park—the impact of having the sacred land taken from them for next to nothing at a time when the Blackfeet were starving due to disease and the demise of the bison.

Annie had no idea what the judge wanted her to see, but she knew from experience that it would be easier to figure it out on her own than to sit through her friend's struggle to communicate it. Besides, she couldn't bear the looks on both the judge's and her mother's faces. The fact that there was a distinct difference in those looks— one exuded sympathy, while the other, the judge's, revealed a state of alarm—hadn't yet sunk into Annie's consciousness.

Her mother's reaction had touched a nerve. It reminded Annie of when she had announced her marriage was over. For weeks, she felt Eleanor's eyes on her, received hundreds of concerned little pats on the hand.

Annie hated pity.

Why would Eleanor be so distressed? Will had been sent out to look for a woman. It wasn't the equivalent of a marriage ending.

It wasn't even logical to equate Will's being gone now to their relationship.

Or was it?

And the other big question eating at Annie's gut, the one making her welcome the chance to get out from under her companions' scrutiny, was what they should do now—go home, or wait for Will to return? Annie's fears about his reaction to her surprise visit had grown in proportion to her disappointment at having him gone.

When Johnny Yellow Kidney's friend, Stacy, passed by, immersed in instructions she was giving an unhappy-looking employee, she gave Annie a curt smile and wave; and Annie suddenly realized she'd been standing, staring blankly at a poster on one of the atrium's giant log columns. A poster that had been tacked up in place of the American Judiciary Conference announcement.

The top third of the poster consisted of a picture of a woman.

Annie moved forward slowly, a darkness creeping into her mind and working its way down her body.

Before she had read a single word, she knew, was absolutely certain, this was what the judge wanted her to see.

MISSING HIKER

The photograph was of a woman with wavy short hair, wearing hiking boots, shorts, holding a ball cap. Big smile. Walking pole in each hand.

Underneath the caption read:

Haldis Beck. 5 ft 6, chin-length, graying hair. These are the clothes she was wearing the day she left to hike Bad Marriage. She hasn't been seen since. Please report any contact you may have had with her.

Annie read it twice, stared at the picture, trying not to resent the woman in it. This Haldis Beck. Imagine how terrified she must be, she reminded herself, trying to put herself in the position—and work up pity for—the woman with the bad judgment to hike a mountain alone.

Inexplicably unsettled by the poster, Annie turned and saw Eleanor and the judge watching her through the windows separating the lobby and dining room.

Resolute, she marched back in and sat down, looking at the judge.

"Poor woman," was all she could think of to say.

Eleanor reached over and patted her hand. The judge turned and stared out at the wilderness longingly. Same expression Annie had seen when he looked at Bunsen Peak.

No one spoke.

Isabelle had just deposited salads on white ceramic plates in front of each of them when Annie jumped back to her feet.

"Oh my god."

Water sloshed over the tops of the glasses Isabelle had just refilled as the table swayed in Annie's wake.

This time she ran for the door. On the other side, Stacy had moved to the registration desk, where she stood talking to a guest questioning his bill.

Seeing Annie, she called out, "Is everything okay?"

Oblivious to anything but the fir column she'd stood in front of minutes earlier, Annie pushed between a couple standing in front of it, reading the poster.

"Hey," the man said.

Annie reached for the poster, tore it free of its staples, then stood, staring at the photograph on it.

Stacy had arrived at Annie's side, while Eleanor Malone hurried through the door being held open by a tuxedoed maître d'.

"Oh my god," Annie repeated softly.

She could not take her eyes off the smile.

"It's her."

The braces might never have been visible if it weren't for the morning sun catching them at just the right angle and the wide smile on the woman's face.

"Who?" Stacy and Eleanor asked in unison.

Behind the two women, Judge Sherburne made his way toward the group, Isabelle at the lifeless arm as the cane in his right hand swept the wood floor, barely landing with each impatient step.

Annie hurried to meet him. The judge would understand better than anyone else.

"We need to go back to our room and talk."

When Annie grabbed his arm, Isabelle stepped back. Eleanor and Stacy had joined them, however, and Eleanor did not like this new plan.

"But we haven't eaten yet," Eleanor said. "And look—the judge is winded."

Annie's eyes took in the judge, which caused a rush of

remorse. He nodded his head, waved his hand, trying to dismiss their concern, but his chest rose and fell dramatically as he tried to catch his breath.

Stacy had been studying Annie.

"Use my office. I'll have your dinners sent in to you."

"Thank you," Annie said, already half-carrying the judge as they followed behind her. Once inside, both women settled the sturdy septuagenarian into a high-backed leather armchair. Then Annie dropped onto the ottoman in front of the chair, straddling the judge's awkwardly placed feet and cane, knee-to-knee with him.

"The missing hiker?" she said, eyes meeting his intense gaze. "It's the same woman we were trying to find a month ago, when that wolverine got killed in a trap up by Thunderer."

The judge's eyes revealed he immediately recognized the significance of her statement. His hot breath brushed Annie's brow, "Hhhhaaa?"

"How do I know?" Annie replied. "I know because I viewed a video of the guy Wylie Darlington cited for the trap. His name was Gladner. Wylie introduced it in court to show he'd lied about when he'd arrived in Yellowstone. It was caught by a security camera at the Mammoth General Store, the day before he told Wylie he arrived in Yellowstone. In the video, he had a woman with him. It was her." Annie held the poster up to the judge. "It was this Haldis Beck. The woman Will is out there looking for."

Eleanor had pulled a chair up to form a circle with Annie and the judge.

"That's quite a coincidence."

Judge Sherburne shook his head while Annie voiced what they both instinctively knew.

"It's no coincidence, Mother. It can't be." She looked toward the judge, saw his expression. "Can it?"

He shook his head again.

"Will's in trouble, isn't he?" Annie asked.

The judge's eyes held the answer she knew was coming.

They both fell silent as their minds raced through the possibilities.

Something else was bothering Annie. Something more than the fact that she intuitively knew they weren't dealing with a coincidence.

Her thoughts went back to the day after the Gladner arraignment and trial. For some reason, she'd done something she'd almost never done before—she'd gone back and reviewed the record. She knew she was second-guessing her finding Gladner not guilty because of Will. Will would have been upset with the ruling. They would have fought about it. And as much as she knew in her heart that she was right, during the middle of the night she'd thought about what would happen when Will returned. How would she explain it to him?

Usually she had adequate time to reflect on arguments in advance, to read briefs prepared by both parties. But Gladner had requested an immediate trial. He had the right to do so and Annie had no choice but to grant his request. Had that caused her to miss anything? Had she made the right ruling? And then, as she was going through the file the next morning, Wylie Darlington had knocked on her door.

"I've found something else," he told her. "More proof that Tony Gladner lied. That he was in the park at least a day before he said he came to Yellowstone."

He'd placed a sheet of paper on her desk triumphantly.

A camping permit. It was issued for a backcountry campsite near Thunderer. Two names were on it. Tony Gladner's, and the name of a woman.

Annie had closed the file she'd been perusing, crossed her arms over it and looked up at Wylie. Had he seen that she was going through the Gladner case file right that moment?

"I'm upset I didn't find that before," Wylie said,

nodding toward the sheet of paper. "It just occurred to me during the night last night. To see if he'd applied for a camping permit. I couldn't sleep."

"Wylie," Annie said, "even if you had found this, it wouldn't have changed the outcome. You'd already provided evidence that Gladner lied. But that still didn't prove he'd set that trap. Nothing you were able to present proved that. And this doesn't either."

She leaned back, rotated the file so that its label faced up, and pushed the file across the table toward him.

Wylie's eyes widened when he saw Gladner's name.

"I couldn't sleep either," she said. "But it was the right ruling, Wylie. I assure you. I had no choice but to find him not guilty."

"I'm sorry," he said so genuinely and sweetly, that his acknowledgment of the mutual anguish they were feeling almost caused Annie to burst into tears.

He stabbed the piece of paper on her desk with his finger.

"Isn't this enough to bring him back and ask him more questions? About why he lied?"

"Lying isn't a crime, not if you're not under oath when you do it. And Tony Gladner's had his day in court. The constitution prohibits double jeopardy. It provides that no one in this country will ever have to be tried twice for the same crime." Annie smiled. "And that's a good thing, Wylie."

When he didn't respond, she picked the permit up.

"I'd like to keep this in the file."

After he'd left, Annie studied the permit. A woman's name was on it. The most logical presumption was that it was the same woman in the video.

But if that was true, there was a problem. The name on the backcountry permit wasn't Haldis Beck. Annie couldn't remember right now what it was, but she would have remembered a name as distinctive as Haldis Beck. Merely seeing it on that permit the day she'd reviewed the records of the arraignment and trial would have triggered instantaneous recollection the moment she saw it on the "missing" poster.

Instead, the braces on the teeth had done it, had allowed her to connect the two seemingly unrelated events—one in Yellowstone, the other in the opposite corner of the state, Glacier.

There was no question in her mind that this Haldis Beck, the woman on the poster in her hand, was the same woman who had accompanied Tony Gladner into the Mammoth store. It now seemed possible, even likely, that it was the woman in whose name the camping permit had been issued.

If that were true, Haldis Beck went by two names.

Annie leaned toward the judge.

"I think this woman went by another name when she and her partner got a camping permit for the second meadow at Slough Creek, the night before Wylie Darlington found the wolverine."

The judge's expression darkened. Annie could tell he was processing this new information. His body might not be what it once was, but Annie had no doubt the judge's mind had survived the stroke as sharp as it had been before it. Now it was traveling back to the little courtroom he'd presided over in Yellowstone for thirty-plus years, the courtroom where Judge Sherburne had earned the reputation for being able to "sniff out" a defendant's motives, and then find a way to make him pay for any harm he or she had done to his beloved park—sometimes using means less than conventional.

Now he pushed back in his chair, filling his lungs.

Both Annie and Eleanor subconsciously stopped breathing, waiting for what he had to say.

"They want Will ahhhh-," he said on the inhale; finishing on the exhale, "-lone. Baaa . . ."

"Alone in the backcountry?" Annie cried, finishing for him.

The judge fell back, emotionally exhausted.

"You're right," Annie replied. "In both places, Will would be in the backcountry alone. If someone didn't know Will had just left Yellowstone—and it wasn't announced, it wasn't widely known—they would have expected him to be the one to find that trap."

The judge nodded.

"Let's say they *didn't* know," Annie continued to more nods. "They found out, too late—after the arraignment—that Will had been transferred to Glacier." Annie stopped. The last piece of the puzzle had just fallen in place. "The missing hiker. It's another ruse—another way to lure Will into the backcountry, this time here, in Glacier."

Judge Sherburne grunted twice. *Yes. Yes.*

"Oh dear," Eleanor Malone cried. At one time she would have thought such an idea preposterous, but she had experienced firsthand just how evil people could be. "But why?"

All eyes turned back to the judge.

He lifted his shoulders in a shrug.

He did not know why.

Annie jumped up, reached for the phone, dialed 0.

"Is Stacy available?" she asked when a thickly Southern male voice from the front desk answered.

"Right here."

Annie pivoted around, put the phone back in place. Stacy stood behind her.

"Do you know the head of law enforcement here," Annie asked, "in the park?"

"Rob Deardorf," Stacy answered. "He wouldn't be in his office now, but I bet I can get his cell phone number. Be right back."

Annie picked the office phone back up and dialed a familiar number in Mammoth as she waited.

"Justine? I need you to go to the courthouse and look through a file. Gladner. The wolverine case. There was a camping permit in the file. A woman's name was on that permit, along with Gladner's. I need you to call me back with her name. And overnight that entire file to me. Along with the Mammoth store video."

By the time she'd hung up, Stacy was back, holding a cell phone to her ear.

"Rob Deardorf," she said, handing Annie the phone.

"Mr. Deardorf," Annie began. "This is Annie Peacock. I'm the magistrate judge in Yellowstone. I'm also a friend of Will McCarroll's."

The revelation that his caller was the Yellowstone judge clearly threw Deardorf off. He hesitated. "What can I do for you, Judge Peacock?"

"I understand that Will's in the backcountry, looking for a missing hiker named Haldis Beck." She eyed the poster.

"Yes. She took off to climb Bad Marriage alone and hasn't been seen since. She failed to make a rendezvous she'd arranged with campers she'd met the night before she left. I sent Will out this morning."

"Haldis Beck was seen with a man who was arraigned for setting a trap that killed a wolverine in Yellowstone. The wolverine was found by a backcountry ranger, Will's replacement, the same day Will left Yellowstone."

The line went silent, then, warily, Deardorf responded.

"When's the trial?"

"It's over. The defendant requested it immediately following the arraignment."

"He was found guilty?"

Now it was Annie who found herself hesitating.

"No. I acquitted him. But my point is, I recognize the woman on the missing hiker poster. She was caught on a security video in the Mammoth general store, with the suspect in the trapping case."

"You're saying this same woman, Haldis Beck, was recently in Yellowstone . . ."

Annie interrupted him.

"I don't think she was going by the name Haldis Beck. But it's her. I recognize her from the poster."

The line went silent. Annie looked at Judge Sherburne, then her mother. This wasn't going well.

"Someone wants to get Will alone in the backcountry," she said emphatically. "We believe the missing hiker is a ruse to do just that."

Deardorf's voice rose with interest.

"We?"

"Judge Sherburne and I. He's here with me. I'm in Glacier. I was a speaker at the judicial conference held in East Glacier earlier today. The judge accompanied me."

"I've met Judge Sherburne on numerous occasions. . . ." Deardorf replied. "Please give him my regards. My . . ."— he stumbled for the right word—"*understanding* was that his stroke left him unable to speak. . . ."

"We communicate perfectly well. Mr. Deardorf, please. I—we—believe Will's in danger. You need to send someone out to warn him."

"Judge Peacock. I . . . Please forgive me for saying this, but it seems to me you're basing a lot of assumptions on a case that ended up with an innocent verdict, an identification you made based on a rather vague photograph and a video you saw some time ago. Will McCarroll is one of the most experienced, savvy, capable law enforcement rangers I've ever worked with. On top of that, I'm shorthanded at the moment—my people are battling a blaze east of Lake McDonald; this afternoon a woman carrying a gun instead of pepper spray took a shot at a grizzly and wounded it, and I've got law enforcement out trying to track it before there's an even bigger tragedy.

I'd be happy to meet with you tomorrow to discuss this, but frankly, my gut isn't telling me that Will's in any sort of imminent danger. I'm sorry."

"Why would this woman show up in Yellowstone using one name, and then, right after Will is transferred here, show up in Glacier, using another? What does your *gut* say about that?"

Deardorf realized he'd offended her. His next realization was probably that Park Service employees—and maybe even judges—move from park to park all the time, and he might just be pissing off the wrong person.

"I tell you what," he said, his tone taking on a condescending note. "What name did she use in Yellowstone? I'll call someone into the office tonight and have them do a background search. We've been trying to find next of kin for Haldis Beck. I'll have them dig further into her background, too."

Annie's grip on the phone tightened.

"I'm not sure what name she used. I just know that it wasn't Haldis Beck."

"Why don't you come in tomorrow? How about ten o'clock? And maybe you can get that video e-mailed to us so we can view it side by side with the poster photo."

"Fine," Annie replied with a sigh.

Dejected, she placed the phone back in its cradle. She could feel all eyes—including Stacy's—on her.

"Will's in trouble," she said, meeting their gazes head on. "I know it. I *feel* it."

She turned intense brown eyes on Stacy.

"Who do you know who can guide me into the backcountry?"

At first, when she rode up on the horse Bridger Brogan had picked for her for their "picnic," Claudette was afraid the trapper had escaped.

The whole ride in, she had been thinking that she should never have gone into Kalispell that day, but she'd felt she had no choice. The night before, when she'd been packing to return to Missoula, she discovered her passport was missing. She'd turned the little one-room cabin upside down, looked for hours, but it was nowhere to be found. Then she'd called her roommate in Missoula to see if she could have left it behind, only to find that he had moved to Bozeman and sublet the apartment. Claudette was furious with him, but she'd known even before making the call that it would be an exercise in futility. She remembered packing her passport in May. Since she was going to spend the summer in such close proximity to Canada, she had felt certain then that she'd need it. For the past four months, however, she'd been so focused on her thesis that she'd never used it. How could she have lost it?

She'd intended to head right back out to the Nyack that morning to check on Brogan, to move forward with her plan, but she couldn't risk being without a passport. If the trapper somehow managed to escape, she would have to flee immediately. The fact that she'd given him the wrong last name wouldn't buy her much, if any, time. Not in a community as small as Glacier Park.

She'd known from the start that if things didn't go as planned, she had to have a last resort option. Her grandparents had always told her she could move to Australia and they would set her up with a job at their luxurious beachfront hotel. She'd laughed at the idea, and she still had no intention of her plot going so wrong that she would have to resort to leaving the country, but ever since hatching it, she'd decided that fleeing to Australia would be her ace in the hole—if everything fell apart. And so she'd raced into the Kalispell post office first thing in the morning, only to learn that it took weeks to get a replacement passport from them. She could, however, order one online and have it shipped within twenty-four hours. This presented a new problem. She didn't dare have it sent to her post office box in Columbia Falls. If Brogan escaped, they'd be looking for her and she couldn't return to Columbia Falls. And she feared that renting a PO Box in Kalispell could also be risky once her name was known, so after leaving the post office she decided to find a local Mail Boxes, Etc. to rent a box. She was also able to have her photo taken there. Finally, she'd stopped at an Internet café on her way out of town to place the order.

All in all, her trip to Kalispell had taken up most the day, and by the time she'd returned to the spot on Highway 2 where she and Bridger Brogan had parked to enter the Nyack, her anxiety was through the roof.

She'd been annoyed to see another truck and trailer, with government plates, taking up the spot where Brogan had parked yesterday, but she was able to fit Brogan's truck alongside it.

Racing along the trail into the Nyack, which was completely shadowed by this time, she began to think about all that might have gone wrong in her absence. It was unlikely, based on where she was able to manipulate Brogan to move their tryst, but someone could have come along. He could have escaped—had the knots she used to tie his hands held?

Her heart thumped against her bony ribcage when she finally entered the clearing where they'd had their little "picnic."

She did not see him.

He wasn't where she'd left him, lying in the dirt, several feet from the bearskin, which she'd moved almost within reach, just to tantalize him—or maybe draw one of its brothers to him.

How was she going to get out of the country without a passport?

Claudette was about to turn and flee when she noticed movement in the brush, just beyond the tree she'd bound Brogan to. Inching forward, still on horseback, she saw his naked, ugly body, curled in a fetal position.

She pulled the mare to a halt thirty feet away.

He hadn't heard her. She sat, staring, evaluating. Breathing again.

She wished she'd chosen another tree, but she'd had to make decisions quickly the day before. All in all, everything had gone even better than she'd planned. But the Douglas fir she'd used to chain the trap to was young and scrawny, and she'd worried during the night that Brogan might just be strong enough to pull it down. Now that she was looking at it again, she realized she'd been worried for nothing. The tree was sturdier than she'd remembered. It stood firm, despite the fact that most of the vegetation within Brogan's reach—mainly deep green bracken ferns, thriving with the cooler late summer nights—had been trampled upon. The scuffle marks on the dirt around Brogan's motionless body also indicated he had put up a significant struggle to get free.

Claudette nudged the mare forward.

"Rough night, huh?" she called out.

Brogan did not move, but Claudette thought she saw his body tense.

The night before she'd left him about an hour before sunset. That's how long the ride in had been. She'd been worried that she'd left too late—that it might get dark as she tried to find the way back to their vehicles, but she'd been enjoying herself so much that the time got away from her; and the horse, such a good horse, had known the way so well that Claudette never even had to make a decision. All she had to do was hold on, which only proved a challenge once, when the gelding Brogan rode in tried to pass them on the narrow trail. That prompted a race that ended at the river. Claudette had thought briefly about jumping off, but in the end, had clung to the saddle's horn and actually found the experience exhilarating. Of course, she was already exhilarated when she left Brogan moaning and cursing her as he writhed on the ground.

Claudette had never been around horses, but already she felt at ease with them. After crossing the river, she'd been able to load them back in the trailer, and was surprised by how easy it was to drive Brogan's truck—she'd found his keys easily in the pants he'd shed—pulling so much weight. Back at her cabin, she'd turned the horses loose in a small wooden pen for the night, and as it turned out, most of the day. She had had no trouble loading them again when she raced back from Kalispell. They were nice horses, and Bridger Brogan had trained them well.

Now she watched as Brogan's gelding approached him, snorting loudly as it pawed the ground next to him.

Still, Brogan did not move.

Claudette dismounted and slowly approached where he lay.

"Brogan," she snapped.

He was lying on his right side, his face pressed against the dirt. She crept closer, watched as the gelding's hoof scraped his left shoulder.

No response.

Something had gone horribly wrong. He wasn't supposed to die. Not yet.

She leaned over him. In an explosion of motion, he lurched toward her, flinging the leg with the trap at her, catapulting the chain her way.

As she jumped back, the metal connected with the front of Claudette's femur.

"You bastard!" she screamed.

The gelding reared, coming down within inches of Bridger's head, then bolted.

Claudette wasn't the only one injured in the attack. The jerky motion had clamped the teeth of the trap tighter around Brogan's thick ankle, and he groaned in pain.

"See what you get for being so clever?"

Crumpled in half, his eyes closed, Brogan moaned, "What do you want? Why are you doing this?"

The night before, while he writhed and swore and screamed in pain and anguish, Claudette had merely watched, refusing to respond, refusing to answer that question, which he'd shouted out time and time again.

Today would be different.

Today, she was here to talk. To begin the lesson she had planned for Bridger Brogan.

School was in session.

"What I want," she answered matter-of-factly, "is to make you suffer like you made Tennyson suffer."

Brogan opened his eyes, turning them on her.

"Who the hell is Tennyson?"

Slowly, eyes glued to his fat, naked body, Claudette reached into the back pocket of her jeans and carefully pulled out the picture she'd chosen. Mentally measuring the length of unused chain to gauge her zone of safety, she stepped closer, hand outstretched, photo facing him.

She'd taken it the day before Tenny disappeared.

In it, he sat looking at her, waiting for the treat she'd held up as a reward for allowing her to photograph him with the new red bandana she'd just knotted around his neck.

"What the fuck is that?" Brogan replied.

"You don't even know, do you?" Claudette practically screamed. "You killed him, and you never even saw him."

A wave of understanding suddenly washed over Brogan, as surely—and as dreaded—as if it were a flash flood bearing down upon him during a summer squall in the mountains.

"You're crazy," he said, staring at her. "You did this to me because your dog got caught in my trap? You planned all this, came to my office, lured me up here, because I killed your fucking dog?"

His voice rose with each word. Once they stopped coming, his lips and chin quivered in disbelief, and a newly found rage. And fear.

"You crazy bitch. You're one of those animal rights nuts, aren't you?"

Claudette knew she had to keep her emotions in check in order to be effective.

"Hard to comprehend, isn't it?" she replied, her voice regaining its controlled tone. "I mean, here you are, out for a nice fuck in the great outdoors, no strings attached, and suddenly your life is in danger. Suddenly, your world explodes. You weren't even doing anything wrong, were you? Why would this happen to you?"

Brogan stared at her, eyes narrowed, waiting, a new sense of dread rising visibly in his bloated, anguished body. He seemed to know better than to respond.

"I imagine my Tennyson felt a lot like that, the day he went out to explore the woods he loved, and ended up being pulled underwater by steel jaws. I bet Tenny had trouble understanding what was happening."

Her face twisted with sorrow, but she would not allow the tears. She had made sure she'd shed them, all of them, before this day. She would not allow Bridger Brogan to see tears. That had been rule number one.

"And I wasn't even there to get him through it. To help him. He didn't have anyone to turn to. Imagine the terror."

She'd crossed her arms, eyes locked with Brogan's, who seemed to know he shouldn't look away. Or say anything.

"Imagine the terror a coyote, or a raccoon, or a pine marten feels when it's just out there, doing what it has to do to stay alive, and SNAP," she unfolded her arms, clapped her hands together so forcefully the sound echoed in her ears, "pain starts shooting through its body. It struggles, terrified, but the iron teeth just dig deeper. Imagine, Dr. Brogan, what that must be like."

Suddenly she giggled, eyes wide and filled with childish delight.

"Well, you really don't *have* to imagine now, do you?" she said with a look of absolute delight on her tanned and freckled face. The face Bridger Brogan had told her was that of a Scandinavian beauty. "I mean, look at you . . ." she said, dissolving into a fit of laughter.

He eyed her like a deer cornered by a barbed wire fence watching a camouflage-clad hunter approach, smirking, with a rifle's crosshairs trained on it.

Back on track, Claudette turned her attention to the backpack she'd left on the bearskin. She walked to it, bent double, and pulled out a bag of trail mix and a nectarine.

Walking to a rock that stood knee high, about ten feet from where Brogan lay, she dropped down on to it, feet planted squarely on the ground, casually tossing peanuts and raisins into her mouth.

"I bet you're getting hungry. We never did get to the food I brought yesterday." She eyed the scuffle marks on the dirt between Brogan and the basket, then the dirt caked on Brogan's feet. "It almost looks like you were trying to reach it last night."

Lifting the nectarine to her mouth, she bit into it, let its juice collect on her lips before swallowing.

"How long do you think it took Tenny to die?" she asked, her tone almost conversational.

"Fuck you."

Brogan rolled onto his side, turning away.

"Of course," she said, undaunted, "Tennyson drowned. You know, I tried to figure out a way to get you in a river, but finally realized this was the next best thing. This is what it's like for badgers, wolves, wolverines—isn't it? I mean, they struggle to get free while they wait for you to come along and club them to death. Or until they die from the heat and starvation. Dehydration.

"You know, when I was in Missoula, I read this letter to the editor from a trapper, and he said that trapped animals don't suffer. That just made me so happy. He said they just go into a state of shock and die peacefully. Is that true?"

When he didn't respond, Claudette picked up a rock the size of the half-eaten nectarine and threw it at him. It thunked off his back.

"Answer me," she ordered.

Without turning to look at her, Brogan said, "They instinctively know to just lay there quietly."

"How the fuck do they know that?" Claudette found her voice rising again. "Maybe because every move they make causes excruciating pain?"

She jumped to her feet, scanning the clearing. When she'd spotted what she was looking for, at the bottom of a stand of trees, she walked toward it, examined it briefly, then picked it up.

A six-foot branch, sturdy, a sharp point where it had broken off the pine's upper branches during a windstorm.

Without warning, like a knight on horseback charging into battle, she ran forward, jabbing the pointed end into the middle of Brogan's back.

His tortured scream filled the air.

"Move," she said. "Get up, you dirty pig. Face me. We're going to talk."

Brogan struggled to his knees, rolling onto one elbow to help stabilize himself before putting one bare foot on the ground, then slowly, agonizingly, the foot dragging the trap.

Once he stood before her, Claudette found herself so repulsed by the sight of his sagging breasts and shrunken penis, all but the tip of which was hidden by the weight of his girth, that she turned away.

Until she heard his voice, choked with fear.

"What do you want from me? What do I have to do to get out of this?"

His terror was such that he seemed indifferent to standing there exposed, which disappointed Claudette.

"Who says you'll get out?"

She said it calmly, as a matter of fact.

"You're going to leave me here to die?"

"Isn't that what you do every day?"

"They're *animals*, for Chrissake."

No longer concerned with his pathetic anatomy, Claudette stepped toward him.

"Animals?" Claudette practically spat back at him. "And that makes it okay?"

Sensing the effect his weakness was having on her, or perhaps trying to retain some dignity, Brogan snapped his head up, stretched his body to its full height, and proclaimed: "Trapping's a tradition. Our heritage."

Claudette had been waiting for this. The dialogue.

"Lynching black men was a tradition in the south. All you twisted sycophants who justify it by talking about tradition—those trappers, the ones you like to picture yourself as, they at least trapped to survive. They ate what they killed. They lived on what they traded for the pelts. It wasn't some game, some twisted recreation for sickos who get off on torturing living beings."

"It's no different than hunting."

"With hunting, there's a chase. And a quick kill."

She could see Brogan beginning to think he might be able to talk himself out of the situation. His body may have been battered, but his mind had cleared.

Perhaps, she could almost see him thinking, this was a game of wits.

"Some trapped animals get free," he replied boldly. "Did you ever think of that?"

Bingo.

Claudette tilted her head. Were it not for the scene in front of her, she might look like a coquettish teen on a first date.

"Yeah, I did. I've actually been thinking about it quite a lot."

Her tone, and demeanor, startled Brogan.

"What do you mean?" he asked.

"Just how do the 'lucky' ones get free?"

Brogan fell silent

Claudette raised the makeshift lance in the air and Brogan knew immediately he'd lost.

"*Answer me.*"

Brogan looked down, at the ground, refusing eye contact as he obeyed.

"They chew off the trapped foot."

Claudette sat there atop the rock, staring at him. He stood motionless, eyes cast downward.

When she saw him begin to tremble, Claudette rose, walked over to the fur. Began rolling it up.

She heard his voice from behind her.

"What are you doing?"

She picked up the backpack, eyed the ground around its imprint, scuffed up prints her boots had left the day before.

She'd worried about this all night, cursing herself for being so stupid.

Brogan was watching her every move.

He seemed relieved when she finally turned to look at him.

"How often do you check your traps?"

He didn't miss a beat.

"Every day."

"Bullshit," Claudette cried.

Brogan began visibly shrinking as she took a step in his direction.

"You have traps all over this valley, all over Glacier. You couldn't check them every day if you wanted. How often?"

He shrugged, shook his head, confusion sweeping his mind again with the fear.

"I don't know."

Claudette dropped her armload and reached for the makeshift spear.

"You *do* know."

"Okay, okay," cried Brogan. "Maybe every couple days."

Claudette stopped. She stared at him for what must have seemed an eternity to Brogan.

Then, gathering up the bearskin and backpack again, she moved toward the horse, saying over her shoulder, "That's another lie, but I'll accept that answer. For now."

When she reached the mare, she tied the roll of fur and backpack behind the saddle. Then, sliding a boot into the stirrup, she used the saddle's horn to hoist herself up.

She could feel Bridger's eyes on her. He'd expected more confrontation. She could almost feel his confusion now.

Turning the mare's head in the direction she'd come from, she said, "See you in *a couple days.*"

She knew he would not miss the meaning in those last words.

"Wait," Bridger Brogan shouted. "I can't hold out two more days. I haven't eaten since yesterday morning. I don't even have water."

Claudette pulled the mare to a stop, threw her right leg back over the saddle's horn and dropped back down to the ground. Donning a sympathetic look, she replied, "Oh my god. You could die. Couldn't you?"

Brogan seemed to know this was his last chance.

"Tell me what I can do to make up for your dog. I'll buy you another one. Same breed."

The offer intrigued Claudette.

"What breed is that?" she asked.

"Lab?" Brogan answered. Then, weakly, "Australian shepherd?"

Slowly, deliberately, Claudette removed the picture from her pocket again, walked toward Brogan with arm outstretched, stopping just short of the chain's length.

"He was a German shepherd, you twisted fuck," she found herself shouting. "A German shepherd. And he was my best friend. You think you can *buy* that?"

She stood there, chest heaving with each breath, sweat beading above her upper lip.

"Please," Brogan said. "Don't leave me here to die. I'll make a deal with you. Any deal. You name it."

Claudette looked at him with absolutely no expression on her face. She might have been a card shark holding a pair of jacks, but about to take it all.

She hadn't expected to get to this point so quickly.

Decision made, she pivoted on the ball of one hiking boot, walked slowly back to the gelding. With measured determination, she reached into the bag tied behind the saddle.

When Brogan saw it, he groaned.

Her hand clasped a saw. Brand new, its price sticker sparkling clean.

Claudette's half-smile blossomed to a full grin.

"You want to make a deal?" she said, lifting it into the air like a fairy godmother's wand. "Okay. Here's your way out. Your key to that trap."

She hadn't moved any closer, but Brogan stepped back anyway.

"You're out of your mind. Insane."

"Insane? *I'm* the one who's insane? Isn't this what you've forced dozens, no hundreds, maybe even thousands of animals to do? Chew off their foot in order to save their lives?" Claudette's knuckles turned white on the saw's handle. "I'm just offering you the same option you give them."

Brogan fell silent, eyes on the saw.

Claudette recognized it—literally saw it—the very moment the thought entered his mind.

"I'll do it," he said resolutely.

She was actually quite impressed with his quick thinking.

"You'll do it? You'll sacrifice your foot to live?"

Brogan's chest heaved with his dramatic sigh.

"Yes. I'll do it. Maybe you're right."

"Thank the lord," Claudette cried, playing along.

She started toward him, saw in hand.

"Lay down."

Brogan's eyes went wild. He stumbled backward, tripping over the chain and falling onto his lower back.

"What do you mean?" he yelled from the ground as she advanced toward him. "Are you crazy? I'm not going to let you cut it off. I meant *I'd* do it."

Claudette kept coming.

"Do I look like an idiot to you?" she cried, rage punctuating each word. "You actually think I'm going to untie your hands?"

The saw flashed out, glancing his skin above the trap's teeth, slicing it as cleanly as a butcher's knife to a side of lamb.

"Stop," Brogan screamed, momentarily frozen with disbelief.

Blood trickled over and around the mottled swellings and just-formed scabs disfiguring his thick ankle.

"Lay still," Claudette ordered again, swiping at him.

Legs flying, Brogan scooted backward frantically on his rear end. When he'd pulled the chain tight and Claudette still continued toward him, he kicked at her, wincing as each thrust of his legs drove the metal teeth deeper into tendons and tissue.

"You crazy bitch. You crazy, crazy bitch," he yelled. "Get the fuck away from me."

Laughing, Claudette jumped back to dodge a kick.

Movement in the trees above—a soft wind, characteristic of recent evenings—suddenly drew her attention skyward. The top of an almost-full moon rose ghostlike behind Mount Henry.

Claudette hadn't realized how dark it had grown.

Without another word, she pivoted in the direction of the horse, took a dozen measured steps—a distance that at least doubled the length of the chain holding Bridger and the trap to the tree—and placed the saw on the ground.

Nodding toward it, she said, "Next time I return, you'll beg me to use it."

Then she climbed back on the horse, patted it sweetly on the side of its long neck, and galloped out of Bridger Brogan's sight.

Based on Johnny Yellow Kidney telling Will that experienced hikers had difficulty finding their way down from Bad Marriage—which meant that a novice would find it nearly impossible to find her way up—Will had decided to do the Bad Marriage Grand Circuit, starting with Mad Wolf, then Eagle Plume, and ending with Haldis Beck's stated destination. Any guidebooks the missing woman had read before making that decision would have recommended taking the circuit. If she'd truly headed out to Bad Marriage, and had not changed course along the way, Will had decided that was his best shot at finding some trace of her—or of hikers who had seen her somewhere along that route.

If she'd made the mistake of trying to find her way up Bad Marriage, bypassing the circuit, then once he reached Bad Marriage, Will would begin working the descent in a grid to look for her.

It was a plan that didn't feel close to good to Will, but after hours and hours, and over a hundred miles of working through it in his mind, he'd decided it was the best he could come up with. And if it reached that point, and she still hadn't shown up anywhere else, he would get word to Rob Deardorf to deploy a full scale SAR.

After fording Cut Bank Creek, which was at its fall low, he'd bushwhacked toward Mad Wolf. He was pleased when he came upon a game trail. A close examination of the tracks along it told him it had been mainly forged by the feral horses, several of whom he'd spotted just before crossing the creek.

When the trail finally broke out of the trees, near the summit of Mad Wolf, Will paused, heart swelling at the sight. While he appreciated their grandiosity, Will had been surrounded by peaks ever since coming to Glacier. He missed Yellowstone's plains and valleys—the Lamar and Hayden, with their rivers lazily zigzagging across wide open space, rolling hills and rounded mountains framing the sight, with the more jagged peaks—more like those that could be found in every direction in Glacier—in the distance.

The view from the gently graded ridge that connected Mad Wolf to Eagle Plume reminded Will of what he was used to—of home. Prairie meeting mountains. Rivers that could be seen meandering in and out of sight. In the distance, a herd of wild horses—as majestic in their own way as the bison that spotted the landscape in the Lamar.

But still no sign of Haldis Beck. The route he initially forged didn't help, as it had few two-legged travelers. But once he got on the ridge, he began seeing hiking parties with regularity. Those returning from a wilderness journey had not seen anyone fitting Haldis Beck's description.

Those who were just starting out had seen the poster with her photo and promised to keep an eye out for her.

How had one woman disappeared so quickly and completely?

The only answer—at first—that came to Will was the one he most dreaded. She had become a victim of an accident, perhaps falling to her death, or an injury so severe she couldn't make her way back to a trail, perhaps having had a run-in with one of Glacier's magnificent grizzlies. That, in Will's eyes, would be a twofold tragedy—for the woman, and eventually, once found and confirmed by DNA analysis to be the attacker, the grizzly. Either situation would explain why no one had seen her.

As he rode that afternoon and into the evening, Will had mulled his conversation with the grizzled old-timer over and over.

Now, as night began to fall, he looked down from his perch on Eagle Plume. He needed to choose his campsite carefully.

Someplace visible.

His tent in place, he began building a fire, one that he would stoke several times during the night.

Will McCarroll *wanted* to be seen.

Fifteen

"Many a night I saw the Pleiads,
rising thro' the mellow shade,
glitter like a swarm of fireflies
tangled in a silver braid."

Johnny Yellow Kidney's melodic baritone drifted through stands of black cottonwood trees—their soft needles just beginning to yellow—and Douglas fir, blending with the gurgle of Nyack Creek. While a nearby cow moose and calf merely lifted their heads, quickly returning to grazing the succulent riparian growth along the water, the melody Johnny had long ago composed to Alfred Lord Tennyson's words would have baffled any weary two-leggeds camping nearby.

Nights like this, when he couldn't sleep, Johnny liked to lie looking at the night sky that played such an important part of the Blackfeet culture Johnny had grown up in. Like other tribes, the Blackfeet had their own stories about the constellations, the "sky beings" who guided them on their journeys. Now, Johnny lay on top of his sleeping bag, eyes glued above, looking at the Pleiades and thinking back to the stories his grandmother had taught him as a little boy.

"The stars, they're people who have died," Thelma Yellow Kidney often told Johnny and his cousins in her singsong voice as they camped in her backyard in Browning. "They're there to teach us respect for all life."

In addition to a respected elder and tribal storyteller, Thelma was a traditional singer and dancer. While Johnny's cousins teased him about how much time Johnny spent with her, he didn't care. He loved watching her dance, was proud of her, and loved listening to Thelma. He could close his eyes and still hear that voice, its cadence. Or at times like this, look at the stars and hear it.

His favorite story had been passed to his grandmother by her friend, Clifford Crane. It was about the Six Lost Boys.

Johnny fixed his gaze on Taurus, the constellation just above and to the right of Orion the Hunter, and traveled back to one of those nights with his cousins.

The rhythm and softness of her voice often lulled his cousins to sleep before a story ended. But not Johnny.

A long time ago a young boy watched as his father went out to hunt buffalos. He said to his dad, "Will you bring me back the unborn buffalo?" But late that night when his father came back, he told his son he forgot to bring him an unborn buffalo calf.

The boy was hurt and sad. He said to himself, "My father doesn't love me. He neglects me."

The young boy didn't want to live in a place where he was not loved, so he left his tipi and he walked out to the prairie. He sees five boys out there and he asks them what they are doing there by themselves. The five boys all reply: "We asked our fathers to bring us back the unborn buffalo calves but our fathers didn't. We don't want to live at a place where we are not wanted. We are unloved. We are neglected."

The six lost boys go out to the prairie and start wondering "what shall we be?"

One boy says, we should be six giant trees.

But the others didn't want to be trees. "Somebody's gonna come along and chop us down."

Another boy says, we should be six swans.

But somebody's going to shoot us and kill us.

One of the boys looked up at the sky and says, "We should go up to the heavens where we can be there and look down on our people."

They all thought this was a good idea.

So the six boys went up to the heavens, where they could see the unborn calves of the bison their fathers had hunted.

Then Johnny's grandmother used to finish by telling them that when they get older and have a family of their own, and when they get mad at their children, they must go out and look up at the heavens and see those stars.

"Those are children who were neglected," she told Johnny and his cousins, *"and not loved by their parents."* She always ended by saying, "Let this be a reminder never to neglect your children."

Perhaps that story was why, when Johnny was studying literature at the University of Washington, before he decided to become a biologist, Alfred Lord Tennyson's sonnet had struck him, stayed with him. It wasn't a poem he would have sung in front of his Blackfeet cousins, but still, it reminded Johnny of their grandmother, and those nights.

Now that he was back home and he didn't need to be reminded of his grandmother or his culture, now that he did not ache for it in its absence, Tennyson's words reminded Johnny of the time when he walked in both worlds.

These thoughts were suddenly broken by the static of the two-way radio he always stuck inside his sleeping bag when he came to the backcountry on horseback. It was against the rules, but Johnny never tied his horse at night, and once he'd had a big old black gelding step on his radio and break it. He'd concocted one hell of a story, after which his supervisor, a good old white man no longer in this world, turned to grab another radio for Johnny, saying, "You have to start tying that horse."

Johnny rolled off the bag now, onto the dry dirt, and stuck his hand inside the bag, fumbling for the radio. He swore it sounded like Stacy's voice, but it was muffled by the down of the bag until he found it.

"Johnny?"

"Hey there. What's up?"

He didn't try to hide the surprise, or the unexpected pleasure, in his voice.

She had only called him on the two-way once before, when she'd been lost on the way down from Sinopah. But when he left earlier that day, she'd told him she had to work practically nonstop this week. One of her assistants had quit suddenly on her, and with the season winding down, it didn't make sense to hire anyone else. So she couldn't have lost her way again.

"Johnny," Stacy repeated. Her tone told him something was wrong. "I have someone here who wants to talk to you. Your friend, Annie Peacock."

Johnny bolted into a sitting position as a new voice, one he'd never forgotten, blended with a light breeze swaying the tops of the trees.

"Johnny, I need your help."

"What is it, Annie?"

"A friend of mine, Will McCarroll, is in trouble and I need to warn him."

"Will?" Johnny replied, almost dumbly. Annie and Will McCarroll? "What kind of trouble is he in?"

"It's complicated. Just trust me for now and I'll explain as soon as I see you. I have to get word to Will. I tried calling Rob Deardorf and he blew me off. I asked Stacy to find someone to take me to find Will but she couldn't find anyone. Then she thought of you. Would you do it, Johnny? Would you take me to find Will?"

Johnny was having trouble absorbing all of this, but he still sensed Annie to be the wise, no-nonsense woman he'd once dated, and he knew to take her seriously.

"Last time I talked to Will, he was headed to Bad Marriage to search for the missing hiker. Does this have something to do with that?"

"Yes. We think the lost hiker's a setup for Will to be ambushed."

Johnny's mind raced back to the last conversation he'd had with Will. Johnny had thought it odd that the missing hiker had approached her climb of Bad Marriage from Two Medicine, and not Cut Bank. It was a small thing, but it had troubled Johnny—enough so that he could tell he'd irritated Will in focusing on it. Johnny had never known anyone to approach Mad Wolf and Bad Marriage from that direction—at least not if they weren't already hiking and camping down toward Flinsch Peak, or farther south. But Will had told him she was just starting out on her backcountry trip. It hadn't passed Johnny's smell test.

"Damn," he said softly.

"Where are you?" Annie asked. "Can we leave tonight?"

"I'm already in the Nyack. I came up here this afternoon because someone reported traps up here. There's nothing I can do tonight, not in the dark, but in the morning I'll head up toward Bad Marriage. That probably makes more sense than coming out and trailering the horse up to Two Medicine or Cut Bank."

"Please, let me go with you."

So it was serious between them.

"It would take you hours to get to me. You'd have to drive down to where I left the horse trailer, and you'd never be able to find me alone."

"Johnny, please. I can't sit here knowing Will's in trouble."

Johnny fell silent.

Would bringing Annie along make sense or should he head out alone first thing in the morning? Johnny had grown to respect Rob Deardorf, so he didn't totally discount Rob's decision to wait before sending someone out after Will.

But Rob didn't know Annie like Johnny did. Or at least like he once had. And based on that, and the fact that she and Will apparently had a history together, Johnny's gut was telling him to take Annie's concerns seriously. Because of their history, Annie might be able to give him information that could be helpful in finding Will, if the missing hiker were indeed some kind of plot to trap him.

"Okay," he finally said, "put Stacy back on."

Even as he said it, he was questioning himself.

Was he doing the right thing? Was he even thinking clearly? After all, he had never thought clearly when it came to Annie.

Wasn't that why he'd headed up to the Nyack so suddenly—why he'd left Annie's presentation before it was over?

He heard Annie utter a charged "he'll do it" as she passed the radio to Stacy.

"It's me," Stacy said.

"Can you bring Annie to where we entered the Nyack the day I brought you with me to the fire cache and the old ranger station? You'll see my trailer. I'll meet you there at dawn."

"That means you'll have to ride down there awfully early in the morning."

"I'll head out now. Couldn't sleep anyway."

"Talking to the sky, were you?"

Johnny laughed.

"Maybe a little." He paused, then added, "I'll be waiting."

"We'll be there," Stacy replied.

* * *

That damn Brogan.

What the fuck had happened to him? He was supposed to meet her at Triple Divide Pass days ago.

She should have known not to count on him.

Still, she shouldn't be so hard on herself. Her initial instincts—sleeping with him at the national ARF conference—had served her well; at least when it came to setting the wolverine trap in Yellowstone. Brogan had provided the scent lure, and despite the outcome, she had to admit it had worked. But this, getting him involved here, in Glacier, had turned disastrous.

Now here was Will McCarroll, no more than a quarter mile away, and no Brogan.

McCarroll's presence meant *her* end of things had gone just as planned. The idiotic couple from the campground had signaled she was in trouble, and with the fires raging in the west side of the park—that had been brilliant, too—Will, and Will alone, had been sent to find her. Once she learned that Will had been stationed in the east side of the park, she'd felt confident that the powers-that-be in Glacier would consider Will capable of handling the job alone.

It really couldn't have gone more smoothly.

And then Brogan didn't show up.

She'd sat at that very spot, first waiting for the crude, brutish trapper, and then, Will. While her partner in this endeavor had failed her, Will McCarroll had not. She watched as he stoked his campfire for what must have been the fourth or fifth time, no doubt for her sake.

This was it. This was her last chance, Brogan or no Brogan.

The decision made, a sense of anticipation and calm began to encompass Haldis.

She settled in for the night.

Sixteen

"You warm enough?" Stacy asked, reaching for the controls to the heater on her Lexus SUV.

As agreed the night before, she and Annie had met in the lobby of the lodge at 5:30 A.M. With two bellmen bolting for the opportunity to hold the door for the boss, they'd stepped outside into total darkness and temperatures near freezing.

Stacy's car was already idling at the curb. Annie let each of the young bellmen grab a backpack. She'd packed two, not knowing what she'd need. The small one held her basic essentials, the larger one contained what little food—mostly trail mix, jerky, coffee and teas—she was able to buy at the tiny store in the lodge the previous night after she and Stacy connected with Johnny. She'd had to knock on the windows of the shop, which was closed, and plead with the young girl working there to let her in. Throwing Stacy's name out had helped.

Now, as steam rose from two Styrofoam cups sitting in the cup holders in Stacy's SUV, Annie buckled herself in.

"I'm fine," she said, reaching for a cup. "And thanks for this."

"I have to confess," Stacy replied, a smile briefly warming her perfect profile, "I'm not the one to thank. I called down and had the car, and the coffee, waiting for us. One of the perks of my job."

"Still, it was nice."

They had just crossed under the railroad tracks and turned right onto Highway 2, when deep within the smaller backpack, Annie's phone let out two beeps. Annie reached over the seat for the pack while Stacy pulled off the highway, explaining, "We're about fifty yards from not having service again the whole drive."

When Annie had retrieved her phone she looked first at the sender's name. Justine. Leave it to her clerk to go to the courthouse in the middle of the night to peruse old files.

Annie's eyes turned to the message:

The woman's name on the backcountry permit was Sally Gordon.

"Everything okay?" Stacy said, looking over at her.

"I was right." Annie didn't try to hide her alarm. "This woman is using two names."

Stacy studied her briefly, then reached over and, in the dark, patted Annie's arm.

"Don't worry. Johnny will get you to Will."

For some reason, the gesture almost brought Annie to tears.

"I don't know how to thank you for all you're doing."

"No need to," Stacy said, pulling back on to the highway. "That's what we do for each other up here."

They drove the next forty-seven miles mostly in silence. Perhaps it was the early morning hour. Or the mission. Or the fact that each was still trying to figure out the nature of the other's relationship with Johnny Yellow Kidney. It wasn't an uncomfortable silence. Each woman respected and liked the other.

In truth, Annie and Stacy had a lot more in common than a past or present relationship with the enigmatic wolverine biologist. They were both successful and driven, women who'd been willing to take untraveled paths that had led to the remote reaches of the states of Montana and Wyoming.

Both had become stronger, more tolerant and more compassionate as a result.

If given the chance, neither would change the decisions that led them to where they were at this point in their lives.

Still, right now Annie couldn't help but wonder how *her* life had taken so many turns since deciding to leave her husband and take the magistrate judge job in Yellowstone.

She'd wanted to flee the city, put out of mind the violent crimes she prosecuted day after day. She wanted to go somewhere peaceful, somewhere she could take comfort in nature, play a role in protecting wild places.

Sixteen months earlier, her mother had been kidnapped, brutally disfigured.

And now the man she'd fallen in love with was in some kind of danger.

So much for the simpler, saner life.

Annie suspected, actually sensed, that Stacy would have similar stories to tell. But both women had one more thing in common: awareness of the hazards of driving highways in places like Yellowstone and Glacier in the dark, so instead of small talk they both stayed alert, Stacy's eyes fixed on the road while Annie scanned the periphery for the wildlife that could at any second step into the Lexus's headlights.

As they started the climb to Marias Pass, the sky

suddenly opened up and the jagged peaks of the park began taking form. It was hard to believe that less than twenty-four hours earlier, on the drive to East Glacier, Annie and her passengers had looked out at those peaks, stretching all the way into Canada, with wonder and excitement.

Now she looked out at them and wondered about Will.

She'd dealt with the criminal mind long enough in her work in Seattle to know better than to underestimate it. False identities, well-planned plots to lure a victim—she'd dealt with both before. She'd prosecuted two cases with similarities in Seattle. Both had ended up with victims murdered.

The difference, she'd been telling herself all day, ever since learning that Haldis Beck was the same person in the video presented by Wylie Darlington at Tony Gladner's trial—which was taken across the state, at the Mammoth General Store—was the identity of the intended victim. Annie's work as a federal prosecutor had also given her the opportunity to get to know plenty of great criminal investigators and outstanding cops, and she recognized immediately (and grudgingly), upon assuming the bench in Yellowstone, that in terms of wit, courage, and skills, Will McCarroll ranked at the top of that list.

For that reason, she had to admit that last night, after arranging the rendezvous with Johnny, she found herself questioning whether the urgency she felt about notifying Will he was in danger might in part be something else.

After all, how could the woman in the photo present a real threat to someone like Will?

She'd finally turned to the one person who could help her sort out her thoughts, the one person whose instincts were immaculate: Judge Sherburne.

Before turning in the night before, she'd knocked on the door to his bedroom. She'd turned the knob even before she heard the grunt.

It almost seemed as if he'd been waiting for her. He sat in his pajamas on his bed, feet on the floor, no surprise whatsoever registering on that kindly face so misshapen by the stroke.

"Am I doing the right thing?" she asked, approaching him, barefoot, in the robe she'd pulled down from the back of the bathroom door. "Or am I using this as an excuse to make sure I see Will?"

She continued, almost as if she were talking to herself.

"After all, how can a lone woman present a threat to someone like Will? What could this even be about that would motivate someone to hurt Will?"

Standing there, she realized that what she was doing was talking herself out of meeting Johnny Yellow Kidney. Not because every fiber in her being did not want to go out and find Will, but because she feared the consequences if she'd been acting irrationally could permanently change her and Will's future.

And then she looked at the judge, saw that he was trying to say something—she hadn't really given him a chance.

"Comm . . ."

"Come home?" Annie finished for him. "You think we should just go home."

His face twisted in impatience, he shook his head. No.

"Hear . . . g," the 'g' was the guttural sound she'd heard him practice again and again.

For the first time she could remember, the judge wasn't making sense.

"I'm sorry," she said. "I shouldn't have bothered you."

She turned to leave, but his good arm shot out and grabbed her, stopping her.

Startled, Annie watched as he pointed to his ear.

"Hear . . . g . . . g . . . g."

"Hearing!" Annie cried. "Are you having trouble hearing?"

Stomping his good foot once, the judge shook his head again, "No!" and then made another pathetic attempt: "wwwww," but Annie stopped him.

"The hearing! The Congressional hearing!"

Falling back, the judge nodded.

"Oh my god," she cried. She fell silent, staring at the judge. "This is serious, isn't it? They want to keep Will from testifying against the guns-in-park policy."

The same weary nod.

Annie dropped onto the bed beside him.

"Who? Who would do this?"

The judge's shoulders lifted in a shrug.

"This woman, this Haldis Beck, isn't working alone."

"No."

It came out just like that, plain and clear. No.

Any doubts or second-guessing had ended at that moment.

Now Annie's stomach felt like a giant hand held a grip on it. She placed the coffee back in the holder on the dashboard, eyes scanning for wildlife as she asked Stacy, "Are we close?"

Stacy didn't respond. She was too intent on finding their rendezvous spot with Johnny.

At Nyack Flats—the long, straight section of highway that paralleled the Nyack Valley—she finally slowed.

"If I blink we'll miss it," she said.

Seconds later, Annie was thrown forward as Stacy suddenly pressed her foot to the brakes.

"Damn."

She looked at the highway ahead. No oncoming traffic. The rearview mirror reflected nothing but blackness.

Shoving the gearstick into reverse, she expertly backed twenty-five yards.

The narrow gravel road wasn't marked. Annie had missed it, too.

As they pulled up to the small parking area, the SUV's headlights swept over Johnny and his horse, who had just shot up the bank from the river. Water still dripped from the horse's massive chest. A pack horse followed close behind.

An older model gray Honda Accord and the truck and trailer Johnny had driven were the only vehicles parked in the small lot.

Annie felt a rush of anxiety.

"You okay?" Stacy said as she turned the key to stop the engine.

Annie nodded, looking straight ahead.

"Yes."

Johnny had dismounted. He approached the Lexus, opened Annie's door. Stacy had already reached his side. Annie watched as she stood on her toes and kissed Johnny on the cheek. He wrapped his free arm around her and pulled her briefly close to him. Then he became all business.

"You'll ride Tucker here," he said to Annie. "I'll take Rusty.

"Stacy, can you adjust the stirrups while I get another saddle?"

Without waiting for an answer, he strode to the front side door on the trailer, produced a ring of keys from his green fleece NPS jacket's pocket, unlocked it and disappeared inside. Annie could hear him tossing things out of his way.

Stacy had left the headlights of the Lexus on. Now she led Tucker into the periphery of their path, the gelding reflexively turning away from the glare.

Annie felt awkward, useless, as she watched Stacy loosen the stirrups from the top of the saddle, where Johnny had tied them, then shorten each side by several notches.

"Want to try this?" she said, turning to Annie.

Trying to remember the instructions Will had given her the time they went into the Lamar on horseback, Annie put her left hiking boot in the stirrup Stacy had just shortened and threw her right leg over the horse's back. This animal was a lot wider than the one Will had given her.

"Try standing," Stacy said.

Annie placed her right foot in the other stirrup and rose.

"Feels just right."

Stacy handed Annie the reins, scooted under the horse's neck, and adjusted the other side.

"I'll get my packs," Annie said, preparing to dismount.

"Nope," Stacy replied. "You stay there. I'll get them."

Annie watched as Stacy and Johnny got the horses ready, Johnny saddling Rusty, a sturdy Appaloosa gelding, and Stacy packing Annie's two packs along with the packs Rusty had been carrying. They were a team, an efficient, experienced team; Annie could see that.

Johnny hadn't changed much. If anything, he looked even leaner and more fit than when Annie had known him. He still wore his thick long hair in a ponytail, and lacking much in the way of an ass, his blue jeans were still held up by a tight belt.

He'd been moving around so silently that Annie began to wonder if he was annoyed at, perhaps even rethinking, her request to bring her along. But once he and Stacy had tested the saddle and packs, he turned to her, and the sincere, familiar smile eased her fears.

"You ready for this?" he said. "It's not too late to change your mind."

"I'm ready."

"Okay, let's head out."

With a quick kiss on Stacy's lips, he mounted Rusty and turned back to the riverbank.

Stacy reached up and squeezed Annie's hand.

"Good luck."

Seventeen

A mournful call broke the silence as Johnny followed Annie on Tucker through the densely wooded trail along Nyack Creek. He'd decided to start out letting her set the pace. Tucker knew the trail. She couldn't get in trouble. He also wanted to assess what he'd gotten himself into in allowing her to talk him into this situation, and how hard he could push Annie in the wilds.

"Ponoka," Johnny said to himself at the sound.

Annie turned, her face silhouetted by the alpine glow of the morning against the peaks in the distance. She'd been quiet, subdued, but the sound of the elk bugling seemed to exhilarate her.

"I have elk outside my bedroom window, and my office," she said. "Can you believe it?"

Johnny smiled.

"To be honest, it's a little hard to believe," he said, then added quickly, "*Any* of this."

Annie's nose was as dainty and perfect as he remembered. She had aged, but she was still the beauty she had been as a serious, and, in Johnny's mind, overly intense college student.

"I know," she replied before turning back to the trail in front of her.

Annie's comfort level on Tucker impressed him. Like most beginners, she rode stiff. She'd end up hurting after what they had ahead of them. But that didn't concern Johnny. As they moved through the Nyack toward a situation that his gut told him was dangerous, he'd been balancing Annie's safety—and Will's.

When their horses stopped to drink from the dark waters of the creek, Johnny broached the idea.

"I know you feel strongly that you want to go with me, but I've been thinking. There's a way for me to get there a lot faster. Red Eagle Pass."

His words sent red flags flying for Annie, who turned suspicious eyes on him.

"What do you mean a way for you to get there? Why wouldn't it be a way for *us* to get there?"

"Listen, Annie," Johnny replied. "Red Eagle Pass isn't something I'd take you on. It was a major thoroughfare through the park, from Two Medicine to St. Mary via the Nyack, a hundred years ago. But it was abandoned after World War II. It's overgrown, and dangerous. Hard to find. I've done it, and I can do it again, but I'm not taking you on it."

"How much time would it save?"

"If you're not with me, maybe four or five hours."

"I'm going with you, Johnny."

"Not if I take Red Eagle Pass."

"Goddammit. You're still as stubborn and know-it-all as you were in college."

"Only when I'm right."

They were standing on the edge of the creek, horses' reins in hand, separated by Annie's horse, Tucker, whose long neck stretched to the cool water. Annie's eyes had the same fire in them they'd had the day he'd told her he was quitting school. Moving back to Montana, to the reservation.

"I can do it, Johnny," she said. "I'm a big girl. I'll make my own decisions."

"You always have."

"What does that mean?"

"Annie, I'm telling you, that trail is dangerous. It's so overgrown that at times there'll be alders and willows taller than our heads—you have to navigate by instinct, hope you come across a game trail. There are drop-offs. Sheer drop-offs. A misstep could be disastrous."

"I'll be following you."

Johnny locked his gaze with hers. Held it for several seconds in silence.

"As nice as that would be—for a change—it's still too dangerous. If what you want is to get to Will as quickly as we can, let me go alone. I don't want to end up rescuing you instead of Will."

"Goddamn you," Annie replied. She turned away, looking into the sky that was just hinting at life with morning sun to the north and east, the direction they were headed. The direction Will McCarroll was heading last time Johnny spoke to him. "Where do you get on that trail, the Red whatever?"

Johnny took his eyes off her. He was making progress, and Annie had never responded to pressure. At least from him.

"Red Eagle Pass. We'd swing over to Two Medicine," he replied. "You could wait for me there, in East Glacier."

Annie looked straight ahead as she said, "We have to head that way anyway." He could hear the resentment in her voice over what he was doing—forcing her to choose between going along with Johnny or getting to Will faster. "Let me think about it."

"That's fair," Johnny replied. A tug on his horse's reins brought his soft, wet muzzle up out of the creek's waters. "Let's keep moving."

They rode on in silence, this time occasioned by Annie's angst and anger.

Had they not, had they been speaking, Johnny might have missed it. Might not have heard the cries, the groans.

He knew the sound.

His gut reflexively twisted in the anger, the horror, moments like this always gave rise to.

Johnny reached for his belt, unsnapped his gun from its holster.

He had taken the lead after their stop at the creek. Bringing his gelding to a dead stop, he turned halfway in the saddle and said, "Stay here."

Annie's horse had already followed suit.

"What is it?" Annie asked.

"An animal," Johnny replied over his shoulder.

Annie apparently hadn't heard it.

"Where?"

"In that direction," Johnny answered, nodding to the west, the direction of the creek. "It's in a trap."

Annie gasped.

"Why do you have your gun drawn?"

"Because chances are, at this point, the only thing I can do to help is use it. Stay here," he ordered again. "This won't take long."

With an almost imperceptible nudge, his gelding continued forward.

Johnny had judged the sound to come from as far away as two or three hundred yards—animals in traps generally fell quiet after a while, but from time to time, either right when they were first trapped, or when they felt the end nearing, they would cry out with desperation and ferocity, fighting back at an invisible foe. Or perhaps fending off another four-legged—a predator like a coyote, bear, or wolf.

The sound may have carried even farther, depending on the victim.

The nearness to Nyack Creek might have indicated it was a muskrat or beaver, but they were quiet little animals. While the trap was probably set for one of them— their pelts weren't bringing in big dollars now, but they were easy, and a reliable way for a trapper to pick up a little cash between trophy catches—judging from the sound, something bigger had stepped into this one's steel jaws.

Something a trapper would no doubt be elated to find. Maybe even a wolf.

As his eyes scanned the undergrowth for signs of recent activity, Johnny at least felt the relief of knowing it hadn't been a wolverine. Not this time.

A trapped wolverine made ferocious, hair-raising sounds. But not something that could be heard that far away.

Trappers liked to say that the animals, when trapped, lie quietly until they die. That they barely suffer. But every animal Johnny had come upon in a trap, if it was still alive, had struggled like hell. Maybe that was because, upon seeing a human, they instinctively knew that the next trauma they'd endure would be the end of a wooden club against their skulls.

These were the thoughts that ran through Johnny's head as he moved slowly, silently, in the direction of the cry. Such an unusual cry.

The trail had turned away from the creek as he and Annie followed it north. Johnny reached it within a minute or two, again stopping to listen. By now he would have expected more cries, unless what he'd heard was the animal's last protest before giving in to death.

Following his initial instincts, he steered the gelding across the creek, continuing in the same direction.

He'd gone another two hundred yards and was about to turn back. The lighting ahead indicated a small clearing. Trappers didn't set their lines in clearings, especially somewhere like Glacier, where they could be seen, both by potential prey and by people like Johnny.

Convinced now that he'd gone the wrong direction, Johnny reined Rusty into a turn. As the gelding turned to his right, something in Johnny's peripheral field of vision moved.

Stopping mid-turn, Johnny steered Rusty back on course. Less than a dozen yards later, he stepped into the clearing.

At first glance he assumed he'd come upon an abandoned campsite. Kids did it often enough—camped, had too much to drink, then stumbled out of the woods, leaving gear behind, too drunk or hungover to remember where they'd left it.

But then he saw the glint of morning sun off the metal, and the next instant, heard the groan.

"*Help me.*"

Shielding his eyes from the sun's glare, Johnny stared in disbelief.

A man lay naked, wounded, on the ground. He'd lifted his head, dirt clinging to his left cheek. His eyes—filled with agony, and something Johnny took to be almost otherworldly—locked with Johnny's.

"Help," he repeated.

Johnny's eyes traveled from his face, down his shriveling, dehydrated body—curled into the fetal position against the high mountain morning chill—until he saw what the sun's rays had ricocheted off. The metal around the man's ankle.

He was secured to the tree behind him by a leghold trap.

Sliding his gun back into its holster, Johnny bolted off his horse, stripping his shirt off as he ran toward the man.

"What the hell," he said, dropping the shirt over the gross, massive torso. It reminded Johnny of a raven- and coyote-ravaged pig carcass he'd once discovered in a ravine on the reservation, just off the highway between Browning and Cut Bank. The animal had apparently stumbled into the ditch and been unable to climb out. Johnny's shirt barely covered the man's shoulders and top half of a gut, the rest of which lay, almost pancake-like, on the dirt.

He moved to the man's feet and dropped to his knees, reaching for the ankle held by the trap. The skin had turned bluish-black. Pus oozed from several spots—mostly places where the trap's teeth had broken through the skin, but also a newer, cleaner slice just above the ankle.

Gangrene appeared to be setting in.

The moment Johnny's fingers touched the skin, the man let out a scream that caused Johnny to shudder. It was the same sound that Johnny had attributed minutes earlier to a trapped animal.

"You have to let me straighten your leg," he said. "Do you understand?"

The man nodded, eyes closed.

"I'll be right back."

Johnny was on his knees, bent over the pack he'd removed from behind his saddle, when he heard the rhythmical pounding of a horse in a run. He rose just in time to see the expression on Annie's face when she broke through into the clearing atop Tucker.

"Oh my god."

"Annie, go back. I can handle this."

Annie had already jumped down, gaze intent on the scene unfolding in front of her.

As she moved toward where the man lay, still curled in half, Johnny grabbed her by the arm.

"He stepped in a trap. He's been there a while. It's not a pretty sight."

Jerking her arm away, Annie shook loose of Johnny's grip and walked slowly but determinedly to the man, who now looked up.

Johnny saw him watching Annie approach, his expression blank, shocked.

Then he heard Annie's gasp of horror.

She must have seen the ankle.

His fingers closed around the wire cutter he always carried in his pack.

He straightened to his full six-two, and followed in Annie's wake.

She had fallen to her knees, hands gently running down the discolored leg, examining it. The fact that she could ignore the man's nude form did not escape Johnny's notice. When she felt him at her side, she looked over, saw the wire cutter.

"Will those work?"

"Let's hope I don't have to use them." Johnny dropped down on his knees beside her, raised his gaze to meet that of the man, and said, "This is going to hurt."

"Just get the fucking thing off me."

"Okay, hold on."

Johnny placed one hand on each side of the ghastly, bloated ankle and without further warning, used all his strength to press on the springs holding the teeth shut.

The man's scream filled the air.

Sweat began streaming off Johnny's chin.

"This looks like a four," he said, aloud but to himself. "It probably has a seven- or eight-inch spread." Even if he could get it to open to its full capacity, would that be enough?

The next sound out of the man's mouth startled Johnny even more than the bloodcurdling scream.

"It's a three," he said. "Six-inch spread. It was stretched to its limits by my foot *before* it swelled up. You're gonna have to cut the fucking thing off."

Johnny realized what he was dealing with now. He looked over at Annie.

"We're going to have to get him upright."

"You mean on his feet?"

The man's eyes widened.

"No. I can't do it. And that's not gonna work. The teeth are too deep. I knew not to move, but the psycho kept coming at me with a spear. . . ."

Johnny glanced sideways at Annie, who quietly uttered one word.

"Spear?"

"He's delusional. Probably from the pain and dehydration. But he may be right about the trap being too deeply embedded. This may not work. We may have to take him out of here with it still on."

Annie's eyes had remained fixed on the man.

"What's your name?" she asked.

"Bridger Brogan," came the response in less than a heartbeat.

Johnny visibly startled. He hadn't recognized him.

"How the hell did you manage to step into your own trap?"

Based on information Johnny had provided after crossing paths with Brogan in the backcountry, Will's predecessor had arrested Brogan the previous summer for trapping inside Glacier. Brogan had hired a lawyer, also known to be a trapper, who, based on ambiguous legal technicalities, had managed to keep obtaining trial continuances.

Johnny had heard through the local grapevine that Brogan had vowed to get even with the wolverine biologist, that he'd even enquired about where Johnny lived.

For the first time since they'd come upon him, Brogan's face came alive.

"The bitch lured me into it," he said angrily. "She tied my hands behind my back, then blindfolded me."

A new sense of horror immediately took seed in Johnny's gut. Over the years, Glacier's backcountry had attracted many unsavory types, people with visions of living in the backcountry, usually on the run, trying to escape the law. Some of them were heading to Canada, with little to lose if someone came upon them.

But in all his years, Johnny had never heard of something as bizarre and twisted as someone luring a stranger into a trap.

"Someone you came upon out here?"

The question seemed to anger Brogan.

"No. We came out here together. For a picnic." He looked up at Annie, half sheepishly. "Hell, I came out here to get laid. That's how she got me to be tied up. She said she was into bondage. I fell for it."

Annie didn't flinch. Perhaps, thought Johnny, in her work as a prosecutor she'd heard things equally as sordid.

She finally spoke up again.

"Why would she do it? What made her want to do this to you?"

"She said I killed her dog," Brogan answered, looking at Johnny as he did so, then quickly turning his eyes away again.

Johnny realized that Brogan wasn't sure yet if Johnny had recognized him.

Johnny finally got it.

"Her dog got killed in one of your traps."

No regret registered on Brogan's dirty face. Only disgust.

"That's what the bitch said."

Johnny turned to Annie, who had removed her hand from the discolored leg. It lingered in the air, as if it had a will of its own and couldn't bear to return to Bridger Brogan's body.

"He's a trapper. He's been arrested before for setting lines in the park."

He turned back to Brogan.

"Who is she?"

"She calls herself Claudette. That's all I know. That and that she's a student in Missoula. She's been up here, staying in a cabin up Paola Creek."

"How long ago did this happen?" Annie asked.

"Two, maybe three days ago. She comes back every day."

This time Annie's voice didn't disguise her horror. "What?"

"She comes back. She taunts me. Asks me how it feels, if I'm hungry. She'll be back again today."

"To release you?"

Brogan actually laughed. He nodded toward the ground just beyond his reach. For the first time, Johnny noticed the handsaw lying there.

"No. She said she'd come back to help me use that."

Annie's expression indicated she didn't understand.

"She told you she's going to let you go today?"

"No. She told me she'd hold that and let me cut my foot off. That's the only way she said I'd get free."

Johnny couldn't see Annie's face in response to this news. While the two had been talking, he had slowly moved behind Brogan's back.

"Just get me the hell out of here," Brogan said now, "and I'll help you find her."

Suddenly, in one swift, continuous motion, Johnny placed a hand under each of Brogan's arms and with Brogan screaming so loudly his roar filled the Nyack, Johnny lifted him to his feet.

He eyed the ground for a stick and found the hand-fashioned "spear" Brogan must have been referring to. Grabbing it, he put it in the trapper's right hand, then turned to Annie.

"I need you to hold him up."

She quickly moved to the other side, pulling his flaccid arm around her shoulder.

Johnny positioned himself back in front of Brogan and, with Brogan stifling another scream, he put one foot on the spring on the trap's left side, then quickly jumped up to place his right foot on the other.

The trap opened enough for Johnny to see that Brogan's tendons and skin had become enmeshed with its teeth. He was about to step off and come up with another plan when the big man jerked his foot free.

Groaning, Brogan fell back, to the ground, Annie toppling along with him. Quickly, she got up and began tending to his ankle.

"We need hot water."

Johnny had already started for his saddle pack. Within minutes he had his camp stove going, and water boiling.

"You allergic to Vicoden?" he asked Brogan, hand extended with a white tablet in it.

Brogan shook his head, grabbed the pill, and threw it back into his throat.

Now that Brogan was free, Johnny couldn't help himself.

"You're the one setting traps in the Nyack, aren't you? And up at Iceberg Lake?"

Brogan eyed Johnny, silent.

"We're going to save your sorry ass," Johnny continued, "but then you're going to jail. No bail this time, not until your trial."

Annie stood up. Johnny expected her to chastise him. Instead she said, "I'll get the water," and headed for the cook stove, which Johnny had placed on a large boulder halfway between the horses and the tree still anchoring the trap.

Johnny followed.

"We need to get him to the clinic in Columbia Falls."

When Annie turned to him, she had tears in her eyes.

"What about Will?"

"Annie, I'll head right back out to look for him."

"No," Annie replied. Johnny was surprised not only by the grief that was so visible in her expression, but also by his response to seeing it. "Let me take him back to the highway. You go on, get word to Will. He's in trouble, Johnny. I feel it."

"I think you may be underestimating Will," Johnny replied. "If he is in trouble, my guess is Will can handle it."

"Damn it, Johnny. Now you sound like Rob Deardorf. I thought I could count on you."

"You can count on me," Johnny replied, an unexplained anger surfacing. "I'm here aren't I? But it's my responsibility to get this man help. And to keep you safe. Will McCarroll or no Will McCarroll."

Those last words, and the tone in which Johnny said them, clearly did not sit right with Annie.

Propped up against a rock, Brogan had been listening.

"Will McCarroll?" he said. "The ranger from Yellowstone?"

In unison, both Johnny and Annie turned to face him.

"Yes," Annie replied.

Brogan fell silent for several seconds. Johnny somehow sensed he was weighing the situation.

What the hell was going on?

When Brogan finally opened his mouth again, nothing could have prepared Johnny for what came out of it.

"I can take you to Will McCarroll."

* * *

Claudette had made her decision. Today was the last day she'd visit Brogan.

Fear had set in.

She'd wanted him to die, but the son of a bitch was too mean and ugly to give up and die.

Now what she wanted was to watch him make that first cut into his ankle.

She believed she'd convinced him that the only way he would escape the trap, the only way to save his life, was to literally dismember himself—amputate his own leg.

If she had convinced him, then maybe he'd do it. Maybe he'd let her hold the saw in place while he got the opportunity to do what the animals he trapped so often did—cut the trapped foot off in order to gain freedom. In order to avoid dying slowly, cruelly, without food or water, or the alternative—a trapper arriving.

She wanted him to know the full horror that animals like Tenny experienced.

Then she wanted him to die.

But she'd realized that she couldn't actually do it. She couldn't kill him.

She'd debated with herself, chastised herself for days now. After all, trappers did it all the time. When they found animals still alive in their traps, they clubbed them to death. Or shot them.

Claudette had planned to do that. She'd been prepared, if need be. At least that's what she thought.

So far things had gone pretty much as she'd hoped. She'd made her point, and Brogan knew she was serious. The last step was just the natural progression of things.

But now that it had come down to it, she didn't have it in her. So her hope for this day was that Brogan would choose to sacrifice his foot. And then, in all of the scenarios that she'd run over and over through her mind, the best one was that he would then bleed to death.

But another reality had also set in. Even if Brogan obliged her today and proceeded with the amputation, he might live. Hell, as miserable as he was, Claudette couldn't believe how strong the bastard still appeared. And if Brogan lived, they would eventually find her.

So last night, a long, sleepless night, Claudette had decided that what she needed was time. Time to return to Missoula, pick up her passport on the way, get her things. Time to make her escape to Australia.

During the night, she'd thought about leaving for Missoula immediately, but one thing stopped her. She'd left one critical piece of evidence behind.

That damn saw.

It still had the price tag on it. The Ace Hardware price tag.

That tag could easily be traced to the store in Kalispell. And wouldn't you know, when she was standing there in front of the selection of saws, a guy who worked there had come up to ask her if she needed any help.

He'd been flirting with her, she could tell.

She'd told him no, she was fine, but he'd persisted, asking her what she needed the saw for.

For some reason, she hadn't planned for that.

Claudette had uttered something about a tree, a branch, that had fallen in her yard in the wind, and he'd replied by showing her a larger saw. Something too big for her to fit into the backpack she wore when she and Brogan went on their picnic.

When he'd finally left her alone, she'd grabbed the smaller one she'd been looking at when he first approached, and hurried to the line at the cash register to purchase it. But he'd passed her again as she stood there, and damn if he hadn't seen it.

"Still think the bigger model is what you need," he'd said with a smile.

And then, stupidly, she'd used her debit card to purchase it. What the fuck had she been thinking? All the thought and planning that had gone into this, and it might all come down to that one error in judgment.

As she was standing in line, she discovered she didn't have as much cash as she'd thought she had in her wallet. She'd debated about stepping out of line, going to an ATM, but with the flirtatious clerk coming and going, she just wanted out of that store. As it turned out, that seemingly minor detail had now changed everything.

She didn't have a choice in the matter now. She *had* to go back into the Nyack.

Not just in the hopes that Bridger Brogan would oblige her by using the saw—which might just end up granting Claudette's wish that he die—but more importantly, to remove it, take it with her.

She felt confident that without the saw, and with what little information she'd given Brogan—most of it false—they wouldn't be able to identify her until she was long gone.

Retrieving the saw, however, was key.

As she pulled Brogan's pickup and trailer off Highway 2, she was startled to see another horse trailer parked there, alongside her Honda.

Her first impulse—to come back later in order to avoid any chance of being seen on the trail—was negated by the fact that the spot she'd used for her plot against Brogan was off-trail, where no one would see or hear him. That, combined with the urgency she felt, caused her to stifle the desire to flee. She hurriedly transferred the suitcase, laptop, box of books, and backpack she'd packed into the pickup the night before into her Honda, started it up, just to be sure it was in working order, then as quickly as the mare allowed, unloaded her horse, leaving Brogan's gelding in the other side of the trailer.

She had prepared signs to leave on the truck's windshield and the back of the trailer when she returned, before taking off in her own car—PLEASE HELP THESE HORSES, THEY HAVE BEEN ABANDONED—but she wouldn't post those until she'd returned.

Despite her many recent crossings of the Middle Fork on horseback, Claudette's fear of drowning hadn't eased. Compounded today by her angst, by the time she reached the other side, her heart rocketed so wildly in her chest that she had to stop, close her eyes, take several deep breaths, and repeat the invocation that she began her yoga practices with:

Om, namah shivaya gurave
Saccidananda murtaye
Nisprapancaya shantaya
Niralambaya tejase

It helped.

The trail had become so familiar to both her and the horse that she was making the ride in record time. That speed, however, almost caused Claudette's downfall. Had the horse not pricked up her ears at the sound of her owner's voice, and then begun galloping toward it, Claudette might not have heard it until too late.

But when she yanked the mare to a halt, Claudette, too, heard the sound.

She knew immediately what it was. The same sound Brogan had made when he backed into the trap.

Had Brogan been able to reach the saw?
Or—better yet—had a predator come upon him?

Anxiously welcoming either possibility as it raced through her mind, Claudette still held the horse back, moving forward at a snail's pace until they'd come within twenty-five yards of the clearing. She was about to dismount and cover the rest of the distance on foot when she saw movement, and then horses. Two of them.

At almost the same time she caught glimpse of a man. Indian, long black hair in a ponytail, bent over something on the ground.

A backpack. Behind him, where she'd left Brogan, she saw a flurry of activity. She did not wait to make it out.

Terror clutching at her throat like some ghoulish character from *Halloween III*, Claudette pivoted the mare. It took all of her presence of mind to force the mare to retreat slowly, in order to prevent being detected.

Once she felt confident they would not be heard, Claudette slapped the horse on the flanks. She practically flew back down the trail, toward her waiting car, repeating the invocation over and over again in her head.

Annie literally put her arm out to stop Johnny from reaching Brogan first.

She crossed the distance between them in seconds, never taking her eyes off Brogan's heavy lidded gaze.

"What do you mean you can take us to Will?"

Brogan did not try to escape her scrutiny.

"I know where he is."

Now Johnny wanted answers.

"Where?"

Brogan turned his eyes to Johnny.

"I'll tell you that when I know we have a deal."

"A deal?" Annie could barely keep her voice under control. "You're sitting there with a steel trap lying next to you, telling me you know something about Will, and you're trying to work some kind of deal? You would be dead soon if we hadn't come along."

Brogan looked up at her defiantly.

"McCarroll will be dead if I don't help you. Hell, he may already be."

It was Johnny, not Annie, who lunged at him.

"You son of a bitch."

It took all of Annie's strength to stop Johnny and try to reason with him.

"Talk to him, Johnny. We have to find out what he knows about Will. Not try and hang him here."

Johnny straightened slowly back up, glaring at Brogan. Annie was right. He couldn't let his feelings about this man who'd illegally killed countless animals, no doubt including wolverines from his study, interfere with helping Will.

"Name your deal," he said.

Brogan was quick to reply.

"I lead you to McCarroll, you let me go free. Tear up the warrant. No arrests, no jail time."

Johnny wasn't buying it.

"How the hell can you lead us anywhere in the condition you're in?"

"Give me some water, food, and another Vicoden and I can do it. It's not the first trap I've stepped in. Hell, I can do it *without* the Vicoden."

"You'd rather risk losing that leg than spend a few days in jail?"

"Yes."

For some reason, Johnny believed him. He was one ugly, ornery man—and one tough son of a bitch.

"Why?" Annie wanted to know. "Why would you take such a risk?"

Brogan didn't flinch.

"Because my wife's due to have a baby any day now. She'd never forgive me if I was sitting in jail when he's born."

Johnny's laughter startled both Annie and Brogan.

"What a piece of work. But she'd forgive you for

coming out here to get laid?" He glanced sideways at Annie.

"I say we let the worthless piece of shit lead us." Turning back to Brogan, he added, "But in the future, I catch you trapping in my park again, the words 'mercy' or 'deal' won't be in my vocabulary. You won't just be fined, I'll make sure you rot in prison. Kid or no kid."

"I can live with that," Brogan replied, clearly unconcerned about Johnny's opinion of him.

"Then you've got a deal."

Annie wasn't ready to give in.

"Wait. There's no deal until he tells us enough for us to believe he really can lead us to Will."

Intense brown eyes drilling the trapper, she said, "Prove to us you know where he is."

Brogan didn't miss a heartbeat in responding.

"Someone trapped a collared wolverine in Yellowstone about the time McCarroll was transferred to Glacier. Right?"

Annie looked over at Johnny.

"Go on," she said.

"Now McCarroll's out looking for a missing hiker. She was last seen heading out to climb Bad Marriage."

Johnny jumped in.

"You could have gotten that from the posters plastered all over the park."

"Yeah, you're right. But did you know the missing woman, Haldis Beck, also goes by the name Sally Gordon?"

Annie's gasp brought a gleam to Brogan's otherwise dead eyes.

"Need more?"

"Why?" Annie asked. "Who is this Haldis Beck? And why is she trying to lure Will into the backcountry?"

"To keep him from testifying before the Senate subcommittee on the guns-in-park law. She works for Guns

4 All, a radical offshoot of the ARF. That's how I met her, at an ARF convention. She worked as a paid informant for the ARF for years, penetrating gun control groups, until a year or so ago, when a reporter from *Mother Jones* magazine started snooping around. The ARF got rid of her, hoping that would be enough to kill the story. But certain people in the upper levels of the ARF felt the information she was gathering was critical, so they suckered the goon who started Guns 4 All into hiring her instead. "

Johnny sensed Brogan was telling the truth, but not all of it.

"How are you involved?"

Brogan was quick to answer. Maybe a little too quick.

"I'm not. She called me to ask me to help her, told me her plan, but I said I couldn't do it."

"But you *did* supply her with the scent lure she used in Yellowstone, didn't you?" Johnny pressed. "Which you stole from my house."

This reminder actually seemed to please the trapper.

"I want immunity for that, too."

Annie had little interest in scent lures.

"What's the plan? What does she have planned for Will?"

"To ambush McCarroll when he comes to find her."

"Oh god."

"Where?" Johnny asked.

"Depends on how it all comes down. Either as he's coming up the north ridge of Eagle Plume on his way to Bad Marriage, or she'll wait till he gets on Bad Marriage."

"This woman wasn't even an experienced hiker," Johnny scoffed. "She took off with new hiking boots on. You expect us to believe she's not only capable of climbing that loop alone, but that she's going to take on a guy like McCarroll?"

Again, Brogan's response came quickly.

"First of all, don't let that picture she had those buffoons take fool you. She's not only an experienced hiker and survivalist, she's a world class marksman. That was all part of the plot, to look like a helpless, stupid woman out trying to prove herself after a painful divorce."

"Is she alone?"

"My guess is she is."

"Then what—after she ambushes Will?"

"Then she flees to Canada. She's been hired by some mining companies there to do the same thing she did down here with the gun control groups. They're under a lot of heat from environmental groups over the Tar Sands project.

"She'd just been outed in her work for the gun lobby, so she knew she had to leave the country anyway. Taking Will out is going to bankroll her new life up there."

Johnny stared at Brogan several seconds before stepping away, leaving Annie still staring. He nodded for her to join him. When they were out of earshot, he looked directly into Annie's eyes.

"What do you think?"

"I think he knows what he's talking about. No one had any idea that this woman had two identities. The only reason I found out is I saw her in a video in Yellowstone, where she applied for a backcountry permit using the name Sally Gordon, and then recognized her in the poster at the lodge." Annie glanced back over her shoulder at Brogan—a furtive, hate-filled glance— and added, "I also think he's in on it."

"That's my take too. So . . . ," he paused, studying her, "what do you want to do? It's your call, Annie. You're the one with the most at stake if we offer him a deal and it turns out he's involved in the plot against Will."

Annie did not flinch.

"Offer him the deal. If it comes down to my job or finding Will in time, I'll have no qualms. None."

Johnny was surprised by the pang he felt at her words, and the determination on her face. He looked away quickly, but Annie had already seen it.

"What?" she asked.

"Nothing," he replied. "Let's do it."

Eighteen

Haldis Beck rolled out from under the protection of the column of rock that, from millennia of hard-driving Canadian winds, leaned slightly southward. That column, near the pinnacle of Eagle Plume and perched high above the prairies to the east, and mountains in every other direction, had more or less been her home now for several days—her lookout, as well as her shelter and safe haven. It took skill and daring to climb to it. In all the time she'd been there, waiting for Brogan—who had helped her choose this spot to ambush Will, and would have known to find her there, if he were still coming—no one had come upon her little campsite. No one knew she was there.

Stars still shone overhead, but the sky had lightened an almost imperceptible degree to the east.

Had she overslept?

Quickly she jumped to her feet, glanced down at the ridge, heart racing.

Relief washed over her at the sight of the tent, fire still smoldering next to it.

The horse still tied nearby told her she was fine. Will was still sleeping.

She had time. Enough time.

She had made her decision during the night.

She could not dispose of McCarroll's body alone. Not without someone to act as a lookout for hikers coming from Mad Wolf. She was confident now that no one was on Bad Marriage, which would have meant they might be headed her way. The last hiker she'd seen coming from that direction had passed below her the previous afternoon and she hadn't seen a party of hikers going that way for days now.

Still, she couldn't know if a hiker from Mad Wolf might be headed her way.

During the night, she'd finally concluded it was too risky to retrieve and dispose of the body.

The only solution, then, was to get out of there before it was discovered.

If need be—if, as she was leaving, she encountered any hikers so close she wouldn't have the time she needed to reach Canada—she'd have to kill them, too.

That hadn't been part of the plan, but it had now become, at the very least, a possibility. At the worst, a necessity. Until now, she hadn't presented a threat to hikers. It had been easy to scout for them from this vantage point, which gave her time to hide when they crossed the ridge Will now slept on. Other than the bum on the trail that one day, who appeared out of nowhere, she hadn't been seen. She could count on that. And she wasn't worried about the bum. He was as eager to avoid her as she was to avoid him.

Still, damn that Brogan. Her exposure to serious consequences had now skyrocketed because he'd let her down. She'd still hoped he'd show up when, through her spotting scope, she saw Will, on horseback, navigating his way up the north side of Mad Wolf.

She'd known immediately there was no waiting now.

Of course, she could have backed down. Deserted the mission. But Haldis believed in her mission. The second amendment was sacred to her and, whether they knew it or not, all Americans. How ironic that her patriotism would ultimately force her to flee to another country.

And if she had to flee, which became a reality when she learned, the day she left Chicago for Yellowstone, that next month's edition of *Mother Jones* magazine contained an article outing her as a paid informant—those lily-faced gun control freaks would press for charges that could keep her in prison for years, and the American Rifle Foundation's powers-that-be would soon be falling all over themselves denying any involvement in the plan for Haldis to go underground—she would need the quarter of a million dollars Tony Gladner had promised her, when she went to work for Guns 4 All, to start her new life.

A quarter of a million should be enough, especially now that she'd made connections with a Canadian mining company that had read of her success infiltrating gun control groups. They had a huge PR debacle on their hands with the Tar Sands project, which had caused numerous environmental groups in the states, Montana in particular, to take up the fight against allowing the project to go forward. The VP she'd met with had jumped on Haldis' suggestion that, with their help acquiring a visa, she infiltrate those groups, who had recently decided to join forces, then feed the company information on protests and plans—in particular legal strategies.

She'd hated leaving her daughters behind in Chicago, but they would be able to visit—once, that is, she told them where she had gone.

At any rate, there was no sense in looking back now.

She had watched Will set up camp the night before. Cool-looking dude. She actually sensed that the two of them had something in common—strength of character maybe, or maybe just that they were both obviously loners—and almost felt a sense of regret at what she had to do.

He'd kept the fire going all night—hoping, she realized, to attract her.

Little did he know he had.

As the sun's rays began revealing the extent of the majesty surrounding her, Haldis grabbed the loaded rifle that was always by her side, padded over to the rock she'd chosen the night before and centered the flap—still zipped shut—to Will's tent in its crosshairs.

The tent was the only thing that threw Haldis. She wouldn't have expected a macho guy like Will McCarroll to sleep in a tent. But what the hell, we all had our idiosyncrasies.

It was a glorious morning.

She took a deep breath of the cool mountain air, reminded herself that she'd have to come back to Glacier for a visit.

And then, with finger pressed to exert just the slightest amount of pressure on the trigger of her rifle, she heard the familiar sound, and in the same instant, felt the cold touch of steel against her temple.

"Haldis Beck?"

She didn't even have to look.

As the horse tethered beside the tent a quarter of a mile below threw its head back into the air, and whinnied, Haldis Beck already knew who stood on the other side of the .45 Sig pressed to the side of her head.

Will hadn't known if he could pull it off. All he did know was that once daylight broke, it would be too late.

He'd started out around midnight, after feeding the fire, laying dry lodgepole branches and scrub brush around its perimeter so it would eventually spread, keeping itself alive long after he'd gone. Then he'd cut a two-foot slice in his tent, where the floor met the back wall, and slipped out the back, the side facing away from the leaning column of rock he'd kept his eyes on all night—the one where, as the sun set and cast its last rays their way before dropping behind the peaks, it had reflected off the glass of a pair of binoculars.

That single glint, lasting no more than a fraction of a second, confirmed everything he'd suspected. Everything he'd gradually pieced together.

The moon's light was adequate to descend the first, gentle portion of the ridgeline, but then he came upon section after section of the scree Johnny Yellow Kidney had warned him about. Several times he lost his footing and tumbled, during the last of which the only thing that saved him from dropping off the side of the mountain and into a canyon carved by a tributary of the Cut Bank was a scraggly lone pine growing out of a crack in the surface of the rock wall, which he'd managed to grab as he tumbled.

Once down on the ground, he bushwhacked his way to a game trail headed up Mad Wolf. Made by and for humans, hiking trails, as much as the terrain permitted, zigzagged their ways up a mountain. Wildlife took a more direct route, which in this case, was just what Will needed in order to beat the clock. But it also meant four hours of steady climbing sometimes forty-five to fifty degree inclines, and rocky terrain that even the most skilled of rock climbers would gear up for.

Will didn't have that option.

By 4:00 A.M., he'd caught sight of the column of rock. By five, he felt no closer to it. A rock ledge, like a roof's overhang, forced him to move horizontally, looking for a break he could use to move upward instead of laterally. But when the ledge's outcropping finally tapered down to meet the rest of the mountainside's rock, it became vertical, impossible to climb. He'd chosen the wrong direction. Frustrated, Will realized he was moving farther away from his destination.

The sky to the east had taken on an alpine glow that he knew spelled failure if the morning's rays were to still find him on the mountain's side.

And then he came upon a scraggly dead whitebark pine that had long ago grown out of the side of the mountain, and sometime over the past couple years, no doubt in a windstorm, cracked at its base. It hung now, thirty feet down the mountainside. Vertical.

Will could not see its base above him, had no way of knowing how securely it was embedded. Testing it first with a couple firm pulls, he finally grabbed hold of it, and—all his weight now held by what was left of the dead tree's skeleton—he worked his way up it, sweat beading on his face as he wondered if he'd just made the biggest mistake of his life.

Above him and slightly to his left, a mountain goat stood watching him. As he continued upward, and then passed her, he saw that she was standing on a ledge, no more than twenty inches in width. He could almost leap to it—were it not so narrow it allowed no margin of error. But what was especially tempting was the fact that it signaled the start of what looked like climbable terrain.

Of course, it was already occupied.

Will was still eyeing it, assessing his chances of making it, as well as whether the mountain goat would abandon or share the space, when he heard a crackling sound. It started slow, high above him, then quickly accelerated to what seemed a deafening explosion.

He knew immediately what was happening.

Just as Will pushed off for the ledge, the lower half of the pine—the section he'd been climbing—broke free of the top half and began a free-fall down the mountain's side.

A second later, heart racing, face smashed against a rocky wall, Will looked directly down and realized that while one foot had hit its mark squarely, the heel of the other hung over the narrow ledge. Slowly, still uncertain of his positioning, he pulled it under him. He stood, taking deep breaths, hands working the rock for a hold. Finding one, he stood motionless, regaining his sense of balance and placement.

Simultaneous with Will's leap, the mountain goat had jumped to a ledge half a dozen feet higher. Will could see her looking down at him, more curious than anything.

"Thanks," he said.

Then after standing there until his legs felt solid once more, Will did something he had never done. He reached into his pocket for the cell phone they had issued him when he arrived in Glacier. He had not yet used it. He knew he didn't have coverage in the high alpine reaches he'd been traveling.

Still, he opened it, began typing.

He had lost Rachel and Carter without warning, and it had eaten away at him after they were gone.

He typed three words, held the phone to his face to find the "send" button and pressed it.

Then he looked up again, past the goat and to her right.

He saw the column.

For the first time since setting out, he now knew it was doable. Once he inched another six yards to the side on the ledge, where alpine ground cover would give him solid footing, with one short scramble up a rock-filled slope, he would be back atop the ridge—this time on the other side of the column.

Will had long ago become so in tune with the wildlife he'd spent his entire adult life protecting, that he'd come to move like them, and once he got on the ridge, he knew that he could move, silent, undetected, toward *his* prey.

One last mishap, however, threatened to give away his presence. When he'd placed his cell phone back in his pocket, he hadn't buttoned the flap, and as he scrambled up the rocky slope, he stumbled once. At first he thought he'd dislodged a small rock, but when he turned, in the faint, early morning light, he could see his cell phone bouncing down the mountainside. He did not move, waited a full five minutes before ascending the rest of the way for fear she had heard it.

He watched on his belly, from behind a boulder, as the woman—he had no doubt it was her, Haldis Beck—rolled out from under the giant column of rock. She was still dressed, her pack ready to go.

He watched her grab her rifle, set its scope on his campsite below.

And then, as silent and smoothly as one of the animals he'd come to resemble, he moved in, gun drawn.

"Haldis Beck?"

He felt her hesitation, the moment during which she actually debated putting up a fight, or swinging around at him and pulling the trigger.

When it passed, when she turned Will's way, he saw it in her eyes. The knowledge of whom she would be facing.

"How?" she said.

"Drop it," Will ordered. When she let go of the rifle, raised her hands and leaned back, Will pulled both arms behind her back, snapping cuffs on her wrists.

"Circled around during the night," he finally replied.

"But how did you know?"

"Glint off your glasses."

"No," she replied, shaking her head angrily. "How did you know I wasn't lost?"

Will took off his hat. The sun had risen over the peaks to the east and he held its bill over his eyes, shielding them as he looked out.

"That took a while. Mostly it was the fact that no one had seen you. That there was literally no trace of you after you made such a show of letting the young couple know where you were going. Everyone leaves a trace behind—unless they don't want to.

"But the real turning point came from the comments the old-timer made about you."

Haldis closed her eyes in self recrimination.

"I should have known he was trouble."

Will could read her thoughts.

"Killing him would've only meant spending the rest of your life in prison. Maybe even the death sentence. Look at it this way," he said with a handsome, sardonic grin that accomplished what he'd hoped—further enraged his prisoner, "you don't have any bodies to worry about disposing. That's the good news."

He yanked her to her feet forcefully, spinning her by her sturdy shoulders to force her to face him.

She refused to look at him.

But Will was used to that.

He was also used to the feeling of satisfaction that the next sentence had brought him, for twenty-eight years now.

"Haldis Beck, you're under arrest."

Nineteen

"Where the fuck are you going?"

Bridger Brogan's recently freed hands reached for the sides of Tucker's mouth and with a rough jerk on the bridle's bit, brought the gelding to a standstill.

In front of him, on foot and holding Tucker's reins, Johnny turned and, with an anger Annie had only witnessed on one other occasion, swung his rifle's butt against Brogan's arm.

"That horse has a sensitive mouth," Johnny told him. "You do that again and you'll need your own dentist."

The trapper didn't cower or cry out. But he did get the point.

"Two Medicine," Johnny answered. "That's where we're going. I'm dropping you off there."

His gaze then traveled past Brogan, to Annie, who had been riding last, behind Brogan, and with an attempt at indifference, which did not succeed, Johnny added, "Both of you."

Annie felt her mouth literally drop open.

"No."

In her state of disbelief at Johnny's betrayal, it was all she could think of to say.

They'd started out with Annie in the saddle of Johnny's gelding, Johnny riding behind, arms around her on occasion, and Brogan following, on Tucker; but several miles deeper into the Nyack, without warning, Johnny muttered something Annie could not distinguish, pushed off the back end of the horse, and sliding Tucker's reins off his sturdy neck, changed positions, with Annie moving behind, on Rusty, and Johnny leading Brogan, on Tucker, by foot, reins in hand.

Minutes later, when Brogan protested the need for his hands to remain tied behind his back, Johnny stopped, and without a word, sliced the rope that had been used to tie them.

They proceeded that way—with Johnny sometimes jogging for two or three miles at a time, and up and down inclines, rocky trail, and an occasional scree field.

It had brought back memories to Annie, images of the long-distance races she'd watched Johnny participate in, usually placing in the top three, during their days at the University of Washington. Johnny had hated that the local sportswriters labeled him the Indian kid who'd grown up running across the reservation— despite the fact that it was true. When they first started dating— during the period when each was eager to give the other some understanding of their former lives—he'd told Annie how, during the summers, he'd sometimes run the thirteen miles to and from East Glacier, where he worked at the Avis car rental shack. But Johnny felt the press's use of that information amounted to one of many acts of racism, and eventually, he'd quit the cross-country team.

He obviously hadn't quit running, however, as only a conditioned athlete could travel the distance they'd covered, on a trail up a mountain pass, over the past two hours. With his long hair and lean body, on the surface anyway, it seemed the only thing that set the Johnny she'd known as a coed apart from this one was the uniform he wore.

And the gun he carried.

He'd given Annie the gun he'd drawn when they first heard Brogan's hideous screams, then retrieved a rifle from his saddle pack, and now he jogged with it in hand. It made Annie nervous, but not as nervous as she felt about what the trapper had told them about this woman, this Haldis Beck, planning to ambush Will.

For some time now, Brogan had grown silent, giving one- or two-word answers to questions.

Annie sensed that Johnny's unease, like her own, grew with each turn of the trail.

And then they came to a fork in the trail. And Johnny took the right fork.

This broke Brogan's silence.

"What are you doing?" he asked again, still smarting from Johnny's rifle, but keeping his hands off Tucker's bridle. "We need to stay left. That's the quickest route to Bad Marriage."

Several inches of the rope Johnny had cut off Brogan's wrist hung from Johnny's back pocket. With the hand holding the reins, he grabbed it, pulled the rope out. Then he switched the rope into the hand holding the rifle, muzzle pointed at the ground.

"We're going to Two Medicine."

"Why?" Brogan replied, voicing the same question Annie wanted answered. Her instincts, however, told her Johnny had an agenda she didn't understand, so she remained quiet, watching their exchange.

But when Brogan added, "That's not our deal," Annie's heart sank at Johnny's answer.

"*What deal?*"

What was Johnny thinking? They *had* struck a deal with the trapper, and Will's life depended on it.

While clearly mindful of the rope in Johnny's hand, Brogan would not back down.

"We agreed that I'd take you to your friend, and in exchange, you'd let me go."

One of the challenges of Annie career was trying to read the logic behind criminal minds. Why would Bridger Brogan be upset at the possibility of being allowed to go free at Two Medicine, instead of having to continue to Bad Marriage in the horrible shape he was in?

For the moment, the quest for what Brogan was really up to took priority over her own objections to Johnny's plan to dump the two of them at Two Medicine.

She urged Rusty forward so that she wouldn't miss anything that would help with that quest.

"Neither of us said you'd be charged," she said, pulling even with Tucker and Brogan on the trail, just before it forked. The trail they'd been on, which veered slightly to the left, continued through forest, but the trail to Two Medicine quickly narrowed, with a sheer drop-off as it started up a steep incline that abutted a rock wall.

The horses seemed nervous about footing.

"Johnny's right," Annie added, trying to keep her horse in check as it inched forward, the two horses brushing sides as Rusty gained a nose length on Tucker. "You've already told us what Haldis Beck's plans are. In the shape you're in, you'll only slow us down. Unless you have more information we need," she added, "something more that could help us find Will before your friend does . . . ?"

Brogan grew silent. He knew he was on trial.

His eyes scanned the trail ahead, as if he were trying to think his way through the situation.

His patience exhausted, Johnny tightened his grip on the reins and took one step to the side of Tucker's neck, one step toward Brogan, rope held high.

"Hands behind your back."

"I do know more," Brogan blurted. "I know exactly where she's hiding, where she plans the ambush."

Johnny paused, rope in midair as he glared up at the trapper.

"I want specifics. Every fucking thing you know. And I want it *now*—or the illegal trapping of a threatened species charges they'll bring against you will look like child's play next to the attempted murder charges I'll make sure they bring—baby or no baby."

"I told you," Brogan responded. "She's waiting for him along the ridge between Eagle Plume and Bad Marriage. There's a rock column there, up a steep incline. No one ever climbs to it. I have the coordinates on my GPS, but that crazy bitch took everything away when she left me last time. It's not easy to find. You need me with you."

Annie saw that Johnny realized Brogan had him.

"I'm not letting you ditch me either," she said quietly but firmly.

Resigned, Johnny stepped back, to go around to Annie's side of Tucker. Unable to tie Brogan's hands with a rifle in his hand, he lifted the firearm, butt first, in the air, extending it toward Annie.

"Here," he said. "Don't be afraid to use it."

Pressed together, the horses still angled for position. Just as Annie reached for the rifle, Brogan's left leg—his good leg, the one with the boot on it—shot out and kicked her horse squarely in the ribs. At the same time, Brogan let out a scream intended to scare the hell out of the animal.

It succeeded.

Annie's horse bolted, mowing down Johnny.

Now Brogan yanked backward with all his strength on Tucker's mouth. Panicked and in pain, the horse reared back on two legs. As Johnny scrambled to his feet, the gelding managed to avoid any contact with him as his front legs returned to earth.

Annie had let go of the reins while reaching for the rifle. Now her horse, even more panicked upon hearing the commotion behind them, raced at breakneck speed up the narrow mountain trail. Clinging to the saddle's horn, Annie managed to grab the left rein, but the right side hung loose, out of reach, except for the times the gelding jumped over an oncoming rock—when, in landing on the other side, the strap of leather would fly Annie's way. She began debating whether to jump off, but the drop-off, and erratic path of the trail, made that option more frightening than staying on. Finally, on the third try, Annie caught the errant rein.

She had just started to succeed in slowing the runaway horse when the trail turned to scree.

Johnny first bolted after Brogan and Tucker, but horse and rider quickly disappeared as the trail turned into the dense lodgepole forest, with Brogan alternately kicking and then brutally whipping the horse's rear end.

Annie had also disappeared, up the right fork of the trail. He knew that trail well. Knew that a field of scree awaited her a half mile ahead.

Johnny Yellow Kidney began running in that direction.

Twenty

Will led Buddy over the rocky trail.

Haldis Beck, hands cuffed behind her, had not said a word since they started out.

Will had to admit, she was one tough little thing. She clearly didn't know horses, could barely reach the stirrups and mount Buddy, and having her hands bound behind her must have thrown her off balance, but that stout, compact body of hers maintained almost perfect posture.

They would get down to the ranger station in a hell of a lot less time if Will had just climbed on Buddy behind her. The gelding could handle it, no problem. But he'd made that mistake eighteen years earlier—climbing on Kola, his loyal equine partner, behind another woman he'd arrested to ride the twelve miles to the Upper Loop Road. It wasn't just the woman's crime, and Will's obsession with protecting the wildlife in his charge—which was still fueled back then by Rachel and Carter's deaths, and more by anger than the true mission it later became—it was the sight of the baby black bear returning to the corpse of its mother to bawl, charging Will and the woman again and again. The poacher also happened to be one of the most repulsive women Will had ever seen—dirty hair, teeth filled with spit tobacco.

Climbing onto that horse behind her had made him want to vomit.

And then, during her initial hearing, she'd accused him of sexual harassment, saying he'd fondled her breasts on the ride back to the road in the Lamar, where the reinforcement Will radioed ahead for was waiting.

Any judge but Judge Sherburne, in order to be politically correct, might have at least let that charge play out in the courtroom. But the judge had responded with, "Take one look at that man and tell me why he'd want, or need, to have anything to do with someone like you. If you pursue those lies, I'll cite you for contempt of court and throw away the key."

Will found Haldis Beck every bit as repugnant, for what she had done to the wolverine in Yellowstone. But on the surface, she'd have a better argument. And there weren't many Judge Sherburnes in the system these days.

Plus, he looked like hell anymore. So who knew how something like that would play out?

And so he'd decided to walk Haldis Beck back to the Cut Bank ranger station.

They were coming down from the ridge, from high alpine country, country almost no humans had traversed, when he saw the telltale sign: the remains of what looked like a muskrat, hanging from a spike in a tree.

"Get down," he ordered Haldis, bringing Buddy to a stop, then reaching up for her elbow to steady her as she swung her right leg over the back of the horse and dropped to the ground.

"What?" she said. "Time for a picnic?"

Will eyed her for several seconds.

"I wasn't sure I needed to do this, but that attitude makes me feel downright good about it. Sit down."

Will thought he detected a flicker of alarm in the cold brown eyes, but shaking free of the hand he offered in assistance, Haldis obeyed.

Then she saw Will reach for a second set of handcuffs, eyeing her ankles.

"You bastard."

Will responded with a smile.

"I may have to leave you here for a few minutes."

With that, he disappeared.

He only had to go ten feet beyond the tree bearing the muskrat remains to find what he was looking for. He heard it, knew what he would see, before he saw it. He just hadn't expected it to be a wolverine.

The animal's front left leg was caught in a leghold trap. He had begun chewing his paw off, just above the trap's teeth.

Will had come upon many animals over the years who had tried to do the same thing, but each of those times, the animal was already dead, unsuccessful in its desperate bid to live, or alive and forced to fight for survival—always a challenge in Yellowstone's brutal backcountry—on three legs and a stump that may or may not have been usable. This was the first time he'd intervened *during* the process, and based on what he was seeing, Will felt confident that if he could release it, the wolverine would be able to survive, even if it ended up three-legged.

But as Will moved toward it, his heart stopped. And then the adrenaline rush of anger took over.

A second trap, behind the first. The wolverine's hind leg was caught in it.

Will had only seen this one other time—a trapper so heinous and cruel that he set two traps.

An animal caught in a trap could just about be counted on to thrash about and end up triggering the second trap, and this way, should it be able to chew its foot off, the likelihood of escaping the second, already injured, bleeding, and in shock, was pretty much nonexistent.

Fury engulfing him, Will circled the animal, trying to assess the damage.

Baring his teeth, growling with a ferocity that had caused early naturalist Ernest Thompson Seton to label it "fierce, a demon of destruction"—which had always pissed Will off, for what animal isn't going to be fierce when caught in a trap, which is just about the only time anyone ever sees *Gulo gulo*?—the wolverine tried to rotate along with Will, in order to keep this new predator directly in front of him.

The back leg looked like the steel trap had snapped it in two.

That meant the wolverine would not only be three-legged, were Will to set him free, but one of those legs, which otherwise looked healthy—it did not appear to be infected—would be broken.

Will drew his gun.

He stood there pointing it at the wolverine, making certain one bullet would do the ugly job, a tear streaming down his face.

He stood there like that, absolutely motionless, for several minutes.

And then, something about the way the wolverine looked back at Will—about the fire in its eye; the throaty growl that voiced its determination to live—caused Will to lower the gun. Place it back in its holster.

"I think I can save you little guy."

Removing his vest and shirt and loosening his belt, Will got within two feet, and threw the shirt over the wolverine's head. Diving for the frantic animal, who no longer could see his enemy, Will wrapped his arms around its torso. The wolverine bit Will again and again, through his shirt, mostly missing but occasionally taking its toll, but Will managed to slide its small, shirt-covered head through the armhole of the opening of his vest, and ripping his belt off, like a calf roper, he wound it around its compact torso, wrapping the animal almost like a present. As he grappled with the springs of first the front leghold, and then the one holding its back leg, the wolverine bit him two more times, growling and thrashing the whole time, but when Will picked him up, he suddenly quieted, almost went limp.

He'd gone into shock.

When Will returned to Haldis and Buddy carrying his bundle, he did not look his prisoner's way.

He tied the wolverine, as gently but securely as possible, to his saddle, promising him silently that if he didn't make it, Will would return him to the mountain.

"Let's go," he said, turning to Haldis. "You're on foot now."

"You've got to be kidding? For how long?"

"Ten miles. Maybe more."

"You're making me walk for a fucking, half-dead animal?" she replied in disbelief.

Will turned on her.

Any trace of humor, any remnants of what might be considered a handsome face, had suddenly disappeared.

"Do you know anything about that animal?" he asked. "Do you know how much courage and strength and stamina that little critter has? That he can hold his own against a bear, or a pack of wolves? That he doesn't want anything to do with you, or me, or any of us who are determined to wipe him and all his kind out?

"All he wants is to find a way to live in these high places. And to be left alone." He looked the animal's way. "And this is what he gets. This is what we do to him."

Haldis was unimpressed.

"I'll bring this up in court. You have an obligation to protect me."

"Yeah, well, just consider this partial restitution for

what you did to that wolverine in Yellowstone," Will replied icily, as he checked the ties on the wolverine one more time.

"And be glad you're not the one who did this to him."

Haldis Beck had been studying him. Making no attempt to hide her disdain, she replied, "What is it with you? What makes a man like you tick?"

Will had been asked that question, in one form or another, dozens, perhaps hundreds, of times over the past two and a half decades. In all that time, he'd only given one person—Annie—an honest answer. He wasn't about to dignify this woman, whom he considered human scum, with a response.

Uneasy, Buddy shifted weight repeatedly as the wolverine resumed its protest—growling blindly, flopping around pathetically on the saddle.

Will eyed the agitated bundle thoughtfully.

Maybe he was wrong. Maybe he should have put him out of his misery when he first came upon him.

Stepping over to where Haldis Beck still sat on the ground, Will reached down, removed the cuffs from her ankles, stuck his hand under her arm, and yanked her to her feet.

"Get up and walk."

With Will holding onto Buddy's reins, his prisoner several paces ahead of him and the bundle on the saddle spasming periodically, the unlikely group continued down the mountainside.

Twenty-one

Each long-legged stride elevated Johnny's fear for Annie's safety as he sprinted along the rocky, narrow trail that first skirted the west side of Mount Henry, then, several miles to the north and east, began its descent to Cobalt Lake, after which the trail flattened out, before ending at Upper Two Medicine.

At the speed he'd last seen his gelding galloping away, with Annie clinging to the saddle horn—and, it appeared to Johnny, only one rein in hand—they should reach the scree field any second.

Johnny always dismounted to cross that field. Consisting of tens of thousands of loose talus rocks deposited by a glacier on the move thousands of years earlier, bordered by a precipitous drop-off into the canyon created by the river below, trying to cross that section of the trail on an out-of-control horse spelled disaster.

All Johnny could hope was that Annie had been able to halt the horse before reaching it.

That hope was nourished when Johnny first felt the reverberations under his feet—hooves and, clearly, the horse they belonged to was running and coming his way—then quickly dashed when Rusty rounded the bend ahead and Johnny saw he was riderless, reins dragging on the ground, nostrils flaring and sweat-lathered.

With the gelding running his way at full speed, Johnny planted himself in the middle of the trail, arms up; but he was forced to sidestep when it became clear the horse would not stop on its own. As Johnny dove for the dragging reins as Rusty ran by, he got a blurred glimpse at its left leg and shoulder. They were ripped to shreds.

His left fingers felt the strip of leather slipping through them. Johnny's right hand took purchase and he held tight, allowing his body to be dragged along the trail for several yards, but a rock threw him into the air and flipped him onto his back. As a teen, Johnny had been a junior rodeo star during Indian Days in Browning and had often managed to flip himself right-side-up again, to the delight of the crowds, but two decades had taken their toll. Johnny lost his grasp and the horse sped off, reins still dragging behind.

The fleeting sight of the damage to the gelding's left side had told Johnny the story: he had fallen on the talus slope, no doubt begun sliding downhill, and somehow, miraculously managed to regain his footing before the drop-off and climb back up to the trail.

As Johnny climbed to his feet, he couldn't shake the image from his mind.

How much of that ride had Annie been along for?

Twenty-two

"We have them in our sights."

High on a ridge, the camouflage-clad gunman, cell phone sandwiched between his shoulder and ear, looked at his companion and mouthed the word "shit."

His arms cradled a 20-gauge shotgun. He actually got it for free when the Hamilton, Montana RadioShack offered a gun for signing up for DISH Network (PROTECT YOURSELF WITH DISH NETWORK the sign outside read). It was the kind of weapon a hunter used for anything from squirrels to deer. Though the debate about wolves being delisted was still raging in his home state of Montana at the time, and the Rocky Mountain gray wolves were still protected under the Endangered Species Act, that first weekend, it had been the instrument of death to an entire pack.

"I repeat," he said now. "We have both of them in our sights. Do we have clearance?"

What the gunman did not say is that the only reason they had their charges in their crosshairs now was because, having failed miserably in finding them, they had

climbed the highest peak in the vicinity in order to find
cell phone coverage so that they could call and report
that they were calling it quits and returning home. Ironically, at the top of a ridge, through binoculars, they'd
spotted the horse first, which they'd actually debated
about shooting—thinking at first it was a moose—and
then the two subjects on foot came into view.

Four hundred thirty-five miles south and east, at the
mouth of Yankee Jim Canyon, along the highway leading
to Yellowstone, another camo-clad male sat atop a cold
woodstove, pressed the mute button on his cell phone,
and turned to the mountain of a man beside him.

Brahma Shields' size alone would have been enough
to make him an oddity—a menacing oddity. But in addition to looking like he'd played linebacker along with
William "The Refrigerator" Perry, Brahma had a facial
deformity that contributed not only to the nickname
he'd been given as a teen, but also to the years of his
being shunned growing up, and feared as an adult. His
forehead was at least half again as big as a normal
man's.

Brahma had grown up in Corvallis, Montana, a little
town down the Bitterroot Valley, south of Missoula. The
Bitterroot was generally speaking a very conservative
place, home to hunters and ranchers and, more recently,
a few highly compensated CEOs. But it was also a pretty
peaceful little place, downright idyllic, so when Brahma's
politics and rhetoric became a little too hateful for his
neck of the woods, he moved south and east, to Wyoming, where he had no trouble finding people as hateful
and, more importantly, as willing to fight for their rights—
especially the right to shoot on sight any fucking wolf
stupid enough to cross Wyoming soil—as Brahma.

Brahma had founded Justice 4 All. You see, Brahma
didn't believe the world was just—not to people like
him. And he had decided to fight for the justice he and

others like him were being denied. One of the rights most dear to Brahma was his right to bear arms—as many and any type that he wanted, just as our forefathers had promised with the second amendment. Brahma joined the American Rifle Foundation as a preteen, lying about his age on the application. He had finally found somewhere he fit in. He rose in the ranks of the local ARF, shot up like a shooting star, and managed to do a fair amount of agitating in the process. The locals down there in Corvallis, Hamilton, and Darby actually liked a lot of his ideas, but when the ARF representative from D.C. came out and saw firsthand the dynamics Brahma had created, the organization clamped down on him. At least, officially it did. That's when Brahma started Guns 4 All, moved to Dubois, Wyoming, and then, two months later, decided that Guns 4 All could be something even bigger, and more noble—"Justice 4 All." A "subsidiary," Brahma came to call Guns 4 All, of an organization designed to fight for other important issues of justice for people like Brahma. Issues like wolves, whom Brahma blamed for forcing him to actually hike and walk, sometimes miles, in order to hunt the elk he loved to kill, when once he'd been able to just shoot from his truck, or worst-case scenario, sit on top of a neighbor's barn. And like the latest cause taken up by radical animal rights freaks: banning trapping in his home state—which everyone knew was just the first step in a broader movement to ban hunting. That was the last straw for Brahma.

And thus was born Justice 4 All. It was a clever name. Brahma had thought of it himself. And with issues like wolves and trapping as J4A's agenda, it was easy to get the locals on board, especially once Brahma got hired on as the local school's head janitor. Hell, it was like being paid to recruit other people who shared his passions and willingness to fight for what was right, especially during basketball season, when Braham lingered in the halls chatting with the locals as he waited for the games to end so he could empty the garbage cans, pick up the sticky nacho containers and candy wrappers the assholes had dropped in the seats, and sweep the floors. Hell, the past year or so, with all the wolf and gun issues becoming so hot, the locals had started to come looking for him—sought him out, during games that were already in the bag.

While some in the ARF loved what Brahma was doing, officially the organization denounced Brahma's radical offshoot, Guns 4 All, and publicly stated that it did not sanction its activities or message. No one but Brahma and a few in his inner circle were aware of the financial support they received from Faithe Unsword, who was not only the former governor of the state of Idaho, but also a board member and ex-President of the ARF.

It was actually Unsword who suggested that Brahma have Haldis Beck go underground and infiltrate the gun control groups. Beck had done similar work for the ARF, Unsword informed him. And what do you know, the ARF didn't exactly turn its back on the information Brahma passed along about gun control strategies, did it? It was through the informant that Brahma first learned that the gun control groups had succeeded in getting an invitation for the famous Yellowstone ranger, the guy who saved the fucking alpha female of the Druids, Will McCarroll, to testify before the commission. Brahma had only stepped foot inside Yellowstone once, when he relocated from Dubois to Emigrant, so he'd never met the guy, but once a wealthy supporter from Pray offered Brahma his cabin along the Yellowstone River for Justice 4 All's headquarters, Brahma had seen McCarroll from time to time, driving through the Paradise Valley in his law enforcement car.

No, his ARF contacts didn't turn down the information about McCarroll being asked to testify, did they?

They, in fact, congratulated Brahma for his "resourceful-ness." And then bestowed a true honor on Brahma. They invited him to join a conference call, laying out the danger they felt could be dealt not only to the guns-in-park ruling, but to other new and up-and-coming gun laws the ARF was pushing, should the popular McCarroll testify.

Nobody told Brahma to stop McCarroll from testifying, but Brahma was no dummy. The message was clear: he'd be a hero if he could.

That's what was foremost on Brahma's mind now, when his assistant, barely a teen himself, turned to the big man and said, "They've caught up with McCarroll and Haldis. He has them in his sights."

A third man—this one dressed in slick gym clothes—sat behind a large worktable that dominated the tiny, crude cabin about sixteen miles north of Gardiner, with the water of the Yellowstone River so close they could hear it crashing against the rocks below.

Quinton Barr had actually been the one to come up with the plan on how to take McCarroll out. As a former law enforcement ranger, Quint used to work with Will. "Used to" because Quint no longer worked as law enforcement in the park.

Quint had loved being LE. But as it turns out, some folks decided he loved it a little too much. He'd already had two complaints by visitors about his overzealousness when McCarroll came upon Quint issuing a citation to some local teens for drinking beer at the Boiling River.

The kids were punks. Quint had pulled them over earlier in the day and ticketed them for speeding along Swan Lake Flats. The driver had an attitude, and as Quint walked back to his Jeep, he heard one of the kids in the backseat call him a fag.

Quint Barr, former golden glover from Phoenix, a fag? He'd been pissed at himself for not pulling the little fuck out of the truck and beating him black and blue. It had eaten at him all day long.

It had been a rotten day anyway. One of those days, hotter than hell, that Quint would have to spend most of standing along the highway, at bear and bison jams, directing traffic. Hell, what a shitty use of his time.

And then, that evening, on his way up the hill to check out for the night, he saw their car at the Boiling River.

There were a couple dozen or so other people soaking in clusters when Quint reached the thermal waters. The group of kids were off on their own, in one of the deeper pockets. Quint had kicked the other groups out, told them the river was closed, something about a recovery operation—a body had been seen floating downstream from the bridge by Tower, where someone had seen a jumper.

Horrified, the people hurriedly dressed, then practically raced down the trail a mile to the parking lot, talking amongst themselves, looking back periodically, horrified—both wanting to be there when the body washed ashore, and not wanting to.

When the kids looked over and saw the mass exodus, then recognized Quint, they instantly became alarmed and climbed out of the river, heading, heads down, for their clothes.

Quint had decided to teach two of them a lesson—the driver, and the one with the mouth. Problem was, he wasn't sure which of them had hurled the insult. So in the end, he decided to teach all of them a lesson.

He was working on the third teen—and pretty sure, from the kid's whimpering apologies, that he'd found the culprit—when his legs were taken right out from under him.

He'd actually thought one of the kids had tackled him. It wasn't until he wrestled an arm free to reach for his gun that he recognized the voice of his assailant.

"Mine's already drawn, Quint."

Will McCarroll.

As it turned out, McCarroll had been driving down the hill when he saw the mass exodus, pulled into the parking lot at the forty-fifth parallel, and heard the frantic telling of the story about a body headed downstream.

Quint had been put on unpaid leave the next day, and after a series of hearings, fired. He'd never been able to find a job since, so he spent his days hanging out at the Blue Goose Saloon, where his brother introduced him to a newcomer to the area, Brahma Shields.

Before Brahma's arrival, Quint had become a pariah of sorts in the community. His former LE colleagues shunned him. The lawsuit that one of the kids' parents had filed against him and the Park Service hadn't helped, but the real bitch was that the Park Service had been found not liable, and Quint's wife's paychecks were still being garnished to pay off the judgment against him.

He blamed it all on Will McCarroll, which is why seeing Will become America's hero had about killed Quint.

Once he connected with Brahma and learned what Guns 4 All was all about, it was Quint who had come up with the idea to ensure that Will would not testify before the commission. But because of their history, and the likelihood, if something went wrong, that he would be on the short list of suspects, he knew better than to participate in its actual implementation. Instead, Quint suggested they use the woman informant Brahma had bragged about one night while drinking at the Blue Goose Saloon. Brahma had let Quint mastermind the whole thing, although the woman had offered a nice touch—the help of a trapper friend she'd met at an ARF shindig.

Unfortunately, since Quint was no longer privy to inside information within the park, he hadn't learned that Will had been transferred to Glacier until after the plans to lure him into the backcountry had gone bust. And now *this*—the fucking woman had let herself get arrested by McCarroll.

All of it just upped the hatred that Quint felt for the man, and his obsession with getting even.

The only good thing was that, more and more, Quint was finding that planting ideas in Brahma's head—and then getting Brahma to believe they were his own—was a piece of cake.

Now Quint cleared his throat.

"We need to take care of both of them. The woman had her chance. Now, if McCarroll takes her in, what's to stop her from pointing the finger at us?" Without waiting for Brahma to respond, he turned toward the teen. "Give the order."

As the boy lifted the phone to comply, Brahma's fist struck out, sending the phone flying.

The boy let out a shriek that was equal parts fear and pain.

"What the fuck's wrong with you, you little shit?" Brahma yelled. "Did I tell you to give any orders?"

Silent, fighting tears, the kid shook his head.

"What? I can't hear you," Brahma screamed.

"No," the kid said, literally cowering as Brahma stepped in his direction.

Instead, Brahma turned suddenly, redirecting his wrath toward Quint, who still sat with running shoes plopped on top of the worktable.

"And who the fuck do you think you are making decisions like that without me?"

Dumbstruck, Quint jumped to his feet.

Holding both hands chest high in front of him, palms facing Brahma in a symbol of surrender, he replied, "Hey, I wasn't trying to make decisions without you. I was just giving my opinion."

Massive chest heaving, Brahma stood there, glaring at him.

"You think you can get me to do whatever the hell you want, don't you?"

Golden gloves or not, Quint fought an acute urge to step backward.

"Of course not. You're in charge. You always will be. But listen, Brahma, it only makes sense. We have a chance to take McCarroll out right here and now. The woman's expendable."

Brahma wasn't convinced.

"I gave her my word. I told her we'd provide backup, in case anything went wrong. My word means something."

Quint had long suspected that Brahma, who to his knowledge had never been with a woman, believed when the two met—which was the plan after she fled to Canada—that she'd fall in love with him. More than once, he'd heard Brahma on the phone telling her, "We'd make an unbeatable team."

"Anything went *wrong*?" Quint echoed. "It's *all* gone wrong. Isn't she accountable for that? Hell, if she talks we're all going down. Think about it. Think what's at stake. All you've worked for. She's botched it."

Sensing Brahma wavering, he added, "She bungled it. Thank God you decided to check up on her right away when she went silent. The whole point was to silence Mc-Carroll, stop him from testifying before the commission. That was the mission. We can still make that happen."

Brahma fell silent.

Quint had seen one other outburst like this, which subsided quickly. Sensing the worst was over, he risked pushing.

"This isn't just about guns in the park. If we let them take that away, automatic weapons will be next. And extended magazines. All the headway we've made— guns in bars, on campuses—*all* of it is at risk if McCarroll appears before the commission. If he's not there, the whole affair will take place under the radar. But if he's there, it will be a media circus. The whole fucking country will be watching, and buying into what he says. The politicians we've been able to count on will cave to the pressure. You know that. You saw how they made a hero out of him after that wolf shit went down."

Brahma's hand went up to his temple, pressed against it. He was prone to headaches, migraines, ever since he was a little kid. The doctors had told his parents it had to do with his oversized forehead. It happened whenever he lost his temper.

Finally, he spoke.

"I need to consult with someone before making a decision."

Quint knew who the "someone" was. The mystery man he'd overheard Brahma talking to several times now, someone named Tony. Quint didn't trust him to agree with his suggestion that the gunmen take both McCarroll and Haldis Beck out.

He shook his head in frustration.

Brahma seemed not to notice. He turned to the kid, who had retrieved the phone from the floor.

"Tell them not to lose them," he ordered. "Tell them to wait for word from us."

"Yes, sir," the kid replied.

Annie knew her leg was broken—she'd heard it snap against the rock she'd landed on when she tumbled off the horse.

What she didn't know was if the bone had pierced through the skin. A boulder in the avalanche of rocks triggered by the horse's fall had landed on her leg, pinning her. It made it impossible for her to see the damage. The only blessing had been that as the minutes passed, the weight of the rock also caused her leg to go numb.

In the first minutes after she'd come to rest, she hadn't known if she could handle the pain.

She could feel herself slipping in and out of consciousness, which is why when Johnny first appeared, she thought she'd fallen asleep and was dreaming. But the voice was real, and it yanked her back to the present.

"Hold on, Annie. I'm almost there."

She watched as Johnny picked his way down the mountainside toward her. When he dislodged a rock that went airborne for several seconds before hitting earth then, miraculously, bouncing over Annie, Johnny moved sideways two dozen yards, to the field of loose scree.

"Johnny, don't," Annie yelled. "There's a drop-off right past me."

Ignoring her, feet out in front of him, heels dug in, rear end on the rocks, he rode the flow of talus rocks down, managing somehow to roll off the tidal wave he created in the process—which continued on to the drop-off— and finding his way to Annie's side.

"Oh my god," he said when he saw her leg pinned under a boulder.

"It's broken," Annie said, almost matter-of-factly.

The boulder sat squarely on top of her lower left leg. Johnny stepped to Annie's right side, positioned himself dead center with the rock and, using all of his weight and strength, tried to roll it off her.

The rock didn't budge.

He tried again. He knew that his weight against the boulder had to be causing Annie further pain, but she remained silent.

Finally, after his third attempt, he heard her voice.

"Johnny . . . ?"

He looked down at Annie. She was in shock, and frightened.

Dropping to his knees beside her, he took her hand, cradled her in his other arm.

"You're going to be all right," he said. "I won't let anything happen to you. Do you hear?"

When she didn't respond, he repeated, "Annie, do you hear me? I'm not going to let anything happen to you."

Annie simply nodded her head in reply.

Johnny wished he felt as assured as he hoped he sounded. As he cradled Annie, his eyes scanned the hillside for what he would need: a sturdy branch and a wedge-shaped rock. The rock, or some combination of rocks, would be doable, but the mountainside was bare of branches of any size or strength. He would have to climb back to the trail to find a tree limb to pry the boulder off Annie's leg.

That alone would present a huge danger to Annie— that the next time he tried to descend, Johnny would keep rolling down the steep terrain and plummet over the drop-off just ten or twelve feet beyond where she'd come to rest.

It was then that he realized the boulder pinning her had probably saved her life as she rolled toward the drop-off.

When Annie collapsed against his shoulder and closed her eyes, Johnny reached inside his vest pocket.

He needed to reassure himself that the one last resort would at least be available to help Annie—if all else failed.

A sense of cold dread enveloped him as his fingers closed briefly around the Buck knife he'd stashed there for emergencies.

Twenty-three

The group of five had set out at daybreak.

Cole Ingram and girlfriend Whisper Little Wolf, Spencer Four Bear, and Tim and Billy Boyd, twin sons of Tom Boyd, tribal councilman, had been talking about a backcountry trip all summer. During many a night of dealing with obnoxious, liquored-up tourists or locals, debating destinations, routes, and comparing notes from past adventures had helped time pass until closing.

All five waited tables, cooked, or washed dishes at the Snow Slip, a Highway 2 bar and restaurant midway between Essex and East Glacier, and since it was Indian Days in Browning, which meant business would be slow, as the locals and tourists all headed for Browning for this annual event, and four of the five of them—all but Cole—were Blackfeet, their boss had surprised them the night before by telling them to take the next two days off.

Their dream trip called for them to spend four days on foot hiking the arduous trails into the backcountry to an alpine lake known as Beaver Woman. The Boyd twins, who were experienced alpine climbers, planned an ascent of Savage Mountain.

With the unexpected gift of two free days—not the four they needed to get to Beaver Woman—as they cleaned up after an especially crazy night at the Snow Slip, they'd begun debating about a closer destination when Cole slipped away to the pay phone next to the Snow Slip's front door. Within a few minutes he'd returned, grinning.

"I just talked to Romey," he announced. "He said he can give us enough horses. We can still make it to Beaver Woman and back."

Romey Harding was the father of Blake, one of two white kids in the class behind Cole and Spencer's at Browning High. Blake got a master's degree at the University of Montana, married, and now taught biology at Salish Kootenai Community College on the Flathead Reservation. He and his wife had been trying to get Romey, a widower, to move down to Ronan, but Romey would have none of it. He was something of a celebrity in the area, though no one could quite say why. For twenty-some years he'd owned a dude ranch on Highway 2, about twenty miles outside of East Glacier, between Snowslip, Montana and the Elk Mountains.

Two days worth of food and supplies, disassembled fly rods, and camera tripods sticking out of the tops of their backpacks, their moods were jovial when the quintet rolled out of Cole's VW van the next morning at Romey's ranch. The only friction that had marred the morning, but only slightly, arose over the fact that when the twins had stopped by Cole's trailer in town that morning to ride with Whisper and him, Cole spotted their climbing gear—and, in a bag of groceries they'd bought, a bottle of tequila and some weed.

"None of that shit goes with," Cole had declared. "There's not gonna be time to climb, and either that other stuff stays, or you stay."

Almost a decade younger than Cole and Spencer, and still finding their way in a land where sobriety was often the exception, and not the rule, Tim and Billy had protested weakly; but like most the guys who worked at or frequented the Snow Slip, they were secretly in love with Whisper, and at her reprimand and reminder that Cole had not touched liquor for four months, they apologized.

"But how about the climbing gear? Even if we don't have time for Savage, there's plenty of good climbing just around Beaver Woman."

Cole smiled good-naturedly.

"I guess as long as you guys carry all that shit, the climbing gear can go."

Always up before dawn, Romey had four of the five horses saddled and ready to go by the time they arrived.

"Hell, you kids look like you've packed enough to make it to Antarctica," he said, greeting each with a strong hug.

"Why don't you join us?" Cole asked.

Tall, ruggedly handsome and hollow cheeked, with eyes that hinted at a few demons still wandering around inside his head from days gone by, Romey's laugh showed he was pleased to think the young folks still liked his company.

"You don't need an old fart like me tagging along." He nodded toward the barn, and the hills beyond it, where another dozen horses grazed. "I've got wolves. I promised my daughter-in-law I'd string up some fladry fencing before I start shooting the fuckers. Then I plan to head into town for the powwow."

The next half hour was spent tying packs onto horses and adjusting saddles.

"Just take care of them," Romey said before directing the group to the trail. "Once you reach Coal Creek, they've got a helluva climb."

The rest of the morning was going smoothly, each person exhilarated to actually be experiencing not only fresh morning air, but also a brilliant fire-red sunrise. All five worked until the wee hours of the morning, and as a result rarely got outside early in the day. After a summer of waiting on tourists who'd just returned from a glorious day in the park, to be climbing a mountain trail on horseback, sun in their eyes—well, it didn't get much better than this for kids who had grown up with Glacier as their playground.

Half an hour after reaching Coal Creek and turning to follow it east, Billy, whose horse had just decided to take the lead, pulled up and called out, "Holy shit."

A lone horse raced their way.

"Hey, that's Johnny's horse," Spencer cried as the animal blew by them, bolting over downed trees as he dodged them on the trail.

"You sure?" Cole asked.

"Hell yes, I'm sure. It's Rusty. I grew up riding him. When we moved to town my dad gave him to Johnny."

Without another word, Spencer turned his mare on a dime and headed in the direction of the frantic gelding.

As he began to catch up with the exhausted animal, Spencer put two fingers to his mouth and let out the whistle—the same one he'd used as a child to call the gelding home.

Magically, the horse slowed, and within minutes, Spencer was riding alongside of him, reins in hand. By the time the others caught up, Spencer was on the ground, examining the gelding's injury.

Whisper gasped at the sight.

"What do you think happened?"

"I'm pretty sure I know," Spencer replied. Then,

looking at Cole, he said, "That scree field, on the other side of Cut Bank pass."

"That's just what I was thinking."

"Last time I saw Johnny," Spencer added, "he told me he'd found traps up that way over the summer. I bet he went up to check."

Another thing common to kids who'd grown up exploring the wilds of a place like Glacier was that they quickly learned about its dangers, grim statistics, and the need to think and act quickly. By the time they reached their twenties and thirties, most were as resourceful and competent as professionally trained responders.

As a whitewater guide, Cole had pulled many a rafter out of the water. Now he took charge.

"We have to go look for Johnny. His horse is still pretty fresh so he can't be far. Once we find him, Whisper can take off and find a place where there's cell coverage to call for help."

He turned to her.

"How does that sound?"

In addition to waiting tables at the Snow Slip, Whisper had long held another job in East Glacier—that of moving the Glacier Park Lodge's horses down from the mountains in the morning to the stables located between the resort and golf course—a task she did bareback, with the grace and athleticism of someone who learned to ride before she walked, glorious black, waist-length hair flowing behind her. On evenings she wasn't working at the Snow Slip, after all the trail rides had ended, sometimes accompanied by a cowboy, sometimes alone, she'd shepherd sometimes as many as thirty horses back up to their night pasture.

It was an image that stuck with a person, and was one of the reasons so many young men in Glacier, as well as those visiting the area for the first time, fell in love with Whisper.

It was also the reason that Cole's plan made good sense.

"Let's hurry," she replied now.

"Don't fall asleep," Johnny said, shaking Annie softly. "Annie, do you hear me? You can't fall asleep."

Johnny had spent the past several minutes holding Annie, keeping her propped up, while he surveyed the landscape—and his options. None of which pleased him.

Annie's eyes fluttered open, but they lacked focus.

Johnny cupped her chin in his hand.

"Look at me."

Holding her face, he willed the brown eyes that were normally so warm and full of expression to meet his—to connect with him. When they finally did, a small part of him, very small, felt just a measure of relief.

Her color was good, but who knows whether she had other injuries, perhaps internal, or maybe a falling rock had hit her head—time was critical.

As he held her, he began removing his jacket, wrapping it around her shoulders.

"I'm going to have to leave you," he told her. "Hopefully just for a few minutes. I have to find something to get this rock off your leg."

He also needed to make some kind of rope to secure both of them when he did come back with what he needed to pry the rock off Annie—to keep them from sliding off the talus slope.

"No!"

In light of how shocked Annie seemed, the force of her reply surprised him. It also gave him hope.

"Don't leave me, Johnny. Please. I'm scared."

"I know you are, sweetheart. But we have to get you out of here."

Annie nodded.

"I know."

He hugged her then, held her close, without saying a word.

As he drew back, his heart literally feeling like it might give out, he reached for the Buck knife. He'd spent the past minutes debating about how much he needed it for the work he had to do to save Annie—or whether she could end up needing it more. For Johnny knew the harsh reality—that there was a chance, a not-insignificant chance, that he might not even make it back up the talus slope to the trail.

Meeting her gaze fully, he said, "You won't need this. I'll make sure you don't. But if something should happen to me, if no one comes . . ."

Annie's eyes had dropped to the knife in the palm of his hand.

Silent, she nodded her head.

As Johnny started to stand—hand steadying himself on a granite rock just above them—the sound of Annie's trembling voice almost took his legs out from under him.

"Johnny, why did you disappear on me like that? Why did you leave Seattle without even saying good-bye?"

He dropped down in front of her. On his knees, he again cupped her chin in his hand.

"It wasn't anything you did," he said. "I was just this messed-up kid from the rez, and I'd fallen in love with this intelligent, beautiful woman from another world. More and more, I realized this was where I was meant to be, and I knew you could do better. I knew you had big fish to fry." His smile was so warm, so beautiful, that Annie's eyes brightened briefly. "And turns out I was right. Look at you. You're a judge, ruling over this nation's first national park. And I'm still just an Indian kid doing what I love, where I was meant to do it."

"No regrets?" Annie said.

Johnny's laugh surprised himself.

"Oh no, that's not true. Lots of regret. But only about you. I never forgot you, Annie. I thought I'd stop breathing when I saw you in the lodge the other day. I couldn't even bear to stay in the room and watch you up there giving your presentation."

He looked away, marshaling strength.

"No regrets about coming back to my people, my land. But lots of regrets when it comes to you."

Standing, he said, "Annie, don't sleep. Please. I'll be back."

"Don't leave me, Johnny," Annie pleaded. "Not yet. Stay for another minute or two."

Heart sinking, Johnny dropped back to his knees beside her, and held her. With Annie silent, eyes closed, he held her close, and a story he'd heard from a seasonal ranger—a young man who'd only worked in Glacier one summer, but prior to that summer, had worked in the Grand Tetons for two summers—surfaced in his mind, where he'd already sensed it lurking.

The story involved a young married couple, climbers, from Spokane. They were part of a mountaineering club, and they'd stayed behind after the rest of the group had departed, to climb the Grand together. On the way up, they'd crossed a scree field, not unlike the one Johnny and Annie now sat upon, and the wife had triggered a rock slide. Her husband had been swept away in it, and she'd watched as a boulder rolled over him as he lay downhill.

She could tell he was badly injured, and in shock, and she wasn't strong enough to carry him out. Nightfall was just hours away.

She'd made the excruciating decision to leave him, to go for help, but by the time she reached radio coverage and was able to put out an SOS, it was already dark. The search and rescue team, which the young ranger had been part of, was assembled and ready to go at daybreak, but when they reached the injured climber, he was already dead.

The woman had broken down in the young ranger's arms, beside herself at having left her husband to die alone on the mountain.

The ranger had confided in Johnny that that's when he knew he wasn't cut out for backcountry work. He'd come to Glacier to give it one more try, to see if a new landscape might make a difference, but he'd decided that summer to quit ranger work altogether.

That story had stayed with Johnny, and now, his greatest fear was that he wouldn't get back to Annie in time. That she, too, could die alone.

Blackfeet are a spiritual, strong people, so much so that they sometimes hear voices, visualize their dreams, their most fervent hopes, in a way that few non-native people could relate to. And so when Johnny first heard the voice, his eyes closed in prayer.

His great-grandfather was calling to him. He would tell Johnny what to do.

But then he actually recognized *this* voice. It belonged to Cole Ingram.

"*I found him.*"

Eyes wide, Johnny stifled a sob at the sight hanging over the rim of the trail above. Cole's moppy head of hair disappeared just briefly, then reappeared.

This was no dream.

"Hold on, Johnny," Cole yelled. "We're roping up to come down to you."

"What the fuck is that thing on the saddle?"

The two Guns 4 All thugs had managed to keep Will McCarroll and Haldis Beck in sight by moving along the ridge east and high above the trail below. The two, still on foot, with one horse, would disappear from time to time from view, but they'd lucked out when they'd climbed this peak, which turned into a ridge, a bridge of sorts, between two mountains, because the ridge seemed to pretty much parallel the trail, and so inevitably, the group returned to the gunmen's sight.

"Let me see," the larger and dumber-looking of the two said, reaching for the high resolution binoculars.

"Holy fuck. It's moving."

"That's what I been telling you."

He fiddled with the focus.

"It's some kind of animal. Why the fuck does that asshole have an animal tied to the saddle?"

"Who knows?" He fumbled in his pocket for his phone, lifting it high above him, watching the screen as he rotated 360 degrees. "The only thing I do know is there's no fucking cell phone coverage out here. I keep checking. And any minute now we're gonna lose them. Then what?"

"I'll tell you then what. We're fucked. 'Cause we're fucked if we do, we're fucked if we don't."

"You're probably right, but I say we're more fucked if we don't."

He watched below as the trio disappeared from sight again.

"What're you thinking?"

"I say we're gonna have to make the decision. She's gonna be charged with attempted murder so you better believe she'll be willing to make some kind of deal."

"You think she'll talk?"

"Wouldn't you? Why would she take the rap all herself? If she tells them they've got bigger fish to fry, they'd probably be happy to let her off for just talking."

"Then I don't see what the problem is. We gotta do what we gotta do."

"That's what I'm thinking. Hurry, we better try to get ahead of them."

He threw a beer can on the ground, spat a wad of juicy chewing tobacco.

"Next time they break into a clearing, we go for it."

Twenty-four

"Annie," Johnny said, shaking her shoulders, "help's arrived. You're going to be okay."

Annie's eyes opened.

"You're not leaving me?"

Johnny smiled. The Creator had just delivered a miracle in the form of his cousin and friends. But how much time did Annie have?

"No, I'm not leaving."

The elation passed quickly as he looked up. Three figures he recognized had now appeared on the crest of the trail above: Cole, Spencer, and Billy Boyd. Johnny could see Spencer helping Billy hurriedly into his climbing harness. Cole stood beside them, winding a rope into a coil. Looking down at Johnny, he yelled, "Here it comes," and with his forceful thrust, the rope flew into the air and came snaking down the hillside as if it were alive.

Johnny reached for it, caught it on his first try. When he finished tying it around Annie's waist, he yelled, "Her leg's pinned under this boulder. We need something to pry it off."

Spencer disappeared before his voice reached Johnny: "I'll see what I can find."

"Cole," Johnny yelled, "is there enough rope to reach a tree on the upside of the trail?"

Cole shook his head no.

"Then keep Spencer there to hold on to Annie while you hold on to Billy. This stuff is incredibly dangerous. And you'd better start down from us a little way. You're sure to trigger slides."

Spencer's freckled face reappeared almost immediately.

"What about you?"

"Don't worry about me. I'll grab hold of the rope if I need to."

Johnny watched as Cole anchored the rope for Billy, who'd moved a dozen feet down trail. As he descended the slope, he set off two small slides that sent rocks flying. Shielding Annie with his body, several rocks that had been launched into the air pummeled Johnny's back.

Several minutes later, when Billy Boyd reached them, Johnny pulled him to his chest in a hug.

"You're a sight for sore eyes."

Billy had already begun assessing Annie's situation.

"Holy shit."

Johnny glanced at Annie, hoping his reaction didn't alarm her, but her eyes had closed again.

"How many more ropes do you have up there?"

"I think this is it," Billy replied, eyes glued to the massive rock atop Annie's leg. "Do you think we could roll that sucker off her?"

"I've tried, but maybe together we can do it."

The two spent several minutes assessing what direction to push in order to minimize the risk of the moving rock doing further harm to Annie. Once they'd made a decision, they positioned themselves and on the count of three, they pushed.

Both men cringed when Annie let out a sharp cry. The rock didn't even quiver.

"Stop," Johnny shouted.

He stood, rethinking a plan he'd come up with earlier, while holding Annie—one which he considered too dangerous to try alone, with Annie not roped for security. He looked up to the trail, where both Cole and Spencer now stood directly above them, ropes tied around their waists, gloved hands keeping tension on the lifelines.

"Let's see if we can get it to roll off on its own."

Dropping to his knees, Johnny began selecting the smaller, key rocks that seemed instrumental in holding the boulder in place. When Billy got the idea, he joined him. Within minutes, the big boulder wobbled. Johnny saw that Annie was suppressing a cry.

"Stop," he yelled, but Annie raised a hand in protest.

"No. It's working. Do it. Fast."

Frantic now, both men began throwing rocks downhill, where they would tumble briefly before cascading into a free-fall off the edge.

"Here she goes," Billy suddenly shouted, and with one last push, the boulder wobbled briefly and then, almost as if in slow motion, began to roll.

Once free of support, it picked up speed and crashed down the mountainside, disappearing from sight, soundless.

Annie had rolled onto her side, clutching her leg, sobbing silently.

When she realized Johnny was hunched over her, she said, "I'm okay. I'm okay."

Johnny had never felt more sick, or more grateful.

"Let's get her out of here."

Billy didn't need to be urged. With one man on each side, and Johnny holding her elbow with one hand and the rope attached to her waist with the other, Cole and

Spencer began pulling the ropes in, hand-over-hand, raising Annie up the hillside.

Half a dozen arms reached for her as she neared the top. Johnny recognized Whisper Little Wolf, who wrapped a blanket around Annie as she was pulled over the edge and onto the trail.

"You're okay," Whisper repeated over and over to Annie as Cole lifted her in his arms and, with Johnny and Spencer guarding against his stumbling and falling on the scree field, carried her toward where Tim Boyd stood with the reins of the horses in hand.

"Johnny," Cole cried, "take my mare. The fastest way to help would be to go back to Romey's. We can call for a medevac about two miles from there. I'll ride with Whisper."

As Johnny put one foot in the stirrup, Annie opened her eyes.

"No," she cried, eyes fixed to Johnny. "Someone else has to take me back. You have to go find Will."

Johnny stepped back to the ground.

He knew that voice, the determination it held, and knew he had to deal with it firmly.

"Annie, we've got to get you to an ambulance. That's the number one priority."

"It doesn't take all of you to do that. Please, Johnny, go after Brogan. You have to catch up to him before he reaches Will. Please. Let someone else take me back."

Johnny drew in a deep breath and paused, but only briefly.

"She's right," he said. "Will McCarroll's in serious trouble. We need to break up. Cole, can you and Whisper get Annie back to Romey's? The rest of you come with me. We need to catch up with Bridger Brogan."

Cole and Whisper echoed his words in unison, "Bridger Brogan?"

At any other time, the expressions each wore would

have made Johnny curious, perhaps even alarmed, but right now all that mattered was that Annie needed immediate help. He didn't give a shit if these kids knew Bridger Brogan or had some issue with him.

That realization was followed immediately by another—the fact that, in all likelihood, they had just saved Annie's life. He owed them an explanation.

"He's part of a plot to kill Will McCarroll," he answered. "He was supposed to be leading us to him, but he deliberately spooked Annie's horse and took off. We need to catch up to him before he reaches Will."

Cole turned to Whisper and with a sternness clearly intended to brook no protest, ordered, "You go with Annie. Billy, you too. I'll go after Brogan."

The tone of Whisper's reply appeared to startle Cole as much as it did Johnny.

"*I'm* going after Brogan."

Johnny watched the two stare at each other for several seconds. Then he'd had enough talk. He had to form a plan to save both Annie and Will.

While he'd known and respected their father his entire life, and Billy had been instrumental in getting Annie up off the mountainside, he knew the person he trusted most with Annie's welfare.

He nodded toward Spencer, who was standing at ready by his horse and seemed prepared for Johnny's order.

"You take Annie back." Then he turned to the Boyd twins, "Tim, you go with them. Billy can come with us."

Stepping in front of Cole, Johnny gently took Annie from his arms.

She had rallied, he could see that, but that could be the adrenaline. There was no time to waste.

"Thank you," Annie said, eyes glistening as she reached up and put a chilled hand to the side of Johnny's face.

At her touch, Johnny felt he might break into tears, but he had to reassure Annie, had to make sure she wasn't frightened. Or worried about Will. Johnny of all people knew the power of emotion and hope.

"I'll find Will," he said, planting a quick kiss on her forehead. "I promise."

Annie nodded as Johnny lifted her into the cradle of Spencer's long arms.

"She'll be alright, Johnny," his cousin said, once he had Annie positioned in front of him, one arm wrapped around her waist, the other holding the reins.

Tim Boyd had already gotten back on his horse and turned it in the direction of Romey's.

Protect her, Creator, Johnny prayed as he briefly watched Spencer and Annie, followed by Tim, retreat back down the trail.

Stepping into the stirrup and swinging his leg up and over the back of the horse he'd taken from Cole, who was now seated behind Whisper on a gray Appaloosa gelding, he turned to the business at hand.

"We need to backtrack to that last fork. That's where Brogan took off."

Cole's eyes, troubled and intense, followed Johnny's nod.

"Where was he headed?"

"Toward Bad Marriage," Johnny replied, turning his horse in the direction they'd last seen Brogan. Billy's palomino was right in step.

"Wait," Whisper cried. "I know a shortcut to Bad Marriage. How big a head start does he have?"

Johnny paused briefly.

"Maybe two hours. It would have to be a hell of a shortcut."

"If I can find it," Whisper replied, "I can beat him there. It's a game trail my grandfather took me on as a little girl. He used to do his vision quests on Bad Marriage. It branches off a couple miles, straight ahead, on this trail." She nodded toward the scree field they'd just left. "Let Cole and me go this way. You two follow behind Brogan."

Skeptical, but also seeing the logic in Whisper's suggestion, Johnny looked at Cole. Once someone deviated from known trails within Glacier's backcountry, finding them again could be impossible.

But somehow he trusted Whisper's confidence.

"You armed?"

Cole nodded.

"Okay," Johnny said. "Be careful on that scree field. We'll look for you up the trail."

Twenty-five

Will McCarroll recognized there was something wrong with the man approaching on horseback the moment he came into their view. To start with, he was obviously injured—his right foot was bare and swung free of the stirrup, and he held it at an angle that kept it from being bumped with the horse's movements. That alone would have been cause for concern, but the direction he was going—toward Will and Haldis Beck—made no sense. If he'd injured himself, he should be headed toward the nearest ranger station, which would be Two Medicine.

And then there was the expression on Haldis Beck's face. When she first saw the grizzled old guy coming their way, not just her face, but her entire posture changed.

The man slowed, waving a hand in the air.

"Thank God," he called. "A ranger. I need help."

As he slowed the black gelding to a halt, even with Will, he lifted his right foot in display.

It was sickeningly mangled, bruised, with a wound that was clearly infected.

Deliberately holding his head down as if to inspect it, Will snuck a look sideways at Haldis.

Instead of looking at the mangled ankle, she was making eye contact with the man.

Will did not look up.

"Let's see if I can help . . ."

Head bent over the man's ankle, Will's back blocked the fact that he was reaching for his holster.

"Bridger, look out," Haldis Beck cried suddenly.

Brogan had just pulled the gun he'd found earlier, inside the pack tied behind the horse's saddle, from the inside of his jacket and pointed it at Will when a bullet shattered his wrist.

Will literally fell back as Brogan screamed, blood spurting from between the fingers of the hand that covered the wrist.

Disbelieving, Will looked at his gun. It had not been fired.

"What the hell?"

Haldis Beck had dived to the ground. She lay there now, staring in horror, certain that her worst nightmare had just come true.

"Holy shit," Cole cried.

Beside him, Whisper Little Wolf calmly reset the lock on her Colt .45 and replaced it in her backpack, barrel still warm.

"We better get down there to help," she said, avoiding eye contact with Cole.

They had crossed over the mountaintop that her grandfather's shortcut entailed and had only a half mile left to descend to the trail leading to Bad Marriage when Bridger Brogan first came into sight below. Fearful of losing him, they'd kicked their horses into a gallop.

The next time Brogan came into sight, he was not

alone. He'd encountered a man and a woman on foot. The man was leading a horse. Even from that distance, Whisper had recognized the new backcountry ranger she'd been seeing around East Glacier: Will McCarroll.

"Hurry," Whisper urged now, as they cut off the barely distinguishable path once traveled by wild horses, and still used occasionally by Glacier's other ungulates, and bushwacked through dense brush to get to the trail below.

When they reached it, they quickly saw that Will McCarroll had the situation under control.

Brogan was on the ground, facedown, as the ranger tied his arms behind him by the elbows. His wrist had been wrapped in gauze.

Ten feet away, also facedown, lay the woman they'd seen from the distance—a prisoner, too, they realized upon seeing her hands cuffed behind her back.

"Will McCarroll?" Cole called out as they approached.

Placing a booted foot on Brogan's back, Will looked up, then finished the job and stepped back to watch the young duo as they approached.

When Cole and Whisper jumped down off their horses, his eyes traveled between the two.

"Which one of you do I have to thank?"

Cole nodded toward Whisper.

"Annie Oakley here."

Whisper seemed not to hear. Her eyes were fixed upon Brogan. Moving with the grace of a mountain lion about to pounce upon its unknowing prey, she approached the trapper and spat on him.

"Pig."

Brogan rolled to the side to look at her, his face blank save for the pain registered in his heavy lidded eyes and the set of his jaw.

"You don't even recognize me, do you?" Whisper asked.

Will had stepped toward the two, but Cole put an arm out to stop him.

"Let her go," he said. "Please."

Uneasy, but having just been saved by this enigmatic woman, Will watched as she locked eyes with the moaning trapper.

"I'm your patient," she said. "How many others have you done it to?"

"I don't know what you're talking about."

"You do know. You pervert. You gassed me and then got your rocks off. You didn't even take the time to fasten my bra. That's how I knew. At first I thought I was just hallucinating. . . ."

"You're crazy," Brogan replied. He looked at Will, "Get her away from me."

Will simply stood watching. Beside him, Cole's hands curled into fists.

When Whisper stepped toward him again, Brogan tried another tack, which was clearly aimed more at Will than at her.

"If I did something like that, why wouldn't you report it?"

"I did report it. But the police said it was your word— yours and your technician's—against mine. They advised me against pursuing it, said it would put me through hell and go nowhere. Especially because your assistant claimed she never left the room."

Suddenly Brogan recognized her. Whisper could see it. So could Will.

"She didn't," he said. His eyes moved to Cole. "Must've been the gas. It can play with your head."

Whisper spat at him again. This time her saliva hit him squarely on the side of the nose. As it slid over its ridge and dripped from its tip to the dirt, which his face was pressed against, she turned away, saying, "You and she both deserve to rot in hell."

She stepped back, joining Cole and Will, who was still trying to figure out why this young couple had come along when they did, and what the hell was happening.

Cole put an arm around Whisper's shoulders. They stood silent, Whisper's face now dead of emotion, until Cole turned to Will and offered an explanation.

"We ran into Johnny Yellow Kidney on the trail," he said. "He's on his way here now, too, to warn you about some kind of plot to kill you. Whisper knew this short-cut so we decided to split up and see who could get to you first."

The explanation did little to relieve Will's confusion.

"How would Johnny have known to warn me?"

"Beats me. The woman he was with got hurt, but she insisted that Johnny come find you."

Will's sense of alarm grew one hundredfold at Cole's words.

"Do you know her name?"

Whisper answered.

"Annie. Her name is Annie."

"How badly is she injured?"

This time Cole responded.

"Hard to tell. She slid off the trail on horseback, on a talus slope. A rock pinned her leg—broke it, but it probably also saved her life 'cause she could've easily gone right over the edge, with the rest of the slide. Two guys from our party took her back to get help."

Will looked over to where Haldis Beck lay on the ground, silent, observing. Somehow she almost looked relieved at Cole's relaying of the information from Johnny Yellow Kidney.

"I suspected someone else was involved. Didn't make sense to me that she'd ambush me without a backup."

"*He* must be the backup," Cole responded, eyeing Brogan, who was straining against the rope Will had bound him with, blood seeping through the gauze at his wrist. "According to what that bastard told Johnny and your friend, he spent two days caught in his own trap. Must've been on his way here at the time. Somehow Johnny and your friend came upon him."

"That explains why she ambushed me alone," Will replied. "She figured he wasn't coming."

Brogan had been listening—but so had Haldis Beck. Both remained silent, but Will suspected that if he got either one alone, he'd hear an earful right now.

That would be his first move when he got them back to Two Medicine.

Cole looked toward the horses, saying, "We'll help you get these two to Two Medicine," when he noticed the bundle on Will's horse shift slightly.

"What the hell is that?"

Will was staring at Brogan.

"It's a wolverine," he replied to Cole, not taking his eyes off Brogan. "And my guess is you're the one responsible for setting the traps I found it in."

Brogan evaded his gaze.

"You are one sorry son of a bitch," Will said, grabbing Brogan by the armpit and lifting him roughly to his feet.

"Bridger Brogan, you're under arrest for conspiracy to commit murder and illegal trapping. You have the right to remain silent. You have the right to an attorney. If you can't afford one . . ."

Will's words were suddenly drowned out by the rapid fire of an automatic weapon splitting the air.

Haldis Beck was the first to cry out, but in the same instant that Will sprinted to protect her by throwing himself on top of her, Whisper, too, screamed.

Cole dived for Whisper, but she had already been struck.

Once the rain of bullets stopped, Will left Haldis to help Cole drag Whisper out of the line of further fire.

Then he returned for Haldis Beck, dodging new fire as he pulled her inert form behind a rock just off the trail.

Clearing her airway, he tried to revive her. Her eyes fluttered open briefly, and Will heard her say, "I knew they'd send someone . . ."

"Who?" he asked, shaking her shoulders gently, trying to keep her conscious. "Who did this?"

But her eyes had closed. Frantic, Will felt for a pulse. Barely perceptible. He began CPR, blowing breath into her lungs, then compressing her chest.

"Come on, breathe. *Breathe.*"

He kept at it for several minutes, sensing all along, from years of experience, that it was too late.

When he turned Haldis Beck over again, he saw why. Lying facedown on the ground, the bullet had hit her in the back of the skull.

Will had forced her to assume the facedown position. It had cost Haldis Beck her life.

Brogan had rolled off the trail and lay half hidden by brush. Will couldn't tell if he'd been hit by this new sniper fire. Ahead, up the trail half a dozen yards, propped up against a lodgepole pine, he could see Cole holding Whisper, cradling her in his arms. She appeared to be alive, but Cole's frantic expression did not bode well.

"Brogan?" Will called out, eyes scanning the ridge above. "Were you hit?"

"What the fuck?" came the reply from under the brush. "How many times am I going to be shot at today?"

Relieved to hear him, Will assessed the situation.

Haldis was dead. He would have to make his way back to Cole and Whisper, see how badly injured she was, and then find a way to get everyone down to safety and medical help.

Will scanned the trail in both directions for the horses. Even if they could carry Whisper the distance, she did not appear to have that much time. He would need the horses to get her the help she clearly needed.

But he did not see a single animal. They had all taken off.

Only 400 feet above them, from the top of a rock formation carved millennia earlier by glaciers on the move, the gunman's grin revealed several teeth missing.

"This is better than shooting wolves," he cried, eye fixed to the crosshairs of his high-powered rifle.

"I dunno," his diminutive companion—who had only fired three bullets to his friend's twenty-five—replied from beside him. "We asked them to give us the okay to take Haldis Beck and the ranger out, not everyone who comes along. We could be in deep shit."

"You moron. Those aren't just people who 'came along.' That Indian bitch is the one who fired the shot that saved McCarroll. If we don't shut her up, too, our whole mission'll be a failure. McCarroll would've taken Beck in and she would've talked. Believe me. She would've spilled her guts in exchange for immunity, or a shorter sentence. Now we just have to finish the job."

"And just how do you propose doing that? Everybody's taken cover."

"Brogan's still in that brush. They're not going anywhere without him. You stay up here, keep them under cover"—he reached into his bag and threw three dozen rounds of extended firepower at him—"and I'll circle around and come at them from the other side."

"This is nuts. Fucking crazy."

The grin on the other's face grew wider.

"I live for this shit."

Grabbing inside his bag again, he smeared black paint over his face.

"Besides, at this point, what do we have to lose?"

Twenty-six

"Something's up."

Johnny Yellow Kidney and Billy Boyd had been moving at a fast clip along the trail when Johnny, in the lead, pulled his horse to a stop.

Billy followed suit, his eyes scanning the thickly forested slopes on either side of the dry creek bed they were following—a trail that was impassable in spring and early summer, when melting snow turned it into a rush of alpine water. Heavy rain, like those they'd had a week earlier, quickly turned the trail soft and undesirable for any travel but wild animals and two-leggeds on horseback. It could also turn the bed into a tracker's treasure, leaving prints, like the fresh ones that told Johnny and Billy they were still on Bridger Brogan's path.

Billy nodded, then said softly, almost to himself, "Silence."

Forests, especially forests in Glacier, were not silent. They were filled with sound, sound that was almost unrecognizable, unnoticeable to many of the tourists whose visits to Glacier were once-in-a-lifetime events; but for those who grew up traversing its trails and mountains, silence—stillness—was dramatic evidence that something was not right.

The horses' ears twitched nervously as the two men sat, taking in their surroundings; waiting, hands moving slowly, instinctively toward their holsters.

"Ahead," Billy cried just as a hair-raising cry sent a cow elk and her yearling crashing through the brush uphill from them.

They moved forward cautiously until it came into sight: a chestnut-colored horse, trapped by a loose rein that had been caught on the branches of a downed tree.

The frantic animal had been fighting for its freedom, and in the process, impaled itself on one of the branches that had broken in the dead tree's fall to earth.

Both Johnny and Billy jumped off their own horses and ran to its aid.

"Whoa, boy, whoa," Billy said soothingly, holding it by the bridle as Johnny sliced the leather strap holding it captive, allowing the gelding to rear back, and revealing a two-inch gash in his underside.

"He must have thrown Brogan," Billy said. Even with the wound, the horse had the strength, and the adrenaline, to practically lift Billy off his feet; but he held firm, bringing the gelding back to the ground, talking soothingly to him as Johnny examined his underside.

"This isn't Brogan's," Johnny replied. "He's a Park Service horse."

It wasn't until he'd calmed enough to keep all four feet on the ground that they realized the gelding carried an oddly shaped bundle, tied to the saddle, and wrapped in a familiar shirt.

"What the hell?" Johnny said, lifting the tail of the shirt—clearly Park Service, and, he realized as he cut through the cord binding it to the contents, one belonging to law enforcement. The name badge that should have been centered over the pocket was missing, but Johnny didn't need it.

Staring at what he'd uncovered, he turned to Billy.

"This is Will McCarroll's horse."

"Doesn't look like McCarroll was actually riding it," Billy said, approaching to get a look at the mare's load.

"Cripes, a dead wolverine."

"He's not dead," Johnny said quickly, lifting it off the saddle as Billy held the horse still.

He laid the limp animal on the ground gingerly, pulled the shirt back and away until he saw the mangled legs.

"Damn," he cried. "Two traps. Will McCarroll found this fella in two traps." He fell silent, struggling to maintain his composure. "He must've thought we could save him."

Kneeling next to Johnny, reins still in hand, Billy shook his head sadly as his eyes took in the wolverine.

Its chest rose and fell slowly, almost imperceptibly. Eyes closed, good legs curled into a fetal–like position.

Billy withdrew his pistol from its holster, handed it to Johnny.

"Here."

Johnny glanced at the gun, shook his head.

"No. He's peaceful. Let's let him pass on his own. It won't be long."

"Yeah," Billy replied softly. "Let the Creator take him."

The reverence in his voice touched a chord in Johnny— one as primal and basic to him now as it had been as a child.

"I've never seen a wolverine up close," Billy whispered. "They're not half as big as they seem. And lots prettier."

He fell silent, and Johnny knew that Billy, too, was asking the Creator to take the wolverine to the other side.

So focused were they on the importance of the journey of the wolverine that they did not hear anyone approach until a voice interrupted them.

"You guys lost?"

Johnny raised his eyes to see a forced smile on the face of a Humvee–sized white man dressed head to foot in camouflage. Specks of spit tobacco filled the crevices between his uneven teeth.

Rising quickly to his feet, Johnny's eyes scanned for a horse, or a pack, that would tell him the man's story.

Nothing.

"You a trapper?"

"Hell no," the man answered quickly. "I know you can't hunt or trap in the park."

"So why the camo?" Johnny asked, then nodding toward the bulk under the man's jacket, he added, "And the rifle?"

The streaks of camouflage paint under the man's chin did not escape Johnny's notice, either. But instinct told him he was about to scare the guy off, so he decided not to push further.

"The rifle's for protection," the man replied, "and your uniform tells me you know it's my right to carry it. And this is how I dress." He sounded civil, almost overly reasonable, but his eyes—Johnny couldn't read exactly what it was, but it was definitely there—told another story. "Listen, I thought you guys might be in trouble. I was just stopping to see if I could help."

Beside him, Johnny heard Billy mutter under his breath.

"This guy's full of shit."

Johnny felt certain he'd found another trapper who'd been setting lines—or, more accurately, the trapper had found him—but the clothing and gun alone, even the hastily removed face paint, weren't enough to accuse him.

And right now Will McCarroll's safety was his priority.

"What direction are you coming from?"

The man hesitated, then nodded his head toward the north.

"Bad Marriage."

Johnny did not flinch.

So, this wasn't about trapping, it was about Will.

In a park with hundreds of climbable peaks, Bad Marriage was not one that people singled out. Only a newcomer would not realize that and would think it was okay to offer up Bad Marriage as a believable destination.

The woman Will was after had chosen it, but from what Will had told him, her selection had some crazy emotional connection with her divorce. This man had some connection with the woman, and Johnny sensed that Will's life depended upon his figuring out just what that connection was.

"Really?" Johnny answered, playing along with the man's story. "We're actually on our way to Bad Marriage right now. See anyone up that way?"

"Not a soul," came the answer, a little too quickly.

"That's odd. A search and rescue operation is under way for a woman who disappeared on Bad Marriage. That's where we're headed."

Johnny was surprised when Billy chimed in.

"We've got an extra horse now," he said, nodding toward Will McCarroll's injured gelding. "We could use your help."

The man's demeanor changed in a heartbeat.

"I'm afraid of horses. Bad back. I'd just slow you down." He looked toward the sky. "Got a long hike ahead of me so I'd better get going."

When he'd disappeared into the trees, Billy turned to Johnny.

"Who the hell do you suppose he is?"

Johnny shook his head.

"I don't have a clue, but he's involved in this in some way. He'd just wiped camo paint off his face."

"I saw that," Billy replied. "Shouldn't we have arrested him?"

"We could've done a citizen's arrest, but we didn't have any real evidence—and a bad arrest could've gotten him off on any charges for anything he's already done. Who knows what he's been up to? Here's what I think we should do. He's on foot. You go ahead on the trail, look for the others, and I'll follow him."

"Sounds a little dicey to me."

Johnny was resolute.

"He's the key. I feel it."

Billy held his gun up, pushed it toward Johnny.

"Here, take this. Brogan's got yours. You're gonna need it more than I will."

"No. I'm okay," Johnny replied.

"You're not armed."

Johnny patted the back pocket of his trousers.

"Got my Buck."

Annie had given the knife back to him when he'd handed her over to Spencer.

Billy shook his head.

"I wish you'd take this, but I know better than to think I can get you to."

Johnny looked at the horses, then the wolverine, who lay peacefully on the ground.

"We'll hobble the wounded horse and come back for him. You take the other two. Now let's get going."

As Billy disappeared down the creek bed on horseback, leading Johnny's gelding, Johnny followed in the direction the camouflaged man had disappeared.

Billy and Johnny hadn't seen him arrive, but Johnny had watched him leave. Now, as he followed his path, it became more clear than ever that the man had a hidden agenda. He could never have seen Billy and Johnny from any trail in the vicinity. He had stumbled upon them as he bushwacked through the woods.

Where had he been headed? And why was he off-trail?

There were only two explanations—that he was hunting or out checking traplines he'd set, or that he was involved somehow in what was going on with Will. The fact that he'd mentioned Bad Marriage made Johnny lean toward the second theory.

But if the other theory proved correct, and he was a trapper, Johnny was just as determined to find a way to prove it and make him pay. Only that would have to wait until Will had been warned.

That very thought stopped Johnny in his own tracks.

The wolverine.

He had left the poor animal to die, still partially bound. He'd been unbinding him when the stranger interrupted him.

He was close on his trail right now, could easily catch up with the man, who looked out of shape—at his size, he had to be slow. Johnny had deliberately been taking it easy, to avoid getting too close to him. It was easy at this point to follow his fresh trail through the brush—to see the broken serviceberry branches and matted-down elephant ear, occasionally confirmed by an actual track in bare ground.

Still, there was risk involved—Johnny could lose him if he turned back, even briefly.

With so much at stake, did his concern for the wolverine—that this animal that Johnny held so much respect and admiration for die peacefully, and free—outweigh that danger?

Johnny's world knew no such thought process, no ability to weigh matters of life and death, how to place one creature's well-being over another's.

It was an impossible question for him to answer.

Hesitating only a second, Johnny turned around and ran at top speed back to where he left the animal.

As he looked down at the peaceful wolverine, all the

emotion of the day boiled up within him. Kneeling to finish unbinding him, Johnny didn't realize he was crying until he saw a drop hit the animal's forehead.

The eyes remained shut, there was no reaction to the tear, nor to Johnny's presence, but the subtle lifting and falling of his ribs indicated the wolverine was still breathing.

"Peaceful crossing, little fella," Johnny whispered.

He stroked the coarse fur, said another short prayer, then stood and glanced at the horse hobbled a dozen yards away. Despite his injury, he had calmed down and now grazed peacefully. Park Service horses were used to the backcountry, and to being hobbled overnight. He would be fine.

Without looking down at the wolverine again, not trusting himself to, Johnny bolted in pursuit of the stranger.

Now, instead of having two minutes on him, the man had ten.

Rifle perched on a pile of rocks he'd constructed just for the purpose—still trained on the trail below—the man's partner's back was to him when he returned, gasping for air from the climb.

"Let's get the fuck out of here," he cried.

His partner turned to him, confusion etched on his face.

"I've been waiting for the signal," he said. "What're you doing back here?"

"I ran into a couple of guys down there, stopped to check them out and see if they were trouble for us. They'd found McCarroll's horse. They were out looking for him and Haldis. The whole fucking park is apparently on its way. We gotta get out of here."

"But what about the mission? What about stopping McCarroll from testifying?"

"The mission's over. We'll be lucky if we get out of here." He turned, looked over his shoulder. "I was sure one of those Indians was following me."

"Indians?"

"Both of the guys I ran into were fucking redskins. One of them had a Park Service uniform on, but lucky for me, he wasn't law enforcement."

"What the hell was he?"

"Beats me. Let's just get out of here. Now."

Twenty-seven

Within an hour of Billy's parting with Johnny, Brogan's horse's tracks had veered east, off the trail, crossing through thick brush and willows before joining an established trail that Billy immediately recognized as heading to Ptmarigan Tunnel, and beyond, Triple Divide, Mad Wolf, and Bad Marriage.

He'd made good time, but he knew that—according to Johnny's telling of the events that led to Annie being hurt and Brogan escaping—the trapper must still be miles ahead of him, which is why, when he first heard voices ahead, none of which he recognized, he thought little of it, until one deep, tension-filled voice yelled, "I can't lay here forever with a broken wrist."

Billy pulled the horses to a stop, tied both to a tree and left the trail, moving silently through the lodgepole and boulder-strewn underbrush on foot.

"How is she?" called another man's voice.

And then, finally, in reply, a voice Billy recognized. "She's bad."

It belonged to Cole.

Billy began running in its direction.

He saw the blood on the trail just as he was tackled.

"Get down."

The man on top of him pressed Billy to the ground, literally rolling him under the brush along the trailside.

Billy realized immediately who it had to be; but all he wanted right now was to see Cole and Whisper. To know that they were okay.

Cole had spotted him. Peering out from behind a rock ten yards down and across the trail, he yelled, "Stay down. We've been ambushed. Whisper was shot."

"Shit," Billy replied, turning to face Will McCarroll, who, now that he'd pushed Billy to safety, belly-crawled under the brush along with Billy.

"You must be the rest of the group," Will said. "Where's Johnny?"

Lying side by side, Will listened to Billy's description of their encounter with the camo-clad hunter, which ended with, "Johnny followed him."

"Both Johnny and the camo guy are on foot?"

"Yeah. I've got two horses with me."

"Where?"

"Ten yards back. Tied along the trail."

"The guy was definitely armed? And traveling off-trail?"

"Definitely carrying. And he'd cut through some dense shit to get to the creek bed we were following."

Billy watched as Will stuck his head back out, squinting at the ridgeline above them.

"Two gunmen fired on us to start with," he said, the puzzle running through his mind. "But over the past hour or so, it was starting to seem like there was only one. My guess is you just ran into the other."

Billy's eyes followed Will's gaze.

"For sure there were two?"

"We found two different types of bullets since we

took cover. My guess is the guy you ran into was circling around on us, and that the other guy's up there, waiting for him to get in place. That when he does, they plan to finish the job."

"He almost *was* in place," Billy replied. "So now what?"

Will was silent for several minutes before calling out to Cole.

"Can you carry your girlfriend?"

"Yes," came the answer.

Now Will turned to Billy.

"We need to get her out of here. I'm going to grab Bridger Brogan and make a run for it, toward your horses. When you see me take off with Bridger, you hightail it over to Cole and the girl to help him with her. Wait for thirty seconds, no more, and if no one starts shooting, follow me. Understand?

"I'm counting on the guy up top not being ready, or willing, to act on his own. But that's a big assumption. I don't want you three in the line of fire till I've tested it."

"Got it," said Billy, eyeing Cole's jacket, which he could just see sticking out from behind a boulder, the base of which had blood spread all over it.

"We'll meet you at the horses."

Will took one more look up toward the ridgeline, then he rolled out from under the brush, into the middle of the trail.

He wanted to be seen. If the gunman or gunmen—while the different bullets confirmed there were at least two, there could be more—were still up there and bent upon killing them, Will wanted to be the one that drew them out again. He had never before been put in a position where he had to choose between inaction that could cost a young woman her life and a decision that put an entire group at risk; while he hoped to hell he'd made the right decision, if he had not, he wanted to be the one that paid for any miscalculation.

Once in the middle of the trail, about where he'd stood when the firing first started, he jumped to his feet and bolted to where he could see the heel of Bridger Brogan's booted foot.

"Let's go," he said, reaching down for Brogan.

"They could still be up there," Brogan cried.

Brogan's size alone could not account for the fact that when Will grabbed him and pulled with his considerable strength, the trapper did not budge.

"He's holding on to the fucking tree," Will heard Billy call.

Will's boot lashed out at Brogan's good wrist, and with a cry, the trapper's body gave way. Once exposed, Brogan was on his feet and cowering under the arm Will offered as protection, almost beating Will as he sprinted toward that portion of the trail Billy had emerged from, where the dense trees on either side offered obscurity.

When they reached the safety of tree cover, Will turned and, with heart in throat, watched as Billy and Cole, crossed arms forming a seat beneath her, ran their way with a barely conscious Whisper cradled between them.

The three were halfway to Will and Brogan when the firing started again.

Will jumped back onto the trail and returned fire until all the rest of the group had made it to safety. The gunman's bullets ricocheted around Will as he dove for cover again and belly-crawled out of sight.

A pause to reload told Will he'd been correct—only one gunman remained above them.

By the time Will worked his way off-trail back to the group, Billy had retrieved the horses. Cole sat atop one while Billy lifted Whisper up to him.

Brogan, still bound at the wrists, was eyeing the second horse when Will grabbed its reins and brought his own face within inches of the trapper's.

"Shoot to wound him if he tries to escape," he said to Billy and Cole before handing Billy the reins and crossing over to Cole and Whisper's horse.

He lifted Whisper's hand, took her pulse. The bullet had entered her upper left chest. When he moved two steps toward the horse's rear end, Cole shifted to give him a look at her back. No blood. The bullet hadn't exited. Her color indicated she was probably bleeding internally.

Billy approached Will and said, under his breath, "Should we be trying to remove it?"

Will shook his head but, for fear of her hearing, did not share his thoughts.

If the bullet had punctured a lung and they were to dislodge it, even partially, she could die within minutes, suffocate.

"I know I don't have to tell you guys to get her to Browning's hospital as fast as you can. And I'm sure you know the fastest way to do that."

"We can have her there within an hour and a half," Billy replied.

"You ride behind him," Will ordered, nodding toward Brogan. "I need your advice. Assuming the guy Johnny's following rejoins the gunman on the ridge, what's the most likely route they'll take to get down?"

Billy looked to Cole, who shook his head.

"There are half a dozen trails they could use."

"I guess it depends on how well they know the park," Billy added, "and where they plan to go."

"They'll be on the run," Will replied. "We can count on that. Canada probably looks good to them about now."

"They'd have to be in great shape to make it that far," Billy replied. "My guess is Spencer's made it back to Romey's by now and there'll be helicopters out looking all over the park for us any time now. They'd have to know how to travel undercover, and a long ways. The guy I saw wasn't in shape for that."

"Then they'll try to get back to their vehicle," Will replied. "Which means either Two Medicine or Cut Bank." He added, "Or the highway, where they can hitchhike to it."

"If it were me," Cole offered, "knowing Johnny's following one of them from south of here, and if the guy he's behind is going back up the mountain, I'd approach from the opposite side, one of the north trails."

Billy nodded.

"Plus we'll be on the trail leading south, till we cut off east, to Two Med. I agree with Cole. You should head north. A trail breaks off about two miles from here. It's not easy, climbs a lot, but the real problem is you'd be exposed a good portion of the way."

"That also means I'd have some vistas," Will said. "I'll take my chances that they won't see me before I see them."

"You know what else it means?" Cole added. "That you might have cell coverage. Once you get high enough to see Cobalt Lake and the back side of Sinopah. I know 'cause I sprained my ankle up there a couple years ago and was able to call my uncle for help."

"I lost my phone up on Bad Marriage," Will said. "And my radio's battery is dead."

Cole reached into his back pocket and extended his hand toward Will. It held an iPhone.

"Take mine. We won't have coverage until we're almost back to Two Medicine and by then, I'll have talked someone along the way out of theirs."

Will pushed Cole's hand back.

"No way in hell I could figure that thing out."

Billy grabbed the phone, holding it in front of Will and him.

"Who would you need to call? What's the number for Law Enforcement?"

"Rob Deardorf. 555-4421."

Billy's fingers entered the number.

"See this button? Just press that to unlock it. Then press the phone symbol. Now take it."

"Got it," Will said. He had already begun digging in his backpack. Now he reached up to Cole.

"Here's my first aid kit. Do you know how to use an epi pen, and when?" He nodded toward Whisper, lowered his voice. "If she gets shock-y enough, you may need it. Or . . ."

"Or if she goes into cardiac arrest," Cole replied softly, soberly. "I'm trained in giving epinephrine, for my whitewater guiding."

He looked down the trail toward Haldis Beck's lifeless body, and as if reading Will's thoughts, said, "What about her?"

Will turned to Billy.

"How far back did you leave my horse?"

"At least an hour. And we were off-trail, in the creek bed. Might take you longer than that to find her."

The decision was agonizing.

"We'll have to leave her," Will said, handing the phone back to Billy. "Does this thing have GPS? Can you get the coordinates?"

A half-minute later, head bent to the tiny screen, Billy read the coordinates on the screen.

He had retrieved a pen from his pocket and now each man took turns scratching the numbers on the back of his hand.

"Whoever gets communication first, send someone to pick her up," Will said, risking one more haunting glance at Haldis Beck's body.

He extended his hand. Each young man took it.

"Get going now. And good luck."

Twenty-eight

"Okay, Tonto, game's over."

In the second before he heard the quiet step on to the trail behind him, and felt the gun's barrel against his back, Johnny already knew he'd made a mistake.

Once he got through the off-trail section the gunman had bushwacked through—following a fresh and easily detectible path of broken branches—he had reached the main trail, where his instincts told him to head south. After that—with the exception of one false turn, where the absence of signs quickly told Johnny he'd made a mistake—regular gobs of saliva and spit tobacco led him up the mountain, where his level of fitness allowed him to quickly gain the time he'd lost.

He could literally feel he was within breathing distance of the camouflage-clad hiker when he crested the trail and saw him.

He'd stopped to urinate against a tree trunk.

About to sidestep into the trees, Johnny was stopped by the voice from behind.

"Put your fucking hands up," it added now.

Johnny did as he was told. Rough hands patted him down, stopping at his shirt pocket, where he'd carried the Buck knife, as the man Johnny had been following walked toward them, zipping his pants up.

"Hell, Lyle," the voice from behind called. "He's not even armed. All he's got is a fucking knife." He chuckled as he pulled it from Johnny's pocket and waved it in the air.

Johnny debated about making a run for it, but the tobacco chewer's eyes were on him. The big man pulled his pistol and let it hang, limp, in his hand as the two men studied Johnny.

"This for sure one of the guys you saw?" the voice from behind said.

"Yep. The older one. The other was just a kid, not much older than my boy."

He turned to Johnny.

"Why you following me?"

"Who says I was following you?"

"Where's your friend?"

"He went back to town. He was homesick for his girlfriend."

"Yeah, right." The big guy turned to his partner. "That means the other guy who knows about me is out there somewhere. If this guy followed me, the other guy's probably headed toward them. Won't be long before they figure it out. I say we waste this one and get the hell off this mountain."

The other guy stepped around Johnny, into his field of vision. He was smaller, almost petite, and more thoughtful than his thug partner.

"Wait a minute," he said. "If they know, they'll have every motherfucker in the park looking for us. We need this guy with us. We can use him."

"Use him? How the hell we gonna use him?"

"For bargaining," he replied. Then added, "Maybe even as a shield."

This seemed to impress the big man, who also wanted to be clever.

"Hey, and he works here. He'll know everything about this park." He turned back to Johnny, eyed his uniform.

"What are you anyway?"

"A biologist."

"See what I mean? Not only can he be a bargaining chip, maybe even a shield, he can guide us out of this place."

"Not bad," the little man replied.

"Okay, let's get going."

Tying Johnny's hands behind his back, the big man in front and the little, armed, behind, they walked about twenty yards to where they'd stashed some weapons and two small day packs. Johnny was surprised not to see more gear.

Once they'd shouldered their packs, they started along a trail that led north along a mostly level ridge, Johnny in the middle.

As they passed a pile of bear scat—probably two days old—the big man stopped, pointed.

"See, I told you. We're in grizzly country."

Johnny opened his mouth to correct him, tell him it had been a black bear—possibly a big one, but nowhere as big as a grizzly—that left the pile on the trail, but the little guy spoke first.

"Holy shit," was all he said, and Johnny remained silent.

"North Idaho never had grizzlies when I lived there. Still never seen one. Ever since I read *Night of the Grizzlies* I've been afraid of camping. And you know where that took place, don't you?"

"No," said the big guy, "where?"

"Here! In this fucking park. Two different bears killed two different people on the same night. Something about the moon."

"What's there to be afraid of?" the big guy replied. Johnny sensed a definite note of fear in his voice. "There are two of us, with guns."

Johnny's harrumph accomplished just what he'd hoped.

The man slowed, turned, glared at him.

"What? What the fuck you laughing at?"

"Not laughing," Johnny said, eyeing their packs innocently. "You guys carrying bear spray?"

"Don't need fucking bear spray. We've got these," the big guy said, lifting the scoped rifle like a little kid trying to prove a point.

Johnny nodded, making it clear he'd heard that line before.

"Know any statistics about human-bear encounters that turn deadly?"

The big man didn't answer as they continued down the trail, but the little one said, "What statistics?"

"Shooting a bear's more likely to get you maimed or killed than anything you can do. Especially a griz."

"What're you supposed to do?"

"Depends on the circumstances, and whether it's a black bear or a grizzly. But if you think guns protect you, you're crazy. They get you killed. Bear spray's the only thing you can count on for protection. Bear spray, and knowing what to do if you encounter a bear."

The little guy shoved Johnny with the butt of his gun and the trio fell silent.

"Shit, it's getting dark. How much farther we got?"

"Ask the Injun here."

"Where are you going?" Johnny asked.

This simple question caused a long discussion between the two, whom Johnny had already come to think of as Mutt and Jeff.

"I say we head right to Canada," said Mutt. "Through the park."

"You know how much hiking that'll be?" Jeff replied. "Hey, Tonto, how long would it take us to get to Canada?"

Johnny didn't answer.

He felt the butt of the rifle hit his back again, but walked on, silent.

"I'm talking to you, Indian boy."

At that, Johnny turned, lifted a leg into the air, and delivered a kick that doubled the little man over.

Mutt was on him in a minute, punching him repeatedly.

"Wait, hold off," the little guy said. "We need him. He's not gonna be able to walk if you beat the shit out of him."

Dragging Johnny back up by the shirt collar, the big guy pulled him level with his acne-scarred face.

"You talk when we ask you a question. You hear?"

Johnny, blood dribbling down his face from a gash over his eye, did not flinch.

"You call me Tonto or Indian boy again and you might as well finish the job, 'cause I won't move another inch with you slime."

The giant hands tightened into a fist again. But then, after an obvious mental debate that stretched the limits of his limited brain, Mutt gave Johnny a withering look, let go of his collar, and shoved him in the direction of the trail.

"How far to Canada?"

"You'll never make it," Johnny replied. "Three nights at least, and your pal's right. Everyone in this park will be looking for you."

"That means we have to get back to our truck," the little guy said. "How long'll it take to get to Two Medicine?"

"You stupid shit," Mutt cried. "You just told him where we're parked. Plus that's probably where everyone's gonna be looking for us thanks to the crazy old lady who worked at the gate there. We're going straight to Canada." He glared at Johnny. "And you're gonna get us there."

The little guy was becoming agitated.

"Holy shit. I forgot about the crazy ranger lady. She's probably told everyone what we look like. What the hell were you thinking about telling me to wear camouflage? We stick out like sore thumbs."

"We can take care of that," Lyle said. "All we need is to find a hiker with clothes that'll fit me." Almost as an afterthought, he added, "And you. Then we'll blend in just fine."

"Not gonna blend in when we got an Indian with tied hands with us."

The big guy clearly hadn't thought of that. He pushed Johnny forward, into the lead position.

"We run into a bear, you'll be the first it gets."

The sun had begun disappearing behind the highest peaks of the Continental Divide, then reappearing as the earth rotated and lower peaks gave it more life. The trail had just begun its descent down the mountain.

Johnny's mind raced. He had to get them to head to Two Medicine. The chances that they'd get apprehended if they went that route were many times greater than if they headed due north, toward Canada. If they turned off in that direction in the next hour or two, they'd join a network of trails popular with day hikers.

If they continued north, they could virtually disappear—become impossible to find.

When Johnny spied more bear scat, he recognized it immediately as the droppings of a black bear.

"Another grizzly," he announced.

"Holy shit," the little guy cried. "You're crazy if you think I'm spending a night out here."

This time Johnny laughed out loud.

"You'll be spending the next three or four nights out here if you're going to Canada. Either way, we'll be sleeping on this trail tonight. If you don't stop to camp, you're gonna walk off the side of this mountain. Doesn't look like you two even brought a tent."

"It's all your fault, Lyle," the little guy said from behind. "You insisted on going down there, finishing everyone off. We'd be almost out of the park by now. Now look at us? Half the world knows we're here, we didn't finish everyone off, and we're gonna be sleeping with grizzlies. Oh shit."

Johnny had begun scanning the mountainside. The trail followed a narrow ridge with a steep drop-off to the left and, on the right, rocky, more gradual terrain.

"I'm not stopping," the big man said. "We'll stay on the move."

"You can't hike in the dark," declared Johnny. "Especially without a moon. We're stopping here. At least there's open ground for a while. If we're lucky, we'd see a bear coming, even if we don't hear it."

"Holy shit," the little guy groaned again.

"Keep moving," the big guy ordered.

Johnny planted his feet.

Once they got below the tree line, with the onset of night, they'd be invisible, but if Spencer and the others had reached Romey's, a helicopter should be out looking for them anytime now. With infrared enhanced night vision goggles, even on a moonless night they could be spotted on the mountain easily.

"We're camping here," he declared.

Taking Johnny for his word, the big man pulled the little man another ten feet down the trail. The two shot furtive glances Johnny's way as they heatedly argued, giving Johnny the opportunity to study the west slope of the mountain. It was sheer, but he detected a slight ridge below, with a trail etched in the rock over decades by sure-footed mountain goats and bighorn sheep.

Before long, the little man quieted some, and finally, even shook his head and smiled at whatever his partner was suggesting.

They returned to where Johnny stood.

"You want to stay on this mountain overnight, huh?" the big man said. "Well, we've figured out we should let you. You're more trouble than it's worth anyway. We're gonna keep going. And since we need something to protect us from grizzlies," suddenly, eyes gleaming, he drew Johnny's Buck knife from its sheath, "we thought you could still help us out. We get attacked by a griz, we're just gonna throw him a little morsel to feed on long enough for us to get away."

The little guy had circled around in back of Johnny. Just as he reached for Johnny's bound wrists to hold him still, with the big guy approaching, knife now pointed at Johnny's chest, Johnny kicked out, connecting solidly with the knife-bearing hand.

The man went down, clutching his chest.

"He stabbed me," he groaned as he rolled onto his side. "Kill the motherfucker."

As he heard the little guy draw his gun and release its lock, Johnny sprinted to the edge of the ridgeline.

He hesitated just long enough to get his bearings.

Then he took the leap.

Sweat poured off Will as he paused, chest heaving, to lift binoculars to his eyes for the sixth time in the two hours since he'd found the steeply inclined trail that switch-backed up the nameless mountain the gunmen had used for their sniper attack. Cole and Billy's directions had been letter-perfect, and just as Cole advised, once above the tree line, the narrow, rocky path allowed Will grand vistas—vistas in which to look for the gunmen and, if he'd caught up to them and succeeded in keeping with them, Johnny.

The only thing Cole had gotten wrong, at least so far, was the cell phone coverage. Will had tried using the phone each time he stopped to scan the landscape for movement of the two-legged kind. He reminded himself of Cole's comment that he should be able to make a call once he saw Cobalt Lake and the backside of Sinopah Mountain, and pushed himself that much harder to reach that spot.

Will didn't know what was eating at him more— concern over Whisper's condition, Johnny's safety, his determination to find the gunmen, or the fact that he'd left Haldis Beck's body on a backcountry trail frequented by wolves, coyotes, bears, and wolverine.

He wiped his brow with the back of his hand as he scanned the area first with his bare eyes. Fresh scat on the trail told him a grizzly had preceded him.

Movement east of him, on the backside of the mountain, suddenly caught his attention. Mere dark dots at that distance, but dots that moved purposefully down the hillside. He lifted the glasses, expecting to see one of a dozen wild critters the powerful lenses had already picked up—two adult black bears, one with a cub of the year, a mountain goat, a small band of bighorn sheep, all of which under normal circumstances would have thrilled Will, but on this hike, only served to frustrate him.

"Holy shit," he whispered as his fingers adjusted the binocular's focus.

Two men, guns in plain view, quickly descended a trail that ran along a sheer drop-off, perpendicular to the one

Will was on. One—a skinny, shirtless man—had a rifle slung over his shoulder. They each carried handguns freely. The other wore a camouflage shirt.

Where the hell was Johnny? He must have lost their trail.

Lowering the glasses to get a perspective on distance, heart and mind racing—was there any way to cut them off at the bottom of the trail?—Will was so distracted momentarily that he took another dark spot several hundred yards behind and below the trail the two men followed to be a boulder. Until it moved.

Raising the glasses again, Will slowly swept the hillside.

Nothing.

He trained the glasses on the two men again. One of them, the one wearing a shirt, walked with one shoulder forward and appeared to be holding a hand to his gut.

Experience told Will not to consider trying to angle directly from the trail Will had taken to the one they were on—thick vegetation and rocks would make the going too slow. And it was likely there were crevasses that he might or might not be able to cross.

No, he would have to retrace his steps to the main trail and hope that they would either turn in his direction, or that he could catch up with them.

He turned to head back down, but instincts—long honed, and tried and true—stopped him.

Lifting the glasses again, he scanned the area below the ridgeline the two men descended.

He was about to drop the binoculars when they caught the movement, dead center in their field.

Focusing again, Will realized it was a person, lying on his side.

He watched as he rolled to his knees.

The long black hair fell forward, obscuring his profile. But Will already knew who it was.

* * *

"Johnny?" Will shouted.

It had taken no more than an hour to reach the spot where Will had first seen the two men. He had to be close.

"Yellow Kidney!"

"Here," a voice called back.

Will bolted the distance. Looking down, over the edge, he saw what he'd been praying for. Directly below him, about fifteen feet down. Yellow Kidney's face twisted into a facsimile of a smile.

"Damn," he said. "They said you were good, but I had no idea you were this good."

"How badly hurt are you?"

"Not bad. Broken ribs. But I can't see a way up there. You got rope?"

"No. Be right back."

Will walked up and down the ridgeline twice, hanging his head over the edge precariously several times before returning.

"I think I found a spot where I can get down below you and climb back up. Then we'll see how to get you out of there."

"No," Johnny replied forcefully. "Go after them, then come back for me."

"No way I'm leaving you," Will replied. "You'd end up spending the night there. One false move and you could go down."

Johnny was determined.

"Will, these guys are going on another killing spree. They'll kill the first hiker who comes along with clothes they can fit into. And if he's not their size, they'll kill him to feed to the bears."

The thought that Johnny was worse off than he looked fleetingly entered Will's mind.

"What?" he replied, carefully observing his friend below. He knew Johnny was right about pursuing the two gunmen. If they weren't caught tonight, chances that they'd get away soared. He knew the grim statistics. Early apprehension was the key, especially in a place as easy to get lost in as Glacier.

But he couldn't leave Johnny behind, injured and alone, unless he had a high level of confidence that he was in the right shape, mentally and physically, to handle it.

Johnny seemed to know that he was being evaluated.

"I'm not kidding," he replied. "That's what they'd decided to do with me. They'd taken me captive. They were planning to use me as some kind of shield to get them out of the park. But then we kept seeing bear scat—some of which was griz, some not. They were scared shitless. Never seen anything like it. Especially when I told them I wouldn't continue down the mountain in the dark. They wanted to hike out tonight. So they came up with a new plan. I was too much trouble, so they decided they'd cut off one of my arms or legs and carry that instead of dealing with me—if a griz attacked, they were going to offer it and run."

Johnny was serious. Will listened, incredulous.

"One of them tried to hold me down while the other came at me with the knife. I stabbed the big guy and rolled myself off the fucking mountain as they shot at me. Hid beneath the shelf and managed to work my hands free. They looked for me for half an hour, then decided I'd fallen all the way off the mountain and they hightailed it out of here." Johnny grimaced in pain as he shifted his weight to get a good look at Will, then added, "Now do you see why you have to go after them? I'll be fine."

Will struggled with one more agonizing decision.

"I tell you, Will, anyone they cross paths with isn't safe."

"Okay. I'll go. Cole told me I'd have cell phone coverage if I climbed high enough. Do you think it's worth my heading uphill for a while?"

"Actually, that's not a bad idea. If these guys change their mind about going through the park to Canada, and I think they will, especially once it's dark, they'll have to get their truck at Two Medicine. The quickest way out—the only way really—is the trail that skirts Cobalt Lake."

"Cole said I'd have coverage as soon as I saw the lake and Sinopah."

"My guess is that Cole got lucky. The coverage's going to be spotty, but maybe you'll get lucky, too. That section's only about a mile up the trail. I say head up there, then, once you make the call and get your bearings, you should see several trails you can use to work your way down to that trail to Two Medicine. You'll be able to see it."

While Johnny talked, Will removed both his socks. Now he used them as flags—tying one to a branch of sage just yards up trail, and the other an equal distant down the trail.

Kneeling over the edge one last time, he looked at Johnny.

"Got any matches?"

"No."

"It's gonna get down to the thirties tonight. If the wind comes up . . ." Will's voice trailed off. There was no need to tell Johnny what alpine winds could do to the already cool temperatures. He finished instead with, "Take cover."

"I'll be okay," Johnny said. "I'm strong and healthy. Just banged up."

As Will reluctantly drew back from his hands and knees to his haunches, he heard Johnny speak again.

"Let Annie know I'm okay, will you?"

Twenty-nine

Eleanor Malone reached across the corner of the table next to the window and, using a hankie she always kept handy now, wiped ice cream off the right side of the judge's mouth.

They had just dug into the steaming "Brownies' special"—a hot brownie loaded with homemade vanilla ice cream—Vilma had placed between them. Eleanor and the judge had become fixtures at Brownies, where they sat by the hour watching cars, RVs, and pickups streaming along the two-lane road between East Glacier and the entry to the park at Two Medicine, as they anxiously awaited word of Annie or Will.

A laptop lay flat and unopened on the table in front of Judge Sherburne. Stacy, from the lodge, had loaned him one of her staff's when she learned that pecking with one finger was his best means of communication.

Late afternoons always found Brownies hopping. Mornings were dominated by newcomers on their way into the park—hungry, nervous about a hike they'd long planned in order to "experience wilderness," and hoping to find a local willing to share advice. But, eager to get started and by late August, pretty much tired of serving as unpaid advisors to novice hikers and sightseers, most of the locals dropped in quickly for coffee or to meet hiking or climbing partners, then took whatever they purchased along, stuffing it into expertly arranged backpacks as they stood out on the wood-planked porch visiting with one another.

Afternoons were a different story.

Exhausted, hungry, and eager to socialize and share the day's experiences, the locals came, sat, and stayed put, often for hours, raising the noise and energy level inside to something akin to a schoolyard playground.

Still, when the tall, weathered cowboy, followed by a tail-wagging, three-legged Stinky, strode in, letting the screen door slam behind them, the place went still.

Vilma, who had seen Romey's truck pull up and already had the pot of black coffee in hand, froze with it in midair as Romey, normally a quiet presence, turned toward the tables.

"Listen everybody. A backcountry ranger's in trouble."

"It's Will McCarroll, isn't it?" Vilma asked from behind the counter. "He's usually in here twice a day but I haven't seen him since Tuesday."

"Yep," nodded Romey, his thick head of gray hair sporting a ring left by the band of his cowboy hat.

"Isn't he the guy who saved Stinky?" one gangly, ponytailed man in his early thirties called out from the back table, next to the glass doors of the refrigerator bearing everything from milk to energy drinks to Kaopectate. His hiking shorts, neoprene shirt, and scratched up knees and elbows announced he'd not only been climbing that day but had also spent some unplanned time rolling down a mountainside.

"That's him," Vilma answered, her expression decidedly unhappy now at the news Will was missing.

Eleanor Malone had jumped to her feet. Leaving the judge struggling to get up, she approached Romey.

"My daughter went to look for Will," she said. She'd grabbed hold of the cowboy's arm and now was squeezing it. "She and a biologist."

She looked toward the judge for the name, which in her panic, she could not remember, but Vilma beat him to it.

"I heard she went in there with Johnny."

"Yes," Eleanor replied. "Johnny. Yellow Kidney. That was his name. He took her into the park yesterday to look for Will."

Romey's expression darkened.

"Is your daughter named Annie?"

Eleanor's hand instinctively flew up to her chest. "Yes."

Having never been one to mince words, Romey didn't start now.

"She's been injured. Her horse slid down a talus slope and your daughter broke her leg. Spencer and Tim Boyd brought her back to my ranch about an hour ago. She's being taken by ambulance to Flathead Community Hospital right now."

"Oh dear," Eleanor cried.

For the first time, Romey noticed the old woman's mangled ear, and suddenly, despite the current emergency, it all came together for him. Annie Peacock, the Yellowstone judge. Judge Sherburne, distantly related to a longtime East Glacier family. The kidnapping a backcountry ranger had solved, while saving the alpha female of the Druids.

By the time the Yellowstone story had reached Glacier, it had become legend.

Reaching out to steady Eleanor, just as the judge caught up and grabbed her other arm, Romey looked her in the eye and said, "She was weak, she'd lost some blood, but I've seen worse. My bet is she'll be okay."

He turned to the tables again.

"These people need to get to Kalispell. Who can take them?"

Several hands went up. The paralysis caused by the sense of surprise now dissipating, people began pushing away from tables littered with food, drinks, and laptops to circle loosely around Romey.

"What about Johnny?" one voice asked.

From another: "And weren't Cole and Whisper with Spencer? And Billy Boyd?"

Romey held a hand up to restore order.

"Spencer said they went on with Johnny to look for McCarroll. You've all seen the missing hiker poster?" Heads nodded, almost in unison. "McCarroll was on a search and rescue for her, but turns out it's a trap for him. And there's more than one person involved in it."

The only one not alarmed by this announcement was Stinky, who had been looking up at Vilma and whining.

"Son of a bitch," Vilma muttered as she reached into a jar on the counter labeled HOMEMADE DOG BISCUITS and handed the last of its contents to him.

Romey's bloodshot eyes scanned the group. Several tourists, still seated, looked on, keenly interested but also clearly not wanting to get involved.

"I just spoke to Rob Deardorf. All the Park Service helicopters are tied up with the fire near Lake McDonald—two backcountry campsites are involved now and they've been dispatched to get the campers out. Rob's trying to get a Lewis and Clark Forest Service chopper in to help find Will.

"Meanwhile, I need a group to go in with me and help look for Will. Once the EMTs took off, Spencer and Tim headed right back out on horseback. My group will be on foot. We only have a few hours left till dark."

Before the next words left Romey's mouth, loosened

laces were already being retied on hiking boots and heavy packs reshouldered.

Vilma strode through the group, pressing food items— sandwiches, cookies, bagels—into hands and stuffing them into pockets. There was a sense that everyone had been through this fire drill before.

"Rob Deardorf has given me authority to deputize anyone who joins the search," Romey said.

Half a dozen people stood deftly texting friends or partners not to worry but they might not be back that night.

Romey gave them less than a minute before putting each of them—perhaps even each of their lives—on the line.

"Okay, who's on board?"

Rob Deardorf's back was turned to the phone when it rang.

Glancing over his shoulder, he cursed the Park Service for the thousandth time for remaining in the dark ages when it came to technology. Everyone else on the planet had caller I.D., but there was no such convenience on NPS office phones.

Rob turned back to the SAR plan he'd been writing.

How had things gotten so out of control? Will McCarroll had been out of touch for two days now. Despite the fact that Park Service policy called for a rescue team to go out on the third day without contact with a ranger, Rob hadn't been overly concerned.

For starters, he knew that the country he'd sent Will into to look for Haldis Beck consisted of huge areas of radio-shaded or dead space. Second, while the radio allocated to Will was one of the new radios the park had recently received and substituted for the old, ironically, they'd learned that they had shorter battery lives. The older generation batteries lasted up to six days while the new ones lasted only two to three days. Rob's older rangers, who'd spent decades using radios with longer-lived batteries, had been constantly complaining about the unreliability of the new radios and asking for their old ones back.

But then he'd received the call from the EMTs, who, at their patient's insistence—he could actually hear her in the background—had put Magistrate Judge Annie Peacock on the phone to talk to him as they raced her to Kalispell, and he'd learned that his earlier decision—not sending rescuers out the first time Annie Peacock had called—had been a terrible error in judgment; that, just as the judge had feared, the missing hiker had been some kind of hoax to lure Will into the backcountry.

Deardorf had been doing his job for so long, thirty-two years, that he'd honed instincts that he'd come to believe never failed him. He'd taken Annie's call the night before, her story about the possibility the missing hiker was using two names, with a grain of salt. And as a result, he'd tossed Will McCarroll's safety, perhaps his life, out with that salt.

With that possibility heavy on his mind, as the phone rang for the third time, hand visibly shaking, he reached for it.

"Rob Deardorf," he said sternly.

At first all he heard was static, but then, even though it was breaking up, he recognized the voice.

"Rob?"

Deardorf bolted forward in his chair.

"Will? Is that you? Are you okay?"

"I'm fine, but I need you . . ." Maddeningly, static blocked out Will's words. Then, his voice came back. ". . . a helicopter. Johnny Yellow Kidney's been injured, and . . ." again, static, and again, Will's voice returned ". . . is dead.

". . . gunmen inside the park . . ."

"Who's dead? Where?" Rob yelled into the phone. "Where is all of this taking place? On Bad Marriage?"

Static took over.

"Will? Keep talking!"

Frantic, Rob put one hand over his free ear, ran to the door and kicked it shut to block out the noise from the hallway.

"Will?"

Nothing. In another couple seconds, the line went silent and Deardorf knew the connection was gone.

Hurriedly he lifted his free hand to press the redial button, but he immediately remembered that on the government-issued desk phones the redial button didn't work for incoming calls.

He slammed the receiver down. Then he checked to be sure it was secure, even picked it up again to make sure he heard the dial tone before he placed it, this time gently, back in its cradle, hoping against hope that Will would call again, but knowing in his gut that would not happen.

The fact that Will hadn't used his radio came as no surprise to Deardorf, since he now strongly suspected that Will, not aware of the shorter battery life, hadn't charged it again before leaving to find Haldis Beck. But there were areas, especially alpine areas, in the park where one could get cell phone coverage, but not radio coverage. If that was the reason Will had used his cell phone instead of the radio, it could end up being a valuable clue to where to find him. In a part of the park that was usually shaded or dead for both cell phones and radios, Will had found a rare pocket where there was satellite coverage—no doubt climbing a mountain to do so—and used his cell phone.

Deardorf pressed the button on his intercom.

"Megan," he barked.

"Yes?"

"I need Will McCarroll's cell phone number. Stat."

Hanging up, he pressed the redial number on his phone. The last call he'd made had been to the district law enforcement supervisor at the adjacent Lewis and Clark Forest Service.

"Leon? It's Rob Deardorf again. I just heard from Will McCarroll. He's okay, but I think he was telling me that one of the park's biologists is injured and needs to be airlifted out. Someone's dead so there's also a body somewhere, but Will and anyone injured will be the top priority."

"I've got a crew returning from that lightning strike in the Bob Marshall right now," Leon Jackson replied. "They'll have to gas up but then they can be in the air again within half an hour. Do we have coordinates?"

"McCarroll called from a cell phone. We got cut off before he could provide his location, but his destination when he left on an SAR yesterday morning was Bad Marriage, which is up by Eagle Plume and Mad Wolf. I have my secretary getting his number. I'll establish a direct line between you, me, and his cell phone carrier. By the time you have your copter in the air, I'll have the GPS coordinates for you."

"I'll be waiting for your call," Jackson replied.

"One more thing," Deardorf said, the gravity of the information he was about to relay to Jackson still sinking in.

"Will said something about gunmen. Have your crew be on the lookout for them, but be sure they do not try to apprehend."

Will's frustration had mounted with his phone call to Rob Deardorf. He didn't know what, if anything, Deardorf had been able to hear, which meant that the detour further up the mountain to make the call had cost him valuable time, with little likelihood of paying off.

Now, he used his binoculars to scour the treetops, trails, and ravines playing out below him. The sun no longer cast shadows, but the sky was putting up a fight, not ready to go black on the moonless night, instead boasting a sea of pastel ripples that enabled Will just enough light to see the trail that stretched between Cobalt and Middle Two Medicine Lake, which was little more than a glint of fading sun off distant waters.

Leaving Johnny behind, injured, ate away at him, especially with nightfall fast approaching. He could see several trails, mostly wildlife passages, working their way down the mountain. Choosing the one that looked most direct, he set off in its direction, crossing off-trail at a diagonal until he reached it at a point just half a mile above the main trail to Two Medicine.

He quickly saw that it wasn't just a game trail. A single pair of boot prints had preceded him. Will's pace quickened, eyes now placing equal emphasis on the trail and the occasional glimpses he got of the passages, still below, along the lakes, which appeared to be empty of human traffic at this hour.

Could the gunmen have split up? Was that their strategy? Or had they argued about which option—fleeing to Canada through the park or returning to their vehicle— with each man following his own instincts? From what Johnny had told Will, they both seemed to share the fear of grizzlies, and a night in the backcountry was inevitable, so their voluntarily splitting up didn't feel right to Will.

Within another ten yards, his heart sank.

A familiar sight, but one he had not seen much of since departing Yellowstone, told him he wasn't on the trail of one of the gunmen.

The person he was following had left behind a cairn—a stack of mostly flat rocks, one piled directly on top of the other. While this one was modest—maybe two and a half feet high—Will had seen them taller than his six feet. Some were remarkable, not just for their beauty, but for the engineering feat.

Such sights were not the least bit uncommon in the backcountry. Whether it be in homage to a Native American tradition—Blackfeet used to construct miles of cairns to direct bison to a buffalo jump—a way to find their way back, a message for a hiking partner, or simply the statement to the Universe that they had been there, Will could never know, but he did know one thing: leaving behind a cairn was not something a gunman on the run would do.

Within fifteen minutes, Will had arrived at the main trail along Cobalt Lake, a flat, easy-to-negotiate path that allowed him to finally break into a run.

A scream ahead stopped him cold.

Voices, shouting, followed.

Will drew his gun.

"Roger, Supervisor Deardorf, do you read me?"

Rob Deardorf pressed the phone to his ear as he paced the darkened office. He had not bothered to turn on the lights when the sun had faded.

"Nothing?" he called into the phone. "You can't see anyone?"

"No, sir," the pilot radioed back.

"Are you certain you're at the right coordinates?"

"Sir, we are directly above a ridge connecting Bad Marriage to Eagle Plume. We are not only certain that we've gone to the correct coordinates, we have a visual on a cellular telephone. It's lying on a steep hillside. We have asked Verizon Wireless to confirm that it is the phone belonging to the number you provided them."

Now Leon Jackson spoke up.

"I would suggest you begin a sweep of the area," he said. "But of course, Rob, you're the one calling the shots."

Deardorf's mind raced. The pilot had just reported that the phone was on a steep hillside.

"McCarroll must have fallen after making that call. There's still an hour of visibility. Can you get someone down there for a ground search? I'll be mobilizing from this end at the same time, but it will be daybreak before I can get anyone safely there."

Another voice broke in.

"Gentlemen. This is Laticia Fuentes from Verizon. We have confirmation that the phone your helicopter located is registered to Will McCarroll."

Deardorf's fist struck the back of his door.

"Okay, let's mobilize."

Thirty

"Step aside," Will ordered as he approached the group.

Half a dozen hikers—mostly young, fit men and women, but also, oddly, an older cowboy—parted. Both women held trembling hands to their mouths in horror.

Their parting allowed Will to see what had caused them to cry out.

A body. Forty-some-year-old male. Heavyset. Naked save for his Jockey underwear and hiking socks.

Without touching him, Will followed the trail of blood on the dirt beside him to his skull. A single bullet wound at the temple.

His killers had barely pulled his body out of the trail. Made almost no attempt to hide it.

Had they left it for bear bait?

Next to the body was a backpack that had been ransacked—clothes spread haphazardly, along with personal items like a pillbox and dental floss. Tossed aside, heavy in the tall grass and native fauna, Will saw the answer he was looking for.

Camouflage shirt and pants—legs inside out, they were removed so hastily.

A little further away, clinging to another bush, another camouflage shirt.

Will straightened, eyed the group as the old cowboy, who seemed to be in charge, said, "You Will McCarroll?"

"Yes."

"We came to find you," he replied. Nodding, but not looking, toward the body, he added, "Didn't expect anything like this."

Will met his disturbed gaze.

"Who have you passed recently?"

The rancher shook his head.

"Nobody."

Another man, in his early thirties, with goatee and hair tied in back in a ponytail stepped forward.

"Wait a minute," he said, turning to the two people standing closest to him—a fit-looking blonde and a male with his arm around her, comforting her. "Those two guys who asked if we had bear spray!"

Clearly shaken, the two nodded their heads vigorously.

"Where?" Will asked.

"We'd split up to go around Cobalt Lake, cover both trails," the young man answered. "Romey," he nodded toward the cowboy, "and the others went around the south side, we three went around the north. We were about halfway along the lake when we passed two guys headed toward Two Medicine. They wanted to know if we had bear spray."

Will looked toward the body on the ground.

"They about his size?"

"One of them, the big one. But come to think of it, that little guy was wearing a fleece that was way too big for him." He turned to the woman. "Wasn't he?"

"Yes." The discussion seemed to be taking her mind off the gruesome sight practically at her feet. "I remember that. I remember thinking he must have borrowed it from the big guy."

Will looked at the body again.

The left forearm bore a tattoo—a Sanskrit symbol Will didn't recognize.

"There's who he borrowed it from."

Will tried not to think about a man so in love with the wilderness, or perhaps so lonely, that he hiked it alone, constructing cairns as he went to memorialize his passage.

He knew it would come back to haunt him later. It always did. But for now he could not go there.

"How long ago," he said, "how far from here were you when you saw the two men?"

"Maybe twenty minutes," the first man said. "So I'd say, a mile and a half. But they were heading the opposite direction, so distance-wise, it'll be more now."

The other male, who, like the woman, was visibly shaken, broke his silence. Voice cracking, he said, "We'll go after them with you."

There were murmurs of agreement.

Will's eyes scanned the group, made a quick assessment.

"Not all of you. If you three could cover the south route this time, I'll take the north. I need the rest of you to find Johnny Yellow Kidney. He's injured, and trapped under a shelf." He looked to one of the men who stood near the back, dressed in Lycra, with skinned legs and arms and a carabiner hanging from the corner of the backpack slung over his shoulder.

"You a climber?"

"Yep."

"Anyone else here do technical climbing?"

The woman who had seen the two gunmen shakily raised her hand.

Will was happy for it. He had debated about not including her in the group heading after the gunmen, but he
could see that the quieter of the two men gave her comfort and suspected she'd be resistant to parting with him.

This was better.

"Then you go with the group looking for Johnny," he
said. "The two of you will need to rope up to get down
to him. Now here's where I left him . . ."

The main trail divided within a mile of where the group
parted ways, one portion going north along Cobalt Lake,
the other hugging its south shores.

Will had bid the other two men good-bye with instructions to stay together, attempt calling or texting
for help along the way, a needless admonition to keep
up a loud conversation to warn bears of their presence,
and under no circumstances—should they encounter
them—attempt to apprehend the suspects. Instead they
were to pass them, on the pretense that—assuming the
gunmen recognized them—they had only accompanied
the woman with them earlier to a rendezvous with her
family, and then they were to press on until they could
make cellular contact with Rob Deardorf, whose number Will had given them.

Will and the two young men were to look for one
another at a checkpoint where the two trails converged
on the east side of the lake, but if there was no sign of
the other, continue toward Two Medicine.

Now, as Will jogged along the trail, total darkness
had descended upon the park. He looked at his watch.
10:15. How far ahead were the two gunmen? By his cal-
culations, based on when the three hikers had encountered them, and the relative shape of the two groups,
they were now at least forty-five minutes ahead of Will.

For someone like Will, Middle Two Medicine Lake

was no more than an hour and a half from the head of Cobalt Lake. The realization came to him that unless they'd stopped, catching up with them might be impossible. The one good thing was that the *Sinopah*, the boat that ferried tired hikers across Two Medicine to the campground and lodge, saving them skirting the shores of Middle Two Medicine, would have stopped running for the night. That added another forty-five minutes to their escape.

There might be only one way to stop the fleeing gunmen.

Will looked to the sky, which was so dark and moonless that he could barely make out the trees at the tops of the mountains surrounding him—peaks that seemingly sprung out of the ground, without foothills. Peaks it would be impossible, likely deadly, for Will to climb. Should he try?

There were two gunmen on the loose. They had killed Haldis Beck, and now the innocent hiker who just happened to cross paths with them. The two young men now skirting the south side of the lake could make it to Two Medicine campground and sound the alarm as fast as Will could. . . .

He stood, staring at the outlines surrounding him, a sick feeling, an intuition, gripping his gut. It was foolhardy, reckless—but he had to try.

Suddenly to the east, hovering over the night landscape almost as if beckoning to him, he recognized the outline of Mount Sinopah. It had been the first mountain he'd climbed upon arriving in Glacier. He'd sat there that first day, grieving for his Yellowstone, but marveling at the rugged wildness surrounding him in every direction— and didn't fully appreciate that it was a wildness that could mean death with one misstep on any one of the sheer-faced peaks surrounding him until now.

At least he'd climbed Sinopah, knew its dangers, but climbing Sinopah—still miles away—in time to be of help would not be possible.

A cloud in that direction parted, illuminating more than Sinopah with the night's constellations, and Will's jaw dropped.

Painted Teepee.

He'd sat there that day, on the small plateau carved on Sinopah's peak, looked east to turn his attention to her "partner," Rising Wolf—thinking about the legend behind the naming of these two dramatic mountains that seemed to spring out of the ground overlooking the waters of Two Medicine Lake.

In Yellowstone, Will had always hated that mountains, lakes, and trails rich with Native American history had been given white names in honor of those who "conquered" the wild people and places. Dunraven, Everts, Bunsen, Chittenden, Albright. In an area where twenty-six different tribes had been the first to traverse, live, revere, and protect everything, its wildlife and wildness, the names were almost uniformly and distinctively those of early white settlers and park administrators. An effort that had been underway for years to memorialize the Bannock tribe's contributions to the park by officially declaring their historical passageway the Bannock Trail had proved to be political, the outcome of that effort still in question.

For those reasons, the story of Rising Wolf and Sinopah had especially pleased Will, and that day he'd climbed Sinopah, it had caused him to turn his attention first to Rising Wolf, and then to another namesake mountain, one to Sinopah's west, Painted Teepee.

While appearing to practically erupt from the waters of Two Medicine, Painted Teepee bore a long, pronounced ridge that worked its way steadily up its west side. Will might be able to climb Painted Teepee's western slope high enough, and in time, to get out of the dead radio and cell space.

He picked up the pace.

No one was at the designated checkpoint on the east side of Cobalt Lake. Will called out three times, then continued, stepping over and on top of pile after pile of bear scat.

Will had passed the trailhead to Painted Teepee's summit several times. It had a marker at its mouth. He slowed to make sure he didn't miss it.

Had he been going full steam, he might have broken a leg, but as it is, when his foot caught on the form, he simply did a face-plant, then tumbled, rolling along the trail twice.

On hands and knees he retraced his steps.

The light filtering from the starlit sky was just enough for him to see: an elk calf, days old. Born too late in the season, as some are, in which case their mothers tended to keep them down low, away from the frigid, windblown peaks.

Shot point blank.

A trail of blood showed where her mother had finally fled, no doubt after fighting for her baby's life.

Will was certain now.

The two gunmen were leaving carnage behind in their wake, as bear bait.

A primal fury overcame Will.

A baby elk, dead.

It could just as easily have been another hiker.

His first impulse was to keep on the trail. He wanted the satisfaction of catching up with the two. The feel of his hands around their necks, instilling in them the terror they had instilled. He would turn his badge in immediately after. Walk away from this job. He didn't have it in him anymore.

Thoughts of Rachel and Carter came flooding into his mind. The sight of their bodies. He'd been the one to find them. A single bullet had killed them both. A poacher, firing at anything that moved in his greed, his desire to bring home a trophy.

They had been out hiking, near Soda Butte. Rachel had been a little reluctant when Carter was born to hike alone, but Will, ever the adventurer and frontiersman, had encouraged it. Told her she was safer hiking in the park than walking down the sidewalk in Seattle.

She had grown to love the daily outings with their baby boy safely ensconced in the carrier she wore on her chest. They had never been happier.

Someone with a gun, an illegally possessed gun, had taken it all away.

Ironically, the men responsible for all the carnage now, the two he was following, carried guns that were now legal in the park, thanks to the new guns-in-parks legislation.

Channeling his grief and anger, Will knew he must make the decision that optimized the chance of catching the gunmen. The shooting pains in his ankle overshadowed by what he felt in his heart, he bolted up the Painted Teepee trail, cell phone in hand.

Rhondie Wilkins sat behind the closed window in the entry cabin to Two Medicine. She'd put up the CLOSED sign half an hour earlier, but somehow, this evening she did not hurry out for a hike around the lake, or head home for a cold beer.

She had been depressed lately. Felt old, useless. No one in the Park Service seemed to want to hear what she had to say. Maybe it was time to call it quits. But that thought—the thought of leaving Glacier—terrified her more than any other.

She had never married. Really had never even been in love. Or, perhaps more accurately, no one had ever been in love with her. But she'd rationalized that she wouldn't trade her life for that of anyone she knew.

Maybe she'd been fooling herself all along.

Now, she reached for her jacket, then fumbled for the keys in its pocket.

She was just stepping out the door into the dark night when the phone rang.

During the day, with all the cars coming and going, other rangers in the booth, and visitors asking questions that never ended, she sometimes didn't even hear the phone when it rang.

Now the harshness of its bell caused Rhondie to startle.

To hell with it, she thought at first. I'm off duty.

But then, on the fifth ring, she turned away from the door, padded back across the cabin's wood floor and picked it up.

"Two Medicine gate," she said in an uncharacteristically somber voice.

"Ranger Wilkins?"

A vaguely familiar voice, male, one that held a clear sense of emergency.

Rhondie's devotion to her job reflexively kicked into high gear.

"Yes?"

"This is Will McCarroll."

Rhondie drew in a sharp breath. She didn't even realize she'd dropped the keys to the floor.

"Everybody's been worried about you. Where the hell are you?"

"I need your help. Two gunmen are headed that way on foot. They left their vehicle there. They're armed and extremely dangerous."

"I knew it!" Rhondie practically screamed into the phone. "I know just who you're talking about. Those two were armed to the teeth. I knew we shouldn't have let them in the park, that . . ."

Will cut her off.

"I need you to get ahold of Rob Deardorf," he ordered tersely. "He's not in his office. Let him know. And you get out of the cabin. Do you hear? Now. I repeat, abandon the entry gate and get word . . ." By now Will was shouting, as a new sound—that of a helicopter—came across the airwaves.

Within two seconds, it had completely drowned Will's voice out.

"Will?" Rhondie shouted. "Where are you?"

"Will!"

The connection went dead.

Rhondie picked up the phone, dialed Rob Deardorf's office, but got only voice mail. She reached for her keys, hurriedly locked the door, and stepped into the night. Her car was parked a quarter mile down the road. She began to run toward it.

But then, Ranger Rhondie Wilkins stopped dead in the middle of the two-lane road.

She looked at the sky. She could hear, in the distance, the sound of a helicopter. Was it the same helicopter she'd heard over the phone?

Will had told her to abandon the entry gate. He was, as always, being gallant, a hero.

Not many heroes left these days.

At that thought, Rhondie glanced back over her shoulder, toward the cabin where she'd spent thousands upon thousands of hours greeting visitors, answering their mundane questions, training young new rangers, season after season. Trying to give as much meaning to the work she had chosen as was possible to do.

She'd read about people's lives flashing before their eyes as they were about to die. It was like that now, only Rhondie's life began and ended in that entry cabin.

It would be her legacy—the old woman at the gate.

Or would it?

Turning back to the darkness of the empty roadway, Ranger Wilkins clutched her Park Service duffel bag that served as a purse against her torso and began running toward the pullout where she'd parked her car ten hours earlier.

Thirty-one

"You Will McCarroll?" the pilot shouted as Will ducked his head to avoid the helicopter's whirling blades.

"How the hell did you find me?" Will yelled as he settled in behind the copilot.

"We were headed back from the Bad Marriage area to pick up more searchers. We were told you were up that way, located your cell phone, and called for reinforcements. But just for the heck of it, we kept our night vision goggles on and that's when Stewart"—he nodded toward the copilot—"saw you, waving us down."

Will put a hand on Stewart's shoulder.

"Thanks, buddy. Listen, there are two gunmen trying to get out of the park. They're killing along the way. They could already be near the campground."

The pilot nodded his head enthusiastically as he reached for his radio.

"I'll call that in to Supervisor Deardorf."

"Let me talk to him when you get him," Will replied.

The pilot, who had already established connection, handed the radio back to Will.

"Rob, we've got two gunmen who are planning to flee to Canada either at or near Two Med already. That's where they've parked their vehicle."

Deardorf sounded both alarmed and elated to hear Will.

"I'm shorthanded with the fire at Lake McDonald but I'll send every available LE that way stat." He added, "You okay?"

"Yes."

"What about Yellow Kidney?"

"That should be your next priority. A group of locals are headed to him right now. They looked pretty competent, but I'd still get a chopper in the air right away. I can give them approximate GPS coordinates once they're airborne. Our biggest concern right now should be the gunmen. They've been on a rampage."

Will sensed, more than actually heard, Deardorf's groan.

"I'll have someone there within half an hour."

"That might be too late."

The lights of the park store that sat on the south shore of Middle Two Medicine Lake first made their appearance on the water's surface, their reflection shattered and dispersed by the gusts from the helicopter's blades as the aircraft cruised along the shoreline, which the trail closely skirted.

"Nothing," the pilot called over his shoulder. "Nobody."

As they cruised just over the park store, which had once served as a residence, Will called out, "Look!"

Lights from a truck showed the vehicle careening out of the parking lot that served both the campground and store. One woman crossing the lot, ice-cream cone in hand, was hit and sent flying.

"That's them!"

The truck picked up speed as it turned onto the road leading out of the park, headed toward the entry gate.

"Where do you want me to put down?" the pilot shouted.

"This thing's not big enough to shut down the whole road," Will shouted. "They'll drive right around us. We'll need to get far enough ahead of them to get out of it and be waiting for them. That means up past the entry gate."

As he said it, Will could see the single light bulb above the door to the entry gate that was always left on overnight. Below it, he knew the sign had been switched to CLOSED, even though the reality was that after the gate closed, people could come and go at will, without paying the entry fee.

The truck roared through the gate as Will prepared for the helicopter's abrupt put-down.

"Holy shit," he heard Stewart, the copilot, shout.

Will looked up just in time to see a car's lights pop on, simultaneous with the truck passing.

For some reason, the car was parked horizontally, perpendicular to the road.

As the truck raced by, the car jetted forward, T-boning it, sending it into a 360-degree spin.

The pilot was already putting down as Will watched the truck skid over the side of the roadway and then, as if in slow motion, begin a roll down the hillside toward Lower Two Medicine Lake.

Lights—flashing emergency vehicles and ordinary headlights—had begun approaching the site from all directions as word spread.

A tribal police car whizzed past Will as he jumped down to the pavement, the chopper still six feet in the air, and skidded to a stop alongside the car that had T-boned the gunmen's vehicle—an older Acura sedan whose front end had collapsed into the dashboard.

Dust from its deployed airbags shimmered like miniature fairies in the lights, and the blaring horn blended with the sound of approaching sirens and the crash of the truck below, against a stand of quaking aspens—just feet short of the water.

It came to rest on its side, pointed slightly downhill.

Seeing that the two tribal police had already begun extricating the driver of the Acura, Will bolted down the hillside, gun drawn, guided by the truck's lights, which danced on Lower Two Medicine's waters.

The driver's door was planted against the hillside. The windshield had shattered. Will watched as the passenger door slowly opened. A head followed, waving a black fleece.

"Don't shoot," the man called. He was bare-chested and skinny.

Just as Will reached for his handcuffs, Will saw the glint of a gun barrel protruding from the shattered front window. Diving for cover, he rolled, then returned fire from the ground, two shots aimed into the truck.

The man waving the jacket was still standing on top of the truck's side, pumping his arm back and forth frantically.

Fearful he might hit him, Will ceased firing.

There was no return fire.

The shirtless man bent over to peer inside the cab. He began wailing.

"You killed him. He's dead! Don't shoot. Don't shoot."

By now half a dozen men and women—most in uniforms that represented either law enforcement or emergency medical personnel—worked their way down the hill toward Will and the truck.

After Will had arrested the man on top of the truck and turned him over to two park rangers, neither of whom he recognized, he scrambled up the hill with a growing sense of panic.

A terrible realization had come to him.

He thought he knew who was in the car—the car that had stopped the gunmen.

The two tribal police officers and a team of EMTs were just loading a stretcher into the back of an ambulance.

Heart pounding in his chest and reverberating up into his ears, drowning out the cacophony of chaos surrounding him, Will rushed to join them.

He saw the frail hand, her tiny wrist, IV tubes already inserted.

And then, just as the stretcher was handed from the ground to two EMTs inside the ambulance, he saw her face.

She was grinning ear to ear.

Will could tell, even though an EMT held an oxygen mask to her mouth.

Rhondie Wilkins' gaze met Will's. She couldn't talk, but seeing his expression of horror and grief, she lifted her other hand and gave him a thumbs-up, just before the doors closed.

Will bit down on his lip, but that didn't stop the tears.

EPILOGUE

Johnny Yellow Kidney stared at the image on his computer screen, oblivious to the noise in Brownies, until one voice caused him to catch his breath.

"I was hoping I'd find you here."

He turned and the sight of Annie Peacock, leg in cast and crutches under her thin arms, staring at the image on his computer screen, caused him to blush.

He started to close the laptop, but Annie reached out and stopped him.

"No, please. Tell me what had you so transfixed."

Johnny rose, pulled out the chair next to him, moving Annie's crutches to the wall as she sat down, eyes glued to the screen.

"It's him," he said. "It's the wolverine that Bridger Brogan trapped. He survived."

Annie gasped, leaned forward to study the photo.

"You're sure?"

"Look," Johnny said, his finger touching the screen, which was filled with the image of a black and brown animal, white tip on the back right leg, which was the only hind leg visible. Its eyes glowed like small suns in his dark face, reflecting the unexpected flash of the camera.

"And here," Johnny said, moving his finger up the compact torso to the front right leg, which hugged the trunk of a tree. Just visible at the top of the photo was the bloody partial carcass of a deer. "Here's the wound from one trap."

When Annie leaned closer she saw it.

"And the hind leg is broken," he continued. "Bridger Brogan set two traps. I didn't think the little guy had a chance, but that leg's apparently healed enough for him to climb up to the bait I set out for him."

Annie leaned back, looking at Johnny.

"You knew he'd survived?"

"When we went back that first day after I'd left him in the creek bed to die, there was no sign of him, but more significantly, there were no signs of predation. No fur, no blood. I scoured the area. Then, over the past few weeks, I've found wolverine tracks that clearly indicated a damaged leg. I was hoping against hope it was this guy. I set up the bait station and a camera two days ago, and just downloaded the photos this morning."

Johnny could feel Annie keenly studying him.

"You really care, don't you?"

He met her warm brown eyes. They hadn't changed in all these years, after all she'd been through.

"It's not just him," he replied. "Wolverines are just . . . there's something I can't even articulate about how I feel about them. The big carnivores—wolves, grizzlies—are what people think about when they think about wilderness, but for me, it's the wolverine. They're so enigmatic, and they have such big hearts. Bears and wolves grow used to cohabiting with humans, even getting dependent upon them, but wolverines—they want no part of us. All they want is to survive. And they're willing to live in the most inhospitable terrain on this continent to do so. All they want is to be left alone. The idea that people like Bridger Brogan might trap a creature like this out of existence . . . well, that about makes me crazy.

"I don't approve of what that woman did to Brogan, but there's a part of me that's felt the same impulse. Almost every time I've found an animal in a trap, I've wished I could make a trapper experience what that animal went through before I found it."

"Maybe, if you believe in karma," Annie replied, "Brogan got what he deserved. That plus the prospect of spending the rest of his life behind bars. Will says they have a strong case."

The mention of Will sobered Johnny.

"Will's a great guy," he said. "And a lucky guy."

Annie reached out and placed a hand on Johnny's forearm.

"He is a great guy," she replied softly. "But I don't know how lucky he is. He wasn't surprised when I told him that seeing you, spending time with you, had revived some very deep, long-suppressed feelings."

Johnny's dark eyes, usually so veiled, could not hide his surprise.

"You did? *It* did?"

Annie nodded, her gaze not shying away from Johnny's scrutiny.

"Being laid up for a while gave me plenty of time to think. I honestly believe now that I married Alistair on the rebound, that I hadn't gotten over you. It's been good for me, but it's definitely caused both Will and me to decide to move slowly. But in the long run, I think we'll be alright." She smiled. "Will's a big fan of yours, you know."

"The respect is mutual. I've never known anyone who takes poaching and trapping inside the park more seriously. Rumor has it he's leaving. Part of me wishes he'd stay, but the other part of me knows that you two are supposed to be together, Annie." He nodded toward the screen. "Plus I'm worried that if he stays he'd eventually come to his senses and kick my ass."

Movement just outside the café's window drew Johnny's attention away from Annie. He added, "Maybe that's why he just pulled up."

"I don't think so," Annie said as she watched Will step out of his patrol car. "We were on our way here earlier this morning, to look for you, but Will got called to an accident on Highway 2."

Felt hat in hand, eyes fixed straight ahead, Will Mc-Carroll strode through the door and headed Johnny and Annie's way.

Johnny was on his feet by the time Will got there. The two men stood, eye-to-eye.

Will spoke first.

"I'm glad you're here. I wanted to tell you in person that I'm going home, to Yellowstone." Will looked down at Annie, who was still seated, and the anguish on his face seemed to ease at her smile. "And I wanted to thank you again for what you did for Annie. I owe you."

Johnny took a deep breath.

"Hell, Will."

Acutely uncomfortable, Annie needed to break the tension.

"How bad was the accident?" she asked.

"A fatality," Will replied. "Someone reported a car in the river, just after the sharp curve past Bear Creek. Turns out it belonged to Claudette Nillson, the woman who lured Brogan into the trap."

Both Annie's and Johnny's expressions registered their shock at this news.

"It's been there a while," Will continued. "We found her passport, other things that make it look like she was fleeing to Canada. My guess is she went in the river the day you two came across Brogan. It looked like she may have been able to survive the crash for a couple hours, there was an air pocket. But she wasn't able to get out of her seat belt."

"Talk about karma," Johnny muttered quietly.

"We were just talking about Brogan and her," Annie explained to Will. "That what she did to him might have been, in a way, karma—for what he'd done to animals all these years."

"If things go like they should in court," Will replied, "Brogan'll be getting plenty more karma."

The conversation sobered all of them into thoughtful silence, but when the laptop screen drew Will's attention, Johnny couldn't help but grin.

"It's him, Will. You saved him. Tough little son of a bitch. He's already climbing."

Will bent to get a closer look. Johnny found himself watching the look of delight on Annie's face as she watched Will study the picture of the wounded wolverine.

"Hell," Will said. "That's about the best news I've had in a long time. That and the fact that Rhondie Wilkins got out of the hospital this morning."

He straightened, paused—as if at a loss for further words—then looked at Annie.

"Ready to get going?"

Annie avoided looking at Johnny as she nodded.

"Wait," Johnny said. "Aren't you two coming to the naming ceremony this afternoon?"

"Naming ceremony?" Annie echoed.

"We're naming the mountain that Whisper Little Wolf's grandfather did his vision quests on. The mountain where she . . ." He could not bring himself to say the words. "Hopefully, over time, the Park Service will do it formally, but from today on, to my people that place will be known as Whispering Mountain. The ceremony and spreading of Whisper's ashes are this afternoon."

This news visibly shook Will. Annie reached out, squeezed his hand.

"How's Cole taking it?" he asked, unable to make eye contact with Johnny.

"Hard, like everybody else. Whisper was one of our shining stars. But this will help. Today will be healing."

"She was so kind to me," Annie said softly. "But I don't feel it would be right for me to be there. I wouldn't want to be an intruder."

The anguish on Will's face said it all. Whisper had died trying to warn him about the plot to kill him. He felt responsible for her death.

Barely able to hold back the emotion, he looked directly at Johnny.

"Please let Cole's and Whisper's families know that I will do everything in my power to ensure that the gunman who survived is held accountable. And I'll also make sure charges are filed against Brogan for what he did to her. When the son of a bitch is done facing all the charges we've filed against him, there will be one more. In Whisper's name."

Unable to say more, he looked at Annie. "I'll meet you outside."

Neither Johnny nor Annie protested.

"He's carrying a heavy load," Johnny observed, watching Will work his way back to the door. Numerous locals reached out to shake his hand, but Will couldn't bring himself to stop and say anything.

"I'm worried about him," Annie replied. Then she added, "I'm worried about us."

Johnny drew back.

"Because of you and me?"

Annie's smile had changed. The radiance was gone, but not the kindness.

"No," she replied. "Well, maybe that's not entirely honest. I know that Will recognizes that being with you brought back feelings for me. We've talked about it. But I think we can get beyond that—neither of us are young and idealistic anymore, and what we have is strong and deep. But we both have our pasts and baggage to deal with, and we realize that's going to take time. Right now, my first priority is helping him heal from all the tragedy that he blames himself for. And Yellowstone is the best place to do that."

Despite the crutches, she managed to stand with the

same grace Johnny had always admired in her. She turned to face him, eyes wet.

"Stacy is a wonderful woman."

Johnny intended his smile to reassure her. To let her know he would be alright.

"She is indeed."

Will's arrival and departure had alerted the locals inside Brownies to Annie and Johnny's presence at the back of the shop. All conversation seemed to have stopped, with many sets of eyes on the two as they stood facing each other now in silence.

"Thank you for doing what you did for Will," Annie finally said. And then, raising her voice, she turned to the others. "Thank all of you."

Some dropped their gazes self-consciously to half-emptied plates, others met Annie's, heads nodding, smiling. Many eyes misted, like Annie's.

A tail thudded against the floor. Stinky's.

"This is one hell of a community," Annie said, taking one last look around before stepping out the door and into the fall sunshine, Stinky following close behind.

"Please, never change."

"Do you solemnly swear that the testimony you are about to give is the truth, the whole truth, and nothing but the truth?"

The room—filled with senators, congressmen and women, and reporters, had been abuzz—but now it fell into silence, all eyes on Will.

"I do."

"Please be seated."

Will lowered himself into the single chair at the table set up at the front of, and facing, the congressional chamber. A panel of twelve senators stretched in front of him, and behind them, a standing-room-only crowd.

At the center of the table, Senator Taylor Cook, Republican from New Hampshire, pressed his mouth to the microphone.

"Thank you for being here, Ranger McCarroll."

Will glanced over the senator's shoulder for Annie, who was seated in the front row and just to the senator's left. Meeting his gaze, she nodded almost imperceptibly as cameras clicked and television journalists whispered commentary.

"No problem," he answered, redirecting his gaze to the Chair of the commission.

His answer brought a crooked smile to the face of Judge Sherburne, who was seated between Annie and Eleanor Malone.

"From what I've heard, sir," Senator Cook replied, "that may qualify as the biggest understatement ever uttered in this chamber."

It started out with a single clap—one person at the back of the room spontaneously bringing her hands together—but like wildfire in a brittle stand of quaking aspen, it spread, thundering through the chamber, whose high ceilings echoed it back down to the floor.

"Order," the senator called, "order," but in the next minute, he, too, was on his feet, applauding.

Several immaculately dressed men seated just to Annie's left remained in their chairs, hands covering their mouths as they muttered among themselves, well aware of the cameras directed at them.

Nodding in acknowledgment, red-faced at the attention, Will wanted to shrivel up and disappear into the cracks on the weathered maple table, which he had glued his eyes to.

"Order," Senator Cook called out again when the applause finally began to die.

"Mr. McCarroll, we've asked you here today to testify before this commission, which has been called in order to revisit what's become known as the guns-in-park ruling that went into effect in February of 2010. As an experienced law enforcement officer in this country's first—and most famous—national park, we, sir, are eager to hear your opinion of this law. Specifically, we would like any insights you may have regarding this law's impact on safety, not only for citizens visiting the parks, but for people like you, who work and serve in the National Park Service."

Straightening in his chair, Will brought his gaze even with the Senator's.

"How many bodies?"

"Pardon me?"

"How many bodies? How many does it take? 'Cause if it's four, that's how many I've personally witnessed since the rule went into effect. People who were alive one minute, gone the next. And every one was killed by guns that were legally brought into the parks."

A stunned hush fell over the room—but not over the front row—as the startled Senator gathered himself.

Will's words had brought the suited brigade to its feet, one of whom rushed to whisper in the ear of the panel member immediately to Senator Cook's left, Senator Nelson Slada from Arizona, who then, in turn, leaned toward Cook and proceeded to whisper frantically in his ear, both men making sure they had their hands covering the microphones.

When Slada stopped, Cook leaned forward, pressing his mouth to the mic.

"I would like to call a brief recess."

This brought half of the members of the commission at the table to their feet.

A stately woman, seated midway to the end of the table, remained in her chair and pulled her microphone forward. Will recognized the name on the plate in front of her: Senator Irene Halliday. The senator from Connecticut who had issued Will the invitation to testify.

"We've been in session approximately three minutes. No recess is necessary"—she looked back over her shoulder, to the brigade of suits in the front row—"whether powerful lobbying interests want it or not. *Especially* if they want it.

"We've invited this man, this hero, to speak today," she continued. "I will not stand for him being silenced or censored."

Emboldened, Senator Cook looked to Slada defiantly, leaned forward, and said, "You're right, Senator Halliday. Unless our guest feels a need for a short break. . . ." He looked toward Will, almost hopefully.

"I'm used to twelve-hour days on horseback in the wilderness," Will replied. "And frankly, that's where I'd rather be. So, no. No need for a recess. No offense intended, but I'd rather get this over with as soon as possible. Sir."

"Very well. Please, Ranger McCarroll, go on. You were giving us your opinion of the guns-in-parks law."

Will paused, his eyes scanning the room.

"I'm sure some of you have done your homework"—he made direct eye contact with several of the men dressed in expensive suits in the front row—"so I'd like to get it out on the table now. Twenty-eight years ago, my wife and six-month-old son were killed by a poacher in Yellowstone." The room had fallen back into silence. "So I'm not exactly neutral about guns in the national parks. But the gun that killed Rachel and Carter was brought into the park illegally. The guns that killed Haldis Beck, Whisper Little Wolf, a man hiking alone through Glacier, and a twenty-one-year-old who was shot by his best friend over a card game in Yellowstone were there legally.

"An entry gate ranger saw the guns that killed the

people in Glacier. She wanted to confiscate them then and there but, of course, she couldn't, and ironically, she ended up being one of the victims of this ruling, though, luckily, she survived.

"Gun rights advocates"—he looked directly at the row of suits—"their *lobbyists*, will tell you that crimes and violence happened in the parks before this ruling, and they'd be telling the truth. And the Guns 4 All suspects may well have gotten their guns into Glacier no matter what. But in my opinion, the parks got a whole lot more dangerous the day the guns-in-park ruling went into effect. In my opinion, not a single one of these deaths would have taken place were it not for that ruling. I can't prove that, but if I'm right—if there's even a slight chance I'm right—how can you justify it?

"You can argue and discredit my testimony with rhetoric that appeals to the growing paranoia of everyone in this country, and figures slanted whatever way you want, but you asked me my opinion, and that's it."

As he spoke, one of the suits in the front row scribbled on a piece of paper. Now he passed it to Senator Slada, who promptly leaned into his microphone.

"Mr. McCarroll, I protest your maligning the fine people in this country and this room who believe fiercely in the need to protect our citizens' second amendment right to bear arms. According to the press reports, the group responsible for the reprehensible events that occurred in Glacier National Park was not part of any legitimate, respectable organization. Let's make that clear. They were the acts of an extreme and small, isolated group—Guns 4 All—that used means that all law-abiding citizens in this country, including the gentlemen behind me, condemn and abhor."

"What about Haldis Beck, Senator?" Will asked. "She is known to have infiltrated gun control groups as an informant for this country's largest gun rights advocacy organization. I believe that, too, is a matter of public record. Is it just a coincidence that she ended up at the heart of a plot to kill me, in order to stop me from testifying here today?"

Rattled, Slada turned and looked over his shoulder, then glanced down furtively at the paper he'd been handed.

"Yes, well," he stammered, "there is ample evidence and testimony that Haldis Beck's actions in the attempt to prevent you from testifying today were part of the plot attributed solely to Guns 4 All. A plot that legitimate guns rights organizations have denounced. I just want to make that clear. There is absolutely no evidence linking legitimate organizations to the Guns 4 All plot to kidnap or harm you."

"With Haldis Beck dead, we'll never really know for sure now, will we?" Will replied testily.

When Will's words caused another storm to sweep the room, Senator Cook, sweat pouring down his neck, pounded his gavel on the table.

"Thank you, Ranger McCarroll, this commission appreciates . . ."

Will leaned into his microphone, clearly not ready to be dismissed.

"Isn't anything sacred anymore?"

"Please, go on," Senator Halliday urged over the protests of Senator Slada and the others.

"A gunman took my wife and my child from me, but you know what got me through? You know what kept my spirit alive?"

Seeing the cameras focused on Will, and the hush that fell over the room, the dissidents on the panel seemed to realize the best course of action would be to allow Will to speak.

"No, sir," Senator Cook replied with quiet resignation. "Please, tell us."

Will looked from Annie to Judge Sherburne.

"Yellowstone," he replied. "Its mountains. Its wolves, bison, and bears. Its elk and otters. Sandhill cranes. Mountains and rivers so beautiful they make me want to cry. So beautiful they *make* me cry. People who feel the same way I do. Who find solace and inspiration and meaning in the world by going there."

Tears were streaming down Judge Sherburne's face as Annie reached for his hand and held it tight.

"So I ask you, all of you. Isn't there anything, any place left, that you people will allow to remain sacred? Can't we take the guns and the violence—and the tension that comes from both—out, and trust that the magic of a place like Yellowstone, a place like Glacier, just might bring out the best in people? That no matter how they behave in the rest of the world, they'll be better human beings, happier, kinder, more thoughtful, for that brief period of time they're surrounded by that kind of beauty and spirit?"

Cameras clicked, videos rolled, as several of the suits in the front row stood and marched out of the room, expecting a crowd to follow.

But no one followed.

As the last of the suits stood to go, Will leaned into the microphone.

"Before you go, can I ask you fellas a question?"

The group hurried toward the chamber's back door, leaving behind a man, younger than the others, who was still gathering papers and files left behind.

Startled, he looked away. But then, as the others disappeared through the door, a spectator yelled, "Answer him," and the young man froze, eyes moving reluctantly in Will's direction. He did not see the one remaining colleague at the back of the room, beckoning him to ignore Will.

"When I was a kid," Will said, "when I was a kid,

I remember the ARF as a non-controversial, public service organization promoting rifle safety for hunters and young people."

The man's expression brightened momentarily, hopeful.

"The name of the organization refers to rifles," Will continued as the man quickly returned to gathering the files he'd placed on his seat and began practically running to the door, "not handguns or machine guns. I'm not sure when, or how, you grew into a political lobbying group dedicated to protecting people's right to own more advanced, military-type weapons and ammunition"— lips practically twitching in anger, the suit at the back of the room held the door open for him as Will finished—"that enable any crackpot to become a mass murderer."

Even after Will fell silent, after he'd been thanked again for his testimony, people remained in their seats.

Panelists remained seated at the table, keenly aware of the cameras still on them, sneaking furtive glances at the tweets flooding their hidden iPhones and iPads— wondering how best to react without yet having had a survey or pollster interpret the public's response to Will's words.

Annie, Eleanor, and Judge Sherburne stood waiting at the gate that separated the panel and witness stand from the gallery.

Will approached them, looking exhausted but relieved.

He reached for Annie's hand, felt the judge's pat on his back.

"Let's go home," he said.

"This is Faithe Unsword. As most of you know, this is my last day on the show. It's been an honor to be here and get to know you folks here in northwest Montana.

Really. I think we made a difference here, you know, that we started folks thinkin' just a bit about what really matters, the rights that are at stake. How important it is what I'm trying to say, how important it is to fight for what's right. What our ancestors taught us. Like trapping. Whoa boy, you trappers have your work cut out for you! That group tryin' to take away your heritage here in this great state. The dentist who had all those fake charges trumped up against him—some plot to murder a ranger, rape, you name it—all in a sick attempt to discredit him. All 'cause he's a trapper. An honest man trying to make a living doing what God meant us to do. Trapping. And did you hear, can you even believe it, that animal rights crazies are actually calling the mentally-ill woman who lured the guy into a trap a hero? That they've created a Facebook page in her honor? I mean, she left him there to die—to die!—and they're making a hero out of her. What's the world coming to? It's enough to make you crazy, isn't it?

"But I know you'll fight on. I know you'll never give up, that you'll protect your God-given and constitutional rights, like the right to carry a gun wherever you darn well please, and the right to rid the earth of . . . to rid the earth of all that's wrong with it, including vicious animals that take away our ability to make a living because they want to kill just for the fun of it.

"And I want you to know that in my next job, as the head of the Department of the Interior under our newly elected President, just know that I'll be fighting right by your side. And we will win, my friends. We will win, because what we have on our side is righteousness.

"Now, let's get to the big announcement you've all been waiting for, the one I've been saving for my last show: the winner of the predator derby . . ."

AUTHOR'S NOTE

While what happens to him in *Trapped* is in part fictitious, one character in the book actually exists. That character is Stinky. He's had his share of rough times, but I'm happy to report that today Stinky is alive, well (and four-legged), and enjoying being lovingly cared for by Jack Marceau, who took him in.

I took this picture in October of 2011, during one of Stinky's frequent rounds of East Glacier, after watching him sit across from Brownies (which had closed for the season) staring at it for most of the morning. East Glacier is in good hands with Stinky.

TOR

Award-winning authors
Compelling stories

Please join us at the website
below for more information
about this author and other great
Tor selections, and to sign up for
our monthly newsletter!